THE
MARKINGS

For those who need an escape…

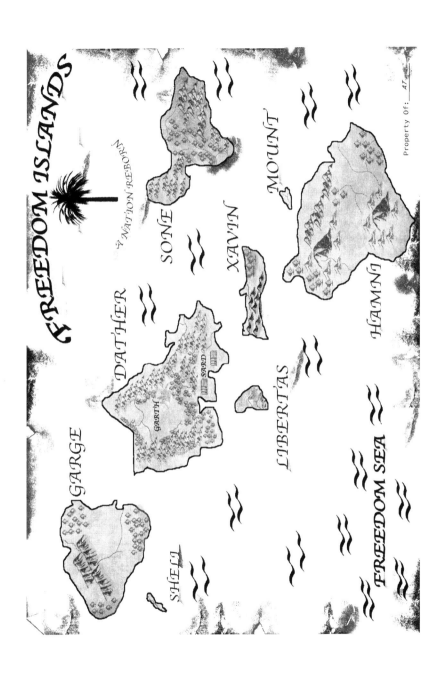

FREEDOM ISLANDS

A NATION REBORN

GARGE

DATHER

SONE

XAVIN

MOUNT

SHELL

LIBERTAS

HAMNG

GARTH

SAND

FREEDOM SEA

THE GIFTED

ENHANCED HEARING
   COMMUNICATOR
   SOUND WAVER
   NOISE ABSORBER

ENHANCED SIGHT
   FUTURE HOLDER
   FORCE LIFTER
   VISION SHIFTER
   INFORMATION SCANNER

ENHANCED SMELL
   TRACKER
   MANIPULATOR

ENHANCED TASTE
   CONSUMER

ENHANCED TOUCH
   SENSOR
   CONTROLLER
   TRANSFORMER
   AEROS

Property of: _AT_

Part 1: The Beginning

Chapter 1

My frail fingers curl around the jagged rock. I press it into the stone wall and drag it up and down until a small groove forms. I drop the rock and step back, glancing over all the lines I've made. It is day 2,436 of being in this prison with my mother and younger brother.

"Adaline, you've got to stop tallying. You've filled the entire cell with your lines," my mother, Rosa Sagel, groans. She sits with her back against the opposite wall, and her eyelids threaten to fall closed as she blinks slowly.

"I need to keep track so I'm ready when we escape," I say in a hushed voice. It may have been nearly seven years of being locked in here, but I've almost finished my escape plan.

"Addie," my younger brother sings in his childish voice.

"Don't call me that, Titus," I say, taking a seat next to him on the old ripped up mattress.

"Will you tell me the story about the rocks again?" Titus asks slowly. He has a hard time finding the words he wants to say. I know he means the story about the asteroids that reset civilization on this planet nearly 100 years ago. When we were arrested Titus was just a baby, and I was only nine years old. I've been trying to teach him about our history and how to read and do math, but he's still far behind where a seven-year-old should be. I really only blame myself.

"Don't you have that story memorized by now?" I joke, poking him in the stomach. He laughs, and just as I'm about to start the story my mother jumps up, alarmed.

She starts spinning around the room and asks me, "Adaline, what day did you say it was?"

"2,436," I say, scanning her worried face.

"Are you sure?" she asks sternly.

"I'm pretty sure," I say gently.

"It's fine. I'll just count them," my mother brushes me off.

"I can help," I say, and together we move around the cell, counting all of my tally marks until we get to the one I made this morning.

"2,436," my mother whispers, tracing the last line with her thin finger. "It's time. It's finally time."

"Time for what?" I ask, my voice trembling.

"You are nearly 16 years old, Adaline. It's time to be strong," my mother says, sitting me down on the mattress with my brother.

"Actually, I'm 15 years and 363 days," I correct. Ever since we were put in prison, I've become a numbers person. I'm always counting up to dates and back from them. It helps to keep time moving in here. Usually, my mother scolds me for correcting her or for bringing up my numbers, but right now her eyes fill with tears, and she gently cups my face with her hands.

"You did such a good job, Adaline," my mother says, looking deep into my emerald eyes.

"I don't know what's going on," I choke out and give my head a soft shake. She seems to focus a bit and rubs her damp eyes.

"It's time I tell you a secret," my mother says.

Titus leans in and his eyes widen, "A secret?" My mother lets out a dry laugh before pulling an old, black diary from her grey prison shirt. "What's that?" Titus asks.

"I am a Future Holder," my mother says gently.

"You have a gift?" I ask, shocked. We never talked about gifts before. I learned about them in school once. A select group of people were infected during the fall of the world before ours, giving them magical powers. As a kid, I'd always wondered what it would be like if my family was gifted, but I had never thought it would be a reality.

"Yes, and so do you." My mother hands me the diary, and I notice a small lock on its cover.

"What gift do I have?" I ask quietly.

"You are a Force Lifter, Adaline. You control whatever you see," my mother says. "There is so much I never told you about how the gifts work. If someone is born with a gift, they will have a sense that is enhanced in a certain way. You have an enhanced sense of sight that lets you control what you see."

All of the information my mother is telling me loses me, and I feel a confused glaze settle on my face. My mother pauses and must notice she's lost me. "I have an enhanced sense of sight as well, but my powers are different. I can see into the future."

"So I can save us?" I ask, as the idea of having magical powers fully processes.

"No!" my mother almost shrieks back to me. "You have to wait to use it until the time is perfectly right."

"I don't understand," I draw out my words, confused.

"You just have to promise me, or else we will all be killed. Do you promise, Adaline?" she asks urgently, her hands squeezing my arms.

I hesitate and look into her icy blue eyes. "I promise," I choke out in a small, almost inaudible, voice. "So you've seen this all happen?" I ask, starting to piece together my mother's information about our powers.

"Yes, as a Future Holder, I've had visions of how our lives play out," my mother explains.

I glance at the ticks in the wall and ask her, "So what does day 2,436 mean?"

"Today you escape," my mother whispers. The ringing sound of the metal prison door slamming open makes me jump. I had completely forgotten it was Parting Day. "I love you both so much," my mother says, tears escaping her eyes.

"Why are you crying?" my voice breaks. I hear cell doors being thrown open as the guards start dragging select prisoners to their executions. An officer appears in front of our cell, and I scream in protest. It can't be one of us, not now.

"It's your time Ms. Sagel," the guard announces before unlocking our cell. My mother stands to go, and Titus begins to scream and sob. They can't take her. I can't lose her.

"Mother what do I do now?" I ask between cries. I hope she tells me she was wrong and that I need to use my powers now. I need her to tell me how to use them, and how to save us.

She looks at me very calmly and says, "Hold your brother's hand, Adaline." I turn to Titus and see him squeezing the air between his shrieks. I grab his hand tight and he continues to squeeze three times, then a pause, and then three more. I had taught him to do this when he got upset and couldn't find the words he wanted to say. It was his way of communicating with us.

I look back to my mother who walks out of our cell and the door closes behind her. "Count Adaline," she instructs. I catch one last glance of her blue eyes and her long brown hair before the guards take her with the other prisoners, and then she's gone. My mind races trying to figure out what I'm supposed to do now. She isn't gone. She can't be gone. "Count Adaline," her voice reminds me again. I do this every Parting Day. It's the same every week. From the moment the guards leave with that week's group of prisoners it's exactly 1,876 seconds until the guards will drag the dead back through the prison so we know the killings were successful, and then bodies are disposed of.

So I start to count softly and evenly. *1. 2. 3.* I now know what my mother had meant when she said I had to wait until the time was right to use my gift. After Parting Day most of the security and help at the castle get the evening off. This will be my best opportunity to escape.

11. 12. 13. Titus continues screaming and squeezing my hand. Three squeezes, then a pause, and then three more. He does this every Parting Day, but today it is so much worse. Parting Day is a way for the King to make room in the prison. Once a week seven or so prisoners are removed and executed in the large coliseum, and everyone in the entire city of Garth, the city I used to live in and the capital of our island, has to watch.

98. 99. 100. Everyone is supposed to attend the killings and is forced to watch us die as a sign to show what happens when the laws are broken. Then, the bodies get brought through the prison to the disposal room to remind us what we have to look forward to.

245. 246. 247. As I count I imagine my mother walking further and further away from us. *451. 452. 453.* I have to be strong. I am a Force Lifter. I am a gifted. I can escape and save my brother. *777. 778. 779.* Titus has finally quit screaming. He sits quietly beside me while we wait for the dead to be brought to the disposal room.

1,206. 1,207. 1,208. I wonder if she's gone already. Was she one of the first to go or did they make her wait and watch everyone else die first? I hope it was quick. *1,505. 1,506. 1,507.* They'll start wrapping up now.

1,874. 1,875. 1,876. I stop and the prison seems to balance on a silent beam. Just a beat later and the doors slamming open rings through the concrete tomb. 93 seconds to the disposal room. 1 body. Then 2. 3. I count as they carry the dead, wrapped in dirty white fabric by the cells. 4. 5. 6. There's a pause, a lag in the line, and then finally my mother's body is carried by us. Her eyes are closed and her skin is pale. She could just be sleeping. "Mother," my voice chokes out. I know what Parting Day is, I've seen this happen hundreds of times, so why did I let my mother go with them? I had thought it was a plan she had. If she had seen this in the future why would she let herself die?

"Count Adaline," her distant voice echoes to me. *83. 84. 85.* I continue, tears rolling down my cheeks until 93 and the guards have cleared the prison and enter the disposal room. We sit in the cell completely shocked. Titus has begun to cry again, but I don't feel upset. I feel anger pound through every inch of my body. Anger at the guards that took away my mother, but mostly anger toward myself for letting her die. She told me I had a gift. Why did I do nothing? I glance down to the black diary she had handed me. When I try to open it, the small lock resists. She gave me a diary I can't read, told me not to use my gift, gave me no other instructions except to count, but there was one more thing. She had said to wait. Now she would say to move.

Before I can act I try and calm myself down, just enough to be able to think straight. I breathe in very slowly until I can't take in any more air and then release it. I do this a few more times until I feel the muscles in my body relax. "Breathe Titus," I mumble and he takes in shaky breaths through his cries.

I don't even have the first clue as to how to do this, but I rise, not wanting to waste any more time. I place the small black diary into the pocket on the inside of my grey prison button-up shirt and take in another deep breath. I waited as mother had instructed and now I need to move. "Run now and mourn later," I instruct to Titus and myself.

I lift my hand and hold it out in front of me. She said I just need to picture it. I see the caged door so I can control it. I can open it, but I feel the nerves building up inside. What if my mother was wrong? What if her visions were wrong? What if she didn't have visions at all, and was just trying to keep me hopeful for when she was gone? I know what this prison does to people, it drives them crazy. For a second I doubt my mother and her visions, and I wonder if she had just completely lost her mind in her last minutes. I look from my shaking hand to the barred door. I clear my thoughts of doubt and just try to believe. I close my eyes and imagine the door sliding open.

"Please work," I whisper. I slowly let my eyes open and I feel my heart drop when I see the door is still closed. "No," my broken voice lets out. I have to get out. I stare into the barred door and squeeze my fists as tight as possible. "Move. Move. Move," I repeat in my head over and over again. I focus harder and harder until my hands shake and my eyes water with tears of frustration, and then I see the bars start to tremble.

"Yes," I breathe, overcome by hope. I continue to think and beg the door to move in my head, and I see it continue shaking and shaking. As the frustration and tension build inside of me I hear myself scream, "Open!" and watch as the barred door flies to the right.

I almost fall over at the release of all the tension built inside me. I did it. I exhale and can't help but feel relief. I do have the gift. My sense of sight is enhanced so that I can control whatever I see. I am a Force Lifter.

The second this thought crosses my mind I'm hit by another wave of panic. I won't only be wanted as an escaping prisoner, but also as one of the gifted. King Renon forces everyone with a gift to work directly under him. I can't get caught. My heart starts to quicken at the thought of the guards catching me and turning me into King Renon crosses my mind. Images of how my mother may have died flash in my head. I won't let her death be for nothing. I turn to Titus who sits frozen on the mattress.

"Run now, and mourn later," I instruct him again and help him to his feet. "Time to go Titus."

"Addie, how'd you do that?" Titus asks, but I don't answer because I don't know.

I grab his hand and drag him from the cell. I begin to turn right to go toward the only entrance and exit I know of, but Titus begins to pull my hand left and toward the disposal room.

"No, that's the wrong way Titus," I say, but he shakes his head hard.

"Mother is in there. We need to save her too." His words crawl across my skin.

"Oh Titus," I say softly and kneel in front of him. Even though nerves and anxiety run through me I try to deliver my words as calmly as I can. "Mother is dead Titus." His face sets in a stone line. "Today was Parting Day and they took her." I can see his eyes shifting. His brain knows what happened, but he's trying to deny it.

"No Adaline," he says, getting my name right. That's how I know he's serious.

"Come with me, Titus. She wants us to go now." Titus gives one more glance over his shoulder, down the hall toward the disposal room. After a second he takes my hand and we move toward the exit. I just have to picture it. I can do this. It's just like I've dreamed about every night for as long as I can remember.

Out of the corner of my eye, I look in the cells of other families. At first, they all look shocked, especially when they don't see a guard with us. Then, they start pleading for help. When I don't offer any they start screaming, "Guards! Guards!" Usually, the prison is filled with guards, but on Parting day there are only ever two.

The two guards turn around the corner, swords pulled and ready to attack. In my head, I try to command the guards' swords to move away from their hands, but it's not that easy. The swords start shaking in their hands and I watch as the guards try to use both hands to steady them. I look around the room at other things to control, but everything in the dungeon starts shaking. Stones in the walls and ceiling fall, crushing the guards in my path. Innocent people in their cells start screaming and huddling for safety from the destruction I'm causing. I stop trying to control things and the prison becomes still again. I tell myself to start running and Titus and I take off down the dungeon hallway to the metal staircase I was brought down seven years ago.

We climb up the stairwell and to my right is a door that will lead into the castle itself. We turn and proceed through it. The hall is dimly lit with lanterns that hang on either end.

"I remember this," I whisper softly. As my eyes adjust to the dim light I feel my heart drop. I look forward and everything looks the same as it did the night we arrived, except for the fact mother is no longer with us. The night we were brought here is replaying in my head over and over again, but I know I have to keep moving, for mother's sake.

I walk forward down the short hallway. The walls are a simple white with gold and red swirls and floral designs. Beneath my bare feet is a beautiful velvet purple carpet lined with gold. It's a rare luxury in Garth, my family could never afford it. Once I reach the end of the hallway I lift my hand and picture the locks on the other side of the door turn and the doors open. I can't tell if the locks on the other side of the door flip open or if I simply just shake the door until it breaks free.

"That's so cool," Titus breathes and I see his eyes light up. He knows what this means. We get to start over and be free. We step out into the main foyer of the castle. Everything looks the same here as in the last hallway except for the hints of purple and blue running through the walls. I squeeze my eyes shut, trying to recall the way out, but it's been far too long. My gut tells me to turn right so I stop trying to force my memory, and just follow what feels right.

Quietly, we move down the hall, our feet silently floating over the lush carpet. Trying to get out on Parting Day was the right decision. The castle seems to be empty after today's events. Everyone from Garth who came to view the killings have returned home, and the majority of security has been off duty. Titus and I continue to move through the castle undetected. We walk past a hall to our right when something catches my eye. About halfway down the hall hangs a large painting of a palm tree. I stop suddenly and focus on it. I remember it from the night we were brought here. The memory from that night surfaces and I see myself and my mother walking by the painting with Titus in her arms. I remember the guards practically shoving us down the hall, and I had peered at the painting through tear-filled eyes.

"We're close Titus," I say softly. We turn and move down the hall with the painting. The way out starts to come back to me and I know the front of the castle is just around this hall.

A slam of a door back the way we came causes my heart to pause. "We need to move faster," I whisper and Titus and I pick up our pace to a jog. Another slam off in the distances sends me into a sprint. I glance over my shoulder and see Titus falling behind.

Then, a guard emerges into the hall behind Titus. "Run!" I scream as the soldier draws his sword. I stop in the middle of my stride and switch to running back to him, but the guard's blade drives through Titus's chest before I get there. Through clenched eyes I picture the blade flying back into the guard and effortlessly it does. I drop to my knees, into the purple damp carpet next to my little brother under the palm tree painting. The guard I threw the sword into makes unidentifiable noises as he falls to the floor and silence returns to the castle.

"Titus," I say gently, tears filling my eyes. He takes my hand in his, wet with red blood, and tries to speak. "It's okay Titus," I try and quiet him.

"We need to go find Mother," Titus gets out.

I drop my head. "You'll be with her soon Titus," I say and meet my younger brother's dying eyes. "You and mother will be free soon." Titus's lips curl into a tiny smile before he takes in his last small breath, and his hand becomes limp in mine.

I fight the urge to make a sound. I clench my teeth and fill my head with internal screams. *1. 2. 3.* I count and squeeze my brother's hand.

1... 2...3

Chapter 2

I don't know how much time passes before I finally let go of Titus's hand. It feels like one or two minutes but the stiff muscles in my legs tell me it's been longer. My tears have dried to my cheeks and my mind is finally starting to accept reality. My mother and brother are both dead. If I don't move soon I will likely face the same fate. Before I stand I gently cross Titus's arms and close his eyes. I hate the idea of leaving him here, but I know I have to.

Abruptly I stand and continue down the hall. I tell myself to move quickly because I know if I hesitate, even for a second, I'm not sure I'll get the courage to go again. I pick up my pace to a steady jog and then I hear two distant voices coming my way. I scan the hall, looking for somewhere to hide, but there's nowhere for me to go.

"Parting Day was a little boring," a man's exhausted voice says.

"I know, the group of prisoners they brought were lackluster at best," the second guard says and their voices grow louder.

Disgust starts to build up inside of me. The executions are just a form of entertainment for them. They never have to worry about facing that terrifying day. No one they love or care about will ever have to experience that. I think they must be making nightly rounds in the castle, but then I hear one of the guards add, "We're ditching tonight, right? Leave it to the newbie to handle. We really only need a single guard on duty outside the maze anyway."

"Couldn't have said it better myself." At that comment the two guards turn into the hall I'm standing in. They stop suddenly and I watch their eyes glance from me to the dead bodies and then back to me. My hatred for people like them, who see Parting Day as a form of entertainment, bubbles over. My eyes focus in on one of their swords. Without thinking I control it, and pull it into the air before slicing through one of their chests. It takes me a second to realize I have just murdered a human being. For the second time, I quickly realize. What have I just done? The disgust and anger that flowed through me steadied out my nerves and my gift, but now those have quickly vanished and I'm left empty and partially scared of myself.

The other guard starts back-peddling before disappearing around the corner of the hall. I hear him yell, "Gifted! An escaped gifted!" My original instinct to fight is overcome by a need to hide. I race to the end of the hall and take in my options. The hall branches off to my left and right, but I hear voices growing on both ends. In front of me is a staircase, and I take each step two at a time until I reach the top. Once I get to the top I'm overcome by numbness. There's only one old wooden door so I run through it and hope I'm not just running into a trap.

I slam the door shut behind me and slide the bolt to lock the door. It doesn't take long before I hear guards on the other side of the door trying to break it down. "Okay, how am I going to get out of here?" I say and try to slow my breathing.

For the first time, I scan the room to make out where I am, and a chill runs down my spine. It seems to be some sort of torture chamber. Along the left wall are two large cabinets holding who knows what, and on the right side there are chains hanging from the wall. There's an odd feeling in the air of the room. Cold and empty; sad really.

There's a small window on the far side of the room. I move to it and look outside through the bars on the window. It's on the front side of the castle and must be thirty or so feet up. I shouldn't have gone up the stairs, that was stupid. I was on the ground level. I should have been looking for a door or window to get out of. I glance out over the maze of hedges that circle the castle and can make out bits of light coming from lanterns in the city. Word of my attempted escape will have reached them before I get out of here so I know I can't go there. Everything outside seems to be so still though. Like a completely different world. The breeze from the cool night air lightly blows against my face.

"I need to get out of here," I say, trying to work out a plan.

"I can help you," a deep quiet voice says from behind me. I whip around and scan the empty dark room.

"Who's there?" I ask, my voice shaking. A tall thin man dressed in a uniform similar to that of the other guards steps out from the shadows of the room. "Don't come any closer," I say, my eyes holding his.

"Don't worry, I'm here to help. It's time. It's finally time," his deep voice says and it reminds me of when my mother had said the same thing when the guard came to take her away.

"Time for what?" I ask and raise my voice to be heard over the banging on the door.

"What's your name?" The man deflects, his face coming to life as he starts to walk around the room looking for something. He opens one of the cabinets on the side of the room and pulls out a sword. He moves back in front of me and hands it to me. "Your name?" he asks again.

"Adaline," I say in an uneasy voice as I take the sword in my hands. I've never held a weapon before. It's heavier than it looks, its cool metal handle piercing my skin sends a chill through me. It's old, not as shiny and clean as the ones the guards in the rest of the castle were carrying. It has a beautiful curling design around the handle, and the letters TM engraved at its end.

"Good. Good name. You'll need that," he says, looking to the sword as he moves around me to the window. "You need to go," he says and looks to me. I can tell he notices the confusion on my face. "You don't know how to get out? You can teleport. You're a Force Lifter, right?"

"That's what my mother called it, but I don't know what it means. I don't know what any of this means," I say and tears of frustration and fear build in my eyes. "What am I?" I ask quietly.

"A gifted. You're a gifted," the man says simply. I look to him with pleading eyes wanting him to give me more information. The man begins to explain, "Every once in a while a child will be born with the gift that gives them the ability to enhance one of their five senses, such as hearing something from miles away, or smelling something or someone and immediately identifying it." He pauses, seeing I'm still very lost. "You've used your gift, right? You've made it this far."

I nod my head slightly but add, "But I don't know how to use it. I don't think I'm doing it right."

"Here," he says, pulling out a small gold coin. "Picture this coin sliding around my hand." I think about the coin moving but nothing happens. "Concentrate. To make your gift work to its best ability, you need to block everything out except the object you want to control. Don't just picture it moving, but tell it to move in your head. You can do it."

I clench my fists, hold my breath, and focus on the gold coin in his hand and see nothing else. In my mind, I tell the coin to slide forward on his hand. "Slide forward," I tell the coin and watch as it slowly but surely moves across his hand. I let out my breath and look to him for a response.

"That was good. This is an easy exercise you should do to help you get better at controlling it. I have one more thing I need to teach you. It seems more difficult, but it actually can be a lot easier. Picture the coin out there," he pauses, glancing out the window, "but don't just move it. You have to see it there and it will teleport."

I look from the gold coin to the ground outside the window. I stare into the ground and imagine the coin lying there until it finally appears. I blink hard amazed by what I see.

"Good, now you need to go," he pushes.

"Why are you helping me?" I say forcefully and turn to him.

He's quiet for a minute as if he were looking for the right words, "Because you are meant for more," he says strongly, holding my stare. "Now go."

I close my eyes tight and try to picture myself outside as I did with the coin. Suddenly I'm overcome by a cold wind. I open my eyes and now I'm on the outside. The sun has just fallen below the edge of the forest and darkness masks the world. I look up and see the millions of stars scattered in the sky, and I can't help but smile. I haven't seen stars in seven years.

I look up to the window where I was just at seconds ago and can make out the man's face through the bars. I realize I don't even know his name. I will never know the name of the man who saved my life. He gives me a small nod and then sinks away from the window.

A glint of light from the ground catches my eye and I notice it's the gold coin. I bend down and pick it up. I hold it between my thumb and finger examining it. On one side there's a beautiful engraving of the castle with the words *Dather* stamped under it. On the other side is an engraving of a tree with the words *Freedom Islands* stamped above it and *A Nation Reborn* stamped below it. I take in a sharp breath when I recognize the resemblance this side of the coin has to the tree painting back in the castle. Tears threaten to fill my eyes, but I can't stop now.

I put the coin inside the pocket of my shirt. Then, the quiet cool night bursts into commotion. The main castle doors fly open and I whip around raising my hand just in time to see a large, much more muscular, guard. I've only ever seen him once before in my life. His name is Paylon. He is 18 years old but is already the captain of all of our nation's guards.

I think of him freezing just like I did to the others, except he doesn't freeze. I realize, almost too late, that somehow he may be immune to my gift because it doesn't seem to affect him at all. Shock and numbness surge through my body, but I am already so close. Guard after guard starts pouring out of the castle behind him. I turn and run down the rocky road into the maze, and I can hear the guards pick up their pace behind me.

I lift my hand and just picture the bushes splitting apart. The cuts in the bushes aren't clean, but it's enough to get me through it. Once I'm through a section I make sure to try my best to close it off behind me so Paylon can't proceed through it. I make it through the last section in no time and I can see the stretch of forest just a few paces ahead, but what I don't see is the inconsistency of the rest of the path. I miss my step and drive my head straight into the rocks.

My vision starts to blur and I can't make my body move. Everything starts to hurt. I can feel my blood trickle down my face. Then I hear the footsteps getting closer to me. At first, I think it's Paylon, and that he's finally caught up to me. Then I realize that the footsteps are coming from in front of me.

This is the end. I can feel it, but what I feel instead of a sword being driven through me is the feeling of the guard's hands lifting me into his arms.

He runs, not toward the castle, but away from it into the woods, and that's when I lose consciousness. My world is filled with black, but my mind seems to move faster. It works its way backward, remembering each tick I had ever made on the prison cell wall until it stops at a memory I blocked out long ago. In my unconscious state, my mind forces me to relive that memory. I used to think that was the worst Parting Day, until today.

***

I press my face between the two metal bars of the cell, watching the nurse grow smaller the further down the hall she goes. Mr. Stevens, the man in the cell next to mine, has finally stopped his hysterical crying and the prison returns to its chilling quiet self. I'm not sure why Mr. Stevens had been screaming, but it was enough reason to have them send medical down to the prison.

We were brought here because my mother didn't pay her dues to the King. My father left my mother to raise Titus and me on her own, but it just wasn't possible. Most of us are in here for simply not paying the King's dues. Some are here for worse reasons, but in the end, it doesn't matter. In the end, we are just collected to be held down here until it's our time to be killed. They take a group once a week to the coliseum and murder us in front of the people of Garth. We are made into a symbol of what happens when the laws are broken.

I wonder if there's something wrong with Mr. Stevens. Not

because I'm worried about him, but because I know being sick just gives them a reason to pick you next. Better him than me. Most people down here have just accepted their fate, but not me. I'm going to get my mother and brother out of here. I turn and check the carved lines on the wall. Today is day 1,966 in the cell. You'd think being here for nearly six years would have given me plenty of time to think of a way to get out, but I haven't been that successful. Now that we have some peace and quiet down here I may get somewhere on my newest plan.

"Sister," Titus's childish voice whispers. I turn and see his cheeks look shallower than normal. His brown hair is matted to his forehead and his grey eyes peek out at me. He hates silence so I should have known it was too good to be true. "Can we learn history today? I want to hear the rock story again." I take in a deep breath and glance up in the cell across from mine. Cindy Sewer meets my eyes and I give an apologetic nod. She's nearly 60 years old and Titus and I have taken to calling her our grandmother. She sits on her mattress with her back pressed against the concrete wall. She looks weaker than normal, probably as exhausted as I am after listening to Mr. Stevens screech all morning.

"I'll make it quick," I whisper across the cell. Granny gives a huff of a laugh and waves me off like she doesn't mind. I only agree to tell Titus the story because I know he'll drift to sleep about halfway through and then we can return to our quiet afternoon.

I move and join Titus on the mattress and hand him one of the few treasures we have down here; a book. I got it for him a couple of months ago. I had a pretty decent relationship with the servant who brought us our meals and I had begged her for books I could use to teach Titus about anything. He's nearly seven years old and I'm the only hope he has at learning our country's history, math, or how to read. Some days my mother helps, but usually she stays fixed in her trance. Today is one of those days. I glance over at her, curled up in the corner of the cell just staring into the wall. She does that a lot. It's like her body's here, but her mind is elsewhere. I don't blame her though, most people down here are like that.

"What's the point?" The servant girl had asked me.

"It'll help pass the time," I had lied. In reality, I knew I was getting us out of here, and I needed to make sure Titus would be ready when I did. So, she brought me one book a week for about a month, but then she was swapped out for a different servant who I haven't quite warmed up to yet.

I open the old book and begin to read the story to Titus. "The year is 4912, and it is early May."

"It is late spring in the state of Colorado," Titus's voice layers over my own. I laugh a little as he stumbles over the word Colorado.

"Better that time," I try and encourage him. "On the television, a news story plays where they are talking about the asteroid shower again." Titus lifts his finger and points to the illustration in the book. The furniture is so much more luxurious than any we ever had.

"I want a television one day," Titus says, imagining a future where we could somehow be given a television in this cell.

"Televisions don't exist anymore," I gently remind Titus. Nothing in this book exists anymore. Before our civilization, the population on this planet was much greater and people lived in places called North and South America, Africa, Australia, Europe, and Asia. Now, these places no longer exist because of the asteroid shower.

The shower happened just over 100 years ago, and it is the reason the world I know even exists. The asteroid shower was predicted to happen years before it did, but no one had thought that it could be so extreme. When the shower started it was too late for most people. The asteroids, as we learned later on, were full of atomic energy. Some say radiation, but the true chemicals in the rocks had never been discovered before. When the asteroids hit Earth they exploded, sending their chemicals into the air. Many were injured if not immediately killed in the shower. This atomic energy mixed in some people's bloodstreams and gave them the gift of having an enhanced sense.

"The news says Hawaii is the freeform home," Titus continues to read the story ahead of me.

"Close," I say and reread the line to him. "The news report claims that Hawaii is the freedom island. Scientists have launched a force field over the islands as a barrier."

"But," Titus says in an overly loud and dramatic voice as he turns the page. He holds up his hand to stop me from speaking. I try and hold in my laugh because he says he does this to build the tension. His eyes take in the illustration on the page. The destruction and death sprayed across the book. Slowly he drops his hand and lets me continue the story.

"But the force field wasn't put up in time to avoid all destruction. The islands were hit for hours before the field was up and running, leaving the cities and towns completely demolished." I scan the graphic image of the rubble island until slowly we turn the page together. "The first few years following the shower were spent rebuilding civilization on the Hawaiian Islands. Society had to completely start from the beginning. During the shower the islands shifted along the Earth's plate until finally settling."

"The Hawaiian is now freedom," Titus tries to read again and lets out a big yawn.

"The Hawaiian Islands were renamed the Freedom Islands," I correct. "And in the new world, there have been three generations of Renon rulers." This is the part where Titus always starts to doze off, but I continue telling the story anyway.

"Our ancestors that were infected by the rock's atomic energy, but survived, sometimes passed down the gifts to their children. The original King and Queen, King Renon's grandparents, were both gifted and they tried to keep the world at peace between those with powers and those without." Titus's head falls heavy against my shoulder. He's surely asleep now, but I keep reading because this is the part I struggle to understand the most. The part where people are given a second chance at society and somehow they messed up again.

"However, when their kids were not born with the gift they became enraged and jealous of those with gifts. From then on anyone with a gift was hunted down and imprisoned to follow the King's command." I was six when King Renon was crowned at the age of 13 so I don't remember much about life under his parents, but the tyranny didn't stop short with them. King Renon is only 22 now, and in many people's opinion he's too young to have all this power. His mother and father reportedly passed in their sleep after both were very ill and a child was made King of the most powerful nation in the world.

"Garth is the capital of our country, Dather, which is located on a small island that used to be called Oahu. Over the past decades, the islands have had many civil war breakouts trying to find who is the most superior." I turn the page, knowing the next image is the worst in the book. I'm always glad Titus doesn't usually make it this far in the story. "We call these the Alignmass battles." Painted across the page is the result of war; death. "Every year each island will send their best group of soldiers to fight to the death to determine which island should rule. Dather has been on top since the beginning of this new world. As a result, everyone follows us, under the rule of King Renon."

The sound of a large metal door slamming shut startles me and I shove the book under the mattress. At my movement, Titus wakes and looks around panicked. He grabs my hand and begins squeezing it three times then a pause and then three more times. Parting Day is beginning.

"It's okay Titus," I say softly in his ear. I know I can't guarantee him that. I know these guards are coming to take some of us to be executed. Together, Titus and I listen to the heavy footsteps as they get closer and closer to our cell. When they appear in front of us tears are already streaming down my face. I have to save us, it can't be one of us. When I look up at the guard I see his stone face turn away from our cell and into granny's. They open the barred doors to her cell and I watch as two men drag her from the mattress. Titus keeps squeezing my hand harder and harder. He can't find the words he wants to say so he starts screaming.

"Titus you need to be quiet," I beg him. The three guards glance into our cell one last time before they leave, taking granny with them. Titus continues to scream and cry and squeeze my hand until he's driven himself into exhaustion. I just hold him and whisper over and over again, "It's okay Titus. She's going to be okay. She's going to be free."

***

I am going to be free.

Chapter 3

When I awake I rocket up into a sitting position. I look around, confused. I'm in the middle of the woods and it is probably about mid-morning. In front of me is the guard who brought me here, he sits with his back to me and is wearing a thin white t-shirt. He has a strong build to his body. His dirty blonde hair is slightly shorter than the common shoulder length.

There is a sword on his belt, two water bottles, his navy jacket, and a ragged backpack lying next to him. In the dirt by my hip is the sword I got from the castle. My hand moves to my head where there is a piece of wet cloth. Tied around my right forearm is the rest of the stained red fabric. Quietly, I grab my sword with both hands and point it at the guard.

"What do you want with me?" I ask, causing the guard to turn around. My blood runs cold as I see his face for the first time. There's something familiar about him, and my mind races to remember where I know him.

"Whoa," he says when his eyes catch the blade in my hands. "I'm trying to help you."

"Drop your sword," I say, my mind still wondering as to who he is. I watch him slowly unclip his sword and it falls to the ground by his feet.

"Adaline," he begins, "It's me. It's Alexander." My mind connects his name to the memories it had been searching for.

"Alexander?" my shaking voice questions. Before I was thrown in prison I used to be close friends with Alexander. He's my age, and he was my only neighbor out in the valleys that surround our town.

His physical appearance is close to what I remember, except now he's not a ten-year-old boy. He's tall, tan with green eyes. His dirty blonde hair just long enough to cover the scar over his left eye that he got one day when we were out on an adventure, as we had called it. Climbing trees, running through the creeks in the forest, and exploring the different antique shops in town.

"I didn't know you were a guard at the castle," I say, still not believing it's really him. Slowly I lower the sword back to the ground, but I keep my left hand on the grip.

"My father was assigned after you were taken and I followed five years later when I was fifteen." He clears his throat, "Passed the test on the first try. Probably because I could find my way around the castle blindfolded. I basically grew up there."

"Guess we still have something in common," I say even though it's a poor joke. "So, why'd you do it?"

"Do what?" his eyes narrow in confusion.

"Save me. It's your job to kill any escaping prisoners. What do you want with me?" I ask again, returning to my original question.

"You think I would kill you?" Alexander asks, shocked.

"Well we haven't seen each other in almost seven years," I say, shrugging my shoulders, even though I know it's an impossible thought. Alexander and I always felt like we had a connection from the very first moment I met him. I actually can't even remember not knowing him, he was just always there. I think our parents already had our wedding planned out if I'm being honest.

"Well maybe we haven't seen each other, but there wasn't a day that went by I didn't think about you. I mean, you've always been seconds away from me, how could I ever just forget you? There wasn't any way I was going to lose my second in command again," Alexander responds, using the titles we had given ourselves when we were little. He was the leader and I was his second. I let him humor himself with the idea of being in command when we both knew I was the real leader.

"Adaline," he says gentler when he sees my face is still processing. "I was on duty outside of the maze last night. I heard a crash and found you unconscious."

"So you picked me up and ran off with me?" I question him.

I watch him grab his bag and out of instinct, I tighten my grip on the sword. He notices and says, "I'm just pulling out a note that explains this." He turns and digs through his bag, but I don't loosen my tight grasp. As he had said he pulls out a thin piece of parchment. "Two years ago I woke up in my room and my father was gone, along with some other guards that were close with my father. For some reason, King Renon told Paylon to end the search for them. 'They were getting too old to work. They wouldn't make it far.' Paylon had said. My father left this under his pillow." He hands it to me and I scan over the words

Dear Alexander,

I never wanted to leave you, but I'm afraid I have to go. When the time is right we will meet again. I know that you are confused and scared. There is so much you don't know, but I don't have much time. I want you to know that I have the gift and I am a Future Holder. Soon you will meet Adaline face to face, and it is your job to save her. The two of you must flee the castle and hide in the woods. You will know when the time is right.

I love you, Alexander.

George Thompson

"Your dad has the gift?" I ask and Alexander nods his head. His father and my mother were both Future Holders, and I feel as though we have both been guided to this moment based on our parents' visions. "You've just been waiting to save me for two years?" I ask him in a lighter tone and he laughs, taking the note back from me.

"So that's why I picked you up and ran off with you," Alexander concludes.

"So how long have I been out?" I ask. I look down at the ground and run my fingers through the soft mud, feeling the warmth of the earth that I have missed so much. My eyes scan up through the canopy of large palm trees hanging over us and I take note of the moving sun. My muted grey prison uniform feels so out of place in this forest of deep and vibrant colors.

"Just over ten hours or so." He coughs to clear his throat before he continues, "I'm sorry about your family," he says and drops his eyes.

"Were you at Parting Day?" I ask softly, even though I know the answer is yes. Everyone was at Parting Day. "Was it quick?" my small voice whispers.

Alexander nods his head and I see his eyes fill with sadness. "She never looked afraid."

"She was always so strong," I say. "How'd they do it?" I ask, knowing that each Parting Day brings different ways for them to kill off the prisoners.

Alexander is quiet for a moment and I can tell the words he's about to say aren't easy. "They had hangings yesterday." Knowing my mother died by suffocation makes my shortness of breath heavy in my chest.

"I'm sorry about Titus too," Alexander offers and my eyes meet his.

"How'd you know about that?" I ask, and the pain I felt when I held my little brother's dying hand washes over me.

"You were calling out to him when you were unconscious," Alexander explains and my eyes threaten to fill with tears.

"We were just so close," I say softly. "I'm fine though, really." I wipe my flooded eyes dry and try to close the feelings out again.

Alexander understands it's something I don't want to talk about so he changes the subject back to our issue at hand. "We need to get moving again, soon. They'll be coming to look for us."

"Who will be? What exactly are we doing?" I ask.

"Paylon and a search team. King Renon won't let an escaped prisoner go, and now a fleeing guard. We don't really have much choice but to keep running," he admits. I know he's right and just as I'm about to agree I hear horses not too far in the distance. Alexander's head snaps in the direction of the sounds and knows we need to hide. He helps me move behind a cluster of trees and we sit and watch.

The sound of hooves pounding into the earth's surface grows louder and I catch a glimpse of three elegant white horses coming our way. The horses stop a couple of paces ahead of us. I recognize the leather saddles outlined in gold fabric. Their reins are a golden color as well. They are horses from our city out to find us. The three guards dismount and step into view. I'm not surprised to see the faces of Paylon, and his 2 best marksmen, Codian and Chadian.

They are two sixteen-year-old trouble making twin brothers that have such great excellence in shooting they could hit a gold coin with a bow and arrow from a hundred feet away. The guards who worked in the prison always talked about how they were jealous of them.

Codian and Chadian both have on their regular navy blue jackets and pants with red and gold ties. Since they are identical twins most of their features are the same; transparent blue eyes, blonde hair, and the fact that both their bodies have a strong muscular build to them. Paylon, however, is not in a regular navy blue uniform. Since he is the captain of the entire nation's guards he is dressed in a tight long-sleeved purple shirt that has a gold-colored stripe running down both sides of the shirt and gold cuffs on the end of the sleeves. He has beige pants with solid gold metal protectors for his legs. He wears a long white cape that has a tall stiff collar that is also purple with hints of gold. He has odd golden eyes and short brown hair.

"Any sign of them?" Paylon asks, his voice echoing throughout the forest.

"Not any that I can see," Chadian and Codian respond, almost in unison. They both take their hands and run it through their blonde hair in confusion.

"Codian, I want you to report a message to King Renon to send the Lost Souls. They should be able to help scent the path they took," Paylon commands.

"I'm on it. I'll be back before nightfall tomorrow," Codian says, obeying everything his leader instructs.

All three get on their horses. Codian starts heading back toward the castle, and Chadian and Paylon continue forward. Once the pounding hooves of the horses have silenced I speak first, "Lost Souls? Who are the Lost Souls?" I turn to Alexander and see the shock and scared look on his face.

"They're enslaved people with gifts," Alexander says softly. I knew that anyone with the gift was required to go in and work for the King, but no one really talks about what happens after that. The way

44

Alexander says that they are enslaved makes me think they don't get much choice in the matter.

"The ones Paylon is calling for will be the Hounds," he continues, still staring forward at where Paylon was just at, and I can see he's trying to make a new plan for us. "The Lost Souls are tortured humans that have the gift with any enhanced sense. Hounds are people that have an enhanced sense of smell that the King has enslaved for tracking. They do exactly what they are told to do and accomplish it in their best ability. They've never lost a search, although their sense of smell can travel a good five miles, their eyesight is average. If we move now we could get out of their reach."

"But I thought you said they've never lost a search?" I respond, trying to bring some common sense into play. "Why would we run if they'd just find us anyway? It'd be better to save our energy for fighting them, right?"

Alexander looks at me and lets a sly smirk fall across his face, "They haven't lost a search, but that doesn't mean they can't."

"So if we are going to move we need to do it now. What's the full plan?" I ask, ready to give Alexander control.

"Well, for one, we know Paylon is heading deeper into the forest so that's where the Hounds will be going," Alexander says, trying to explain his idea. He should know best since he's been working with the patrol for over nearly two years. "That means we should turn right and head deeper toward that part of the woods," he starts rambling as if trying to convince himself.

Alexander sees the confusion on my face and pushes, "Adaline trust me I know what I'm doing. We need to get started now because we will be walking all day to get enough distance between us."

I reluctantly obey since I don't have any better ideas. He folds his jacket, shoves it into his bag, and slings it over his shoulder. Then, he hands me one of the water bottles and says, "Besides, it will be a way for us to catch up." He helps me up and we start heading in the opposite direction of Paylon and Chadian.

"Start from the beginning," Alexander says, cueing me to update him on where I've been the last seven years.

"The beginning would probably be the night I was taken," I say and let out a heavy breath. I never stop thinking of that night. I glance at Alexander out of the corner of my eye. In my gut I know I can trust him and he really is here to help me, but I don't really know him. I haven't seen him in years, am I supposed to just act like that time apart never happened?

"You don't have to tell me," Alexander starts to object, seeing my hesitation to talk with him.

"It was November 12th, 5012," I interrupt him. "I was nine years old." I know he is practically a stranger to me now, but I do want to walk through that night out loud again. My mother never wanted to talk about it. I start to explain the night to Alexander and as I do I feel myself relive it all over again.

My heavy eyelids fall open and I gaze over the worn wooden walls of my bedroom. A wet and moldy smell fills the heavy air. My eyes are straining to make out much else in the room. It must be 1:00 or 2:00 in the morning. I prop myself up on my elbow and can make out a very dim glowing light creeping under my door. My mother must be up with Titus again.

I swing my feet over the edge of the bed and carefully place them on the icy floor. I walk over to the door and the wooden floor creaks beneath my feet. I pull open my door and the dim yellow light from the fireplace pours in. I look out into the kitchen, and once my eyes adjust to the dim light I see my mother is sitting in one of the kitchen chairs rocking my younger brother Titus in her arms.

"Adaline you should be asleep," my mother says, not looking up from Titus. This has become routine for us. Almost every night for the past few weeks I'll wake up and come out to find my mother with Titus.

I don't respond to her. Instead, I just walk over and sit in the chair across from her. I lay my head on the table and trace its wooden swirls with my finger while flattening out the wrinkles in my thin nightgown with my other hand.

"Is father home yet?" I ask her in a soft voice.

"Adaline, it's been three months. Your father isn't coming home," my mother says with no emotion in her voice. She tucks her beautiful long brown hair behind her ear and turns to face me.

"Sometimes I think that's what you do in the middle of the night. You just sit up and wait for him," I pause and a wall of silence settles between us. I add, "I wait up for him too."

"Well you shouldn't," she says shortly. "Trust me, Adaline, I'm not waiting for him." I look into her empty blue eyes, and I can see the lies swimming in them. My mother stands and walks into her room to lay Titus back in the nest of blankets on her bed. She comes back out and pulls me into a tight hug.

Together we walk back into my room, and I crawl under the heavy blankets. My mother kisses my forehead and says, "We're okay without him." I watch as she leaves and closes the door behind her. I reach over and pull open the drawer of my nightstand. I take out an old picture of my father, Titus, and I.

"I miss you," I say in a hushed voice, thinking somehow he'd be able to hear me.

I remember when we took this picture like it was yesterday. It's the last moment I spent with my father. We were celebrating his birthday. Well, all of our birthday's really. Titus, my father, and I all had birthdays throughout July. My mother said she wanted to take our picture so she had my father and I sit on the couch and he held Titus in his arms. He made some joke about how old he was getting, and my mother captured the picture with us both in mid-laugh, but only half of my father got captured in the picture. My eyes scan the photograph, looking in my father's face for some explanation to his disappearance, but the answers aren't captured here. I place it on top of my nightstand and roll over on my side.

Slowly, I start to feel myself drift back to sleep until I hear a loud bang on the front door. A second later I hear the door being smashed down and booming voices fill the house. "This is the Garth Patrol. You are under arrest for failure to maintain your payments to the King." Suddenly my door is swung open and a guard grabs my arm. He yanks me out of bed, and at the last second, I grab the photograph off of my nightstand.

In the loud chaos that rings throughout my house, I feel my mind fall distant as I watch the world around me crumble away. I wish I had known that night was the last I'd ever get to sit at that dinner table with my mother. The last night I'd have a bed of my own or a bed at all. The last night I would get to be a kid.

"I remember you telling me your father was missing," Alexander says to me. "I hadn't realized he left."

I nod my head. "I hate talking about him," I say harshly. "He's the reason we were ever thrown in prison in the first place." When I say this I realize he is also the reason my mother and brother are dead. I hadn't thought my hatred for him could grow anymore, but it does. I still have the photograph from that night in my pocket and I feel as though it burns against me.

"So what all happened after you realized my family had been taken in as prisoners? You were in a similar situation except it was your mother that left you," I ask, turning the conversation off of me. I realize my comment about his mother leaving may have been a bit harsh but he doesn't seem to think so. I vaguely remember her just telling them she wanted to live a different life and left. At least he got some explanation and she actually said goodbye. I don't need to explain the rest of what I've been through. He isn't interested in hearing what it was like living in a cell for seven years.

"Well, like I said, after your family was taken in my father went to work for King Renon. I went with him since my mother was gone, and we worked together. We got to live in the castle," Alexander says as though it is something to brag about. "Although I didn't work much, I mostly explored the castle, but of course I had my boundaries. Like no going down into the prison, and no going into the treasury," he pauses and glances to me. "I wanted to walk down and talk to you. To let you know you weren't alone. I wanted to make sure you were okay, but that didn't mean I didn't have people doing the checking on you for me. Alyssa got you those books, right?"

Silence settles between us and I stop walking. "You got me those books?" I ask and scan his face. Those books kept my brother and me sane. Alexander has been trying to help me all this time, but I had no idea.

"Yeah, I found out Alyssa was in charge of taking meals down to the prison and I'd ask about you and your family all the time." Alexander drops his head and his cheeks flush a light pink. If I'm being honest I haven't thought about anyone from the outside of the cell for seven years, but he has been doing the exact opposite. Alexander begins walking again and I follow. "She told me you had wanted books to help pass the time so I collected some and had her sneak them down to you."

Alexander continues to talk about living in the castle and how he still attended school until his father disappeared. He has definitely lived a much more luxurious life than I have. He always had enough food to eat, a bed of his own to sleep in, and a constant feeling of safety. When I imagined escaping the prison hiding in the woods with a former guard was not what I was expecting.

As Alexander tells his stories I catch myself scanning him, and I realize I'm going to need to decide if staying with him is my best option. I want to trust him, but he is the spitting image of the kind of people I hate. The ones who get everything handed to them, and have never had to worry for their lives. As much as my mind tries to place Alexander in that role though, some things stick out to me. Like the books he got me, the effort he put into knowing I was okay, and the way he talked about my mother's death. My brain sees him as a threat, as the enemy, a guard at the castle, but my heart feels he is a friend. The question is, which one is right?

Chapter 4

The sun is starting to set and we need to find a place to stop for the night. Up ahead I see a formation of large boulders. As we get closer I notice that there is an opening, creating a small cave.

"We'll stop here for the night," Alexander says, examining the makeshift shelter.

"Good, looks sturdy enough and right next to a creek. That'll be good for food and water," I list off, trying not to be completely useless to him.

"We can eat these berries too," he says and points to a bush full of colorful yellow berries. They are common in our town. Almost everyone can afford them, but my family was lucky enough to have bushes of them in our backyard. We call them ray berries. Not only because of their bright color but also because of the warm juices inside. "We will start our fire once it is completely dark. That way the smoke is as hidden as possible. No one will be close enough to us to see its flames either. We'll put out the fire at the first signs of daylight, and cook any fish we catch in the morning on the hot coals.

Okay?" he asks bluntly. I agree, feeling just as useless as I had before.

As Alexander starts to collect wood for the fire I go over and fill my hands full of ray berries, and refill our water bottles that Alexander had brought with him. I have been dying to use my gift out here. There are so many possible things I could do, things I could build, but I resist. I'm not ready to tell Alexander about my gift. I've always had a problem with trusting people. This is just another one of those cases. Plus, I don't even really know how to use it and that's kind of embarrassing.

Once my hands are full of berries I return to the cave. "Maybe we should see how your injuries are doing," Alexander says and I go and sit next to him.

He starts to unravel the first bandage on my arm and I ask, "What exactly happened last night?" My mind starts to walk through the night's events over Alexander's voice; me running through the castle, learning how to teleport, running through the maze, my mother and Titus being killed, and then my train of thought stops. Mother and Titus. I suddenly feel the sorrow and pain I told myself not to have wash over me, but I need to be strong.

"Well, for one, all the injuries came from your fall on the rocks," I hear Alexander say and I let the thought of my mother and Titus go. "Everything after that was running through the woods downhill. I found a place to stop and bandaged everything up. Unfortunately, I'm not a trained professional so I couldn't tell you how severe the wounds looked. Plus, it was dark so cut me some slack." The first bandage falls off my arm and I can see that the wound is just a scratch now. I exhale with relief.

"So I can tell you that you shouldn't worry about this wound," Alexander says. Then he unties the one on my head and thankfully, according to what he says, it isn't bad at all. "There are only a few scrapes that are scabbed up and a couple of bruises. So this one should be just fine."

I respond, "It's a good thing your survival skills are better than your medical skills or else we'd have a problem." I turn my head and take a look at the scenery around us. Alexander starts the fire and it comes to life in front of us, giving off immense amounts of heat. It's the only source of light in this pool of darkness. I look up through the thick arch of tree branches and see the thousands of stars that I have been dying to see again. Alexander notices that I'm looking at the stars and he knows that I've missed being out here.

He throws his arms over my shoulder and says, "Just like old times, right? Remember when we used to go out and camp in the woods?"

I turn my focus from the stars to him. "Of course. Especially when you would get scared and cry, begging me to walk you back home. I hope you've outgrown that fear of the dark," I say, reliving the memory. I look back up at the stars and for the first time in over seven years, I feel happy and free.

I can barely remember the feeling of both happiness and freedom. *Freedom* I think to myself and for the first time in a while I let myself think of being free; running through the grass, playing in the creeks, and climbing the trees. I actually think I might even miss school.

This would be my last year since our school levels stop at 12th grade. After that, you have to get a job or go to work with the castle. Then I realize I won't even get to finish school or get a job in the town I was born in. This freedom I have been granted with is going to be much different from any life I had once pictured having because now I'm a fugitive. Now I have the nation's best commanders searching for me.

"Alexander," I say, my weak voice cracking.

"Yeah?" he asks, turning his head to me, but I don't meet his eyes.

"How long do you think they're going to search for us? Will we spend the rest of our lives running from them?" I ask as the haunting thought settles in my mind.

He tightens his arm trying to give me some comfort. "It's hard to say, Adaline. I know that there has to be something important about us if King Renon has sent Paylon out here, but maybe if we can stay hidden long enough they will call off the search." I can think of a few reasons why King Renon would send someone as important as Paylon out to find us, and my mind lingers on the two soldiers I killed during my escape last night.

"Where are we even going? Do you even know what's out here in these woods?" I ask.

"Not much I'm afraid. Here," Alexander pauses and pulls out a tattered piece of cloth from his bag. He unfolds it and I see that it is a map of Dather and all the surrounding islands. He hands the map to me and I hold the fragile piece of fabric in my hands as he continues, "You can pick where we go."

I let my eyes gaze over the old map. There isn't much on the map for Dather. I see Garth labeled and the forest. There's a small town that sits on the very edge of the island called Sard. I've heard of it before, it's where all the factories that produce the clothing we wear and the warehouses that store the food we buy are located. King Renon will have word of our disappearance there before we even wake up tomorrow, and even though Alexander's survival skills are quite excellent I'm not sure how long we can live off of ray berries. I haven't even seen a single animal out here.

I'm about to admit that I'm out of ideas when I notice an island just off the shore of Dather by Sard. *Libertas* is written in a small cursive print next to it. A small memory starts to return to me. I close my eyes and my father's face swims into view. I watch as he hands me a small book. I see my little hand reach across the cover and open the book. The first page is a map of a single island. Scribbled across the top of the page is the title *Libertas*.

The island is broken up into five sections with the capital placed directly in the center. I hear my father's voice say, "This is where we are moving to Adaline. This is where our new home will be." There's a loud knock on the door and I see worry rise in my father's face.

I open my eyes and see the orange flick of a fire in front of me. I'm back in the woods. "Here. We are going here." I let my index finger grace the map where *Libertas* is located.

"All right, then that's where we are headed." I look up to him and see a confused look on his face.

"What is it?" I ask.

"Nothing, I just realized I don't think I've ever heard anything about that island," he says perplexed.

"I think I remember my father talking about it before," I mumble. I hand the map back to Alexander and he places it back in his bag.

"Tomorrow will be another long day of traveling so we should get some rest," Alexander says between a large yawn. He stands and starts to move his things into the small cave.

"In a second," I say and lay down on the forest floor. I lay here on my side, watching the glowing orange fire dance against the black night backdrop. The thought of putting myself inside a small and closed space makes me sick. So instead, I lay out by the fire. It doesn't take long for the bright orange flames to pull me into a heavy trance, and after a while my eyelids fall closed.

I awake to oddly familiar surroundings. The cold stone ground, being surrounded by a dark and dim light, the feeling of soreness in my back, and the eerie silence. It all suddenly reminds me of the cell my mother, Titus, and I were in for seven years. Then, pictures of Alexander and I in the woods appear in my mind. Did I just dream all of that?

My heart quickens as flashes of my life in the prison mix in with those of Alexander and I can't keep the two straight. I'm caught somewhere between reality and what's in my head. I hear the screams of the other children in the prison, slowly dying from starvation, their cries ringing in my ears. The man in the cell next to mine, Mr. Stevens, crying over the loss of his wife and daughter still haunting me. "I didn't want to do it," he cries over and over on an endless loop trying to force himself to believe he did the right thing by killing them so they wouldn't have to suffer. All of these horrible things aching inside of me, but there's one light. I see Alexander's face, pure and comforting. It's like coming home after being lost for so long. The flashes from the prison cell stop coming and the only sound in the dark room is my heavy breathing.

I roll over, half expecting to see my mother and Titus lying in the corner on the old torn up mattress, but find myself coming face to face with a sleeping Alexander. Relief and sadness wash over me. Relief that the memories from last night were not a dream, that I actually am here with Alexander, but sadness because it just reminds me again that my mother and Titus are really gone.

Alexander must have moved us into the cave after I had fallen asleep. It's still dark outside, but I can start to make out rays of sunlight. I crawl to the entrance of the cave and try not to wake Alexander. I take in deep breaths of the morning air and remind myself that I am not locked up. I am not trapped. I look out of our small quiet cave and I see that our fire has died off overnight. I can still make out hints of smoke coming off the still warm stones.

There's a soft sound of running water from the creek to my left. I look back into the cave and see Alexander still asleep, and then

I turn back to the creek and see fish swimming through it. My first thought is to use my gift to move the fish from the creek to the hot stones. I look into the creek and follow the slimy creatures with my eyes. I focus harder and harder and try to see them from the creek to the stones. The creek starts to ripple and splash, but I can't get control of any of the fish. It's no use. The adrenaline from escaping the castle made using this gift much easier.

When I was younger my father used to take me out into the woods all the time. I remember one specific summer day when we had gone together. I was only five so my father carried me up on his shoulders. We had been walking along a creek that day and I remember looking down over his head at the little fish swimming in the currents.

"Daddy, I want a pet fish," I squealed and kicked my feet against his chest.

"Adaline, we can't take these little guys back with us. We have nothing to carry them in. Plus this is their home," I remember his warm voice had said to me. He stopped and looked down to the river for a moment. I think I remember crying. I always used to throw tantrums when things didn't go my way.

He put me down next to the river and started digging a shallow hole at the edge. I remember him explaining to me that he was going to build a fishpond for my fish. He dug a deep round hole next to the river and left a little sliver of dirt between the two. Then he removed the barrier wall and let the water flow into his hole. I remember kneeling there with my face inches from the water, waiting for a fish to swim into it.

Then, the current brought this little shiny yellow sliver of a fish into it. As soon as it did my father got a big rock and put it between my pond and the creek.

"There you go! Your own little fish," he had said and I'm sure I jumped up and down with excitement. I remember after the excitement had worn off I got really sad because the fish was all by himself so I told my father we needed to get him some friends.

We spent the rest of the afternoon pushing fish into our little pond and I remember lying next to it on my belly, just poking my fingers in and out of the water, watching the fish swim around me. "We're playing," I remember telling my father. The memory starts to slip away and I'm back to staring at this creek that has calmed since my gift sent ripples through it. I miss him... but I hate him. I realize I hope he's dead because it's not fair he gets to live and my mother and brother don't. If I ever find him he's going to wish he were dead.

I kneel next to the creek and watch the fish swim around. I try to push my father from my mind as much as I can because I don't have the energy to waste on thoughts of him right now. Then, I start digging a deep hole next to the river. If it worked for my father maybe it'll work for me. After I've got a deep enough hole I tear down the barrier between it and the creek. I watch the water slosh into my hole filling it to the top. I grab a large rock to use as my barrier and wait for a fish to swim into my trap.

It doesn't take long until a small baby fish swims right into the hole. I quickly push the rock down between the hole and the river and catch my first fish. I soon realize I now need to get this guy from here to the hot coals. I remember the bag Alexander was carrying yesterday. I return to the cave and find it lying inside the opening. I dig through it, not taking note of everything inside, until I find a smaller bag that is empty and a handheld knife. I take them and return to the creek. Carefully, I scoop the fish into the bag. The water drains through the cloth material leaving just the little fish flipping around.

For a second I feel like I should let the fish go, but food is so scarce right now, I don't have much choice. I've been living on bread and a poor excuse for soup for seven years. This fish will be the first real food I've had in years.

I lift the rock barrier and wait for another fish to swim inside. While I'm waiting I take the knife and begin to prepare the fish to eat. I used to watch my mother do it all the time with the fish my father would bring home. We could hardly afford to buy anything so most of the food we ate came from the woods. I know I'm doing it wrong, but I think it's close enough. I continue to catch, wait, and prepare until I have 8 good-sized fish. I return to the warm stones and carefully lay the prepared fish out to cook. Once the bag is emptied I rinse it in the creek and then lay it out next to the fire to dry. The smell of real food comes almost instantly, and I am not missing the one piece of bread I got back in the cell. I try and push all thoughts of that place out of my mind.

I hear Alexander stir and wake behind me. "So I see you're making breakfast," he says still half asleep.

"Well, I thought I'd try and not be completely useless to you," I respond.

"Hey! You're not useless. You make great company," he says. I can tell he can't come up with anything more to say. Yet, he continues to try and persuade me to believe him, "And apparently you're great at fishing. You're also good at collecting ray berries," and I see him pull out the rest of our berries from yesterday. He had wrapped them in leaves and set them inside the cave with us last night.

"I hope you don't mind I used this bag to catch the fish," I admit, glancing at his extra bag. "And your knife," I add and hand over the knife I had used.

"That bag's for you, so I don't mind," he says, grinning. A bead of sweat rolls from his hairline and he looks up toward the sun. "It's going to be hot today," he concludes.

"It's July, right?" I ask.

"Yeah, but it's hot enough it could be August," he says. I can already feel the sweat beginning to bubble on my forehead.

"Can I see that knife again?" I ask him and extend my empty hand out to him.

"Yeah, sure," he says and hands the knife back over to me.

I take the knife from him and stick it into the fabric on my pants, just above my knee. "I think shorts would be more suitable with today's weather," I say as I finish cutting one leg of my grey pants. I move to the other leg and do the same. When I hand the knife back to Alexander I watch as he glances from the knife to his pants, considering cutting his own clothes. "What's wrong?" I ask.

"Nothing," he says quickly, and I watch him cut an even line around his pants at the knee.

"What else do you have in that bag?" I ask since I didn't take an inventory of it earlier.

"Not a needle and thread if that's what you're looking for," he says back, laughing as he hands me his bag. I take out its contents and see what we have to survive on. There's his navy jacket, his father's letter, the map, and a deep purple folder. I pull the folder out and Alexander's eyes land on it.

"That's nothing," he starts to says. *Hunting Gifted* is written in gold print across the front. I open the folder and sift through the collection of papers inside. Most are torn or extremely worn, clearly passed down from soldier to soldier.

The last paper in the folder is titled *THE GIFTED*. Printed down the aged sheet are the signs of all five senses and the multitude of gift titles. I never knew there were so many combinations of gifts. My eyes hang on the symbol for enhanced sight, feeling drawn to it.

"It's nothing?" I ask and hand the folder back to him. "Have you ever caught one?"

"No, I don't hunt people," Alexander says disgusted. "They're just papers from the castle." He shoves them back into his bag and pulls out the last of his items, a first aid kit. I open the kit and see there are some more wraps like the ones I had on my arm, different medicines for fevers and the common cold, and a thick stainless steel needle and rolls of nylon.

"You should take some of those wraps," Alexander offers.

"Thanks," I say softly and take a roll of the white bandages. He's given me my own bottle of water, doesn't mind that I have sword, let's me borrow his knife, and now shares his small amount of medical supplies. His kindness is comforting and I'm starting to feel bad for questioning whether I should stay with him.

"What do you think?" I ask, and we stand up to examine our makeshift shorts. We both laugh as neither of them are very proportioned to our bodies. The muscles in my face feel tight and I wonder when the last time I really laughed like that was.

"They're great," Alexander lies and takes his seat next to me again. "Here are some ray berries," he offers, handing me the bright yellow berries. I take one and place it between my teeth popping it and sending warm sweet juice across my tongue. I place one after another in my mouth until I have devoured my share of the berries. Almost telepathically we both reach down and collect our fish at the same time.

The taste of real food nearly brings tears to my eyes. I want to eat it all in one bite, and as slow as possible all at the same time. I go for the later and savor every bite of real food. When I'm finished eating I collect the scraps of fabric and place them into my bag.

Then, I suddenly remember what is in the pocket of my shirt. The journal my mother had given me before she died. I'm about to pull it out when I stop myself. I'm not sure I want Alexander to know. This is kind of something I want to keep to myself. Although I don't see the point since the diary is locked and I can't even open it, but there

64

has to be a reason she would give it to me. If she was a Future Holder then she must know I'll figure out a way to open it. I take the journal, the old family photograph, and gold coin from my pockets and shove them into the bag Alexander said I could have. It's still a little damp and smells of fish, but it's better than nothing.

Alexander is the first to break the silence, "So I think we've traveled far enough east, thus saying the castle is north, that we can start heading south, and deeper into the woods. If I'm predicting right the Hounds, Paylon, Codian, and Chadian will all head into the western section of the woods. While we are in the eastern section."

"You know, it's horrible that they're called Hounds," I say, and my nose wrinkles up with disgust.

"I hadn't given it much thought," Alexander admits. I glance up to him and his face looks distant and sad. He was trained to call them that. I know he isn't responsible for their title.

"I didn't mean you were horrible for calling them that," I say gently, trying to make him feel better. "I meant the King is disgusting for treating them like dogs."

I think about how literal my statement is. They are prisoners in their own body, forced to use their gift of enhanced smell to track. I know if we get caught that's what will happen to me since I have a gift. I won't be one of the Hounds because I have an enhanced sense of sight, but my mind starts to imagine the different ways I could be used for my gift and my stomach threatens to give up the fish I just ate.

"We better get started," I say as I stand, determined to never have to be a prisoner again.

I can feel my internal clock telling me I'm running out of time to make my decision whether or not I want to continue this journey with Alexander. The more time I spend with him the more I realize I don't want to be alone out here. He's starting to feel like a friend, like a teammate in this mess. I know now that I've made my decision, and I lend him my hand.

Chapter 5

Alexander and I have been moving deeper into the woods all morning. We've been steadily moving up in elevation and have entered a section of the woods that is thick with different types of trees. Alexander says some of them are pine trees, which is good. He thinks their strong smell will cover our scent and make it more difficult for the Hounds to find us. We start talking about how each of our lives was, inside and out of the castle. Alexander hands me one of the water bottles and tells me to keep drinking as we go. I don't go into much detail on my end, more so to spare myself from reliving the past.

Alexander seems to have lived a much more luxurious life on the other side of the castle. He tells me stories from the different training camps he had to go to, and about how life in our city progressed. He continued to go to school and he tells me about some of our classmates. In our school system, you are separated and assigned to a class and a teacher at the grade zero level and that is the class and teacher you advance with until you graduate. We had been assigned the same class and teacher. He says he would have graduated first in our class this year, and our teacher Ms. White is even engaged now.

"Did you ever fight?" I ask and glance up to him, the afternoon sun glowing on his face. "All that training, did you ever use any of it?"

"I wish I could say no," he says and his voice falls dry.

"You don't have to tell me about it," I say, cutting him off. It's easy to talk about the good stuff. I only shared the best moments of my time in prison. The days mother would smile and fix my hair. The times Titus didn't break down. When the prison was quiet on cold nights, mostly because we were freezing to death, but any time there wasn't screaming or crying it was a good day.

Suddenly I hear the needles in the trees in front of us rustle. I step forward and stretch out my right arm in front of Alexander. If I have to use my gift I'm going to. Well, I'm going to try to. Alexander will have to know I have the gift eventually. Now that I've decided I want us to be a team I'm going to need to start trusting him with this information. The woods fall silent again, but I don't move.

"Adaline I'm sure it's," Alexander starts to say but is cut off as an arrow flies toward us. I watch it as if I'm in a trance. It whizzes right by my face, just barely grazing my cheek, and sticks into a tree behind me. My hand touches the spot it brushed. I pull my fingers from my face and they are red with blood. I look back up into the tree the arrow came from and can see a dark small figure getting ready to load another arrow.

"Run!" I yell to Alexander and he breaks off our path to the right.

I know I have two choices, run away and hope we get out of reach of the arrows or take out the shooter. Running around the forest like an animal being hunted is the last thing I want to do, so I run straight ahead to the tree the arrow flew from and begin to climb up it. The dark figure tries to shoot an arrow down at me, but it can't make it through the maze of branches before snapping. As I get closer the figure starts to climb higher into the tree. I move faster than they do and as I reach up, my hand clasps onto their ankle.

"Let go!" I hear a female voice call out. I yank down on her ankle and rip her from the tree. She loses her grip on the branch and begins to fall through the tree hitting every branch on the way down. I drop to the ground after her and see her lying on her back. I run over to her and sit on her stomach, pinning her arms above her head. I take my right hand and brush the hair out of her face.

"Why are you hunting us?" I say and I take in the number of purple bruises forming on her arms and face from the fall.

"Adaline?" she struggles to say and her eyes scan my face.

"What do you want with me?" I say and I feel my blood pounding in my ears.

"It's Zavy," her voice cracks on her name. My eyes widen and I scan her face again until my eyes land on the three dark circle freckles under her right eye.

"Oh my gosh, Zavy what are you doing out here?" I ask and get off of her. I help pull her to her feet and wait for her explanation. Zavy and I were in the same class as well. Her, Alexander, and I were such a tight group I can hardly believe the three of us are together again. Alexander meets me at my side and Zavy's eyes flip between the two of us as equally surprised as I am.

"What are you guys doing out here?" she asks, turning the question on to us. "I thought I'd never see you again."

Alexander explains, "Well, basically running to freedom. Adaline escaped the castle, which I just realized she hasn't explained," he pauses and gives me a wondering eye before continuing, "I'm a guard at the castle," he stops himself when Zavy's eyes widen. "Well, was," he corrects. "I was on night duty outside of the maze and we came across each other. Now we're off to find freedom, and there's also the fact that we are running from a search group led by Paylon and his two best marksmen, Codian and Chadian."

"That would be the really summed up version," I step in and say.

"Well you guys seem to be in a messy situation," Zavy says. "Sorry about the arrow," Zavy apologizes for shooting at us.

"Where'd you get that bow?" I ask, examining it.

"It's a long story. Come on, I'll show you back to our camp. Toby and I just moved to this part of the woods." I recognize the name of her younger brother and wonder why the two of them would be living out in the woods.

Zavy spins on her heels and starts walking deeper into the woods, but Alexander and I share a quick glance before following her. I am still too in shock to have both Alexander and Zavy here with me I can't even try to decide whether or not going with her is the right idea. It helps she's moving in the way we were traveling anyway, but I don't want to get distracted with Paylon hunting us. We follow her for a good mile or so and again I ask her how she has been since I last saw her seven years ago.

"So what happened to you, Zavy?" I ask.

"Well I, like most people, didn't find out about your family being taken until school the next day. Then questions started to arise and trust me I freaked!" she says, being as overdramatic as I remember her. "As you know my family was in the same situation yours was, financially. We were soon going to be thrown in the prison too. As we had suspected, we were the next ones to go." Zavy's voice grows a bit harsh and I can tell she's fighting to keep her emotions at bay. "Except only my mother and father were taken. My little brother, Toby, and I managed to escape. A search group was never put together for us, I assume, so we've just been living out here."

She stops suddenly and I see the emotions she's trying to hold down surface. She turns to me slowly and her wet eyes meet mine.

"Are my parents okay?" she asks and I realize she thinks I must have seen them in the prison.

"The prison under the castle is a maze of cells, Zavy," I start saying and she nods her head, knowing what I'm going to say. "I never saw them. I'm sorry."

"It's okay, I just thought maybe you would know," she says and turns back to leading us to her camp. She wipes her wet eyes and I watch her transform back into her stiff self. "Is your mother and brother out here with you?" she asks over her shoulder and I feel the blood drain from my face.

Her question in sincere, but it makes my chest hurt. Zavy glances

71

back because of my silent pause and sees my ghostly white face. "No," my voice breaks out through my tight throat.

"Oh, Adaline," Zavy starts, but I don't need her sympathy. "Parting day?" she asks and I just nod. I don't want to give her any of the details. Not because I don't want her to know, but because I don't think I can get them out.

After a bit longer of hiking we come upon a clearing. In the center is a fire pit with a small boy sitting next to it. The boy has dark brown hair and is dressed in an overly large white t-shirt and black shorts.

"Zavy. What's going on?" The young boy asks in a high-pitched voice, obviously curious.

"Toby this is Alexander and Adaline. Both of them are very close friends of mine," Zavy says, introducing us to her little brother that I haven't seen since he was just a couple of years old.

Toby stands and moves toward us, hiding behind his older sister not exactly sure if he can trust us. I give him a slight wave and he sinks further behind Zavy.

"He's usually not this shy," Zavy says, pausing for a moment. "They used to come over a lot when you were little," Zavy tries to explain to Toby. He scans us both, trying to remember who we are. He was only five or so when I was arrested so I'm not surprised he can't remember us.

"You're a guard," Toby's small voice says and he points to Alexander. "You said not to trust anyone. Especially someone wearing navy blue," he says to his older sister.

"I know, but this is different, Toby," Zavy starts to say.

"I used to be a guard," Alexander admits. I watch as he kneels down to Toby's height. He pulls out his thick navy jacket from his bag and Toby's eyes widen at the uniform. Alexander carefully unclips a gold pin from his jacket and holds it out to Toby. "I can't be a guard without my badge, right?" Toby considers this for a moment and then nods, agreeing. "You take this, and as long as you have it you can trust I'm not a guard."

Toby gently takes the badge in his small hands and examines it. "It's really cool," Toby says. I watch as he pins the gold badge onto his tattered white shirt. "I'll be guard Toby. You all answer to me now."

"Don't get ahead of yourself, kid. I'm still in charge," Zavy says and ruffles his hair. "But you can give Alexander all the orders you want. Obviously we can't just leave you two on your own," Zavy says, turning the conversation back to our predicament. "So, you guys are more than welcome to stay here with us. Toby and I were just talking about needing to build a shelter to last us a couple of days until we move to another location. So, why don't Adaline and I do that while you two go hunting," she pauses, handing Alexander her bow and arrows, then adds, "but Toby, no weapons." Before I even have time to accept or decline her offer she already has our day planned out.

"Got it, I won't use any," Toby says, pulling Alexander along with him.

Once they are out of earshot Zavy speaks first, "So what kind of gift do you have?"

At first, I'm confused by the question. Only I know that I am a Force Lifter. "Excuse me?" I ask, trying to get some understanding out of this.

"Oh come on Adaline. Your father left you, your mother and younger brother are dead, King Renon knows you have no one left. The fact that you can cause him to put a search group together means you have to be of some use to him. No offense, but you don't have all that much to offer on your own." Zavy laughs like this is some sort of joke.

"Wait what? I don't understand. That would mean Alexander would have the gift too. I mean, they're after both of us," I stumble over my words, trying to keep my secret as long as I can.

"Well, maybe. I think the fact that one of his own guards betrayed him would be enough reason to find him. But, I want to know what gift it is that you have," she says as she stares at me, her light green eyes pleading for an answer.

I feel sweat begin to bead up on my forehead. I knew I shouldn't have been so quick to follow her back here. While Zavy and I were friends I have a keen memory that she never did anything that she didn't think would benefit her. "I don't have a gift Zavy," I say very flatly.

"I have one," Zavy offers and she catches the curious light flicker in my eyes. "I'll tell you if you tell me."

I weigh the decision in my head. I do want to know what gift she has. I need to understand who I am working with. I know that if we stand a chance at staying hidden from Paylon and his search group we're going to have to work together. "Ok, fine. So I'm a Force Lifter. I mean that's what my mother had called it. She said I have an enhanced sense of sight," I mumble, upset that I'm not the only one who knows anymore.

"Yeah I know what a Force Lifter is, but I don't believe you. That's one of the most powerful gifts," she says as she turns and points up into the trees. "Ok, if you're a Force Lifter build us our shelter. I can tell you're just dying to use your gift out here." She smiles as she looks back at me, her eyes full of excitement.

I look at her and then to the trees that surround us. "Zavy, I don't," I pause, not wanting to admit that I don't even know how to use it.

"You don't know how to use it do you?" Zavy asks me, her eyes wide.

"I just found out yesterday. My mother told me right before they took her. She said she was a Future Holder," I explain to her.

Zavy shrugs her shoulders and says, "Well then show me what you can do. I won't judge."

I look back up into the trees and try to picture the branch snapping off and falling to the ground. The branches begin to shake and pine needles start to rustle and fall to the ground. I pause and take a breath as the forest falls still.

"Let me try again," I say. I hold my breath and squeeze my hands into fists. I stare at the branches above, focusing on snapping them. I hear a small crack and exhale, adrenaline rushing through me. "Did you hear that?" I say and turn to Zavy.

"Wow, you cracked a branch," Zavy says, rolling her eyes. "Are you going to drop some or do I need to go up there and do it myself?"

I flip my head and look back at the trees. More small cracks click through the canopy of branches above until some of them start to fall to the ground.

"There you go!" Zavy says. I keep breaking branches until there are tons of them scattered around us. "That should be enough. Do you think you can form them into a shelter for us?"

I look from Zavy to the branches. "Absolutely, not. I didn't think it'd be that hard to use. I can control it better when I get my adrenaline going. I can't just turn it on though."

"You'll figure it out, don't worry," Zavy says, brushing me off.

"What about your gift?" I say, stopping her from turning away from me.

"I'm a Communicator," she says simply and tries to pull herself from my grasp.

"What does that mean?" I ask her and she laughs.

"You must not have paid very much attention to Ms. White's lecture," Zavy says, referencing our school teacher.

"That was seven years ago," I say defensively but she cuts me off.

"I have an enhanced sense of hearing. I can communicate with people and animals." Before I can ask her any more questions or have her show me she pulls from my grasp. She goes and starts to collect the branches and looks back at me. "Well come on, are you going to help or just stare at me?" I start to walk around and pick up branches. We begin to form a pile in the center of the clearing. On my next trip out I head to the far edge and scoop up the last of the branches. I spin to head back to our pile when my foot gets caught on something and my face meets the dirt.

"Are you okay?" I hear Zavy ask, but the laughter in her voice tells me she isn't all that concerned.

"Yeah I'm fine," I groan out. I roll on my back and sit up to see what my foot had gotten caught on. Peeking up out of the light dirt is a thick metal ring. I squint, examining its muted silver surface. I move onto my knees and start cleaning the dirt off around it.

"Zavy, come look at this," I call over to her. She appears over my shoulder and I show her the metal disk that was hidden beneath the dirt. It's fairly large, about two feet across. "What do you think it is?" I ask and look up to her. The wicked grin on her face tells me she knows exactly what I've just found.

Zavy kneels beside me and loops her hand through the metal ring, "It's a bunker," she says and pulls up on the disk. Slowly the metal disk hinges up, exposing a dark hole.

"A bunker? Like from the showers?" I ask, referencing the asteroid shower that ended the world before ours.

"I've been out here for years and I've never found one," Zavy says, still taking in our discovery. "It has to be like a hundred years old."

We're quiet for a moment until Zavy looks up to me. "I'm not going down there," I start to say defensively.

"This is the perfect shelter," she cuts me off. "I'll go down first and check it out."

"Zavy be careful," I start, but she has already lowered herself on to the ladder of the bunker.

"What do you see?" I holler down and her face swims back into view as she climbs up.

"Nothing, I need some light." She crawls out of the hole and moves to the pile of sticks I had dropped when I fell. She opens the bag she had been carrying over her shoulder and pulls out a line of dirty white cloth. She takes leaves, wraps them in the cloth, and then wraps the cloth around the sticks.

"What are you doing?" I ask and watch her pull out a large knife and piece of metal.

"Making a torch," she says as she strikes the metal with her knife. Sparks shower from the metal and onto the cloth until it finally catches and an orange flame engulfs the torch. "Hand it to me," she says and crawls back down the ladder. I see her tan hand peek up in the light and I hand down the firing torch.

"Adaline, come down," Zavy's voice echoes up to me. The narrow and dark stone hole makes my stomach turn. I have to remind myself it's not a prison cell. Eventually, curiosity takes over and I climb down the dirty cool rungs of the ladder. My feet hit the stone floor and I spin around and take in the glowing room.

I breathe in sharp, taking in the space. It's a square concrete block with a low roof. It looks as though it was never even touched. It does resemble a large cell and I have to keep my heart calm. Out of instinct, I catch myself glancing back toward the ladder to make sure I still have a way to get out.

We dig through the room, taking a mental inventory of what we find. Along the wall to our left are cabinets full of grey slick bags. I pull one from the cabinet and the word *BACON* is printed on it. I rip open the bag and my nose is filled with a smoky scent. They're food packages. I scan the cabinet and see that there are enough to last for years.

My stomach has been begging for more food since this morning. I pour the bag's contents out on my hand and find that it's a clumped together white powder. I place it on my tongue and as the powder dissolves a smoky meat flavor takes its place.

"What did you find?" Zavy asks, coming up to my side.

"Try this," I say and offer her some of the powder food.

"Oh, that's pretty good," Zavy offers. "The texture is horrible though," she adds and I agree.

"There's enough here to feed us for years," I add showing her the cabinets full of the grey bags.

We continue to search the room while eating some of the food rations. On the back wall there are four beds with thick blankets. On the other side are two couches facing each other and a couple of extra chairs. There are a lot of things I've only seen in books or heard about in stories; a television, lamps, cooking machines, and clothes I would never imagine seeing my mother tailor.

I let my hand rest on the glossy black television and I remember just yesterday Titus had said he wanted one. Just yesterday I had told him they don't even exist anymore. Tears well in my eyes at the thought that if he had made it out he would have actually gotten to see one in person and not just in the old school book we read.

"They really thought they'd have electricity during an asteroid shower?" Zavy scoffs, dusting off one of the side lamps.

"How do you prepare for something you don't know anything about," I mumble, trying to understand what these people must have been thinking. "It doesn't even look like anyone lived here."

"They must not have made it before the shower started," Zavy says and I think it must be awful to spend your time organizing this space to be dead before you could even use it.

Hand-woven rugs are placed around the bunker as well, trying to soften up the stone space. Zavy and I dig through the last crate in the back of the room and find it mostly full of books and children's toys, but at the bottom we find a pile of candles. Zavy spreads them throughout the bunker and lights them with her torch before putting out its flame. From up on the surface we hear leaves and sticks break and a distant child's laugher. We surface to find Alexander and Toby are back from hunting.

"There you are," Alexander says, turning to face us as we walk up to them.

"Have you ever seen a bunker before?" Zavy asks and a coy smile grows on her face.

"No," Alexander says, trying to figure out where this is going.

"Adaline may have just found the hidden gem in these woods." She turns and we follow her back to the bunker. Toby drops to his knees and speaks down into the hole to hear his voice echo back to him.

"Whoever prepared it never used it," I say. "We were thinking we should use it as our shelter. I'm not sure if it will stop the Hounds," I say, remembering the group of Lost Souls looking for us at this very moment, "but at least it will keep us hidden from view." Alexander nods and we file back into the bunker to show him.

"This may have just saved our lives," Alexander says, walking around the bunker. It doesn't take Toby more than a few minutes to find the crate of toys in the back. "This is really amazing," Alexander says and turns to me.

"I didn't actually find it intentionally," I admit but the happiness on his face only grows. "We aren't staying here though, we're still going to Libertas, right?" I ask in a hushed voice to Alexander.

I see a drop of joy escape from his eyes at the thought of leaving the safe haven we just discovered. "We'll discuss it more tonight," is all he offers.

"How about we go and see what kind of food you got us?" Zavy asks as she makes her way back toward the ladder.

"You guys go ahead. I'm going to stay down here a little while longer," I say. I watch the three of them climb up the ladder. The quick remark Alexander had made about our plan to go to Libertas sits heavy in my head. While this bunker is the ideal hiding spot, I feel as though I've spent my entire life sitting underground, hidden from the world. This is the last place I want to stay. I'd much rather take what's useful and move out tomorrow.

Now that Zavy knows about my gift I don't want to leave her behind, because I don't know who she'd spread that to. If Paylon found her and got it out of her, or if she took the information back to King Renon himself then I'd lose my advantage in this hunt. So now I know, no matter what, the four of us are in this together until the end.

Chapter 6

From down in the bunker I hear everyone is back to laughing and catching up, leaving me by myself. I sit down on one of the old couches along the wall and pull out the journal my mother gave me. *Forever* is written at the top of the book. The lock almost reminds me of a belt buckle, except there's the symbol of a gifted engraved on it. I can remember seeing the symbol on some of the uniforms around the castle. The age of the journal is obvious with its withered corners and the wrinkles across the face of it.

I try and picture the lock opening, but nothing happens. I try again and use all of my strength. I see the lock start shaking almost giving in, but it's no use. I stop and take in a deep breath, extremely exhausted.

I need to get my mind off this. It's causing too much stress, and too many questions I don't have the answers to. For example, what's written in the journal? What gift does Alexander have, does he even have one? Did my father have the gift? Did Alexander's mother have the gift? Where are they now? Where is Paylon? Did Codian get the Hounds? Are they headed toward us? I really need something to get my mind off this before I go insane.

My eye catches on the racks of clothes across the bunker. I get up and shuffle through the shirts and jackets. On the ground are totes with pants, shoes, and even more clothes. My eye is drawn to a bright yellow top, but I think better of it. I should probably choose something more muted that won't call me out as a target. Instead, I pull on a plain black t-shirt and pair it with long denim shorts. The quality of the clothes is unlike any I've seen before.

The black shirt is a bit big on me. I take a small black band from a little metal box and tie the front up into a knot so it fits better. The shorts are a little large as well, and I think they may not have been designed to be as long as they are on me. In prison, we weren't given shoes to wear. I think about keeping it that way, but my feet are already starting to blister from the harsh terrain of these woods. I find a pair of socks and odd-looking white shoes. They are a cloth material on top with thick rubber on the bottom. They are already scuffed with dirt, and not nearly as new as the other items in the bunker. I return my sword to my hip and I grab my small bag and throw it over my shoulder, always careful to keep them close. I climb up the ladder and see that the sun has started to set. Alexander has two wild turkeys ready to be cooked on the fire and Toby is sitting in the pile of ray berries they were collecting.

"Who are you and what have you done with Adaline?" Zavy jokes. She approaches me to see my transformation.

"They're a lot more comfortable," I say, gesturing to the clothes.

"Toby," Zavy calls and her little brother joins her at her side.

"Let's go see if we can find some new clothes." The two of them head to the bunker and I join Alexander by the fire.

"Didn't like our makeshift scraps?" Alexander asks and I laugh.

"We didn't do a good enough job to have them last more than today," I explain. "Are you going to change?" I ask and Alexander nods.

"I figured I'd give Zavy and Toby a chance to find something and I'll take what's left," he says and continues to place the firewood.

"Are we eating soon?" I ask, my stomach making me unable to think of anything else.

"When it's dark," Alexander says and I nod, agreeing it's safer to conceal the smoke. Zavy and Toby emerge from the bunker just as transformed as I am. They both have found dark green shirts and black shorts to wear. Alexander goes to take his turn and Zavy takes his seat by the unlit fire while Toby continues to sort the ray berries.

"He wanted to twin," Zavy says in a hushed voice and rolls her eyes.

I smile and say, "That's cute Zavy. He really looks up to you."

"Did you find out what gift Alexander has?" Zavy asks, changing the conversation suddenly.

"No, I'm not just going to ask him," I say and look to her. "I want to keep mine a secret," I add, but she shakes her head disappointingly.

"I won't tell him, but it doesn't seem like the best idea. We're supposed to be a team. You should be able to trust him," Zavy lectures.

"At the end of the day, he's still one of King Renon's guards. Someone at ten-years-old is a lot different when they're seventeen-years-old," I shoot, cutting her off. It's about Alexander, but if I had my way Zavy wouldn't know either. Yes, we were all friends when we were younger, but a lot of time has passed. I know I've changed.

Alexander emerges from the bunker and Zavy and I turn away from each other. He approaches us wearing a dark brown t-shirt that is tight across his chest and black long shorts. I'm reminded again just how different Alexander is. Not only is he one of King Renon's guards, but he has been fed and trained like a soldier. I don't think he's ever missed a meal. What little turkey meat and berries we have tonight will probably leave him starving. I'm a scrawny prisoner and he's a trained warrior.

Toby brings us each a pile of ray berries to snack on while we wait for night to fall. We all sit in a circle around our unlit fire and Toby is glued to Zavy's side at all times, like usual.

"So what are our official plans as a group?" I ask.

"Well, Toby and I have never had official plans of moving to safety. Just to survive. It's been a struggle," Zavy says and I can see the sadness in her eyes as I'm sure the first days after her parents were taken were miserable.

She gently runs her fingers through her brother's hair. I thought my job was hard, keeping my mother and brother alive in the cell, I could never imagine what Zavy has gone through. At least we were given the food and shelter we needed to survive. She's had to do it all on her own.

For the first time in as long as I've known Zavy, I feel like I can actually see her. She isn't being the sarcastic girl who makes everything out to be a joke. Her guard has fallen and I can see her, as a real person who has gone through something tragic.

But as quickly as her stiff guard falls it returns and she continues, "But after seven years out here we've pretty much got the hang of it. We try to move camp around as often as we can so we are harder to track if anyone were looking for us. What about you guys? You two seemed like you were heading somewhere specific," Zavy asks

"Alexander and I were thinking we could head to Libertas. It's an island that isn't too far from Dather. We'd need to get a boat," I start to say.

"Or steal one," Zavy offers.

"Or the bunker could be our home," Toby's soft voice offers. Zavy nods her head, liking the idea. Alexander glances at me and I can see he likes the idea of staying too.

"We can stay for now," Alexander offers as a medium. "Hiding in a hole in the ground isn't much of a life, but at least it's somewhere safe." I feel my stomach drop, but I remind myself it's just for now. We'll start moving again soon. Darkness starts to engulf the area so Alexander lights the fire and he puts some of the meat from the earlier catch, which was neatly cut and cleaned, onto the hot stones.

"So, Alexander," Zavy begins, "did you ever see Paylon when you were a guard at the castle? He is sort of famous."

"Yes, I actually did, quite a lot," he says.

"What was it like? Do you have any good secrets on him? You

know everyone has a good secret," Zavy says, emphasizing *everyone,* meaning that I have yet to tell anyone else about my gift. Her emerald eyes glance my way.

"Well, it was definitely interesting. I actually never worked for him, but more so hung out with him and I'm extremely grateful. Turns out Paylon has the gift. No surprise really. King Renon has to have nearly every person with the gift under his control," Alexander explains.

"What was his gift?" I ask, eagerly wondering if that had something to do with the reason why my gift had no affect on him.

"He has an enhanced sense of touch. He's able to control anyone he comes in contact with," Alexander says shortly.

"A Controller?" Zavy asks and her eyes widen.

"What's that mean exactly?" I ask her.

"A Controller is someone who can control the minds of any human, but not someone that holds the same gift," she says shortly. So still no explanation of why my gift didn't affect him.

"So he could still control some gifted, but not one's with enhanced sense of touch?" Alexander asks and Zavy nods.

"You know, you would think King Renon would have something that would allow a person to be unaffected by someone's gift. That way him and the other regular people could be protected from their power," I say, hinting at the fact that Paylon did.

"Well they do," Alexander says. *Bingo* I think. Then he continues, "It's a green stone that the guards wear as a necklace. The guards can't have it on at all times though. If they wear it too long it will start to kill them. It's a pretty poisonous substance. It's not perfect. It can only block out a certain amount of force, but it's definitely something."

"So gifts have no power around them?" Zavy asks.

"No, gifts still work," Alexander clarifies. "They just can't directly affect the person wearing it."

At the mention of the green rocks, I'm reminded of the guards who wore them when I tried to escape. I hadn't noticed if Paylon was wearing one or not, but he must have been. We grab our share of the meat and eat it with some of the ray berries as we continue discussing.

"So why weren't you taken under control of Paylon?" Zavy asks, scanning Alexander up and down.

"Well, I think it's because I never actually worked for him. I was just someone that ate lunch with him, so I guess he never thought he needed to control me." Alexander says through bites of food. We finish our meal in silence and once we are done the sounds of the woods surround us.

"We should be more prepared in case Paylon finds us," I mumble to myself, but my group nods, agreeing. "Alexander and I each have a sword, and Zavy has the bow, but that's hardly enough. We should look in the bunker for anything else we can use," I say. Alexander puts out the fire and we file back into the bunker for the night. Zavy pulls the heavy lid closed and my heart jumps to my throat. My breaths come short and I have to lean against the cool stone walls to steady myself.

Zavy relights some of the candles and Alexander is at my side. "Are you okay?" he asks me and his strong hand holds my shoulder tight.

I take in a few more short breaths and try to get my words out, "It reminds me of." I don't have to finish my thought because Alexander knows exactly what I'm trying to say.

He quiets me and motions for me to take slower and deeper breaths. "You aren't locked up anymore, Adaline. We are free. It's okay." Alexander helps me to one of the soft couches in the bunker and sits with me. He pulls out his water and tells me to take slow sips between my deep breaths and eventually I feel my heart slow back down.

"You good?" Zavy asks in a not so concerned voice as she leans over the back of the couch. I catch Alexander shoot her a disgusted glance, clearly annoyed with her tone.

"I'm fine," I start to say and Zavy stands and interrupts me.

"Good, help me find some more weapons we can use," Zavy commands and moves around the bunker.

"You don't have to," Alexander begins to offer, but I stop him short.

"I'm better, really," I say, even though it's not true. My stomach still threatens to give up what little food I've eaten today, but I'm hoping that searching the bunker will take my mind off the thought that I am currently several feet below ground. We dig through the bins throughout the bunker, looking for anything useful. We don't find much except for a set of four kitchen knives.

"It's something," Zavy says, twirling it through her fingers. Toby is far more interested in the bin of toys than looking for weapons. His favorite seems to be a little family of colorful squishy frogs. While looking for the weapons I do come across a crate full of bags. We distribute a backpack to each of us and fill them with the extra knife, and food rations.

"Have you tried these yet?" Alexander asks, shaking the ration. He tears it open and similarly to the one I had earlier, it is filled with white powdery chunks. Alexander pops one in his mouth and wrinkles his nose.

"Not good?" I ask with a light laugh.

"It tastes like nothing," he says. He turns the bag over in his hands and the word *EGG* is printed on it.

As I suspected Alexander continues eating the dried rations, not use to the lack of food. The difference in our reaction to the rations is obvious. I saw them as a miracle, an endless supply of food that could keep me alive. I've lived off of prison food for years so this white powder seems like a luxury. He's always had the privilege of getting to choose what he wants to eat.

Additionally, I move over my mother's journal, the gold coin, and my photograph to my new bag and scrap the old one Alexander gave me. After we've sorted our things we settle in for the night, each getting our own bed.

"I'm blowing out the candles," Zavy says, glancing at Toby who is hopping around the couches with his new frogs. He scoops them up and places them in a line at the foot of his bed before crawling under the thin sheets. She blows out the candles on her side of the bunker, leaving one flickering flame at my bedside. "You can get that one," Zavy says, letting out a large yawn before curling down into her own bed. Almost instantly, Toby and Zavy are asleep with their backs turned to us.

Down in the bunker, swallowed in almost complete darkness, it's surprisingly chilly. I turn my head to Alexander and say with a light laugh, "I didn't expect it to be so cold down here." Alexander doesn't respond, but he takes out his thick navy jacket from his bag and hands it to me.

"Better?" he asks as he crawls back into his bed.

"Somewhat," I say as a smile forms across my lips. Wrapped up in the coarse material thick with Alexander's scent I'm overcome with the feeling of safety. Tonight is the first night I've laid in a bed with blankets and pillows in nearly seven years.

I prop myself up above the last lit candle and stare down into its flame. I'm about to blow it out when I'm hit with the thought that today is my birthday. I am sixteen years old today. Outside of the cell, I let myself lose count. I let go of my numbers, but the flickering flame pulls up memories of past birthdays before the prison with my mother, father, and brother. My heart hurts that they aren't here with me for this one. "Happy Birthday," I whisper in my head before blowing out the flame and letting the bunker fall into complete darkness.

I drift into the deepest sleep I've ever reached, and my mind places me in one of my last memories with Alexander and Zavy. It was just three months before my family was taken, and my father had already been missing for a week. I move through the dream as if it was in real-time and I can't help but think how simple my life was then. How simple all of our lives were then.

***

I drag my heavy feet into the overcrowded wooden school building. The sun has just begun to peek over the trees, a sure sign it's much too early to be awake.

"Welcome back," Ms. White's voice rings through the hallway. She floats effortlessly down the crowded hall, her beautiful pink dress glowing in the dim morning light. She's all dressed for the occasion, the first day back to school.

I follow her into our classroom and take a seat in my usual spot. The same wooden desk as the last two years. I'm in fifth grade and this will be my last year in this building, at this desk. Then, all of us, Ms. White included, will be moved to the newer school building next door for the older kids. I'm told I should be in fourth grade, but I tested out of my first year. I drop my patched together bag to the floor under my desk and let my head lay on my folded hands.

"Too early for you too?" I ask Zavy, my best friend. She skipped her first year of school just like I did, so we've pretty much stuck together since day one. Zavy sits with her face flat on the desk with her long jet black hair blanketing her shoulders. For a moment, I think she may actually be asleep until she gives me a small nod in return. Then, there's a loud smack on both of our desks and we rocket up.

"Why the long faces?" Alexander asks, taking his seat behind me. Zavy drops her head back to her desk, determined to get a few more minutes of sleep before Ms. White begins teaching.

"I don't know how you can function at this time of day," I say and turn to face Alexander.

"Well," he begins and his light green eyes dance with excitement, "I may have just happened to have heard something life-changing."

"What?" I ask and I sit up straighter in my chair. The weight of exhaustion seems to lift as curiosity floods my veins.

"They're letting fifth graders take training classes," Alexander whispers to me.

"Like to work for the King?" I ask and wrinkle my nose.

"Isn't that really cool?" Alexander boasts.

"No," I say simply and turn back to the front of the room. In actuality, I do think the idea of getting training to be in the King's army is really cool. It's the idea of Alexander being on the other end of a war that makes me want to throw up. Of course, none of us can be sent to war until we're fifteen, but just the thought threatens to break me.

The scratching of chalk against the green board pulls my attention up. *GIFTS* is delicately scratched out in Ms. White's clean handwriting. The loose chatter in the room subsides and even Zavy lifts her head from her desk. We don't talk about the gifts very much, not in class, not with family, and not with each other. This is mostly because there are too many mixed emotions that come with that conversation.

"It's time to talk about the gifts that some of you possess," Ms. White says as she walks in front of her desk. "I know this is a hard conversation to have, and many of you have a lot to learn." She pauses and scans each of our faces. The silence in the room makes my ears throb.

I know that gifts are powers that get passed down to certain people based on their ancestors. I have a feeling Ms. White is going to finally tell me all the things I don't know.

"Have you ever thought about what it would be like to have a gift?" Ms. White asks the classroom. I don't need any time to think about my answer, I know it's yes. I thought of it every day for a long time. I mean, what kid wouldn't think about having cool powers?

"I think many of you would jump at the opportunity, but I'm here to give you the full explanation of what happens to those with gifts." Ms. White stands and moves to the board. She carefully writes out the five senses around the word GIFTS. "Sight, taste, smell, touch, and hearing," Ms. White reads off. "These are the five categories that gifts fall into."

Ms. White begins to ramble about how each gift is unique and while two people can have an enhanced sense of hearing one person may hear people better and one may hear animals better. In the end, she tells us that it is truly up to the skill of the gift holder to unlock the full potential of their gift.

Zavy's hand next to me shoots in the air, "Have you ever met someone with a gift?"

Ms. White nods her head gently. "I'm getting to that," she says and I see her face set in a solid blank stare. "You all know so little about gifts because you have probably never interacted with someone who had a gift. Have you ever found that strange?" Her words settle across the room and my skin begins to crawl. "This is because everyone with a gift is taken to live in the castle and work for King Renon."

"My father told me if you're taken in for a gift they kill you," Miguel, one of my classmates says. The murmur of hushed whispers causes Ms. White to raise her voice to quiet us.

"Rumors are just that, rumors." Ms. White clears her throat and I can tell these next words are hard for her. "The truth is, no one knows what happens to you when you get taken into the castle. I've heard stories of the gifted going off to fight in our wars to protect us. They use their powers to keep us all safe, and to keep the rule in Dather undisturbed."

"But they don't go willingly. They are forced," Miguel spits back.

Ms. White simply nods her head. She knows that what he is saying is true and she doesn't want to lie to us. "At the age of ten, which many of you are or are soon to be, you must be tested for a gift." Ms. White's words sound like a death sentence. I glance around the room and wonder how many of my classmates I won't see again soon. How many of them have these gifts?

"So who did you know that had a gift?" Zavy asks again.

"My son," Ms. White says softly. I tilt my head confused, I hadn't known Ms. White was ever married or had kids. "My husband died in the Alignmass battles over 20 years ago, and in that same year my son was taken for his gift."

"You don't know what happened to him?" Zavy asks softly.

Ms. White silently shakes her head no. "I know he had an enhanced sense of sight. He was a Force Lifter."

Chapter 7

When I awake I realize I'm alone. I roll onto my back, remembering what had happened last night. For starters, I finally figured out why Paylon is immune to my gift, and what gift Paylon has. The thought that he could control someone with a single touch makes my skin chill. That has to be one of the most powerful gifts, especially to King Renon. This information will definitely help me if we ever meet up with his search group in the forest. Zavy's sarcastic comment is still echoing throughout my head, "You know *everyone* has a good secret."

I unwrap myself from Alexander's navy jacket and smile. Is there something going on between us? I mean the connection has always been there, but we're practically strangers now. When I hear Toby's laughter and catch a scent of freshly cooked meat all memories of Alexander and last night fade away. I drape the jacket on Alexander's bed and grab my sword and bag. I make my way out of the bunker and across the clearing to join them.

When I reach them, I'm welcomed by a handful of ray berries and a couple pieces of meat. I sit next to Zavy and watch Alexander and

Toby run through the forest. Zavy sees me looking at them. She leans over and whispers in my ear, "Don't think I didn't see you two last night. I know what's going on," I look at her and laugh, shaking my head no.

"Nothing is going on between Alexander and me, Zavy. I can promise you that," I say and eat my breakfast.

We finish eating the meal in silence. Soon Alexander and Toby walk over and sit by us. I'm about to ask what we should do today when I hear the gallops of horses not too far off. Alexander and I leap up and draw our swords ready for the attack. We already know what we're up against, but Zavy and Toby look at us confused.

"What's that sound?" Toby asks, his voice shaking.

"It's Paylon," I say beneath my breath, as my mind is elsewhere trying to figure out a plan.

Zavy sends Toby down into the bunker for safety. As the gallops grow near I start working out a plan. I position Alexander to my left and Zavy up in a tree with the bow and arrow, with all three of us surrounding the bunker Toby is in. I'm about to tell Alexander that I am a Force Lifter and they just need to follow my lead, but the gallops are getting faster and louder by the minute so I don't waste my breath.

Three large horses leap into the clearing with Paylon, Codian, and Chadian as their riders. Their leather and woven riding mats hang heavy with swords. Behind them, I can just barely make out the Hounds. There are five of them with heavy chains linking them together at their wrists. They are incredibly thin, their eyes sunken back in their heads. My eyes land on the youngest of the group, just about my age. The sight of her causes fear to build in me. That is what will happen to me if I get caught.

"So what do we have here?" Paylon's eyes scan Alexander and me before glancing up and seeing Zavy in the tree above us. "An escaped citizen, a prisoner, and an un-loyal officer," Paylon says, leading his horse just inches closer to us. I step forward, ready to use my gift, when he starts laughing at my stupidity, and then my eyes land on the glowing green rocks around all three of their necks. "Don't tell me you haven't already figured out that I'm immune to your gift."

"Paylon what are you talking about? Adaline doesn't have the gift," Alexander says, stepping forward with me.

"Of course she does, Alexander. Let me tell you a little secret. Statistics show that almost every child with green eyes has the gift." My heartbeat quickens and I feel ashamed to not have said something to him earlier. Tears brim my eyes and I can barely make out the hurt expression on his face.

"I know how you must feel Alexander," Paylon says, "Betrayed, unwanted, not trusted. Go ahead Adaline, tell him what gift you have. Let's just start getting the truth out." Paylon's immaturity of only being 18 shows in the tone of his remarks.

I'm silent for a moment longer as I take in a deep breath, "Force Lifter," I mumble.

"What was that Adaline? I couldn't quite hear you." Paylon smirks, bleeding with arrogance.

I lift my head and stare at him. My eyes are red from the tears, and immense amounts of anger are starting to build inside of me. I respond one last time as I shout, "Force Lifter. I am a Force Lifter." As I scream the words the ground beneath my feet shakes with the powers in my body coursing through my veins.

With that out, I'm ready to battle. I raise my hand and snap thousands of branches off the trees, and launch them straight at Paylon and the search group. I'm taken aback by how seamlessly my gift worked. I don't even remember processing the thought it just happened. Even at the intense speed I throw the branches they are deflected by the armor, but I do happen to hit their horses. I watch as the horses stand on their hind legs, flipping Paylon, Codian, and Chadian off their backs and fleeing into the woods.

"Get them!" I hear Paylon shout, aggravated that I have outsmarted him. The horses have run into the woods taking Paylon and his partners' swords with them. Defenseless I watch Paylon, Codian, and Chadian sink back into the woods for cover.

I whip around just in time to see an army of about 20 soldiers coming toward us, all with the green glowing rocks around their necks that Alexander had described last night. I know my gift can't affect them directly, but I can still control the objects around us.

With my gift, I take hot stones from the fire and launch them at the soldiers. I break down tree branches smashing groups of soldiers, stopping everyone in my path. Most of the trees I break down aren't on purpose, I still can't control this gift, but the mayhem and destruction are working.

On the other hand, Zavy and Alexander aren't doing so well. Alexander is good with his sword and many men have fallen injured from him. I watch him fight and he is focused too much on where his sword hits so he just injures and not kills these soldiers. There are too many men though and his careful tactic is his weakness. Just as he's freed himself from a group of guards another has pulled Zavy from the tree.

The lid to the bunker flies open and I hear Toby scream and run out of the shelter, prepared to save his sister. We should have covered the lid so he couldn't run out.

Zavy rolls on her back and fires her bow and the three guards who had pulled her from the tree. As Toby runs to his sister another guard catches him and throws him over his shoulder.

"Toby!" Zavy screams and she tries to fire at the guard who begins to run off with her brother. Paylon joins him and they begin running away with Codian and Chadian following close behind. An idea comes to mind too late to save Toby, but just in time to save us.

I start to picture all of the guards' swords being moved to their hearts. I might not be able to control the soldiers' movement, but I can control their weapons. All of the swords start shaking in the air, and the guards scream and retreat into the woods. Alexander and Zavy fall to the ground breathing heavily, showing how exhausted they are, and for a second I hesitate killing the guards. For a second I let my heart into battle, but I know deep down that if I don't kill them they will just be back to kill me.

So, I focus on the swords. One deep breath in. Hold it. My mind flashes back to the gold coin and the guard in the castle. Focus. I stare into the array of swords and they become still in the air. I stare so hard into them their surroundings become blurry and I can feel my eyes pulsing in my head. As I let out my breath I push the swords through the guards' bodies and watch as they all fall to the ground around the perimeter of the clearing. Once the soldiers have quieted I fall to the ground and take in deep breaths of air.

It is silent except for our breathing. Zavy pulls herself to her feet and starts stumbling across the clearing. "I have to get him back," she says and tears are running down her face.

"Zavy wait," I say and meet her in the center of the clearing. "What's wrong with your foot?" I ask, noticing her heavy limp.

"It got pulled when they ripped me from the tree," she says and pushes around me.

"You can't go after them on a twisted ankle," I say and grab her wrist. "You'll never catch them."

"Are we just going to let them have him?" she asks and looks at me shocked.

"No," I say and my brain searches for a plan. "We're going to go get him together. Let's just get your ankle wrapped before you make it worse."

Alexander clears his throat across the clearing, and I turn to look at him for the first time since the battle ended. "So when did you plan on telling me you were a Force Lifter? Did you ever plan on telling me?" I turn away from him as the tears start to form again. The pain and betrayed look he has is too much for me.

"Of course I planned on telling you. Just not at the moment. I mean, I just found out the day we met. It's not like I've known my whole life," I say sheepishly, trying to come up with an excuse. I help Zavy to the ground and we carefully work on getting her shoe off her swollen ankle.

"But why Adaline? Why not at the moment?" Alexander pushes me. "I thought we were in this together." The hurt tone in his voice makes my heart tighten.

I turn around and raise my voice to a deathly scream. I rise to my feet and make my way across the clearing, tears streaming down my face as anger and pain mix into one. "Because Alexander! Because I had just lost my mother and my brother. I ran to freedom for myself. I ran so I wouldn't have to be taken in for my gift that I've only known about for a few days. I ran so my gift wasn't wasted. My life is different from yours, Alexander.

And you might not understand where I'm coming from, because you never had to try for anything! It was all handed to you from the day you were born. You had the most perfect family. They gave you everything! While mine fell apart. My father left me to figure things out on my own. Unlike when your mother left you. She stood there the day she left and told you how much she loved you. Do you know what my dad said to me when he left? He said nothing! Nothing, Alexander!

So don't stand here and question me about trusting people with my most treasured secret. You don't even belong here with us, so you might as well just go back to the castle. And don't act like you are any better than me. You have green eyes too! So what's your gift? And Zavy has a gift too! Her eyes are just as green as the rest of us. I'm not the only one here who kept my gift a secret!" The world around us falls completely silent as the words I've just said settle and it physically feels as though the connection between Alexander and me that I have felt my whole life is broken.

I watch as Alexander looks at Zavy and understands that she is not in the least bit surprised to hear that I'm a Force Lifter. "You told Zavy?" he spits at me. "You trusted her?"

"She's not the one I can't trust, you are. You're the one who worked for the castle. You're the one who worked side by side with Paylon. Who knows, you could just be some spy. You could take the information about where we are and what gifts we have back to King Renon and get us killed." I say back to him, but I can't get my eyes to meet his.

"Adaline, I don't know what hurts more. The fact that you all kept secrets from me, or the fact that you think I would turn you both into King Renon." Alexander turns and runs toward the forest, but stops and looks at me one last time, "I'm a Sensor. I have an enhanced sense of touch," he says, choking on his own tears as they pour down his face. Then, he spins back around and continues into the forest.

Frustration swells in my chest. I pick up my black bag and throw it across the clearing towards Zavy, letting out a huff of anger. When it hits the ground my mother's diary launches out and lands by Zavy's feet. I look at her and see her staring off into the distance where Paylon, Codian, and Chadian ran.

"We're going to get him back," I say. I rub my damp cheeks and make my way back to her. "I promise Zavy. They won't hurt him, he's not who they want."

Zavy's eyes meet mine and I can tell she blames Alexander and myself because if we hadn't been together Paylon would never have found them. I can see the words sitting tight in her throat, but she doesn't speak them. Instead, she picks up my mother's journal, "What's this?" she asks with a tight voice.

"It's my mother's old journal," I explain, "She gave it to me right before she died. I haven't been able to read it yet because I can't get it unlocked. I don't even know what could be in there."

"Well from what I know, all Future Holders are given journals, and that's where they keep all the information on what they see in the future," Zavy says as she hands me the journal and takes in a deep breath. I can tell she is debating whether or not to say her next thought to me so I push her.

"What else?" my eyes squint and I can see her distant face contemplate her next words.

"Nothing, I just think I know how to unlock it," she says. My pleading eyes are enough to get her to continue, "Someone with an enhanced sense of touch would probably be able to take off the lock."

Her words hang in the air as my thoughts move to what Alexander had just yelled before he left. He has an enhanced sense of touch. The one person who can open my mother's journal will probably never talk to me again. I lift my bag and shove the journal deep inside.

I feel Zavy's eyes trying to read my thoughts about never getting the journal open without Alexander. "We don't need him, Adaline," Zavy says, but I know we do. I pull out the white bandages Alexander had given me the day before and begin to wrap her ankle.

"Zavy, we'll get Toby back, okay? We'll regroup and go after them," I say, dismissing her idea to leave Alexander behind.

"I know Toby can survive," she says more to try and convince herself. "The only thing he would have to do is find a weapon. He's an Aeros, by the way." She sees the confusion on my face and explains, "An Aeros is someone with an enhanced sense of touch. They can handle any weapon they come in contact with to absolute perfection." I watch her next thought register on her face. "He can probably open the journal for you!"

I shake my heavy head. "I still have to make things right with Alexander." I see her face tighten and can tell she disapproves.

"He literally lied to our faces last night. When I asked why Paylon didn't take control of him I was trying to give him an opportunity to tell us what gift he had," Zavy says with a stiff voice. "He has an enhanced sense of touch, same as Paylon, and that's why he wasn't taken under his control. He knows that's why, but he lied to us." I don't know what to say to her because she's right. She lets out a heavy breath and says, "If it was up to me, I'd say we leave him, save my brother, open your journal, and move on by ourselves," I try to say something, but she throws her hands in the air in frustration. "It's fine. Go fix things with Alexander, and then we'll go save my brother. I'll clean up this mess." She turns and gestures to the dead soldiers scattered through the woods.

"We're going to get through this," I say softly and she just nods in agreement, but her frustration is obvious.

I turn and head off into the woods to clear my head about Alexander. Once I'm far enough in the woods I sit under a large tree and lay my head on it. I let my eyelids fall shut, and I sit here for a long time and think about a lot. The quiet woods are a sudden change from the chaotic battle we were just in. The amount of soldiers I just killed weighs heavy on my mind.

For the first time, I hate myself for clinging to numbers because I feel the internal tally of how many people I've killed in the last two days tick away in my head. I take in deep shaky breaths and try to calm my anxious mind. They would have killed me if I didn't kill them. I repeat it over and over trying to justify the killings. Now it's us against Paylon, Codian, and Chadian. Three against three. The only back up they'll have are the Lost Souls.

When my beating heart slows my mind shifts and I think about mine and Alexander's friendship. We used to be so close. I told him everything. He knew everything there was to know about me. I feel ashamed of myself for keeping my gift a secret, but I was only nine the last time I saw him. I would say Zavy feels the same way, but I know she doesn't. She only thinks she is right. She'd never apologize to him in a million years.

Although we are practically strangers now the last couple of days were still real. He is the only person I've been with in the last seven years besides my mother and brother and both of them are dead. I didn't trust him from the beginning and I questioned whether I even wanted us to be a team out here, and yet he sacrificed so much for me. A single tear escapes my tightly locked eyelid and rolls down my cheek.

Suddenly, I hear someone say, "You really like him don't you?" It's Zavy. She's probably been here all along.

I open my eyes and fight to hold back the loose tears, "I don't know what I feel for him. I know he was my friend. I've been dancing around the connection I started to feel for him, but it's broken now. There's nothing left." Once I hear myself say it out loud I know it's the truth, but Zavy doesn't believe so.

"Adaline I can tell he cares for you. The way he looks at you," she starts to explain.

I stop her short and interrupt, "The way he looks at me? Did you see the way he looked at me when he found out I had kept my gift a secret? He never wants to see me again, to see either of us again."

"You'll never know unless you try. Go find him. He can't be far, but honestly Adaline, he's just a boy," she says flatly as she walks away.

I let the words she said settle. There is something greater between Alexander and me than some childhood friendship. He's a part of me. Alexander and Zavy are all I have left from my life before the prison. I can't explain the connection we had, it was as if we knew each other from a different life, or that outside forces were pushing us together. I have to try to fix things with Alexander. If I still can. I rise and start to wander through the woods, hoping to find him and have some chance at restoring our bond.

Chapter 8

I've been walking aimlessly around the woods when I finally find him. He's sitting on an old fallen tree by the river. I watch as he fails at attempting to skip rocks with one hand while the other holds his head. I picture a hand full of rocks lifting into the air. They more or so just bobble around in the air and I try to skip them down the river. Most just sink, but a couple of the rocks make two or three hops on the brown creek water.

Alexander turns and looks up at me, but doesn't offer a smile. His eyes are puffy and red. The tears have stopped coming, but only because he has no more left to cry. I step over the log and take a seat next to him. I lift a rock and try to skip it without using my gift, but it immediately sinks.

"You know, without my gift I'm nothing," I look at him, and then back down before I add, "Even with my gift I'm nothing. I don't know how to use it." I pause and he doesn't say anything so I keep talking, "I didn't have the right to speak to you that way. I'm truly sorry for what I said back there, Alexander. I didn't mean any of it."

He still refuses to look at me and I don't blame him. I take out my mother's journal, I don't have a use for it anymore anyway, and I put it on the ground by his feet.

We are silent for a second until Alexander says with a broken voice, "Just go away."

"I'm not going anywhere Alexander," I say but he cuts me off.

"I said go away," he repeats harsher, but there is no hatred in his voice.

"What if I don't want to?" I struggle to say back to him, my voice growing and beginning to shake.

"Adaline it doesn't matter if you want to or not. I need time to myself. Whether you meant what you said back there or not, the fact is you're not who I thought you were," he says, and his words pierce my heart, leaving my chest aching.

"Alexander, I'm still that girl you knew. I'm the same girl that went on all those crazy adventures with you, running through the woods and the city." My voice is so weak I can barely make my words audible. I don't believe the words I say and neither does Alexander. I'm not the same girl and he knows that now.

"The Adaline I knew would never have kept something like her gift a secret from me," he says coldly and I know he's right.

"Alexander," I start again, but he stops me.

"You put my life in danger Adaline. I not only helped a prisoner escape and defied my oath to the King, but I helped a gifted escape," he says, shaking his hanging head.

"So you're saying if you knew I was a gifted you would have

turned me in?" I ask shocked at what I am hearing.

"No, of course not," he says, his eyes meeting mine for the first time, "But I should have known what I was getting myself into. Do you realize how much of a fool I look like to Paylon now? I didn't even know the girl I have been best friends with my whole life has the gift. She didn't even trust me enough to mention it," he says under his voice, more to himself.

"How do you think I feel?" I say softly. "You didn't trust me either."

Alexander doesn't respond so I stop fighting him. I'm about to get up and leave when I see Alexander toss the journal back by my feet. I bend over and pick it up. I try and open the journal by lifting the cover and find it magically unlocked.

"Leave and get to freedom, you have what you wanted," he shoots.

"But what about you? Where will you go?" I say.

"Back to the castle I suppose," he mumbles.

"Alexander, are you crazy? If you return you'll be killed!" my panicked voice says.

"Adaline you have what you want, now just leave!" he shouts back at me. He's trying to sound forceful, but I can hear the shakiness of his voice.

"But you're wrong. I don't have what I want," I say in a small voice.

"Then what could you possibly want?" He shouts and turns to face me.

"I want you, Alexander. I need you." My grip tightens on the journal as I get up to leave, not wanting to hear what more he has to say because I know it's nothing that will make this any better.

I make it back to the clearing and into the bunker, my eyes full of tears but not letting any go. I sit down on my bed and open the journal, the only thing I have left to turn to. On the first old tan page is one sentence in bold letters. I can't believe what it says. I wipe my eyes clear of tears as I reread my mother's handwriting.

If I could only tell you one thing it would be: Never Let Alexander Go.

I turn to the next page in the journal. "Why can I never let Alexander go?" I think to myself. The words start to magically appear down the page as if they were being written right now.

Adaline, if you let Alexander go your life will be over. I've seen the future happen in many different ways, but any without Alexander by your side ends with an early death for you. Alexander is the reason you have made it this far. He is the reason you have survived. If you let him go you will die. Together you have an immense amount of power. Each of you contribute in a certain way, and even without one, you will all fail. If you are reading this it may be too late. Adaline, you have to hurry.

"But I already know he won't come back. I've tried everything," I whisper to no one in particular, almost as if I was talking to my mother. I flip through the rest of the journal, but all the other pages are blank. It registers to me that this journal will only give me information when my mother would want me to have it. Knowing too much about the future would surely change its course.

I close the journal and put it back in my bag. My eyes catch on Alexander's navy uniform jacket, still lying on his bed where I had left it this morning. How naive I was to think a jacket could make me feel safe. I truly hadn't understood the level of forces King Renon had sent after us. I rise and make my way out of the shelter and sprint through the forest.

I go to the one place I know he might still be at, the river. When I reach it I'm terrified to see that he isn't there anymore.

"Alexander," I hear myself choke out. What if I am too late?

"Alexander," I shout.

"Alexander!" I hear myself scream with a deathly shrill, sending birds into the sky, but still nothing. I look on the ground and notice a path of where the leaves have been parted heading down deeper into the forest along the river, right in the direction of Paylon. I turn and run down the path.

As I run my mind starts to bring up memories of the two of us before my life in the prison. Birthday parties and weekend adventures flash in my head. A particular memory starts to surface, the last time we were together before I was taken to the castle. We were so young back then.

The morning of the day my family was taken in as prisoners

Alexander and I went out in the woods behind my house. We just walked in silence, listening to the song of the forest. We walked into a clearing full of white daisies. To us, it looked like they stretched on for miles.

"I've never seen this before," I said as I reached down and pulled up a small daisy. I examined its white petals closely.

"We've been all over these woods, how have we not seen this before?" Alexander asked confused.

"It's beautiful," I said. I took a seat on the ground in a nest of daisies. Alexander sat down next to me and plucked up a flower. He turned to me and gently placed it in my hair behind my ear and said, "You're my daisy princess."

I laughed and leaned against him, "Then you're my daisy prince." The memory starts to fall away. I can't lose him.

After running for what feels like hours in the burning summer sun my speed is now nothing, and I'm losing hope since I lost the trail a couple of yards back. The sun has started its descent. It's early afternoon, but I know there's no way I'll find him in the dark. Just when I'm about to turn and go back I hear a low laugh coming from up ahead. I move closer, making sure to stay hidden. I kneel behind a tree and try to make out what is going on.

Looking at the scene it's hard to make out what's happening. In front of me is Paylon and the twins standing in a triangular formation, Paylon is front and center as always. I can see the Lost Souls lurking closely behind. Suddenly Alexander steps in to view and I take in a sharp breath.

Paylon and the twins are laughing hysterically at the stupidity of Alexander. All I want to do is leap forward and beg him to come back, but that wouldn't help. I hear the laughter die down and Paylon begins to speak.

"What do you think you're doing back here?" he asks, his confident voice booming through the forest.

"I have nowhere left to go," Alexander responds with a very hoarse and cracked voice. He lifts his head back, making sure to keep eye contact, and reveals his cold, red, swollen eyes.

"What happened? Your girlfriend found out you're a Sensor and kicked you out?" Chadian spits at him. I watch as he and his brother break into another round of laughter. Alexander's face twitches and I know he's trying to process how they had known he had that gift, but he can't let them faze him.

"She's not my girlfriend," Alexander says as he rolls his eyes in frustration, "and she was never even my friend. We needed to get to the same place and that's all. I'm here to be turned into one of the Lost Souls." Immediately the forest falls silent. My eyes are filling with tears, and I'm not even sure why. Was it because of what he said about our relationship? Or because I don't want to lose him and have him be a Lost Soul.

"Really? You're going to go down without a fight?" Paylon asks, not believing what he is hearing.

"I have nothing left to live for," he says, hanging his head. I can see it in his face. He is without his friends and his family. His mother and father have both left him, and he can't return to his hometown.

"Fine. You know the procedure," I watch as Paylon pulls out a small container that conceals a purple potion. Alexander walks forward and falls to his knees, letting his head hang back with his mouth open. Paylon removes the cap and an eerie purple mist floats out.

I can't let this happen. I scan the clearing confirming that they still haven't found the horses, which means they don't have their weapons. I act quickly, and just as the first drop is about to be poured I fling the bottle out of Paylon's hand, smashing it into a tree. I blink hard not sure what I just did. I'm starting to feel as though this gift controls me more than I control it.

Codian and Chadian whip around in confusion. In seconds Paylon flips out a long knife he had concealed on his belt and slices it across Alexander's leg. Alexander screams and falls to his side, red blood running from his thigh I try to freeze Paylon, but it's no use. I see the glowing green rock around his neck and I know I won't be able to stop him.

Alexander sees me through the trees, but relief is not on his face. Instead of staying to fight I clench my eyes shut and try to teleport Alexander back to our camp. I remember the night in the castle with the coin. I focus hard and picture him lying back in the clearing by the bunker.

"Where'd he go?" I hear Codian yell and when I open my eyes I see that it worked. I scan the clearing looking for Toby, but he's not here. Paylon's gold eyes see me through the cluster of trees and I feel the blood leave my face. He races toward me, and my adrenalin builds. I close my eyes and just like I teleported Alexander, I also send myself back to our camp.

When I open my eyes I'm back at the campsite. Alexander is sitting next to me. His hands are pressed against his thigh, and I can see a distant and painful look on his face. At first, I'm confused, but then I realize the blood seeping through his fingers and running down his leg.

Out of instinct, I run over to him. I place my hands over his, but he shakes me away, "No! Adaline, you can't help! I don't want your help!" Tears start slipping through his tightly closed eyelids.

I ignore him and place my hands over his. Before he can push me away I make him freeze with my mind. It feels wrong to use my gift against him. Suddenly I feel the warm blood start flowing through my fingers. I need to move fast, even though I'm not sure what exactly I need to do. I move his hands and see the slash down his left thigh where Paylon had cut him. He's going to need stitches. I rip his backpack from his shoulders and take out the first aid kit.

My hands start shaking as I dig through the kit. I grab the needle and nylon thread I had seen earlier. I grab my water bottle and try to twist off the cap but my hands won't stop shaking. I take in a deep breath and my hands fall still. I twist off the cap and pour water over the needle and thread to try and clean them. Then, I pour what I have left on Alexander's leg. His red blood washes down into the ground. I attach the needle to the thread and position myself above his leg.

I try to remember back to the night my mother gave me stitches.

I had fallen and busted my arm open on a rock on my way home from Alexander's. My family couldn't afford to go see a doctor so my mother sat me down in the bathroom and gave me stitches.

"I'm going to squeeze now and it's going to hurt but you can't pull away Adaline, okay?" my mother had said to me. I sat on the chair in the bathroom while my mother knelt next to me. I shook my head and agreed. She squeezed the spot on my arm and I remember screaming really loud. "It's okay, Adaline. I'm sewing it shut now, don't look and don't move."

I clenched my eyes closed and felt the cool needle pierce my arm and weave itself in and out. When my mother finished she told me I could open my eyes. I did and watched her tie off the end of the stitching thread. She handed me a small blue pill for pain, but I remember it didn't seem to do much. We never got to take medicine since it was too expensive. That was one of the only times I ever did.

I look down at Alexander's thigh. I take my left hand and squeeze the wound together. Then, with my right, I send the needle through the bottom of the cut and out the top. I pull the thread through and then send the needle back through his skin. I do this until I've made my way down the gash and then work my way back, making sure to cross the stitches so they make a little "x". Just like my mother had done with me. When I get back to the end I started at I tie off the stitching thread and cut the extra away with the small pocket knife from Alexander's bag. I unfreeze Alexander and he lets out a scream of pain. He looks at his leg in disbelief. My hands are stained with his blood. I take his water bottle and pour it on the needle to clean it.

"Look, Alexander, there's something I need to tell you," I pause, waiting for him to ask me to continue, but he doesn't. He just looks at me with red swollen eyes. So I continue anyway.

"I'm really sorry I kept my gift a secret. I know it could probably take years, maybe even forever before you even consider forgiving me. I want you to know that I truly am sorry and that it will never happen again," I look at him and see that his facial expression hasn't changed and I know that it is pointless.

I place the needle back into the first aid kit, my bloody hands shaking. Tears are forming in my eyes, and I just can't take all this right now. I rise and take off into the forest. I think I hear Alexander yell my name, but all my senses are muffled. I can't change his mind so what's the point of trying? I'm so frustrated with myself that I just keep running, and running. I'm telling myself I'm breaking down because I don't want to lose Alexander, but it's more than that. His blood on my hands, the needle in and out of his skin, it sends a nauseous wave over me. I keep running trying to get away from it. Make it to the river. Wash the blood. I keep thinking over and over again. I almost got him killed. The thought seeps into my head and I'm sent into another wave of panic.

When I can't physically run anymore I collapse to my knees, sending a shooting pain up my back. I fall to my side, letting out a shrieking cry of pain. My breath comes fast and shallow. Tears are streaming down my face, and suddenly I'm overcome by a feeling of exhaustion.

It feels like someone has dropped a hundred pounds on my chest knocking the air out of me. I suddenly can't move any part of my body. I'm about to scream for help when, suddenly, I seem to have lost the ability to speak. Soon I can't hear anything either, each sense slipping farther and farther away. I'm starting to panic more, which isn't good, especially when I'm already paralyzed on the forest floor. Another shot of pain courses through my body, and then everything goes black. The last thing I see is the quiet world above me.

Chapter 9

When I regain consciousness it's dark all around. I try and sit up and find my body able to move again, but extremely sore. Slowly I brace myself on a tree and drag my body to my feet. The river. I see it through the cluster of trees. I'm not overcome by panic from the blood and death from this morning anymore.

I walk to the river's edge and clean Alexander's dried blood off my hands. I can't do that anymore. I can't freak out. I have to stay in control. I try and lecture myself, but how do you control waves of panic and anxiety? One step at a time I make my way back to our camp.

When I step into the clearing the first thing I see is a fire brightly lit. I move closer and see Alexander and Zavy sitting near it. Zavy stands and races towards me, still limping on her foot.

"Where have you been?" she asks, her hands gripping my arms.

"The river," I say and my tired eyes meet hers. "I'm sorry, I said we'd go get Toby," I start to say but Zavy stops me.

"We have another plan." Zavy leads me to the fire and hands me some meat and berries. I try and catch Alexander's gaze through the flame, but he doesn't look at me.

"What's our plan?" I ask and scan the rest of the clearing for the first time. The dead soldiers from this morning's battle still lay scattered around the forest rim. We are camped out on a battlefield, and I have to avoid looking at them to keep myself from getting sick.

"We're going to stay in the bunker tonight," Zavy says and I look to her in disbelief.

"Paylon knows that's where we've been hiding. That's the first place he'll look," I say between bites of food.

"That's the point." Zavy tosses another piece of wood on the fire and it explodes with sparks. "You and Alexander will be in the bunker. We'll lock it from within so you are protected. I'll wait up in a tree and when Paylon comes I'll shoot him." She drives the small stick she'd been holding into the soft dirt by her foot. "He'll never see it coming."

"Why don't Alexander and I stay out of the bunker and help you in the attack?" I start to question.

"The Lost Souls will smell your scent. They're here to track you, not me. They'll know you're out of the bunker and the plan will be ruined," Zavy says and I nod understanding.

"And if Paylon doesn't come?" I ask.

"Then we'll go after him," Zavy says flatly and I nod agreeing. It's better for us if he comes here. Then we have the advantage.

"Toby wasn't at his camp," I say, remembering that I had looked for him when I saved Alexander.

"Alexander says they're holding him at one of the Stake Points," Zavy says.

"What's that?" I ask and direct my question to Alexander.

He still doesn't look up when he answers. "They're camps set up throughout the woods with cages. We use them to lock up the runways we find out here until transports can be sent to get them." While I may have struggled to trust Alexander in the beginning because he was a guard at the castle, I now see how valuable it can be to us. We have inside knowledge.

"So we take care of Paylon and then go save Toby," I say and finish off my late dinner.

"Let's get into position," Zavy says and stands. Alexander begins to move toward the bunker, but I stay put. My eyes stare into the bright red flames of the fire and I am fighting the wave of nausea setting in at the idea of going down underground again.

"Take a minute, but you need to go soon," Zavy says when she reads the fear on my face. They both leave the clearing and I watch Zavy climb high into a tree just over the bunker lid.

I reach into my bag and pull out my mother's journal. I lift its worn cover and turn to the page where I left off. Again the words appear to form down the parchment as if my mother is writing them now.

The next step you need to take is getting to freedom. I have seen so many wonderful things happen for you, but I'm afraid if I let you know it might interfere with how they eventually turn out. I want to let you know that you were very right in going to Libertas. There you will find freedom and so much more. Just like any other adventure, you will run into more obstacles that will challenge you, and force you to use your gift.

Adaline, you need to be careful about how often you use your gift. As you have just witnessed if you overuse your gift you will freeze up and be incapable of moving. The biggest risk you face is that there is a large chance that you can't regain movement. Also, I'm sure you know now that you can transport people to places you want them to go. However, this only works if you know what the place looks like. I could explain everything you need to know about your gift, but I'm afraid it'll overwhelm you. Make sure Alexander gets this information as well. Pace yourself, Adaline. It'll all be okay.

The words end and my mother cuts me off again. I close the journal and place it back in my bag. Reading it always seems to leave an empty hole inside. I know it's because I would much rather have my mother actually here with me to help me through this. I still can't get myself to be okay with her or my brother's death. I know I need to move into the bunker, so slowly I pull myself to my feet. As I walk across the clearing I take in as much fresh air as I can. When I descend into the hole I pull the lid closed and lock it. I stand on the ladder for a bit and have to convince myself that I'm not truly locked in. I can still get out. When I'm convinced I continue down the ladder and scan the bunker.

Alexander is lying in his bed. I can catch the light of the candle reflecting on his eyes. I don't say anything to him though, and he says nothing to me. I go over to my bed and crawl under the covers, feeling dirty in the clean linens. I bring my knees to my chest and hold myself there in a tight ball. My heart feels like it's been smashed to pieces. I've not only lost all of my family but possibly even my best friend.

I lay here for around an hour and nothing has changed. I roll onto my back and I stare up at the ceiling of the bunker. The stone has small sparkles in it, dusted across its surface. The glowing candles make the shinny flakes dance, and it's as if we have our own sky of stars above us. But even the fake shining stars can't make me feel better. I don't know what to do. My life feels like it's crumbling apart again. The ceiling begins to blur as more tears begin to stream down my face. I don't hold them back this time. I just keep letting them come.

I hear Alexander shuffling and the next thing I know he's by my side. He takes his arm and wraps it around my shoulders.

"It's beautiful isn't it?" he asks as we look up at the sparking ceiling stars together.

"Incredible, and breathtaking," I say through the tears.

"Just like you," he whispers. I turn my head and look at him, our eyes meeting just inches from each other. He takes his thumb and gently wipes away the tears on my cheek.

Suddenly Alexander leans in kisses me lightly on the forehead, and I'm overcome by a swelling in the pit of my stomach.

He pulls away and says, "Thank you for saving me."

"You're not mad?" I ask, wondering what changed his mind.

"No, I can't believe I was just about to hand myself over to Paylon. I've done a lot of stupid things, but that would have topped them all." I feel his arms wrap around me as he holds me tighter. "Adaline, promise me you'll never leave me. I can't lose you again," Alexander whispers.

"I promise."

I don't know what time it is when I wake up, but I do know that it is as painful as it was when I woke up on the forest floor. Slowly I roll to my side and come inches from Alexander's face. This is the first time in a while that I've gotten a good look at him.

He's relit the candles and it's easy to see the dried tear stains on his cheeks. His face is completely washed of color and his brilliant green eyes are like none I've ever seen. In the blacks of his pupils, I can see my own reflection and I don't look much better.

"Sorry, I didn't mean to wake you," he mumbles as he drops his eyes from mine. He starts to move away, but I place my hand on his shoulder and pull him back toward me.

"No, you didn't," I choke out, and I'm surprised at how my broken voice sounds.

"So, you didn't come back to camp until late last night. Where'd you go?" he asks, his voice much stronger than mine. Now those green eyes can't leave mine and I don't want them too, but I know I can't let him close to my heart in that way. It's only going to get more painful the deeper we get in this fight with Paylon.

"I'm not sure what happened. I was running and then I completely passed out. Here, my mom explains it better." I take the journal out from my bag and hand it to him. He takes it without saying a word. I watch his facial expression change as he reads through it.

"It's going to take us a while to master these gifts, isn't it?" he asks, handing the journal back to me. "I've known about mine for a while. I can use it, but sometimes I feel like I'm not doing something right."

We are quiet for a minute until I ask, "Alexander, if green eyes mean you have the gift then why are Paylon's gold, and my mother's blue?" It's the first time I've really given it some thought.

"I heard that once you turn 18 you get the power to change your eye color because you need to hide your gift more as an adult," he pauses for a minute and then sits up straighter. "Adaline," Alexander's voice draws out, and a questioning look falls over his face.

"Yeah?" I ask.

"Zavy should have been down here by now, right?" he asks and looks to me. Worry starts to rise inside. She was supposed to come down and get us early this morning. I don't know what time it is, but I feel like I've slept late into the day.

"How long has it been?" I ask and Alexander doesn't know.

"You slept for a long time," Alexander admits. "We should go check on her."

We don't waste another second. We throw our backpacks on and grab our swords. I climb the ladder first and Alexander follows close behind. We race out of the bunker and into our clearing, the morning sun beating down, but I freeze when I see him. Alexander nearly knocks me over when he doesn't stop. He doesn't have to ask why I stopped running because he sees him too.

In front of us is Paylon. He holds a fighting Zavy. The quick unexpected attack from behind me sends a shriek out of me. I fall to my back and see Codian kneeling above me.

Next to me, Chadian has Alexander in a headlock, struggling to get a brown sack over his head. Before I know it Codian has one over my head and my world goes black.

My face is in the dirt when I wake up. I take in deep breaths and I've broken out into a sweat even though I'm shivering from the icy air. The cool air burns through my throat, but it seems impossible to calm my quickening heart.

My muscles all ache and I remember passing out in the middle of the woods, unable to move any part of my body. For a moment that's where I think I am until I remember my conversation with Alexander when I awoke and found him next to me.

Slowly I pull myself to my knees, and I'm caked with dusty dirt. I try to understand my surroundings, but it's all unfamiliar to me. When my eyes adjust to the darkness of the forest I am terrified when I see the metal bars of a cage enclosing me. Out of instinct my hand launches up and strokes the slick metal surface, freezing my fingers, but I don't stop, even when they become numb.

I'm caught in a trance from when I lived back in the prison. I would spend my days running my hands over the smooth surface repeatedly wanting to break through them. I stand and pace the edge of the cage, running my fingers across each bar, and I count. *1. 2. 3.* When I get completely around the cage I hit 38, and then I do it again. I don't feel strong and brave like I did the other day when my mother and Titus passed. I don't feel invincible with my gift that gave me such strength. I feel small and worthless. I cling to my numbers again, as if I were still in that prison.

"Freedom has been taken from me again," I think.

I feel empty like my gift has been stolen from me. This thought makes me suddenly stop stroking the metal bars. Have I lost my gift? I feel so weak I'm not sure, even if I had it, I could accomplish anything. I see small rocky pebbles scattered around me, pressed into the dirt. I focus hard and picture them rolling around and I am able to move them, shaking them around on the ground with my mind. I relax a little knowing my worst nightmare is not in fact true.

I see a spark out of the corner of my eye and raise my head. Codian has started a fire not too far from my chambers, ten maybe fifteen feet away. I don't see anyone else out here with us. Not even Alexander and that startles me for a minute, but before I try to worry about saving him I need to save myself.

Even though it doesn't seem like anyone is around I still don't risk raising my voice. "Codian," I hiss.

He looks around frantic and sees it was only me that called his name. He ignores me and turns back to his fire. My hand moves to my hip and I notice my sword is gone. My bag is laying in the corner of the cage I crawl to it and reach into it to take out my mother's journal. I pull out the photograph of me, my father, and Titus, and the gold coin from the guard in the castle, food rations, but find the journal and knife missing. A chill creeps through me as my heart skips a beat. I fight to steady my breathing and stay calm so my mind can start searching for ideas to get out of here, but my thoughts are frantic. How can I find a way to escape? I need to get out of here. I start to feel as if my small chambers are pressing in on me and I realize I will do whatever it takes to get my freedom back.

The first question is how do I get out of this cage. I don't see any locks or keyholes visible. The bars seem to be coming out of the ground. I could try and dig down under them, but I don't know how deep they go, and I'm sure Codian will notice that. I try to see if Codian has a key on him but the only thing out of the ordinary is a silver necklace that he has been constantly pulling on and no sword. I wonder why Paylon would leave him here with no protection unless they were running low on supplies. This must mean they haven't found their horses that ran off in the battle. I know they took my sword, and I'm sure Alexander's was taken too. Three of them, our two swords, I guess Codian pulled the short straw. They've underestimated me to think he won't need protection, I need to use this to my advantage.

I'm trying to think of some way to get Codian over here when I remember a story I had heard back in the prison about him and his brother. The rumor was Chadian was appointed to be Paylon's right-hand man first and Codian was supposed to be left behind to tend to less important matters at the castle. A rivalry between him and his brother may be all I need to get his blood pumping. I pull on my backpack and get ready to outsmart him.

"Codian," I hiss at him again. When he looks over at me, I wave him toward me.

He rises slowly, throwing another piece of wood on his fire before walking to my cage. "What do you want?" he asks, kneeling face to face with me.

"I just wanted to know if the rumors were true," I say through gritted teeth and I watch the curiosity flash in Codian's eyes.

"Rumors about what?" he asks and draws out his question, trying to figure out where I'm going with this.

"About your brother being Paylon's first pick," I say and tilt my head innocently. I watch the muscles in his face tense and his lips press into a straight light.

"If that were true then why am I here?" he questions back to me. He stands and I match his movements to stay at his level.

"I heard it was because your parents paid Paylon to take you both." At this comment he squints his eyes at me. He's losing sight of why I'm asking these questions and is getting lured into defending his integrity.

"Who told you that?" Codian huffs back to me.

"Your friends that work in the prison at the castle talk a lot," I say and take a step back from the bars. He rolls his eyes and starts to turn away from me, but I can't lose this opportunity.

"They said you failed your first three attempts to be a part of the army," I call out and he freezes with his back to me. "They said if it wasn't for your parents' money you would be nothing." His hands close into tight fists and I know I'm getting to him.

"What's it like to share everything with a twin that's better than you?" I question and raise my voice. "Birthdays, first days of school, holidays," I list off and I watch the muscles in his neck tighten. "All while everyone around you is saying how he is the better twin. He is the successful twin. He is the one who will make the family proud."

Codian spins on his heels and comes straight at my cage. "You have no idea what you're talking about!" His voice roars and I watch him fly through the metal bars of the cage. The silver necklace around his neck burns bright red as he effortlessly passes through the bars. That's the key.

Codian reaches for me but I use my small size to my advantage. I drop and miss his grasp. I come up behind him and rip the silver chain from his neck. Swiftly I clasp it around my own neck and launch myself through the bars. Just like before, the necklace glows red and allows me to fly though the metal cage, and Codian is left, shocked, behind bars.

With my blood pulsing through me I start to regain strength and confidence in my gift. "Where's Alexander?" I ask sternly.

"Why should I tell you?" he spits back in my face. His cheeks are flushed red with embracement that he fell for my trick.

"Look, you're going to answer the question. Where is

134

Alexander?" I growl.

A look of fear passes through his eyes and he mumbles, "Just around the lake, to your right." I look over my shoulder, and through the trees and tall grass I see the lake off in the distance. I'm about to leave when I stop and ask, "And my mother's journal?"

"Paylon has it, I swear," Codian says. I turn to leave and he calls after me, "You're just going to leave me here?"

"Be happy I didn't kill you," I say, my voice low and scratchy. I turn away from Codian and make my way off to my right.

I don't have to walk far when I see the hint of flames a few paces ahead. I drop to my knees and crawl the last few steps. I peek through the bushes in front of me. It's just a small clearing, almost looking identical to where I was being held captive. Chadian is sitting around a fire wearing a similar necklace to the one I now have on. Alexander is trapped in a steel cage just behind him.

I crawl over to Alexander trying my best to keep quiet. He sees me out of the corner of his eye and relief spreads across his face. I put my pointer finger to my lips to remind him to keep quiet. Then I notice the black eye and gashes on his face. What happened to him?

I take the necklace and slide it through the bars. It glows red as it passes through. Alexander seems to understand what to do. He puts on the necklace and quietly comes through to the other side. I gently touch the black circle under his eye and give him a questioning look. He nods toward Chadian and I notice the sword in Chadian's belt. Alexander's sword.

I stand and walk into the clearing making my way to Chadian.

Alexander hisses at me to stop, but I ignore him. I have to get to Zavy somehow, and Chadian is the only one who will know where she is. Alexander urges me to stop but he is being too loud and Chadian turns around and gets to his feet.

He draws his sword, but the next thing he knows I have it in my hands. I'm grateful my gift is coming back and getting stronger as the adrenaline pumps through me. I draw the sword and hold it to his neck.

"Where is Zavy?" I ask.

He swallows and I can see the fear in his eyes, similar to Codian's. "About a days hike up ahead. You'll have to cross a bridge over a river. Her brother is with her."

"And my mother's journal?" I ask, just to see if it lines up with Codian's answer.

"Paylon took it with him." I think about killing him right here, but I just can't seem to do it. This is different than the guards at the castle or the army back at our camp. Killing Codian or Chadian just seems wrong. I realize I not only need to stop using my gift so often because of how tired it can make me, but also because of the monster I'm starting to turn in to.

"I'll let you go this time, but don't follow us." I turn behind Chadian and with the sword to his neck I lead him to Alexander's cage. The key around his neck allows me to shove him inside and I make him throw the unlocking necklace back through. He does and I clip it around my neck so Alexander and I each have one.

I slide the sword through my belt, and finish, "I won't be so forgiving next time." I return to Alexander and help him to his feet. "I suggest when you dig your way out you go back and let your brother out of my cage." Then, Alexander and I move further into the forest in the direction of where Chadian said Zavy is being held.

Chapter 10

I match my pace with Alexander and instantly I feel the need to explain to him how I escaped from Codian. It's almost as if I'm now always second-guessing whether or not he trusts me. If I don't tell him every little piece of information about me will he get mad again?

"Do you want to know how I got away from Codian?" I ask him and he glances down at me.

"I just assumed you used your gift," he says coldly, although I don't think that was his intention. I tilt my head for a second and realize that I didn't. I didn't even try to.

"Actually no," I say to him and he's curious as to why not. "It wasn't my first instinct. I just brought up how much better Chadian is than him and he went into a fit."

"You outsmarted him," Alexander says and I see a smile cross his face. "That was smart."

We continue to walk in silence for a mile or so, just letting the sounds of our footsteps speak. Finally. Alexander says he thinks we should stop and make camp because it's better to sleep at night and move in the daytime when we can see where we're going. I nod and say that I think we would be safer staying up in a tree. I know that doesn't seem the most comfortable spot, but if Codian or Chadian come after us I know we'll be better hidden up there.

In the mix of tall palm trees are beautiful trees clothed in bright pink and yellow flowers. We come to a stop next to one that has thick branches that start low enough for us to climb. Alexander goes up first and I follow directly behind him. He stops midway and straddles a thick branch. He pulls me up and I sit in front of him. The shower of beautiful flowers conceals us up in the tree. I keep the sword I took from Chadian on my belt, ready to draw at any second. I lay my head back into Alexander's chest and his arms instantly wrap around my waist.

"I'm sorry about your mother's journal," Alexander says in a weak voice.

"It's okay. We'll get it back," I say, and my eyelids fall shut.

We are quiet for a long time until he says, "Adaline what's wrong? You're crying." My eyes bolt open and my hand rubs my cheek. It is damp with tears. "What are you thinking about?" Alexander asks.

"Nothing," I say, remembering what I was thinking about.

"Please, Adaline, you can tell me." He places his hand under my chin and turns it so he's staring into my eyes.

"I'm just scared," I admit softly.

"Scared of?" Alexander asks, but I don't know what the answer is. Maybe it's the fear inside me that we are on the run for our lives. Maybe it's the paranoia that I feel like I could take a wrong step, keep one thing to myself, and lose Alexander instantly.

"I just want to get to Zavy and Toby and get as far away from Paylon as we can." I turn around and Alexander tightens his arms around my waist, trying to give me some comfort. "And it's also the paranoia that I may do something to lose you again."

He's quiet now and I glance over my shoulder. His eyes look hurt and he chokes out, "I don't want you second-guessing yourself, Adaline. You won't lose me, we're in this together."

"I'm not the girl you remember as a kid," I whisper and turn back around.

I sink further into his chest and he says, "I know, and I'd choose who you are today over her anyway."

I gaze at the stars through the canopy of leaves and flowers and ask, "Do you regret helping me escape?"

"No, no of course I don't. I was planning my own escape from that horrid castle," he says between a deep yawn. We are quiet for a minute and I can't help but wonder if he doesn't regret it because he may actually still have feelings for me. Could there still be a chance those feelings could be there? I don't know if I want that, I know I don't need that right now. If it's true though that would mean he's really forgiven me for keeping him in the dark about my gift.

"I also just feel protective over you, that's all. You're my responsibility as my friend," he says, letting his voice destroy the hope I had that he really did still have feelings for me. He lets his eyes fall shut and slows his breathing down. It wasn't the answer I was looking for, but it's better than having him hate me. Maybe he isn't the right person for me either. I match my breathing to his rising and falling chest, and I fall asleep to the beating of his heart in sync with mine.

Waking up to Alexander gently breathing behind me sends a warm and comforting sensation down my skin. I think to myself that this wouldn't be such a bad way to wake up every day. Slowly I let my eyes fall open and I'm blinded by the sunlight seeping through the tree branches above. It must be nearly noon.

My chest rises and falls with Alexander's. His arms hold me close to him as if someone might have come to try and steal me away in the middle of the night. I lay my head back on his chest and Alexander wakes up from my slightest movement.

"As much as I want to stay up here all day, we need to get to Zavy and find food," I say, remembering how long it has been since we had last eaten.

We slowly make our way down from the tree and walk in the same direction we were traveling in last night, and Alexander was right, it is a lot easier to travel in daylight. With the sun up, the woods that surround us seem to take on a new life. We haven't been to this section of the island before and I wonder how far Paylon carried us after they captured us. It doesn't look like they were taking us back toward the castle because I don't recognize any of this area. The dirt beneath our feet is dry and baked with the sun's heat. The palms are taller here and they are scarce with fruit. The trees with flowers I had seen last night have a very dry and white bark. The muscles in my legs throb and I try to stretch them out as we go. We each pull out one packet of dried rations and eat as we walk.

"So what exactly can a Sensor do?" I ask him, bringing up his gift for the first time since he told me. "Besides open locks. I mean you already know I can basically just control anything that I see."

"Well, I'm not entirely sure what I can do with it. All I know is that anything I touch I'm able to know all the information about it and its history. Like, for example," he starts as he takes his water bottle from his bag," I can tell you that this water bottle has been carried by ten other soldiers, it was produced three years ago, and currently holds exactly 8.3oz of water."

"That's incredible!" I say at all the knowledge Alexander can simply generate by coming in contact with an object.

"I don't know," he says. "It all seems kind of pointless if you ask me. Like, what am I supposed to use that for? At least your gift can help you in combat. Lucky for me, I've had some training or I'm sure I'd already be dead."

"I just feel like these gifts hold more meaning to their use if we only knew how to use them," I say. "Like the fact that I can use mine for fighting isn't its only purpose, because I can also teleport items and people."

"Yeah, I get what you're saying," Alexander says and we fall back into our quiet manner as we continue walking through the trees of the forest.

"What happens when you touch people? Do you just instantly know their life story?" I ask Alexander curiously.

"No it only works on objects," Alexander says shortly.

"I mean, yeah that makes sense or else you would have known about my gift a long time ago," I say more to myself than him. Again silence settles between us and we continue to walk and finish off our rations.

"Well, maybe it works on people, and I just can't do it yet," Alexander says and he gives me a questioning glance.

"Maybe we can try to see if we can figure it out," I say. "Right after we find freedom and aren't running for our lives."

"Can you tell me Zavy and Toby's gifts or do they not trust me either?" Alexander asks. His voice is soft like a child's, afraid he may get scolded for asking.

"Toby can master weapons with an enhanced sense of touch. Zavy called it an Aeros, I think." I pause and Alexander nods. "Zavy said she was a Communicator with an enhanced sense of hearing."

"So she can talk to animals?" Alexander asks amazed.

"She said so," I say. I nudge Alexander slightly with my arm and add, "We're all in this together now, Alexander." He gives me a soft smile. I know Zavy doesn't particularly want to work with Alexander. I remember she had tried to convince me to leave him behind, but if she knew he was here trying to find her she may change her mind.

"How many different combinations of gifts are out there?" Alexander asks me and I tilt my head confused. "Like Toby and I both have an enhanced sense of touch, but can do completely different things. I know we have this list we are trained on, but could there be more combinations?"

"I'd say the combinations are endless," I admit and remember the dream I had a few nights ago about when Ms. White had lectured on gifts. "I remember Ms. White saying it was up to the power of the gift holder to unlock their full potential."

"So maybe I could use my powers to master weapons like Toby if I was trained and had enough practice with it," Alexander works out and I agree. Alexander begins to list off all the information we have about gifts, "You are a Force Lifter. Your mother and my father were both Future Holders. Zavy is a Communicator and Toby is an Aeros."

"And Paylon is a Controller," I say, finishing off the list.

"You must have enhanced sense of sight because your mother did," Alexander says. Talking about her makes my heart ache, but differently now. The fact that I may have this power inside of me because of her makes me feel like I have a part of her with me.

"Maybe your mother had an enhanced sense of touch then," I offer to Alexander and he nods. "Did you ever hear from her again?" I ask him, trying to recall everything I remember about her leaving. I was over at his house after school as normal. Alexander's mother had told me I needed to go home and as I was packing up my bags she sat Alexander down to tell him that she needed to go away too.

"No, she never came back," Alexander says and his voice is dry as he chokes out the words.

"Why did she leave?" I ask, wondering if I remember it correctly.

"Something about my father needing to protect me so she had to go away." He pauses and adds, "It was a long time ago. I don't really remember." I wonder if he's telling me the truth because I know the day my father left me is still clear in my head.

We've been walking for hours and still, neither of us has really said much other than a few comments about our gifts and families. We trade off on who carries the sword since we only have one to protect or hunt with. We've started to make our way out of the dry woods and are now back to lower ground where the trees seem to be more green. The air feels heavy with humidity and the dirt beneath our feet turns to a stiff mud. We stopped once to refill our water bottles earlier, and are about to stop a second time to take a break when I hear a branch snap up ahead.

"Alexander," I whisper, my voice hoarse from not using it. Suddenly there's another snap, and another, and then it sounds like our intruder is simply running through the woods, breaking anything in its path. A small baby deer runs out right in front of us and I flinch back. My mouth drops, as I watch two arrows fly down from a nearby tree and run straight into the deer causing it to crash to the ground.

My first thought is somehow Zavy got away from Paylon. I watch as someone drops from the tree where the arrow came from and by the strong muscular build I know it's not Zavy. Another boy, slimmer, follows down the tree. Instinctually my hand finds the grip of the sword on my belt. The first has short brown hair that is just barely peeking through the off white colored hood he has pulled up over his head. He turns and faces us, letting his hand with the bow fall to his side. He takes his other hand and pushes his hood off his head revealing not only the fact that his hair has an intricate swirling design cut into it but also his odd caramel-colored eyes.

I take in a sharp breath when I realize how much they remind me of Titus's eyes. When the guy speaks to us I can hardly believe what he says.

"Adaline, we've been waiting for you," his strong voice booms.

"You've been waiting for me?" I hear myself ask, not recognizing my own voice.

"Yes, come with us and I'll explain everything," he says as he positions the bow on his shoulder. Him and his partner make their way toward the deer. They carefully remove the arrows from its side, and lift the deer together. They start heading deeper into the forest, not bothering to wait for us to go with them.

I start to step forward, but Alexander grabs my arm. "Whoa, where are you going?"

"He said to follow him," I say and Alexander gives me a bewildered look.

"Do you know who he is?" Alexander asks, trying to understand why I'd go with this man.

"No I don't think I've ever seen him before, but he knows who I am. He could help us, Alexander." When he still hasn't loosened his grip on my arm I continue, "Do you have a better idea?"

"Yeah, we ignore him and continue toward Zavy," he says stubbornly.

"Alexander, trust me on this. I really feel like I need to follow him," I say, locking my eyes with his. When he still hasn't let go of my arm I add, "Can we at least find out how he knows who I am? Aren't you at least a little curious?"

"I thought you wanted to get Zavy and Toby and get as far away from Paylon as possible," Alexander says, still fighting me.

"I do," I admit and bite my lip lightly He's right, maybe we need to keep moving to Zavy, but how do we do that knowing this guy is just here and knows me.

"Your father told me about you," I hear the mysterious man yell from deep in the woods, still not waiting on us.

My gaze with Alexander falls heavy and now he knows we have to hear this guy out. My father left me years ago and I have gotten no explanation as to why or where he went. I know Alexander understands that I need to go just for the chance I could learn something about my father's disappearance. Alexander reluctantly lets go of my arm and we hurry to catch up with the hunter.

"How do you know my name?" I ask when I've matched my pace with his.

"It's a pretty long story. I'll tell you everything once we get back to my camp," he says shifting his eyes between Alexander and myself.

"Are you with anyone else?" Alexander questions, taking in the two hunters.

"Yes, there are ten of us. We've been living out here for just under seven years," the hunter explains shortly, being sure not to share more information than he wants. I look at this guy's facial features more closely and realize that he can't be any older than I am.

"What's your name?" Alexander pushes.

"My name is Cooper, and this is Bren," he nods to his silent partner. "I assume you're Alexander?" Cooper shoots to Alexander and his eyes widen.

"How do you know," Alexander begins

"Like I said, long story. So how exactly did you get out here?" Cooper asks.

"Oh, so finally something you don't know?" Alexander mumbles.

"I know a lot, but not everything," Cooper says as he glances between Alexander and me.

"Well, it's a long story," Alexander says, mocking Cooper.

"Well, how about you enlighten me with your story of how you got here? We still have quite the hike back to camp. I can take us back the long way," Cooper says.

"We aren't saying anything," Alexander starts to say before I cut him off. I don't know what it is about Cooper, but I'm starting to think I've seen him before. I just can't place where. There's something oddly familiar about him.

"Seven years ago I was thrown in prison with my mother and younger brother," I pause and try to steady my breathing. Talking about my mother and Titus hasn't gotten any easier for me.

"You don't have to do this Adaline," Alexander cuts in.

"No it's okay," I say to him and then continue. "Just about a week ago they ordered for my mother to be killed on Parting Day," I stop and take in a deep breath. She's already been gone that long. "My mother told me I was a Force lifter and I used my gift to escape with my brother Titus, but he was killed." I stop as the words start to feel thick in my throat. I decide to leave out the fact I don't know how to use my gift, he doesn't need to know that. In case this is a trap he won't know I can't use my gift.

"I'm sorry," Cooper starts to say, but I cut him off, not wanting to talk about their deaths anymore.

"When I was making my way out of the castle I ran into Alexander, he was on duty outside of the maze," I glance over at Alexander and see he's hurt that I have just told these complete strangers about my gift and I hadn't told Alexander until Paylon forced me to, but if we want Cooper to share what he knows about us I have to give him something.

Cooper stops suddenly, dropping the deer. He shoves Alexander against a tree, pressing a small knife he had concealed to Alexander's neck. "Are you still working for King Renon?" Cooper asks forcefully.

"No, he helped me escape," I say and try to reason with Cooper.

Alexander chokes out, "I did work for him. I don't anymore, I'm being hunted, same as her." Cooper is hesitant for a second before backing away and releasing Alexander. He lifts the deer and starts walking again. I fall back in step with him, but Alexander has decided to stay a few paces behind us.

"Continue," Cooper instructs me.

"Since then we were traveling south when we ran into our other friend Zavy and her younger brother Toby. We were heading to Libertas when the search group lead by Paylon found us and took us as prisoners. Alexander and I escaped and they locked Zavy up just a couple more miles south of here. We were on our way to help save her and her brother. That's the summed up version of everything we've been through." Cooper simply nods his head in approval.

We step through some underbrush and into a small clearing. There are three small tents propped up around the clearing and a large fire pit in the middle. Around the clearing different people are cleaning shirts and pants or collecting firewood. Some are cutting up a couple of rabbits and a deer and two others seem to be standing over a large map discussing some sort of plan. However, all actions stop as soon as we step into the clearing. Everyone is completely silent and staring at us like they'd just seen a ghost.

Cooper nods to everyone and they continue to do whatever they were previously doing, but we have definitely drawn everyone's attention to ourselves. Two guys about my age run over and take the deer from Cooper. Bren joins them in taking the deer and Cooper starts leading us toward one of the far tents across the clearing. When we enter, Cooper motions for us to take a seat on a cloth that has been thrown down and then Cooper sits down across from us.

"So are you going to tell us what's going on now?" Alexander pushes.

Cooper nods and begins speaking, but he can't bring himself to make eye contact with either Alexander or myself.

"Seven years ago I was taken from Garth with the other nine

people you see around here. An older man planned our escape and brought us out into the woods. Back then I was only ten years old, like many of the others. Mio and Cinder are the only two adults and they basically raised all of us. The man who brought us all out here told us that in seven years a girl named Adaline will arrive here and that when she does we had to help her." He stops suddenly and I know he's leaving something out.

"Cooper," I say, trying to figure out my own question. "Who was the man who planned all this? Who brought you here and told you about me?"

"Adaline." There's a long pause before he continues, "It was your father." He takes in a deep breath and says, "Our father."

Part 2: The Truth

Chapter 11

"Wait, what?" I ask, probably more forcefully than necessary. Instead of answering me I watch as Cooper reaches into his pocket and pulls out a small folded piece of paper. I watch as he unfolds the paper and I realize that it's actually a photograph. He hands me the wrinkled photograph and I gently take it and examine it. It's a picture of a young kid who I can only assume is Cooper. He is sitting on a couch next to a man I instantly recognize as my father, even though only half of him is in the photograph. Both of them have been captured in mid-laugh. I take my finger and run it along the ragged edge of the image where my father sits.

Something seems oddly familiar about this picture, and then I make the connection. I reach into my own bag and pull out my own photograph of myself, Titus, and my father. When I hold the two next to each other I see that they make a perfect match. I can feel Alexander tense up next to me as obviously shocked as I am.

"You're my brother?" I question, barely audible. Cooper just nods and lets me continue, but all I can manage to say is, "What?"

"It's a pretty complicated explanation, Adaline. Maybe you want to eat something before I get into it," Cooper stumbles over his own words.

"No," I force, tears brimming the edges of my eyes. "I want to know everything. I'm tired of not knowing anything. No more half-answers. I want the whole story. Every single detail," I say, frustration building inside of me. Mostly because of everything I have been left out of, my father's elaborate secret group waiting for me in the forest for example. But I'm also frustrated because no matter how hard I try I can't ever remember having a brother, besides Titus.

"All right," Cooper continues, coughing to clear his throat. "Our father, Derith, dedicated his life to helping people with gifts escape Garth. This way they wouldn't be taken in by King Renon. Mother and Father were both Future Holders, and so the odds of them having a child with the gift was very high." My skin tightens at the knowledge that my father was also a Future Holder. Both of my parents had an enhanced sense of sight.

"Before we were born, Dather was ruled by King Renon's Father, King Lexon. He, similarly to King Renon, took in children with gifts but was much more secretive about it. When he passed away rule fell to his son. King Renon tripled the number of gifted prisoners in just a couple of months. That's when Derith decided he had to find a place of freedom for people with gifts. There was an underground operation that had been going on for a while where gifted people were being smuggled out of Garth and to an island known as

Libertas." I nod my head connecting the memory I had about my father calling that our new home.

"Our father joined the operation and began to help move other families to Libertas. We were born about a year apart and when I turned ten years old we confirmed through the testing process at the castle that I did not have the gift."

"They took you in to be tested?" I ask confused. If he did have the gift he would have been targeted and hunted for sure.

"We knew before based on our mother and father's visions that it would be you who had the gift. They needed me on record to keep suspicion away from our family while our father continued to work for Libertas," Cooper explains, and I realize how precise and detailed this entire plan really had to be.

"During one of Derith's journeys to take another gifted family to freedom, he ran into a group of King Renon's guards. Father managed to escape and make it back home, but he knew that the guards had identified him and they would be there by morning. So that's when he made this plan."

"Why didn't we just go to Libertas?" I ask and Cooper raises his hand to calm me.

"I'm getting to that," he says gently. "The journey to Libertas is hard. It's a minimum of a three day hike from Garth. You have to get through Sard and then survive at sea for another two days. It was too dangerous to make the journey with so many kids. So, our father decided he needed to hide us."

Alexander clears his throat, "Where do I come into this?"

"Right," Cooper says and rubs his face with his hand. "I'm sorry it's so confusing." He takes a minute to collect his thoughts and says, "Our father and your mother, Marin, were good friends growing up. When our father went undercover to work for Libertas Marin joined him."

"She had an enhanced sense of touch didn't she?" Alexander asks and Cooper nods.

"Your father, George, had seen visions of you with similar powers to Marin and they knew they needed to protect you too," Cooper explains.

"So our families worked together," I say, trying to hold on to what seems real because I am still struggling to even remember Cooper's existence.

"They did and when our father was caught they knew they needed to hide all of us until the time was right to move to Libertas. So, they put us where King Renon would be least likely to look," Cooper says and glances between Alexander and myself.

"In his own castle," Alexander processes out loud.

"Correct. Then he put together a group to wait in the woods until we would be old enough to make the journey together. He took me with him and we went around the village asking families to send their children with us," Cooper begins to explain but I stop him.

"And they just did?" I ask.

"We explained to their families that we needed their children to come with us so we could have a group waiting for you when you escaped the prison. If their families agreed to send their children with us they would be considered as possible candidates to reside in Libertas. This in itself was enough for the parents to agree because only people with gifts had been allowed to make the journey away from Garth." Cooper pauses when he sees me open my mouth to say something but I close it and just shake my head, not sure what I should even ask now.

"After we had gathered the other kids we met up with Mio and Cinder, both of them have helped Derith and Marin with previous journeys," Cooper begins to explain faster and faster spilling out the details of that night. "Father said he had one more family to talk to before he was ready to leave. So we all went with him to this house outside the village. A man and a woman came and talked to our father in hushed voices. I'm not really sure what they said, but then this kid walked outside and I remember the older woman telling the boy to go back inside. It was you, Alexander. She said, 'Alexander go back inside' and then my father said 'Marin we have to go now. You should go and say goodbye and grab whatever you're bringing with us. You both know the plan and if we just keep doing everything according to the plan it will all work out.'"

"Wait," I interrupt him again and he lets out an exhausted breath. "If you're really my brother then we would have grown up together. You talk about Alexander and his parents like you don't know them, but as far as I can remember they were like family to us," I say, trying to keep straight what I can remember about my childhood and what Cooper is telling me.

"No, Adaline we never talked to Alexander or his family before.

Just our father had, secretly on trips to Libertas," Cooper says, confusion in his voice.

"But don't you remember that one summer when I was eight I came home from building forts with Alexander in the forest and I had gotten poison ivy so bad I had to stay in bed for a week and Alexander basically lived at our house. He insisted on taking care of me because it was his idea to build the forts in the poison ivy."

"No, that was me, Adaline," Cooper says defensively. "I told you that was the best spot,"

"Because we could see our intruders from all angles," I say, finishing his sentence and the memory finally comes back to me clearly. I see Cooper up on top of a hill and he's yelling down to me that this is where we should put our fort. "It was you," I say confused.

"But that doesn't make sense," Alexander says. "Because I remember myself being there."

"I get it," Cooper says suddenly and Alexander and I look to him to continue to explain. "Father told me when we left that mother was going to take away all your memories of me, one of the many things Future Holders are capable of doing. She must have substituted all of the memories with me in them with Alexander in my place."

"But why?" Alexander asks.

"That way Adaline would trust you as soon as she saw your face when she ran out of the castle. She would instantly think you were her childhood friend and then you would go with her to Libertas."

"Continue the story," I say after a moment of silence because I'm

160

starting to realize that everything I thought I shared with Alexander was actually a lie. I don't even know the person sitting next to me.

"We waited as both of Alexander's parents went inside, and then Marin came back outside and said she was ready to go. So we left. We hiked through the woods until we got to this point. Derith told Mio and Cinder to set up camp here and that if everything goes as planned Adaline and Alexander would be here in seven years. Then our father and your mother left and headed to Libertas." Cooper stops speaking and the questions start pouring out of Alexander and me again before we can stop ourselves.

"Why didn't my mother just take me with her?" Alexander asks.

"For the same reason our father didn't take Adaline or me. We were too young to survive the journey." Cooper explains.

"Well, I'm pretty sure I could survive some boat ride!" Alexander says back, floored at his mother's decision.

"But it's more than just that," Cooper argues with him. "The sea is full of the atomic energy from the asteroid shower years ago and that has filled the waters with these inhumane creatures. They are similar to the animals that inhabited the sea before the shower, but they are far more deadly. I'm not even sure we could survive them now."

"Okay, but I'm confused about why our father brought all these kids out here into the woods to what? Just wait for us?" I ask.

"The idea behind this was that if guards found us Mio and Cinder were supposed to tell them that we were just sick kids from the village and that we were sent out here because they wanted to lessen disease in the village. The reason we had to do this was because we couldn't keep moving camp around to keep away from the guards. We had to stay in this exact spot so that you would find us. Plus, the guards had no good reason to bring a bunch of sick kids back into Garth. We made sure all of us were non-gifted and not wanted by the King," Cooper says.

"So you're telling me our father put a camp of children in the woods with Mio and Cinder to just wait seven years for me to show up because there was a good chance I'd have the gift according to their visions?" I ask, unable to believe his story.

"Yes," Cooper says sharply. "Look, he was right wasn't he?"

"Okay, so father knew that mother, Titus and I would get thrown in prison? He knew mother and Titus would die? Alexander and George going to work in the castle was all part of this plan to help us get to Libertas once we were old enough?" I ask, bewildered by the thought that my entire life is some plan.

"It was a fairly good plan. In the dungeon no one would see your green eyes to know you were highly likely to have the gift. Our father never mentioned the fact that mother and Titus would die. I don't think he ever knew that would happen," Cooper stops, letting his eyes drop.

I realize that he never even got to really meet our little brother. He probably doesn't even remember what our mother looks like or what her voice sounded like. I reach and grab his hand, and a sense of belonging rushes through me. Like I finally put in the missing piece of a really messed up puzzle. Cooper looks up at me and I can see the tears forming in his eyes, those caramel colored eyes.

"You have his eyes," I say. "You and Titus had the same caramel colored eyes." I smile slightly, remembering Titus and how alike they really are.

Cooper gives me a slight smile before I pull my hand back and he continues. "Since Alexander worked for the castle, King Renon didn't need to capture him for his gift. You were already following his orders."

"But something still doesn't make sense," Alexander says, "Why did my father flee from the castle and leave me behind?"

Cooper clears his throat before continuing. "I heard Derith and Marin discussing it the night we came here. Since George was a Future Holder he had seen a time where King Renon had ordered for him to go through a mental restoration. It's a process that would allow King Renon to take all of the visions your father has had and put them into his own head. It also would have resulted in your father's death. After King Renon takes all his visions and disposes of his memories it leaves the body brain-dead, so George left once you were old enough to fend for yourself. If King Renon would have gotten hold of George's visions of the future then he would have seen all of this. The plan would fail and we all would have lost our lives."

"Well have you seen him since then? My father?" Alexander pleads.

"No, I'm afraid not, but that doesn't mean he didn't make it to Libertas," Cooper adds shortly. "I don't know what instructions

Derith gave him."

"Why do you have to have the gift to get into Libertas?" I ask, realizing I hadn't thought it to be weird at first, but now I see that all these ordinary people wasted seven years of their lives living in the woods just to get a chance to go to Libertas. And there were more guards that fled with Alexander's father, not all of them or maybe any of them had gifts. An act like that would get you killed if you were caught. "All of these people who don't have gifts are risking their lives helping Alexander and I get somewhere that they aren't even allowed to live in?"

"I don't know much about life in Libertas, but when people first started to flee to the island it was known as a place of freedom for people with gifts. But that's all I know. That's all anyone knows really. People who go to Libertas and make it there don't come back unless they are helping others escape to the island."

"But that doesn't make sense, why would all these people risk their lives for our freedom?" I urge.

"Well, what would you do if a group of Future Holders got together and told you that if you helped get their children to freedom the future would be much better for your kids?" Cooper says simply.

"I mean, I guess I would have to believe them," I agree.

"Their only alternative choice is to continue living under King Renon. I think I'd take my chances in the woods too," Alexander agrees.

"Have you heard from our father since he left?" I ask Cooper, finally finding the question I'd been wondering this whole time.

Cooper is silent for a while before he forces out the answer, "No. We have connections living in Sard that said they arrived. Usually, groups stay overnight with our sources in Sard before heading out onto the ocean. A couple of days after they left Sard someone said they'd found washed up remains of what seemed to be a boat." Cooper senses my body tense up and he reaches over to put a hand on my shoulder.

"We don't know for sure if it was their boat. Our father has made that journey dozens of times, right?" I ask him and I'm finding that I don't know if I really want my father to be dead. I spent all this time hating him and wishing he were dead, but now I don't know if that's what I really want.

He drops his arm and pulls out a gold chain from his pocket. My heart tightens at the sight of it. My father's gold compass. Cooper doesn't have to say anything, and he hands the heavy metal memory to me. "They found this in the ship wreckage." My father would never go anywhere without it. I hand the compass back over to Cooper, haunted by its past. From the distant look in Cooper's eyes I know that, just like me, Cooper has had to accept the fact that our father is gone and out of our lives. At the confirmation of my father's death, I'm surprised relief and joy aren't what I feel. Hadn't I wished for this? Just the other day in the woods I begged the universe to let it be him instead of my mother.

I look up to Alexander and see the blank expression on his face. "I'm sorry about your mother."

He shakes his head and says, "It's okay Adaline. She's been gone a long time, this doesn't change anything."

We are all quiet for a moment. I try to process all the information that has been poured out to me. Out of the corner of my eye, I can see Alexander processing all of the information as well. We look at each other for the first time and hold each other's gaze. Who is he? I can't even answer this question anymore. When I look at his face I still see him with me as my neighbor. I still see him running through the woods and the town. I still see him as the boy who sat behind me in class, who could finish my every thought, who came over with his family for Christmas and Thanksgiving. All the birthdays we celebrated together, all the school projects and presentations we did, every memory I still see his face. I try to make myself picture them with Cooper instead.

No Alexander wasn't at my 5th birthday party where we dressed up as princesses and princes, that was Cooper, my brother. And as soon as I make myself make this connection I feel as though a string holding the bond between Alexander and I snaps, and it physically hurts my heart. I'm torn between not wanting to lose him from my memories and wanting to know the truth about my past. But I'm not the only one whose memories have been infused with Alexander. I remember that Zavy believes that he was just as good of friends with her as me. Was it really Cooper in all those memories?

"Mother messed with Zavy's memories too?" I ask, still holding Alexander's stare, both of us looking at the other trying to figure out who they really are.

"Yes. All those days it was you, Zavy, and I in the city.

Alexander was never there," Cooper says gently.

"So where was I?" Alexander asks Cooper, but still not dropping my gaze. "You can just replace me with Cooper in all your memories, but what are my true memories?" Alexander asks his voice weak and empty.

"They're in there somewhere," Cooper says, obviously holding back information.

"But how do I access them?" Alexander says more sternly, frustration building in his eyes.

"We have something that can return all of your memories back to normal," Cooper says flatly and Alexander and I both break our stare and turn to him.

"You what?" Alexander asks.

"When we left that night, the night we were all brought here, my father gave us supplies that we would need in the future," Cooper says as he rises and starts looking through some of the bags in the tent.

"We have a couple of swords, some knives, cooking equipment, maps of the island, and this rock. It's enchanted and is supposed to hold the power to recover all lost memories. Don't ask me how or where he got it from, I'm only the messenger. He told us we would need to use it to fix the memories our mother had altered in Adaline, but I bet it would work for you as well," Cooper says pulling a large, perfectly round, grey rock from a beige bag. Then he comes and sits back down across from us. "We can fix your memories now," he starts to say before I stop him.

"Wait," I interrupt. Alexander and Cooper look to me. Alexander sees the fear in my eyes and reaches for my hand. Already his touch is more empty and cold than before. "I don't want to forget you," I say quietly.

Cooper clears his throat and says, "I don't need to be present for this so when you both are ready you can do it on your own. You just need to each place a hand on the rock and recite this," Cooper says, laying down a piece of fabric next to the rock as he leaves the tent.

A moment of silence passes between us before Alexander speaks, "Adaline, you can't forget me because you don't even know me." Alexander tries to say it gently, but his words pierce my heart like a sharp blade.

"But I do know you, I do. I thought I did," I say, my mind slowly wrapping around the situation we're in.

"But you don't. You know Cooper," he says. I look into his breathtaking green eyes and try to convince myself that I don't truly know them, that the memories with him aren't real.

"We're in this together now," Alexander says. "Once we erase the lies we can start getting to actually know each other. We will have real memories together. All this time in the woods, me helping you escape, that is all true Adaline. So what if I didn't know who you were when I saved you? I wouldn't change any of this."

"You say that now, but what if, when you get your real memories back, you wish you could have your old life back? What if you wish you never had met me and never had saved me," I say stumbling over my own words as the horrible thoughts cross my mind.

168

"I won't," Alexander says sternly. "I promise," he says as he places his hand on the rock while keeping my hand in his other. He gives my hand a tight squeeze of reassurance and I gently lay my other hand on the rock. We both look down to the piece of fabric and start to recite the words in unison:

Help me see the truth in me
Erase the false and bring forth the real
Take me back so I can see
All the past and set me free

I clench my eyes shut as the room begins to spin. My head starts to pound as I see old memories fade and new ones form. There's a loud pounding noise in my ears accompanied by a high pitch squeal. I squeeze Alexander's hand tighter and tighter until finally everything comes to a halt and the room falls silent.

I slowly let my eyes fall open and look down at my hand in Alexander's. In unison, we both pull away. I hardly know anything about him why am I holding his hand? I look into his green eyes, how peculiar they look to me. I search my brain for everything I know about him and all I can grasp is that he saved my life and helped me leave the castle. My mother had messed with my memories and I used to believe he was my childhood best friend, but in my head he isn't the boy I grew up with. I don't remember any feelings I've had for him in the past, but somewhere in the pit of my heart there's a tiny piece that cares for him. I remember that he was given completely false memories of me and he truly had no idea who he was before he was put in this mess. He must be so lost.

"Alexander," I say and his name feels foreign on my tongue. "Are you okay?"

He looks at his hands for a while, the memories obviously flowing through his head.

"Alexander?" I ask again.

"I'm fine," he says shortly, rising from the fabric on the ground. "Let's go find Cooper." I stand and follow him out of the tent, scanning his face to see how he really feels, but his face is expressionless, stern, and cold. That's it, I think. He truly hates me and regrets ever coming on this trip. He can't even look me in the eye anymore, but what do I care if he hates me? I didn't mess with his memories, and I didn't make him flee the castle. While I do have a part of me that's, I suppose, sympathetic toward him, I can't be consumed with how this stranger feels about me. Cooper is standing right outside of the tent and his eyes pass from Alexander to me. "We're good," Alexander says flatly. "Everything's how it's supposed to be."

"All right then," Cooper says gently. "Come on, I want to introduce you to everyone. You are kind of famous around here," Cooper says still not sure how to treat Alexander and me, and honestly, I don't know how to act either.

Chapter 12

Alexander and I follow Cooper into the center of the clearing, both of us standing on either side of him like somehow adding distance from each other could make the heavy space between us more bearable.

"So this is where you've been living for seven years?" Alexander asks, his face relaxing and his mind drifting from whatever he experienced with the return of his memories.

"Yes, I'd give you the grand tour, but we won't be staying here much longer. I'll just introduce you to everyone," Cooper says as he starts walking toward one of the tents in the clearing. "Over here we have the health center. It's not much, but we have some basic medicines. This is also where we turn in our dirty garments in exchange for clean ones." Cooper stops and waves us to follow him behind the tent.

On the other side of the tent, a group of three girls are busy scrubbing dirty fabric and hanging them on a line to dry. When they look up and see us they instantly stop their work.

"Oh, come on now. Don't treat them like you've just seen a

ghost. They're just like the rest of us," Cooper says.

"My apologies," one of the girls says. She has a short blonde bob hair cut and shining blue eyes. She places the shirt she was cleaning on the edge of the old wooden bucket and wipes her hands on her own old dress. The ends are tethered and covered with loose strings. Dirt patches, I'm sure they've tried scrubbing clean, rim the dress.

I realize they were kids when they were brought here, but in the seven years, they've grown. They had to gather old thrown out garments from Garth and sneak them back here for them.

She extends her hand out to me and says, "I'm Essie. It's an honor to meet you both." I accept her hand and she gives it a tight squeeze. She does a similar gesture for Alexander and I am almost certain I can see tears brimming her eyes. I realize how crazy it must be to finally see the faces of the people you've been waiting seven years for. We are their key to freedom, to finally leave these woods. Essie lets a smile fall across her lips and I can see the happiness in her eyes.

She gestures to the two girls behind her who have also dropped the shirts and pants they were cleaning and stand to greet us. "These are my sisters. Cassandra," she gestures to one of the girls who has very long and thick blonde hair and brown eyes. "And this is Sarah," Essie says, gesturing to her other sister who has thin red hair.

"It's nice to meet you all," I say and smile as I shake Cassandra and Sarah's hands.

"That's an excellent stitching job," Sarah says, looking down at Alexander's leg. "Who did that?"

"Oh, Adaline did," Alexander says and my name sounds odd coming from him.

"Where did you learn to do that?" Sarah asks, impressed.

"We'll I watched my mother do it on me once before. I really wasn't taught," I admit.

"It's a very nice job. You probably saved his leg," Essie says to me. "What medicine have you taken for it?" she turns and asks Alexander.

"I took medicine for the pain right after we stitched it up. That's it," Alexander says to Essie, thinking back to now two days ago.

"You should take some more pain medicine and some others too, in case of infection. Giving stitches in these conditions is dangerous," Essie says. She walks around us into the tent and then emerges with two pills. Alexander swallows each of them and thanks Essie. "If you need more for the pain let me know. You should take the one for infection every 24 hours."

"I'm fine really. I don't want to use up what little medicine you have," Alexander says sheepishly.

"But you're our key to freedom," Cassandra says shocked by how humble Alexander is trying to be. "We would give up anything for you." I look around at the makeshift home they have here in the woods and recognize that they already have.

Her comment leaves an awkward feeling between the group and Cooper steps in, "We will be leaving first thing tomorrow morning so make sure to distribute the rest of the garments out and pack up whatever you have to take with us."

We make our way to the second tent in the clearing and encounter a very similar greeting. This tent serves as the kitchen and food storage area. There are four guys working here. Two of them, Albert and Andy, are brothers and the other two, James and Bren, were neighbors before coming here. They ask what we've been eating and we explain to them it has been a mix of ray berries and turkey meat. We show them the rations we found at the bunker and they are as confused as we were.

"You found a bunker?" Cooper asks curiously.

"Yes, not far from here. Just over a days hike probably," I say. "We took most of the useful items. We could have brought more clothes if we had known," I say, trailing off. I don't want to insult the conditions they are living in. It's far better than the prison cell I was in, but the quality of clothes Alexander and I have are leaps and bounds from theirs. "We could go back," I start to consider. It's honestly the last thing I want to do. I want to find Zavy and keep moving forward. Cooper said their plan is to get me to Libertas which is where I was headed anyway, but I feel responsible knowing there are better resources not too far from here.

"Not necessary," Cooper says, interrupting my thoughts. "We'll leave tomorrow for Sard and replenish our supplies then."

"But the rations have been safe to eat?" Albert asks, cautiously sniffing the bag.

"We've been eating them all morning," Alexander offers.

"It's just dried food, it doesn't actually taste like anything," I say and watch the four boys test the rations for themselves. They shrug their shoulders not, nearly as interested as they were before.

"They'll still be good to have, in case of an emergency," Albert nods.

We follow Cooper out of the kitchen tent and over to the two people I had noticed before leaning over a table looking at a map. We walk around the edge of the clearing and I glance at the trees. I stop at one and scan the thin lines carved in its trunk. My eyes sweep to the neighboring trees and I see they are covered with gashed lines. My finger lifts and rubs over the groove.

"Just something to keep time moving," Cooper says softly. My eyes feel wet as I remember the cell I left behind, marked with thousands of lines.

"I used to make a tally on the walls of my cell," I say and my voice cracks. There's a comfort that falls over me at the thought of knowing each day I scratched that stone wall my brother was out here making his own tally. We've each been counting our days, together.

When we reach the table the man and woman standing over the map turn and look at us, smiles spreading across their faces.

"And this is Mio and Cinder," Cooper says, introducing us to the two in charge. We exchange greetings and end up circled around the table with the map. I look down and study the aged fabric. I'm amazed by how detailed this map really is. I see a tiny black "x" in the center of a tan circle. "Home" is written under the "x", and I realize that's where we are now. It's pretty centered between the center of the island and the southern shore. I let my gaze move up the map and see "Garth" written out in large red letters. I start to take in how much space there is between the two points.

On fabric the space seems so basic; just green forest. But what I have actually gone through from one point to the other is much more than a couple of green painted trees. My life has changed from the starting point to here. I lost my mother and my younger brother. My family was ripped away from me. I was forced to save myself and use my gift for the first time. I was reunited with my best friends, and for the first time I felt like I actually belonged. And then it was all ripped away from me just as fast. I learned my father didn't actually abandon me, and I learned I have an older brother who has given his entire childhood to saving my life. But when you look at it on the map it's just a couple of painted trees, that's all it will ever look like to anyone else.

I realize there are many other points on the map all around the point labeled home. One has a drawing of a cave and another a creek.

"We've had a lot of time to map out our surrounding areas," I hear Cinder say in her soft high-pitched voice, her dark blue eyes meeting mine.

I drop my eyes from hers and nod my head before asking, "So we're leaving tomorrow to save Zavy and Toby, right?" The silence that follows my question leaves me uneasy. "Right?" I ask again.

"Adaline, we were never given any instruction to help a 'Zavy'. Your father only told us about you and Alexander," Cinder says.

"Well, I'm not going to leave her out here," I say, gesturing to the humming jungle around us. I can't believe what they're telling me.

"They need to get to Libertas." I'm hesitant to say my next words, but I think it may be the only way I can convince them. "Toby and Zavy are both gifted. They need help fleeing to Libertas."

I see Mio consider this just for a second before he says, "Adaline we can't risk going off from the original plan. If we do anything that your father didn't tell us to do it could throw everything off."

"But," I start before Mio cuts me off.

"The answer's no Adaline. Look around you. All these people have given their lives to make sure this plan is followed out perfectly. Don't make all they gave up for nothing. I'm sorry about your friend, but we can't afford to take any chances." He looks at me sternly and adds, "I was given a job seven years ago and I plan to see it through exactly how I was instructed to. You follow me now." His command makes me stiffen. I'm not in chains or locked behind bars, but his statement leaves me feeling like a prisoner.

I drop my gaze from Mio's and feel my hands clench into fists. I feel Cooper place his hand on my arm and I slowly relax my fingers and let out a long breath. "Fine," I breathe.

"Maybe she'll get out on her own and meet us at Sard. She knows that was where we were heading," Alexander says and I let my eyes meet his and he immediately drops his gaze from mine, but I can tell he doesn't even believe what he's saying.

"Maybe," I mumble. "So then what's our next move?" I ask as I gesture to the map.

"I think the best course for us to take will be to follow this river all the way south into Sard," Mio says. "That way we will always have a supply of food and water." Mio drags his finger along the painted blue squiggling line that he refers to as the river.

"I mean that makes sense to me," I agree. Then I hear a low-tone bell ring. I look around in confusion.

Cooper explains, "That's our sign that dinner's ready."

"We'll pack up the documents," Mio says as he rolls up the map.

"Go ahead and take them to the dining tent," Cinder says in her soft sweet voice. I can't help thinking of how different Mio and Cinder are. Cooper starts heading back toward the tent that I had previously referred to as the kitchen. My mouth instantly begins to water at the aroma in the room, and I realize I haven't had a decent meal in almost two days.

I move and stand in line with the others. The food has been laid out in front of us and I don't hesitate to take my fair share of the freshly cooked meat. There are also a large variety of greens and berries, including the familiar ray berries we've been living off of.

I take all my hands can hold and follow Alexander outside. I notice that everyone has broken off into groups to eat their dinner. Alexander and I head toward the edge of the clearing together without even thinking, and sit and eat our dinner in silence. It's the first time we've been alone since we've put our memories back in place and I don't know what to say to him. The only thing I can even think of right now is Zavy.

After a while of eating in silence, I ask him, "We aren't actually going to leave Zavy and Toby are we?"

Alexander looks at me confused, "Well, how do you plan to

change Mio and Cinder's minds? They seem set on not going to save them. I mean, if we had your mother's journal then maybe we could convince them, but we don't have anything to show them that Zavy and Toby are supposed to be going with us."

I sit for a moment, getting my thoughts organized before I speak again. "Then we'll just have to save Zavy and Toby without them," I finally say and continue eating.

Alexander has stopped eating altogether and a worried look sets across his face, "No, Adaline. No, we can't do that."

I look at him and wonder what the old Alexander would have done. I wish I was able to still remember the feelings between us, but I can't remember anything except for factual information about the last few days of our journey.

"You may not actually know who she is Alexander, but she is my best friend, and she still believes you're hers. We can't just leave her here to die. You can't possibly be okay with that," I say shortly and when he doesn't respond I add, "I have a plan."

"No, Adaline," he says again, almost begging.

"Look, Alexander," I say more harshly than intended because I'm not letting Zavy go again. "We'll leave in the middle of the night and we'll be back with Zavy and Toby by morning." We sit there in silence, holding each other's gaze. "Or I will just go alone," I threaten, and even though the past bond between us is broken I see a flicker of possible fear flash across his eyes at the thought of me going to fight Paylon on my own.

He drops his eyes from mine and says, "Fine. What's your plan?"

Chapter 13

Convincing Alexander to risk his life to save Zavy takes less work than I thought it would. I shove a handful of various types of berries into my mouth before explaining. "We leave after everyone has fallen asleep. I was studying the map earlier and it looks like if we just follow the river they mentioned we will come along a bridge that should take us right to where Chadian said Paylon was keeping Zavy and Toby. Then all we would have to do is get this key to Zavy," I say as I twist the necklace around my neck.

"What if Codian and Chadian are there? We can't take all three of them," Alexander questions.

"Well, I'm hoping they won't be," I say simply.

"You're hoping?" Alexander asks shocked.

"We left them locked in those cages. I doubt they've dug their way out that fast." Alexander gives me a look that says he thinks I'm being naive. "I'm really just hoping they can think for themselves for once and leave while they can. Although I doubt that will happen so I'm just really hoping we get there first." I finish off the meat and berries and wait for Alexander to say something.

"All right, we'll do it," he finally says and we both nod to each other in agreement. I get the feeling he agrees more so he can protect me rather than save Zavy. I wonder if it's because he wants me safe or because he wants this search group to help us to Libertas. If I go and die that could ruin his chances of getting there. I believe Cooper when he said our father died in the ship crash, but I can tell Alexander is not one to ever lose hope, about his mother or his father. But they left him the same as mine left me and Cooper. Life's better when you accept the dead are gone.

A large crash in the middle of the clearing pulls my attention from Alexander, and I watch as Cooper and some of the workers from the kitchen, Albert and Andy I think, stack a large pile of wood in the fire pit. I watch the other two guys from the kitchen, James and Bren, work on getting the wood to catch fire.

It doesn't take long for the wood to catch, and I watch as the smoke rises past the trees until it touches the rose pink and orange sky, fading away. I study the colorful sky for a moment longer and see the stars slightly peeking through the colored sunset.

I take a deep breath of the cool night air to slow my heart rate. There's no telling what will happen to Alexander and me tonight. Life long best friends or not we have already been through a lot together. I trust him with my life and yet I don't know the first thing about him. I don't know what his favorite color is or what his dreams were, but I do know I need him and he needs me and we both need to get to Libertas.

Tonight we're going away from the plan that has seen our safety in the future for an unknown outcome. I felt like I had done things on a whim before, but now that I know what the actual plan is it's harder to make those half-second decisions to do something crazy. I watch as the four guys from the kitchen set a wall of logs around the fire to try and conceal most of the bright orange flames

"Come on," I say and stand to face Alexander. I extend my hand out to him and help him up. "Might as well try to make some friends while we're here."

We walk over toward the fire and see the others do the same. We all take a seat around the campfire, soaking in its warmth. I look up and see that Cooper, Mio, and Cinder are handing out a variety of pillows and blankets. Most people are laying their blankets out and sitting on them so Alexander and I do the same. Cooper, Mio, and Cinder then head back into the tent with all the documents to finish packing.

Everyone breaks off into their own conversations. James and Bren wave Alexander over to them and Alexander stands to walk to the other side of the fire. I catch a glimpse of his face through the flickering flame as James and Bren talk with him.

I close my eyes and rest my head in my hands. The memory from reading my mother's journal for the first time swims into view and suddenly the pages turn and more text appears. Shocked, I breathe in sharply and my eyes fly open. Can I control my memories? I close my eyes again and call up a memory with my mother's journal.

I recall the memory of myself sitting in the bunker back at the camp we had with Zavy and Toby before we were ambushed the first time. I'm flipping through the journal as the words appear on the page about not letting Alexander go. I'm about to close the journal to go after him when I freeze the moment. Something about this memory seems strange; it all seems very fake or pixilated. With my mind I try to see the page turn, and in the frozen dream it does just that.

I'm so sorry Adaline.

These are the first words that form on the page and I can't help but feel tears start to form. This can't be good. I don't know what it is, but something about Alexander gets to me. I can't remember how I felt about him. I know it was a great bond of friendship, and I fear I will never get to feel that again. The memories I shared with that person didn't really exist, but Alexander is a real person who I had real feelings for. I know deep in my heart that Alexander means something so much more to my life than just a stranger going to the same place.

I wish there was another way for me to have altered your memories from Cooper, and you may never forgive me for messing with your and Alexander's relationship, but you have to believe me when I say I had no other choice. His mother needed him to get to Libertas and I knew you would one day escape the castle and meet him for the first time outside the maze. Your father and I thought it would be too dangerous to introduce you to each other any earlier, in fear that you would somehow alter the future. For everything to go as planned I had to follow my visions exactly.

As you've just discovered you can access this journal through your memories. If this is true then you have started to truly master your powers. I know it's hard to do alone, and I am so proud of you. You are so strong and brave, and you have to remain that way for what is ahead of you. The one catch here is you can only do this magic if my journal remains in one piece. If it's destroyed the visions and notes here are gone forever.

Please, Adaline, you can't give up on Alexander. You should take what I have to say with a grain of salt because what is next for you is very grey. I have no clear vision of your journey to Libertas, there are far too many factors that could alter the future, but you should know that Alexander is important to you and you should not let this stop you from building a real relationship with him. The memories that have been returned to him are not pleasant. He may never share them with you, but you have to be patient with him, Adaline. When I altered his memories it was for the better so he could be happy. It is not my place to tell you what he has been through.

That's where the words stop. I flip through the pages faster and faster, wanting to know more, needing to know more, but they are all blank. I feel a hand on the center of my back and my eyes flash open as more tears roll down my damp cheeks. I quickly wipe them away as I look up and see Alexander kneeling next to me. Everyone around the fire has stopped talking and they are all staring at me.

Alexander gently asks, "Do you want to go talk." I look into his empty green eyes and beg them to mean something to me again.

"It's nothing," I say, and I regret the words as soon as I speak them. How can I expect Alexander to open up to me when I can't let myself open up to him?

"Are you sure?" he asks.

"Actually, can we talk?" I ask softly, trying to force myself to lean on him. He nods his head gently and lends me his hand to help me up. We walk to the edge of the clearing and sit against a tree.

"It's my mother's journal," I say.

"What about it?" Alexander asks, and in his voice I can hear that he is genuinely concerned. Perhaps I miss read his anger after our memories were returned. Maybe he doesn't hate me. Could it be all the negative parts of his past that my mother had told me about?

"I'm able to still read it in my thoughts. Something about her enchanting the journal allows me to pause a memory with it and flip through its pages so long as they still exist and haven't been damaged."

"Well, what did it say?" Alexander asks cautiously, preparing for the worst.

"It was just her apologizing for messing with our memories and how she said she had no other choice," I stop, catching my breath before continuing. "She just told me not to lose hope for us," I say and look up and meet his eyes. "What are we supposed to do?" I ask him and my voice shakes no matter how strong I'm trying to be.

For the first time, he doesn't drop his eyes from mine and he says,

"I'm not who you think I am."

"I know that your old memories aren't good. My mother said changing your memory was for the better, and I get you truly don't know me and I'm not someone you'd tell these things to, but I know that in the past I loved you. I cared about you more than I could have ever thought possible, and I understand that the memories of that person weren't real but you are. You are a real person who I had a real friendship with, and I can't let that go. I can't help but think that you're who I'm supposed to be with. So I can't stop fighting for us. I don't need you to tell me all your dark moments from your past, but we have to start somewhere," I say, my voice so shaky and weak I can hardly control it.

Alexander takes my hand in his and says softly, "Then let's get to know each other, for real this time. I understand everything you feel and all the confusion you're going through because I'm going through it too. I don't remember anything I used to know about you. We're in this together Adaline. I want to make this work, but I'm afraid once you learn about my real past you'll want nothing to do with me."

"Then we'll take baby steps. Learn the little things first, save the rest for when our relationship is stronger," I say simply. His green eyes sparkle in the light from the distant fire and there is a spark in my heart when I look into them; a sign of hope that those feelings can return.

"Alexander. Adaline," I hear Cooper yell to us. We turn and see him waving us back to the fire. We stand and walk back over

186

together and sit back down on our blankets.

"What's going on?" I whisper to Cooper, and I realize everyone has started humming a soothing tune.

"Some nights we'll tell different campfire stories or play games, but tonight we're singing campfire songs," he pauses and looks at my confused face. "Oh don't tell me you've never heard of campfire songs before."

I shamefully shake my head, not remembering our mother mentioning any before. I don't want to make him feel bad, but we didn't have campfires in the prison obviously.

"Our father used to sing them to us all the time. The memories are in there you just can't recall them all right now," Cooper adds. Of course, that's why he had expected me to know what was going on. "Mio and Cinder said they would do this with our father when they were moving families to Libertas."

"Well, then it's quite fitting to be singing them tonight," I hear Alexander chip in. I turn my attention back to everyone humming and hear Cooper join them when they start singing.

See this city in all its horror
Let us leave this tyrant power
Through the woods and across the waters
Walking where our fate desires.

Gather now, sisters and brothers
Listen to our journey's travels.

We've traveled long, we've traveled far

Left behind what we know

Here we sit strong and steady

And off we'll go when we are ready

We'll travel long and travel far

Until we reach our new home

Many will leave, few will arrive

Whatever we face, we will survive

We've seen each other at our worst

But in the end, we'll be the first

Gather now, sisters and brothers

Listen to our journey's travels

We've traveled long, we've traveled far

Left behind what we know

Here we sit strong and steady

And off we'll go when we are ready

We'll travel long and travel far

Until we reach our new home

And so they're here to sit and wait

For a Queen to accept her fate

Our current King will crumble someday

And the Queen shall find her way

Gather now, sisters and brothers
Listen to our journey's travels

We've traveled long, we've traveled far
Left behind what we know
Here we sit strong and steady
And off we'll go when we are ready
We'll travel long and travel far
Until we reach our new home

When the song finishes the group continues humming along to the melody. "Some say it's a message from a Future Holder, right?" Alexander asks, looking at Cooper to answer him. "I can remember reading this in a book at school." The lesson must have been after my schooling was interrupted because I don't recognize the words at all.

Cooper nods and explains, "Well, sort of. It was believed to be something like a prophecy from the first Queen who used to rule Dather, King Renon's grandmother. Queen Sift was a Future Holder. Many professors have tried to decipher it but it really just sounds like a song kids would sing when they made it to the Hawaiian Islands during the asteroid shower. That's where the Queen had said she'd discovered it, so it wasn't exactly a vision she'd had, but yeah, the song came from a Future Holder I guess."

"Do you think that's why King Renon hates kids with gifts so much?" I ask, "Since his grandmother had one, but then he and his parents didn't have one?"

"I assume so," Cooper agrees. Suddenly the group changes their hums to a different melody and I take in a sharp breath.

"Stay," I whisper. "I remember our father singing this." He was putting me to bed, and he said he had a new bedtime song for me.

"Why doesn't Cooper have to go to bed?" I hear nine-year-old me ask my father and point to Cooper's empty bed while he stood in the doorway.

"I need him to come to town with me to refill our food supply," my father forced out with a broken voice as he pushed my hair off my face and kissed my forehead.

I can hear my father's voice as he sings the song, overlapping with the singing around the fire.

I want to stay
A while longer
A while longer so I'm with you
But it's that time of night
For you to close your eyes
And dream of endless seas of blue
And when the morning comes
I'll be right here with you
This is goodnight and not goodbye.

The memory starts to fade away as nine-year-old me starts to fall asleep and I watch as my father and Cooper walk out of the room. I feel Cooper put his arm around me and it pulls me fully to the present. "Cooper, our father sang this the night he left," I choke out.

"You can remember," is all Cooper says.

"What do you mean 'can remember'?" Alexander asks.

"Our mother had to block all memories of me in her head so that she wouldn't ask where I was. The guards would have made the connection that our father was actually making a plan not just running away," Cooper says.

"Right, but why did you say 'can remember' of course she can remember we got our memories fixed," Alexander asks.

"Since she has all her old memories back now things like this song can trigger these memories. It's difficult to recall these memories on your own because of how long you've been without them, but they can still be triggered by things such as music or pictures," Cooper explains, but I don't even hear his voice. I'm tuning everything out except for the captivating humming.

No one talks for a long time after that. The sound of the groups humming and the forest surrounds my thoughts. Suddenly, Alexander is squeezing my hand and I become aware of the fact that the humming has long since subsided and everyone has started to get ready for bed. Cooper has gone to Mio and Cinder and they seem to be discussing last minute travel plans.

I glance at Alexander with a questioning look in my eye and he knows it's about our plan to go get Zavy. Alexander just nods, lets go of my hand, and says, "Get some rest. I'll wake you when it's time."

I lay my head down on the soft pillow. Before I fall asleep I look at my hand, where Alexander had squeezed it just seconds ago. There is a sort of warmth and comfort that came when he touched my hand. I might not be able to recall the feelings I had for him before, but I do know that I am starting to fall for him now and then I fall into a deep sleep.

Chapter 14

"Adaline," I hear Alexander's hushed voice in my ear. I slowly open my eyes and look around in confusion until I remember where I am. The idea that my father put this entire camp together is still new to me.

"Everyone's asleep. If we're going to go we need to do it now," Alexander whispers. I nod silently and struggle to get to my feet. I pull my backpack on and slide our sword through my belt.

It's nearly pitch black with the slight exception of the little moonlight coming through the tree branches. Alexander takes my hand in his. I look down at our hands and then up at his eyes. He holds my stare for a moment and then gently nods his head for me to start moving and leading the way. I tighten my grip on his hand and maneuver around everyone sleeping.

We walk away from the rest of the group and deeper into the forest. We're completely silent as I lead Alexander toward where I believe the river I saw on the map should be. We inch ourselves forward slowly, careful to make as little noise as possible. With the twisted tree roots growing up out of the ground it's a challenge, and we have to move a lot slower than I would like. We continue like this for what seems to be hours. Maybe it just feels like time is drawing out because of the heavy awkward air between the two of us. His hand in mine, the butterflies in my stomach, and yet I still don't know the first thing about him. At first, we walk in silence for the simple fact that we don't want to be heard, but now we are miles from the campsite and still don't speak. It's not that I feel like I need to speak to him because I think he understands me without me having to explain myself, but I also wouldn't know what to say if I did need to talk to him.

"Adaline, are you sure you know where you're going?" Alexander whispers, finally breaking the silence.

"Shhh," I hush him. "Listen." We both become silent again and stop moving. Off in the distance I can barely make out the sound of rushing water. I look back at Alexander and smile. "Yeah, I know where I'm going." I turn and try to walk forward but Alexander pulls me back.

"This isn't going to work," Alexander breaks out.

"What?" I question back to him.

"What are we doing Adaline? Do you really think we can show up with some magic key and free Zavy and Toby? You know better than I do that it's not going to be that easy, and we don't have anything but gifts that Paylon is immune to," Alexander pushes. I'm silent for a while, knowing that he's right. I take the sword out of my belt that I had taken from Chadian and give it to Alexander.

"We'll figure it out when we get there," I argue and rip my hand free of his as I walk toward the sound of rushing water.

Eventually, I hear Alexander following me. With the sword in his hands it leaves me completely defenseless and as much as he may want to turn back he knows he can't let me walk into face Paylon with no weapons. After a while longer of walking, the sound of water has grown to a roar and we've come through the edge of the forest into a clearing. The cool mist being blown off the rushing water settles on my face, and I'm reminded how extremely hot it's been these past days.

"There," I say to Alexander and point just a bit north of where we are to where the bridge is crossing over the water.

"Looks safe," Alexander mutters as he walks around me toward the bridge. I roll my eyes and continue after him.

"What do you think?" I ask when we make it to the bridge. On the tops of the two side posts is the Dather emblem. The tree of freedom that is on my gold coin sits deep in the wood. It's a reminder that this is all forbidden land to anyone besides the King and his men. No one is ever supposed to be out of the city limits, but I also wasn't supposed to leave my cell. Clearly, I don't care where I am or am not supposed to go. I look to Alexander when he doesn't respond and nudge him with my arm. Alexander still doesn't say anything but instead just starts to walk across the bridge and I follow him, knowing he's just mad that my crazy on a whim plan is working.

While my knowledge on Alexander is limited I believe Alexander and I have been through a lot of the same stuff, but sometimes we couldn't be any more different. Alexander is a planner, and he needs to know exactly what he's getting himself into. I'm different. I just jump into whatever I want and work my way through it. Sometimes I think it's because I had everything ripped away from me at such a young age. I don't feel like there's anything to lose. I mean for the past seven years I didn't even feel like I had a life left.

Once we are on the other side of the bridge Alexander suddenly stops and points to something above the trees. I follow his finger and realize it's a trail of smoke from what can only be coming from Paylon's camp.

I try to steady my breathing as I feel the fear creep inside of me. Slowly, Alexander and I make our way back into the forest, closing in on where the smoke is coming from. I can barely make out what looks like a fire up ahead through the trees. Slowly we inch forward until the entire clearing comes into view.

I feel my heart drop as my plan crumbles away. Codian and Chadian are here, and now Alexander and I are in trouble. Not only have the two marksmen returned to Paylon's aid, but one white horse has also found his way back to his owner which means they've gotten some weapons back. Paylon is sitting down holding my mother's journal in his hands. The sight of him with a piece of her makes my stomach turn upside down. He is facing me and I can see the glowing green rock around his neck, making him invincible against my gift. The twins are sitting with their backs to me and I watch as one twin sits sharpening the end of his sword by striking it with a stone while the other is carefully using a small pocket knife to cut away at a piece of wood. All three are wide awake, clearly keeping watch over the camp together.

Zavy and Toby are both sitting in a similar cage to mine and Alexander's. Toby is lying on his side, probably fast asleep, with his head in Zavy's lap. She is stroking his hair while she sits wide-awake, staring off into the woods and scanning around the clearing. When her eyes land on mine, they widen. I put a finger to my lips to keep her quiet.

My eyes scan the rest of the clearing and I see the Hounds are chained together at the edge of the area. All of them are as spread out as they can be, trying to sleep. I hold my breath at the thought that they could surely smell that Alexander and I are near, but I don't see any realization stir in the group.

Alexander presses his lips against my ear and whispers almost inaudibly, "Now what?"

"I'll just freeze them, right? I don't remember Codian and Chadian having the necklaces with them, and maybe they don't have them on right now," I pause and think back to the two clearings we were kept prisoners at, but can't recall clearly if they had the rock necklaces or not. I swallow and continue making my plan. "And then we'll just have to move fast from there because Paylon will notice them frozen and know it's us. I'll get their swords and you'll take care of Paylon while I get this necklace to Zavy and Toby."

Alexander nods his head and we both look back out to the clearing. "Wait," I start to say.

"What is it?" Alexander cuts me off, his nerves showing.

"Look. On the other side of the clearing. In the woods." We both stare across the clearing. Slowly the form of a person's face comes into view, their caramel colored eyes staring back at us.

"Cooper," I say. What is he doing here? He looks from me to the twins and I know he understands where Alexander and I are at in our plan.

Out of a subconscious instinct, I reach down and grab Alexander's hand. "Ready?" I whisper. He nods his head and I turn back to the twins. I picture them freezing, and just when I'm about to run out into the clearing I hear the ringing sound of rock against metal. Chadian is still sharpening his sword, not frozen like I'm trying to force onto him.

"It's not working," I whisper through gritted teeth as panic surges through me. I look over to Cooper and he can tell by the fear in my eyes that something isn't right.

"What?" Alexander asks, his eyes widening.

"My gift. It isn't working," I say, fumbling on my words.

Suddenly I hear Codian say, "I think your sword is sharp enough." He turns toward Chadian and I hear Alexander take in a sharp breath. I turn to Alexander and give him a questioning look.

"The necklace," Alexander whispers. I turn back and can barely get a glimpse of a glowing green rock around his neck. "That's what's keeping them immune to your gift now." Alexander and I are quiet for a moment, trying to figure something out. We need to get to Zavy and Toby so they can use this necklace to get out of the cage. Paylon has his back to them, but Chadian and Codian will see us for sure. It's three against three, but we only have one sword. I take count of their weapons and see one hanging on Paylon's side, and the one I was given from the castle the night I fled is being hammered by Chadian. We'll need to even the playing field somehow. Just as the thought of needing a distraction crosses my mind Alexander leans in to whisper in my ear.

"All right here's the plan," Alexander starts explaining. "I'm going to go around the clearing and deeper into the woods. I'll start making a lot of noise. I'll start a fire and I'll cut down trees, I'll just get their attention, okay? And then at least one of them will have to come after me, right? So then it'll be two on two and I think you can handle that."

"Are you crazy? That's the dumbest thing I've ever heard," I push my words out, trying to keep quiet.

"Adaline, we don't have any other choice," he says sternly.

"Just a couple of hours ago you didn't want to come here at all," I say, confused by the fact that Alexander is willing to risk his life for Zavy and her brother when she really isn't the best friend he thought she was. Alexander looks at me, but doesn't respond. "What is it?" I ask, knowing there is some reasoning behind this heroic act he feels he needs to perform.

Alexander drops his eyes from mine and says, "They are important to you so they are important to me." I lift his chin and force him to look me in the eye and I know there is more he isn't telling me, but before I can push him further he says, "I'll make sure to get out of there as soon as I can, but you can't wait for me, okay?

You get Zavy and Toby and get back to the camp and get everyone out of here. I'll meet up with you, okay? I promise." He stops and we both look at each other for a long time. Something flashes in his eyes and suddenly I feel as though I have known him all my life and this is the moment I have to lose him. Maybe it's a glimpse as to how I felt toward him before my memories were restored, but as quickly as the feeling comes it fades twice as fast. I throw my arms around his neck and he pulls me into a tight hug. I hold on to that quick spark of love for Alexander; a man I know nothing about but can love with my whole heart.

"Get out of there alive okay?" I mumble into his shoulder, feeling my throat tighten up.

"I promise," he says again. "Take this." Alexander pulls the sword from his side and hands it to me.

"You take it," I push it back to him. "You need to protect yourself."

"I'm not leaving you here without a weapon," Alexander starts to say defensively, but I stop him.

"I'll take one of theirs," I tilt my head to their camp.

Alexander considers this for a moment before nodding in agreement. "I'm going to stop and tell Cooper the plan when I get to the other side, and then you just need to wait for one of these guys to leave." He turns and walks deeper into the woods, fading out of sight.

I pace back in forth, not being able to keep myself still. I look out over the clearing again and see that Cooper has sunk deeper into the woods, probably because Alexander made it over to him. I turn my focus back to the clearing. Paylon is still flipping through the journal and Codian and Chadian are still bickering.

"Give me that rock," Codian says to his brother who refuses to quit striking it against his sword. My sword.

"No I'm using it," Chadian responds as Codian launches forward trying to rip the rock from his hands. The two start wrestling the other to the ground over the rock.

"Enough!" Paylon shouts over at the twins. Chadian freezes with his fist targeted for Codian. Instead of striking his brother he grins, taking victory in the wrestling match. They both fall silent and sit back down. Paylon continues to complain, "I'm trying to decipher this journal and I can't do it with you two acting like children." He huffs and turns back to my mother's journal. What does he mean by decipher?

"What's it say? Does it say if Alexander and Adaline are coming?" Chadian asks as he drops the rock and walks over to Paylon. I start to feel a bit uneasy with his statement. Are we coming? Is this supposed to be a trap? They're expecting us?

"Not in those exact words," Paylon says as Chadian takes a seat next to him. "It looks like the diary is written in some sort of code. It just has random letters all down the pages."

Paylon hands the journal to Chadian. I see him look at it for a second and then hand it back. My mother must have it set so only certain people can read the journal. I lean back against a tree and wait for Alexander to get his plan started, hoping we truly aren't walking into a trap. Through the forest night sounds, I listen as Chadian and Paylon try to decipher what two letters here and two dashes there could mean. I'm thankful that my mother was so clever.

Listening in on their hushed voices reminds me of when I was little and I could hear my mother and father out in the main part of the house talking one night. A night I had lost in my previous memory, but it returns to me suddenly. It was late at night when I was supposed to be asleep, and I had woken to hear their muffled voices through the wooden beams of the walls.

"You shouldn't eavesdrop," Cooper had said in the dark of our room. I glanced over to the far corner against the window and made out his caramel eyes with the moonlight.

"I can't hear them anyway," I had lied. I had heard them. They were talking about how they were going to take us to Libertas one day.

This was before my father had been caught transporting a family the night he had fled with Cooper. Before this crazy plan ever existed. It was simple then, my father would keep working for the current ruler of Libertas to bring them more gifted from Dather, and when my brothers and I were old enough to survive the journey we'd join them. Because of my father's services, we'd be set for life. He wouldn't have to be away from her or us anymore. We could grow up and live together safely and never have to worry. How nice that would have been.

Back then little me didn't understand what he could mean, and I had thought he was talking about us taking a trip to see the ocean. I had been begging my mother and father to take me to the island's edge. Hardly anyone ever gets to leave Garth unless they are sending or collecting goods and supplies from the neighboring islands. I remember having a girl in my class that got to go to the edge of the island with her father because he worked for the King. She talked about how blue the water was. Of course, my mother and father had always told me no, that they couldn't take me outside of the safe ten foot radius of woods I was allowed to play in.

But that night I had really thought I had heard my father say we'd get to go to the edge of the island, and I would get to see the blue water. I remember waking up the next morning shaking with excitement but trying my hardest to hold it in so I could act surprised when they told us about the trip. My father left with Cooper three days later and my memories were wiped. I never got to see the blue water. Not yet, I remind myself. We're going there now. My mother, father, and Titus may not be there with me like I had envisioned in my head, but I will see the island's edge. I will see just how blue the water is.

Chapter 15

I'm not sure how much time has passed when I hear a tree crash to the forest floor. My eyelids had fallen shut, but they jolt open at the sound of the destruction. Alexander. Toby has risen from Zavy's lap, flipping his head in confusion.

I look at Paylon and see that he has dropped my mother's journal to the ground and jumped to his feet, drawing his sword. He turns his back to me so he's facing the direction the sound came from.

"It's got to be them," I hear Codian say.

"I'm not waiting around here anymore for them to show up," Paylon growls. "I'm going out there and getting them myself." Paylon starts to walk toward the other end of the clearing and turns to Zavy and says, "Guess you weren't good enough bait. Shows how little they care about you. They were just going to leave you. Chadian, come with me."

Chadian stands and walks to his brother. "You can keep this piece of junk to protect you." I watch as he drops my sword at Codian's feet and draws a much more deadly looking blade from the supply bag on the horse. Paylon mounts the horse and Chadian follows on foot. Paylon takes two of the Hounds with him, leaving three still chained here with Codian. I watch as they sink deeper into the woods, waiting as long as I dare before moving.

I hold my breath, anticipating my next move. Alexander's plan is working. Now it's two against one. The Hounds aren't here for fighting so they won't get in our way. We have the odds in our favor now. *Get the necklace to Zavy and Toby and get out,* I repeat in my head, and I pull off the necklace off. Once I feel like Paylon and Chadian have walked a good distance from us, I see Cooper resurface at the edge of the clearing and know this is our cue.

Cooper reaches for a sword he must have brought with him. Smart. I hadn't thought to take any from the tents around his camp. I was too worried about getting away undetected to think they would have weapons. Of course they would. They've been hunting and protecting themselves for seven years. So, two against one, and we have a sword and my gift. Confidence builds in me as I weigh the scenario in my head. This is going to work.

Cooper nods to me, and I nod back and mouth the words, "Three, two, one." We sprint through the clearing. I immediately run to the cage encasing Zavy and Toby. As I run toward the cage, Cooper runs from the trees and I watch as Codian jumps to his feet and draws his sword. He flips his head between Cooper and me, not sure who to attack first. The sight of Cooper, someone he doesn't recognize seems to panic him even more. He wasn't expecting an ambush, but he definitely wasn't expecting someone besides Alexander to be helping me. I turn my attention back to Zavy as I hear the clashing of metal behind me. Codian has chosen his fight, and it's not with me yet.

"You came for us?" Zavy asks, crawling to the edge of the cage, pulling Toby with her. I pass the necklace through the bars and it glows red.

"Of course I did. Put on the necklace. It'll let you pass through the bars." Zavy does and then passes it back to Toby, who does exactly as Zavy did.

"Thank you," Zavy says, throwing her arms around my shoulder.

"You would have done the same for me," I brush off.

Suddenly, the sound of clashing metal behind me stops and I whip around to see Codian holding Cooper in a headlock with a sword at his neck.

"Codian," I start to say as I raise my hands until I remember my gift won't affect him. Slowly, I rise and walk toward him. At my movement, he tightens his arm on Cooper's neck and I watch as Cooper struggles to get air to his lungs. He's suffocating, just like my mother, our mother, had died. Furry and fear mix in my chest as my emotions swell at the thought of her death.

"Adaline," Codian mimics back to me. I see tears brimming in his eyes and his hands are shaking. Something's not right. He's not the confident killing machine I've been made to believe he was.

"What's going on?" I ask, trying to calm him down. Why is he crying? He looks as though something inside him snapped.

"I can't do it anymore," Codian says in a hysterical voice. "I can't do this anymore." He pauses, then says, "I need you to kill me.

Adaline, please kill me." The tears are running down his face and he's almost brought his voice to a shriek. I'd be surprised if Paylon and Chadian haven't heard him.

"What are you talking about?" I ask.

"Paylon's been controlling me," he yells out between his sobs. "Since I have this necklace he can't control me anymore, but I don't know how to live any other way. I've done so much harm to so many innocent people, Adaline. Please, just end this for me." I imagine all of the awful things he's been controlled into doing. All the lives he's ended with a clouded mind full of Paylon's voice edging him on. I would hate myself, too, when I finally woke up and had to accept the monster I had been. That's when I confirm in my head that he hadn't had the necklace on at the camp earlier. He would have asked me to do this then. The thought that Paylon's control could reach that far makes me sick, imagining how many other minds he's infiltrated. My guess is the entire army. I had no idea the kind of power he really has.

"Okay, but Codian, I can't do anything when you have that necklace on," I lie, trying to buy some time to let my brain process what is happening. Codian slips my sword to the necklace and cuts it from his neck. It flies across the clearing to my feet. Then, he returns the blade to Cooper's neck.

"Okay. Now do it!" he pushes and I watch as his head begins to tick and his eyes squeeze shut. "He's taking control back. You have to do it now!" Codian roars at me, and I instantly regret making him remove the necklace.

"Codian, I don't think this is what you want," I say, because I honestly don't want to kill him. I don't want his blood on my hands. He isn't what Paylon made him do. I truly believe if he had been given control of his actions, he never would have done those awful things.

"Do it!" he yells, and the blade presses on Cooper's pale neck. I process how drained Cooper's face is becoming. He's not getting enough air. I'm running out of time.

"There are other options. You could just come with us," I offer, but I know that will never work.

"I swear Adaline, do this or we both die," Codian says back to me, and I can see how broken he is in this state. I could probably freeze Codian, get Cooper and us out of here and not have to kill him. Somehow I know I'd be hurting him more if I leave him here alive to do Paylon's bidding. Codian let's out a shriek of pain as he continues to fight Paylon's voice that is threatening to return now that the necklace has been removed.

I take a breath in and tell myself what I'm doing is right. I watch as I move Codian's blade to his own neck and watch him drop Cooper to the ground. The sword is shaking and I try to control it with my gift as best as I can. Codian seems to move the blade to his neck more than I do with my gift.

Cooper falls to his knees, gasping for air. Codian mumbles between his cries, "Thank you." He breathes in one final time and holds in his last breath. Even though I feel that this is wrong and right at the same time I choose to see it through. I hold my breath with him, push the blade through his neck, and watch him fall lifeless to the ground. I gasp for air after it's over. My hands are shaking at my side and my cheeks are damp with tears. I bend down and pick up the necklace Codian had been wearing. You can't save everyone, my thoughts echo.

Suddenly Cooper runs to my side, grabs my hand, and runs back toward the woods. We run past my mother's journal and at the last moment I reach down, pick it up, and shove it and Codian's necklace under my arm. The last thing I grab is my sword and I return it comfortably back to my side.

"We have to go, now!" Cooper says over his shoulder to Zavy and Toby. They share a glance of confusion, not sure if they should follow someone they don't know, but when they see that I trust him they oblige. They stand and run to match our pace. Before we leave the clearing I steal a glance over at the three Hounds, huddled and shocked by the tree. For a second I think about stopping to help them, but Cooper's strong grasp on my arm continues to pull me forward and I lose sight of them.

I don't even remember crossing the bridge or hearing the rushing water of the river, but before I know it we are crashing through the woods into the clearing where everyone is still sleeping.

"Up!" Cooper yells. "Everyone up now!" Mio and Cinder run out of the tent to Cooper who tells them he'll explain later, but we need to go now. Everyone grabs their bags they had packed the day before and struggles to get their pillows and blankets rolled up. The group moves in a groggy haze trying to understand what is happening. I find myself wandering over to my own blanket and pillow that I had been given and I shove them along with Codian's necklace and my mother's journal into my bag. Cooper runs by me and throws more items into my bag, zips it and stands me up.

He waves Zavy over and I hear him distantly say, "I don't know what's wrong with Adaline, but keep track of her." Cooper takes off and moves around to other members of the group.

"What is this place? Who are these people, Adaline?" Zavy asks me. She grabs my arm and forces me to look at her, her grip squeezing around my arm. I don't have time to answer her before Cooper calls the attention of the group to him.

"We leave for Libertas now. Garth soldiers are closing in on us and we can't miss this window of opportunity," Cooper yells to the group, pulling their attention. Many of them give Zavy and Toby a curious glance, but Cooper pulls their focus back to him. "I know this isn't how we were told this would happen. We aren't following the visions anymore." A wave of hushed worries spread through the group, but Cooper silences them immediately. "This is our best option. Move now before they close in on us and delay us even more. We'll be moving fast tonight to get as far from them as we can. Keep up, don't slow us down." His voice is strong, and I wonder when the boy I played in the woods with grew up to be a leader.

Cooper turns to leave and I grab his arm. "Stop!" I yell at him, louder than I intended. "We have to go after Alexander."

"Adaline, we don't have time," Cooper tries to explain and I can tell he is already very frustrated with me.

"We can't leave him. He's outnumbered. He'll never get away from them on his own," I say, and the words come out fast and panicked.

"He had a huge lead on them, Adaline. He'll be fine. You have to let him see his plan through." That's the last thing Cooper says before he turns back to commanding the group.

Everyone falls into line and Cooper leads us out of the clearing and into the thick dark forest. We come out to where the river is and start a steady jog along its edge like Mio had suggested we do yesterday. Was that yesterday? I guess it was just a couple of hours ago. By the grey sky fading above us, I figure it's early morning now. My eyes train on the other side of the river, in the thick forest where Alexander is. My gut tells me we shouldn't be leaving him, but I know I need to trust him. He'll find us. He has to.

Zavy and I have brought up the rear of the group. Toby is a little in front of us trying to keep his tired legs moving. I can barely make out the backs of Cooper, Mio, and Cinder's heads at the front of the group. I see Mio and Cinder glance back to us and know that Cooper is telling them about tonight's events and our new additions.

"Where's Alexander?" Zavy asks, her voice drawing my focus.

"He's the one who knocked the tree down. He had to go and distract Paylon so that I could free you. He's supposed to meet up with us," I say in between deep breaths.

"Adaline," Zavy says, her breathing hard. "I need answers."

"It's a long story," I tell her.

"Please, Adaline," she pushes. "I need to know what I'm getting

Toby and myself into."

"Okay well, my father brought all these people out in the woods to wait for me to come to them in seven years because he was a Future Holder and he predicted this would happen. So all these kids have been sitting in the woods waiting for me to come here and that," I say and point to Cooper, "Is my brother."

"Your what?" Zavy asks shocked.

"Like I said, it's a long story." Zavy doesn't ask any more questions and I know it's because we are both having trouble running and talking at the same time. I'm not sure how long Cooper expects us all to run, but I just tell myself to keep putting one foot in front of the other.

I look down at my hands and panic when I see them encrusted in blood. It reminds me of how they looked after I stitched Alexander's leg up. Caked in red thick blood. I blink my eyes hard and then my hands appear clean.

"Kill me," I hear Codian's voice echoing in my head. I keep blinking and seeing my hands bloody and then clean and then bloody. "Kill me. Kill me. Kill me." Over and over and over again. I take in a deep breath of cool night air and force my mind to focus on running. Right foot. Left foot. Right foot. Left foot. Breathe in. Breathe out. Right. Left. In. Out. Right. Left. In. Out. I fall into a steady pattern as the sounds of our feet smacking against the wet mud consumes me.

Chapter 16

I can see hints of daylight breaking through the trees when Cooper finally calls for us to take a break from running. I close my eyes and try to slow my heart rate. It pounds, shaking in my chest, waiting to burst. I watch as Cooper reaches to the side of his bag and unclips a water bottle. I look at my own bag and find my old water bottle still clipped there.

I unclip my water bottle and drink it slowly until it's empty. I look around at the rest of the group and see many of them are filling their water bottles up at the river. I assume they would know what water is safe to drink so I go to the water's edge and dip the bottle into the water. The cool and clear water runs into the mouth of the bottle and over my dirty fingers washing away the dusty brown layer that has coated my skin.

I put the cap on my bottle and lay it and my bag down on the river's edge. I pull my sword out and examine it. Dark dried blood cracks on the blade. My breath is caught in my throat. I instruct myself to clean the blade first. I rinse it in the river and the blood washes away, but it doesn't make me feel any better.

I untie the worn white shoes and take off the thin socks I had found in the bunker, and walk knee-deep into the water. Even though there is no blood to wash off of my body from murdering Codian I still feel as though my skin is caked in it. I rinse my legs, arms, and face with the cool water and do my best to bring my heart and brain back to being steady. When I've calmed myself and feel numb instead of broken I walk out of the river, grab my things, and find a place to sit in the shade. I walk to the edge of the forest and sit next to a tree letting my legs relax from the hours of running they've just encountered.

"I can't even feel my legs," I hear Zavy say as she collapses to the ground next to me, acting overdramatic as usual. Quiet Toby follows and softly sits down next to her.

For the first time, I notice that my bag feels heavier than normal. For a second I pass it off as exhaustion messing with my head but I take it off and confirm its fuller than before. I unzip the backpack and unpack its contents. On top, I find the necklace and my mother's journal that I shoved in before we started running. Under that, I find a neatly rolled blanket, a small pillow, a clean t-shirt, and a pair of shorts. Cooper must have added them to my bag after I had fallen asleep. Maybe while I was still in shock from killing Codian he found time to pack my bag. I vaguely remember him coming by me before we started running, but my mind was elsewhere at that moment. It's a gesture that makes me feel safe but small. I'm glad my older brother is back to look out for me, but I can't rely on that. I need to be able to take care of myself.

Across the clearing, I hear Cooper and Mio are arguing about the lack of weapons they grabbed last night. I notice there are only two swords, a couple of spears for fishing, and one bow with a set of arrows. Cooper gestures my way and I'm sure he's blaming it on me. If I hadn't snuck off last night we wouldn't have been forced to leave in such a hurry. I watch as Cooper, Mio, and Cinder turn and start walking over to us so I repack my belongings and zip the bag closed.

"I don't believe we've met," Mio says as he, Cooper, and Cinder sit across from Zavy, Toby, and myself. "I'm Mio, and this is Cinder and Cooper. Apparently, Adaline thought it would be a good idea to go against my advisement of not bringing any other guests with us."

"I wasn't going to leave them," I say as I take another sip of my water.

"Well, I hope you're glad you went and saved them. Hope it was worth losing Alexander," Mio says, disgust in his voice.

"He's not dead," I say and hold Mio's stare.

"You don't know that Adaline. All I know is that the plan was to get you and Alexander to Libertas, and now you've gone away from the plan to rescue your friends and Alexander is gone." Mio carefully lectures me, trying to keep his voice steady so the panic won't rise in the rest of our group.

"He'll meet up with us. He said he would," I say more to reassure myself than anyone else because he should have been here already. He was supposed to cut straight across to the river.

"Well I hope for all of our sakes that you're right," Mio stands and walks away. We watch as he walks over and starts talking with

James and Bren, and then they disappear into the woods to find food for today.

"I'm sorry about that," Cinder finally says, breaking the silence in her sweet voice. "He just doesn't like it when things don't go the way he plans." She pulls a large bag off her shoulder and hands Toby and Zavy each a blanket, pillow, and change of clothes. The same extra items I had found in my bag. I know Mio may not agree with me bringing them here, but it's a good sign that they are treating them like everyone else and sharing their supplies. I don't know if that was Mio's idea or Cinder's.

"Yeah, I can see that," Zavy says harsher than she probably intended. "Sorry. Thank you for these," she says taking the items from Cinder. "I'm Zavy and this is my brother Toby." Cinder just lets a small smile fall on her face. She nods her head and gets up to go check on the others.

Zavy and Toby pack their supplies into their bags. I notice each of them still have rations from the bunker as well as additional clothes. They were smart to pack those. I hadn't thought to do that. I guess that shows how different we are. Zavy and Toby have been surviving off of nothing but the woods for seven years. They know when they come across clean clothes not to take them for granted. I wonder what other items around the bunker Zavy saw as treasures while I only saw as useless.

"What were you thinking, Adaline?" Cooper mumbles with his head hanging in his hands.

"I was thinking my friends were in trouble, and they needed my help," I say strongly.

"Do you realize if I wouldn't have followed you, you and Alexander would be dead?" Cooper says, looking up and meeting my eyes.

"What do you want me to say? Thank you?" I ask sarcastically.

"No, I want you to stop making selfish decisions. Do you realize how many lives you put in danger?" Cooper asks, and I can see the fear in his eyes from when Codian had almost killed him.

"I didn't ask you to follow me," I tell him.

"Well, I kind of had to," he says under his breath.

"No, you didn't. I didn't make you do anything," I shout back to him because I can tell this is becoming more than the fact that he followed me last night. This has to do with the fact that he's had to give up his entire life to make sure I survive.

We hold each other's gaze for a long time until Cooper finally says in a weak voice, "I had to. I'm your brother." Cooper stands and walks into the woods in the direction that Mio had gone, and eventually everyone else returns to making small talk.

"Well, that was a warm welcome," Zavy scoffs.

I let myself smile and say, "Yeah, well that's my brother."

Zavy and I exchange small talk and I tell her about the others who are traveling with us. She doesn't ask me any questions about why we are with these people or how I never told her about Cooper, so I don't bring it up either. I'm physically and mentally too exhausted to have to go into it right now. She doesn't mind anyway, as long as she's alive that's her only concern. From her point of view, she's free from Paylon, has food, water, clean clothes, and sleeping components.

I feel guilty because I know she needs to get her memories back so she can remember Cooper too, but I don't see the harm in letting her believe in her fake memories just a little while longer.

Later, Cooper and Mio emerge from the forest with James and Bren, each pair carrying a deer over their shoulders.

"Zavy, look," Toby says, pointing to the deer. "We've never been able to bring one that big down."

"That's pretty impressive," Zavy agrees and notices Toby sitting in shock.

"They must be really good hunters," Toby thinks aloud.

No one has much to talk about anymore so we all end up sitting in silence and my mind can't help but think about Alexander. I watch Albert and Andy clean the meat and start up a fire. I cringe, knowing that the smoke from our fire will broadcast our location. That may be a sign to Paylon as to where we are, but maybe it will also help Alexander find us.

When the meat has finished cooking, Cooper calls us to come and take our share for breakfast. I see that they have only laid out half the meat, and the rest they've packaged to take with us. Zavy and I grab some of the meat and go back to our previous spot. Cinder walks around the group and distributes some berries to everyone.

"At least we won't starve," Zavy mumbles between mouthfuls of food.

"Don't speak so soon. You don't want to jinx it," I say. When everyone finishes eating, Mio announces that it's time to get moving again.

"We'll walk for now and then break again for dinner, and after we'll rest for half the night and then we'll run again until morning. We should get to Sard sometime tomorrow," Mio orders. Since Mio has been caught up to speed he's taken over command of the group. I watch as Cooper sits like a silent shadow behind him. He doesn't seem to mind that Mio is back to giving the orders. He looks almost relieved.

I look out at the river and can see the heat rising from the water. Now that the sun has fully risen, the temperature on the island has seemed to double. I forgot how hot it gets after being in the cell for so long. I know the temperature rises and falls so drastically as an effect from the asteroid shower, but we don't experience these temperature differences deep underground in the prison. I know it's uncontrollable and almost unpredictable when these heat waves will hit. Zavy doesn't seem too fazed by the sudden wave of hot thick air. I'm sure she's lived through hotter days than this.

She and I stand and walk out from under our shade canopy and into the hot summer sun. Toby has become very interested in James and Bren and has been shadowing them ever since they came back with that deer. When the group begins to move again he falls in step with them and Zavy and I take up the rear again.

Once we start walking out in the sun I realize how truly scorching hot it is. This must be why we are walking, there's no way we could run in this heat. Mio was smart to want to walk near the river. It doesn't conceal us as well. If Paylon or Chadian were waiting in the woods up ahead we'd be easy targets. However, in this heat, the constant source of water will save our lives. Granted the once cool stream is now as warm as bathwater, but water is water. Not only that, but we will have a constant supply of food, whether that be fish or other animals using the river as a drinking source.

As hard as I try to keep my mind occupied with history, the science of the heat waves, nature, and resources it immediately starts to move back to Alexander. He should have reached us by now. We must have been sitting there for a couple of hours while they were hunting. Hours of sitting and having a smoke signal and still he never showed. I can't help but start thinking of what Paylon might have done if he'd gotten to him. If he knows we killed Codian I don't think Paylon would have thought twice about returning the favor to Alexander.

"You know it's only going to drive you crazier to think about him," Zavy says.

"I know. I just can't help it," I say bluntly after I've imagined the tenth way Paylon could have killed Alexander if he found him.

Toby runs up and interrupts us and asks, "Zavy are we staying with these people forever?"

Zavy lets out a small laugh and says, "Well, we are both going to the same place. So, for now, we'll be staying with them. Why?"

"Well, James and Bren said I could help them hunt since I'm an Aeros," Toby says, his words running together.

"Toby, you told them?" Zavy says shocked, fear coursing through her.

"It's okay Zavy," I say gently. "They know we all have gifts. We can trust them."

Zavy seems to be hesitant, but eventually says, "Okay, just be careful."

"I will," Toby responds, and he goes back to walking with James and Bren.

"Are you sure it's okay to trust them?" she asks.

"I'm positive, Zavy. All of these people gave up their chance to live a normal life. They are taking us to a place where only people with gifts can live," I say and every time I think of these people risking their lives to go to a place they may be turned away from my stomach sinks deeper. "They may have a chance that they get to live there, but maybe not. I trust them with my life because, honestly, they're the only reason we're even going to make it to Libertas."

"Yeah, I suppose. So, Cooper's really your brother?" she asks, finally bringing up the subject I've been avoiding.

"Yeah, he really is," I respond simply.

"And you didn't remember him until now?" Zavy gawks.

"It's complicated. I need to tell you something, Zavy," I say as I glance up at her.

"Should I be worried?" Zavy asks, concerned about how serious my tone is.

"Well, I don't think you're going to be very happy," I admit.

"Well, go ahead and tell me," she says.

"All right," I hesitate and take in a deep breath before continuing,

"My mother had to block my memories of Cooper so that I wouldn't risk exposing my father's plan to the guards," I say finishing the easy factual part of the problem.

"I can understand that. Continue," Zavy says, knowing there must be more to the story.

"She didn't exactly block out my memories though. Instead, she put Alexander in place of Cooper in all my memories, and she did the same thing to you. And now that I think about it there are a lot of other people that had to have known Cooper. My mother must have done this to everyone that ever came in contact with him," I say trying to understand the logistics behind this elaborate plan we are mixed up in.

"Explain?" Zavy asks, trying not to let herself jump to conclusions. I'm surprised she hasn't completely overreacted to the whole situation.

"Every memory you have with Alexander is actually Cooper. We don't truly know Alexander. At least, I don't think I did before this whole mess started. It's fuzzy, everything before I was in prison. I can't recall any memories because of how long I've been without them, but they can be triggered," I start explaining.

"But, he's our best friend Adaline," Zavy says, and the girl I know to blow everything into a bigger problem begins to show.

"I know. It's really hard to grasp, but it's actually Cooper in all those memories. We have something that can return your memories back to normal. When we stop again I can ask Cooper to give it to you," I say. "This whole situation was even worse for Alexander because it wasn't just a piece of his memory that was wrong, but all of it. He had no idea who he truly was or what life he really lived before going to work at the castle."

"But he knows now? You restored his memories?" Zavy asks and I confirm. "And he still risked his life to save Toby and me?" She can't believe the great gesture just like I had questioned it too.

"He did," I admit and I hope that him saving Zavy and Toby isn't the reason I never get to truly know him. We are quiet for a moment and I'm sure Zavy is rethinking every situation she remembers with Alexander and pretending that it was Cooper instead.

"I'm really sorry, Adaline," Zavy says softly. "Everything from this journey with him is all true though."

"I know. That's what we keep telling ourselves," I say.

"It must be pretty weird, right? Having feelings for a guy you don't even know the first thing about," Zavy says perplexed at the idea.

"It's kind of been driving me crazy," I admit and muster out a light scoff. "Zavy, what if I never get to know him? Who even knows where he's at right now? I don't even know if he's alive!" I say a little louder than I should have, and some people glance back at me.

"Adaline," Zavy starts to try and calm me down.

"I know, I know," I brush her off. "It's just, I don't know how long I can let myself hope he's going to come back," I admit, and my wet eyes meet hers. I don't like holding on and wishing for things that may never happen. After I spent months hoping my father would come back to us just to be left disappointed and angry, I've learned that hoping will only drive you crazy.

"I think we give it until tomorrow morning," she offers.

"Okay, we'll give him until then," I say.

"He'll be here, Adaline," she tries to reassure me.

"I hope so," I say weakly, and my heart continues to deny what my brain keeps saying.

Chapter 17

We walk for nearly the rest of the day. When the sun has sunk deep behind the canopy of long palm branches Mio finally calls for us to break for the night. Zavy and I sit along the forest wall in silence, sipping on the warm water and trying to slow our breathing. We look out into the river and see that Toby, James, and Bren are trying to catch fish with the spears they managed to grab. Toby is very fond of James and Bren, instantly bonding over their drive to hunt and master weapons. Zavy jokes that he's one of the guys now, but I can tell she wishes he wouldn't trust them and just stay by her side. It's easier for her to protect him that way. However, Zavy and I both laugh when Toby brings in a net full of fish and James and Bren are empty-handed. He could teach them a thing or two it seems.

"I don't think I've seen him this happy in a long time, Adaline," Zavy admits, wishing she hadn't been so quick to judge James and Bren.

"Well, he hasn't even interacted with another person in seven years," I point out and try to rub the beading sweat off of my forehead.

Zavy and I go back to sipping on our water in silence until Cinder comes over and asks if we want to help her collect berries. She hands us each a wooden woven basket and we both put our water bottles away and follow her into the woods.

"These are what we're looking for," Cinder says, kneeling next to a bush with a mix of yellow, blue, and red berries on it. Zavy and I nod and spread deeper into the woods to find more bushes. I come across 4 or 5 of them soon and start picking them one by one and placing them in the basket.

"Why don't you just use your gift?" I hear Cinder ask from behind me.

"What?" I question and turn to her.

"I just don't understand how gifts work. Is there a reason you don't use yours? You're a Force Lifter, right?" She asks tenderly.

"Yeah I am, but no, there really isn't a reason I'm not using it. I'm still really new with it, and if you overuse it, it can lead to extreme exhaustion. But that's more with fighting with the gift, not with picking berries," I say and smile.

I turn back to the berries and imagine all of them being pulled off the bush and into the basket. They start shaking from the bush and fall to the forest floor with only about half of them actually landing in the basket. "Ideally they were all supposed to just move to the basket, but I can't work my gift just yet," I say. I quickly scoop up the rest of the berries, stand, and grab the now full basket, turning to see Cinder with a shocked look on her face.

"Need more than this?" I say, joking.

"No, I'd say that should be plenty," she says with a light laugh.

We walk back through the woods and find Zavy with about a hand full of berries in her basket. She turns and sees my full basket and says, "I really hate you sometimes, you know?"

I laugh and say, "Hey, I didn't ask for this gift." Zavy stands and interlocks her arm with mine, just like we used to do when we were little, and for a moment I forget where we are. It's just Zavy and me in the woods. For a moment I can forget that Paylon is hunting me down, I can forget that we have no real shelter, equipment, or survival resources. I just let myself enjoy this moment and wish that it could truly be this simple. We make our way out of the woods and see that Albert and Andy are cooking the fish that Toby caught.

"We're going to use these berries to make a sort of jam," Cinder says and we follow her to a tan piece of fabric that has been laid out next to the fire.

"Just dump out the berries in here," she instructs as she pulls out a wide wooden dish from one of the kitchen bags. I do and then she hands Zavy and I a pair of cloth gloves that are stained purple.

"Use your hands to smash and mix all of the berries," Cinder says as she stands up. "I have to go find one more thing for the jam, so I'll be right back." Zavy and I kneed the berries into a runny purple jam. The aroma of the fresh berries instantly reminds me of my home where we lived out on the edge of Garth. My mother and I would pick berries together.

"Adaline, do you want to come out and pick some berries with me?" my mother had asked me many times. This time, in particular, I jumped up from the floor in the living room and ran out the door with my mother. I remember being barefoot and kicking up dirt with my little toes while swinging our basket that was too big for me to carry. I skipped circles around her as we walked to the edge of the forest. There were tons of large bushes with bright yellow berries on them. I would pluck one and place it in my mouth and my mother would pluck one and place it in the basket.

Then, when the basket was filled, we'd go back to the house and make a ray berry pie for my father. It was always his favorite. The happy memory seems to shatter in my mind. My mother loved him so much, and he just left her to die in prison. How could he have done that?

Cinder walks back over to us with a handful of green leaves and explains, "It's called cental-straw. We're going to rip it into tiny pieces, and it'll act like a sugar in the jam," Cinder hands Zavy and I some of the leaves and we shred it into our jam. I examine them a little closer and realize I recognize this plant. In the last days before we were arrested my mother had gathered a lot of this. Money was extremely tight and we didn't have very much food. She and I would chew on the sweet grass to try and trick our stomachs into thinking we were eating. I don't know if it worked. I think we were just so hungry we stopped feeling it.

"Where'd you get this?" I ask and twirl it in my fingers.

"Across the river, I can go get more if you'd like,1" Cinder says sweetly. She doesn't wait for me to respond. I watch her walk through the shallow warm water to the bank on the other side to pick some more of the cental-straw. When we finish making the plant and berry mixture I stuff the extra cental-straw into my bag. I know we have rations and plenty of food to eat, but you just never know.

When we are finished Cinder goes over to the same bag she'd pulled the wooden dish out of, and pulls out a handful of small wooden bowl. She carefully starts ladling the jam into the bowls and asks, "Can you hand these out to everyone?"

"Sure," I say. Zavy and I take off the gloves and pick up two of the bowls. "What exactly do we eat this with?" I ask.

"Oh, I'm sorry I never said," Cinder says, clearing her throat. "We use it to spread on the fish. The fish in this area of the island has a very bitter taste." I nod and pass out the bowls of jam, grateful that we have someone like Cinder with us. She has a lot of valuable information that others may think is useless. Yes, we need to be strong and be ready to fight and defend ourselves. Yes, we need to be able to hunt and gather food, but if you don't know what you can and can't eat, that will kill you just as easily as a sword.

Mio has everyone move to sit around the fire to eat dinner. He says after dinner we need to try to get some sleep and he will wake us when it's time to move again. It feels kind of weird to have Mio and Cinder here playing the roles of parents after traveling with just Alexander and Zavy. More than that, I haven't had a parent figure since my father left. It's almost comforting, but I struggle with depending on others and warn myself not to get too comfortable.

Everyone moves to sit around the fire and Albert and Andy hand out the fish. We all sit in silence while we eat the fish with the berry jam. The flavors that spread across my tongue remind me of my mom's cooking long before we were in prison, and before my father left us. I haven't eaten anything with this much flavor in years. While we eat, late afternoon slowly shifts to night. The sun has sunk deep behind the trees and the only light left is coming from the fire as it flickers off our faces. Once we've all finished eating everyone breaks off into his or her own conversations.

I wave Cooper over and ask him for the rock to return Zavy's memories. There's an awkward tension with Cooper. He still hasn't forgiven me for last night, but he nods and returns a moment later with the rock and piece of fabric.

"Just put it back in my bag when you're done," Cooper says.

I turn to Zavy and place the rock in front of her. She gives me a questioning look, confused about how a rock can control her memories. "All you have to do is place one hand on the rock and recite this, and your memories will be restored," I say, explaining the process and handing her the piece of cloth.

"How," Zavy starts to say.

"Magic," I say simply and cut her off. She squints her eyes, giving me the look that says she doesn't believe in magic even though she has a gift controlled by magic. I know it's not really magic because scientists say it can be linked to the asteroids, but can they prove that? No, and magic is an easier explanation in my head.

Zavy places her hand on the stone and recites the words off the paper like Alexander and I had done.

Help me see the truth in me
Erase the false and bring forth the real
Take me back so I can see
All the past and set me free

Zavy takes in a sharp breath when she finishes. After a moment of silence, she looks at me, her eyes wide. "I remember. I remember Cooper."

"Did any of your other memories change? There's no telling what my mother altered," I ask cautiously.

"No, I don't think so. It's just Cooper instead of Alexander," she says simply. "This is so weird Adaline," she says, fully understanding what this means. "Who is Alexander?"

"If I knew I'd tell you," I say, running my hand in circles on the dirt. I take a deep breath in and say, "Just think of it as a fresh start to get to know him. There's nothing else we can do." It's the same phrase of words I've been repeating in my head since the memories got fixed.

"Cool magic rock," Zavy jokes, handing it back to me. She's trying to lighten the mood now that we've started talking about Alexander. I return the rock to Cooper's bag and then return to Zavy who stares distantly into the fire. She's probably trying to reanalyze her entire past now that she knows the truth. The moon has risen far in the sky and I know I should rest before Mio has us up and running again. I reach into my backpack and pull out my blanket and pillow and when I do my mother's journal falls out too.

"Have you read any more of it?" Zavy asks, scooping it up in her hands.

I zip my backpack back up, unroll my blanket, and sit on it. I take the journal from Zavy and hold it tightly. "No, not really." We're quiet for a second until I add, "I kind of don't want to read it anymore."

"What do you mean?" Zavy asks shocked.

"I know it must sound crazy. This is the last thing I have of my mother, but I don't want it. I don't want to know what different things she's seen in the future. I don't want to read it and know whether or not Alexander is dead or whether or not we ever make it to Libertas. I don't want the constant reminder of life in the prison or the life where my father left me, and I lived not knowing who my older brother was.

I feel like I have this fresh start now. Like I don't have to have been that girl who had to take care of her family, and I'm not that girl who grew up in a prison, and I wasn't some little girl who lost her father. Now I just feel like I'm Adaline, and I'm going to find my freedom. I'm brave and strong. I feel like I became this new person and I have my entire life ahead of me."

I pause for a second trying to figure a better way to explain it to Zavy. "It's like this book," I say and hold up my mother's journal. "This is my old life that was set in stone and already written out. But I want to be in this new life where my future isn't written down in some dusty haunted book." I stare at my mother's journal for a little bit longer and then toss it into the fire. "I don't want to be that

Adaline anymore. I'm not her and that's not my life."

I watch the fire slowly eat at the brown book. I'm glad I threw it in the fire, I'm glad to be rid of it. It's a constant reminder that I need to live my life in a certain way. It's just like Mio had said, he didn't want to go and save Zavy because it wasn't in the future my father had seen. But if I hadn't gone against that vision then her and Toby would still be trapped with Paylon. Worse even, by now he probably would have killed them knowing we weren't coming to save her. I can't have this book in my bag, spelling out the future because I will always be second-guessing if what I'm doing will mess everything up.

Slowly the dark brown book corners turn a dark ashy black. I imagine my mother as a little girl learning about her gift. She would have been given that book on her tenth birthday to write down all her visions. I never got to meet my grandparents, but I wonder if they had the gift. I wonder how they learned about my mother's and where the book came from. Maybe it used to be theirs.

I have to rid myself of it, but it still pains my heart to watch a piece of my mother burn. Not only a piece of her but my only piece of her. She'd understand though, I have to make myself believe that. Images of my mother sitting in her room scribbling away in the book fill my head. All the visions she saw; like her own future or maybe herself in school. Did she see herself marrying my father? She must have known that he was going to his death when he left us. That's why she was okay with giving her life for this mission too.

As the flames creep further across the binding of the book they finally catch on the light tan pages. They burst in flames and burn quickly, being eaten before my eyes. I hate watching it burn, but I won't look away. I need to know it is completely gone. I need to be sure that there is not a piece left of it. If I can be sure of that then I will be able to stop second-guessing all my moves.

There's no way for me to see the future, to know if the moves I make are correct. I have been wondering if Alexander was alive or dead for two days now. The answer is right there, burning before my eyes. I want to open the journal and see that he's alive, but the fear that he is truly dead wins out. So I won't know, I won't confirm or deny the inevitable. When he finds us then I'll know. When he's not here by morning like Zavy and I had agreed to hope until, then I will know. In seconds, the paper pages have completely turned to ash and I watch the flames continue to work away at the thick old book cover.

Zavy doesn't respond and I can tell she knows it isn't her place to. I wonder if she held onto anything from her mother or father. Does she carry a small piece of home with her? I remember Zavy was never a very sentimental person so I doubt it. Finally, the last of the book's cover turns to ash and it's gone. Every piece of my mother is gone, forever.

The future will remain unknown. It will remain a secret. A blank page that I get to write myself. I fall back and place my head on my pillow. My eyes stare up into the sea of stars above me. I breathe in steady cold breaths of the night air and slowly fall asleep.

Chapter 18

Slowly I start to wake up, but I still feel like I'm in a haze, and then I hear his voice in the distance.

"Adaline! Adaline are you there?" I hear the voice call very faintly, but I would recognize it anywhere.

"Alexander," I choke out. I jump to my feet and run toward the sound of his voice, thankful I sleep with my sword on my hip in case of instances like this.

"Alexander, it's me! It's Adaline! I'm here, Alexander," I call out to him, running aimlessly through the dark forest.

"Adaline!" he calls back to me. "Adaline, I need your help."

"I'm coming Alexander. Don't worry." I pick up my pace and keep running toward him, his calls to me getting louder and louder. I crash into a clearing and see Alexander kneeling on the ground holding a sword to his neck. His hair is matted to his face with mud and sweat. His green eyes looking deep into mine.

"Alexander, what's going on?" I say between my gasps for air.

"Adaline, I need your help," he says in a steady voice.

"Alexander," I start.

"Adaline," he mimics and this all feels too familiar.

"What do you need, Alexander," I hear myself ask him and I'm not in control of my own words.

"Kill me, Adaline. I need you to kill me," he says, but his voice no longer matches him. It sounds different.

"Alexander, I don't think this is what you want," I hear myself say to him.

"Do it!" he yells back to me.

"There are other options," I start to say, my words still not being controlled by my own mind.

"I said do it," Alexander commands, cutting me off.

I feel myself start to lift my hands and as hard as I try to force them down I can't. I've lost all control of my body. "No!" I yell inside my head, but nothing comes out of my mouth.

I watch as the sword pushes against Alexander's neck and I hear him say, "Thank you." I picture the blade going through his neck and hear myself scream.

I feel my body jolt up and my eyes fly open. "A nightmare. It was just a nightmare," I say and take in deep breaths of the cool air. My eyes adjust to the night and I see that everyone is still sound asleep around the dying fire. I have to repeat to myself over and over that the dream doesn't mean anything. We still have a couple of hours until morning. A couple more hours to hope he'll be here.

I feel a drop of water hit the top of my head and look up into the canopy of palm leaves above me. All thoughts of the dream fade and my survival instincts take over. I turn to look out to the river and can see the hundreds of rings appearing on the water. It's the first rain I've encountered since getting out of prison.

I relax my tense shoulders, and slowly get up and walk out from the canopy of leaves. I feel the rain pour down on me, and I'm overcome with excitement. I hold out my hands and can't help but smile in awe of something as simple as rain.

I sit on a large rock by the river's edge and just let the rain keep coming down on me. It's refreshing, and it feels like it's washing away all the pain and emptiness I feel. As quickly as the happiness of seeing rain comes, it vanishes. My mind is drawn back to Alexander, and the dream I had. I thought the hole in my heart from my father leaving me was bad. Now it's grown three times its size with the loss of my mother, Titus, and now Alexander. The thought that Alexander is dead makes my throat tight and this time there's no hope in trying to keep the tears in. My heart finally snaps and the tears and sobs come in waves, and I let the pouring rain wash them all away.

When it feels as though I couldn't get any emptier, the tears finally stop, and my breathing starts to even out again. For the longest time, the only sounds are my breathing and the taps of rain on the river; a mix of beautiful sounds that consume me. I'm empty and raw. I'm not sure I could ever be whole again. I don't think I'll ever let another person in again, because every time I do they are always ripped away from me. I just sit here, in the rain and let its beautiful sound fill the emptiness inside of me.

The loud sound of a branch snapping pulls me out of my

thoughts. I feel my heart beat faster and my blood runs cold. I sit very still and listen. Did I just imagine that? After a couple seconds another snapping branch brings me to my feet. It's not far, just north of us. Quietly, I move in the direction of the sound. As I go I continue to listen, but I don't hear anything new. I've wandered nearly a mile from camp and haven't seen anything.

There's a snap of a small branch behind me. I turn, quick on my feet and draw my sword. I extend my blade and it comes inches for her face. It's the youngest of the Hounds.

"Stop!" she pleads and puts her hands up. "I'm not tracking you."

"Then what are you doing here?" I ask and scan the woods around her, looking for the rest of her group.

"We escaped," she says softly and the two other Hounds who were with her the night I rescued Zavy come out from behind the trees. "The night you killed Codian we got his key and escaped."

"How'd you do that? Aren't you being controlled by the King?" I question her, and her eyes seem to grow sadder.

She brings her hand to her neck slowly and pulls out a glowing green necklace. "He can't control us anymore." The other two behind her show their necklaces and I lower my sword.

"How'd you get those?" I ask, knowing I've only seen the guards wearing them.

"At the battle," she says and I remember all of the soldiers wearing them. "We took them before Paylon had us retreat.

"That's why he didn't know we were at his camp," I say, understanding how we have gone undetected for this long. "Are you following us?"

"No, I promise. We are just trying to find somewhere to hide." She seems to relax now that I've lowered the sword and her young personality starts to come through.

"You all have a gift of enhanced smell, right?" I ask and they nod. "You should come with us to Libertas," I say and am about to explain how it's a place for fleeing gifted but she stops me.

"We know what Libertas is," her smile is soft as she thinks of the proclaimed safety island. "My sister is still being held captive at the castle. I can't leave her."

"You're going to try and save her?" I ask. She's practically asking to be killed.

"With these necklaces we might be able to," she says and her friends nod. She must read my expression and knows I think she's crazy. "I know what she's going through." Her eyes mist over with tears and her voice shakes. "I can't leave her to endure that torture any longer."

I scan the three of them, taking in their incredibly thin state. At least in the prison I was left alone. I didn't get to eat much, but I got to be with my mother and brother. No one was trying to torture or control me.

"Here," I start to say and I pull off my backpack. I hand them each a couple of my bags of rations. "These are food rations we found in the bunker." They take them and thank me.

"We should get going," the youngest says and she falls in line with her friends. "Thank you again, Adaline. Travel safe."

I watch as the three of them sink further into the woods and I wish they would come with us. I wish there was something more I could do to help them; something more than just giving them dried rations. I make my way back to my sleeping group and go back to the rock by the creek. I sit here and think about how much I hate the King for what he does to people, and what he's taken from me.

Soon after I return to camp Mio is starting to go around to everyone to wake them up. The sky has just broken into a light grey glow, warning the morning heat will be here soon.

Zavy stretches and walks over to sit next to me. "It feels like I just closed my eyes," Zavy mumbles as she looks over at me.

I can't help but let my eyes gaze around the group, wishing Alexander's face was in the mix. "They got him didn't they Zavy?" I say with a weak voice. It's finally morning. We need to let the hope go. It's more than just that though. Before I had been okay with hoping because I had a feeling he was alive, I could feel him still here with me. The feeling's gone now, cut from my body like the sword through his throat in my dream. I know deep down he is gone, just like my father.

For a brief second rage consumes me and I'm sure if Paylon appeared at the edge of this river right now I'd kill him in seconds. I take a deep breath in and let the rage go. My job is not to kill Paylon. I need to get to Libertas so these people can have a home. I need to go because Alexander doesn't get to have that second chance anymore. I can be strong and keep moving. Even if I can't, I have to tell myself that I can.

Zavy puts an arm around my shoulder and says, "I'm so sorry Adaline." We sit like this in silence for a long while until Mio calls for everyone to pack up their belongings and get ready to leave.

"Did it rain?" she asks, lifting my damp hair with her dry fingers.

"Yeah, it did," I say and look up to the sky letting out a heavy breath. Letting the last of the pain go.

We walk back over to where we slept. I pack up my blanket and pillow and throw my backpack over my shoulders. I don't say anything to anyone else, but I can tell they are all thinking the same thing; that Alexander is never coming. The fact that I'm not the only one to have this feeling makes me know it's even more true.

Mio has us jogging at a steady pace along the muddy edge of the river. I look ahead of us and can see we are closing in on a large mountain range. I'd seen it on the map at Cooper's camp, but it is so much larger than I had imagined. Surely we won't be climbing it. I assume they must know a way through the mountains since they have made this journey many times before. Not too long after we start jogging Cooper slows his pace until he comes side by side with me.

"Look, I'm sorry about going off of the plan," I force myself to say to him between deep breaths. He must still be looking for an apology from me so I'll give it to him.

"It's already done, Adaline. We can't change it. I just wanted to tell you, you should probably keep your distance from everyone else," Cooper says smoothly. He has no difficulty keeping a steady breath and it registers to me he's spent the last seven years training his body for this journey and these conditions.

"Why?" I ask and nervously glance at him.

"Because it was all of our jobs to get you and Alexander to Libertas. Without Alexander, I doubt any of us will be allowed to stay," Cooper says bluntly.

The truth of what Cooper has just said settles in my brain. These people may not get their freedom. The past seven years were just for nothing. "Well, what will happen to them?" I ask.

"I'm not sure. I've overheard a couple of people already talking about needing another plan," he admits.

"No, I'll make sure you all get to stay in Libertas," I say sternly.

"With all due respect sister, I don't think you have that kind of power," Cooper says sarcastically.

"I'll think of something," I say. "It's not their fault Alexander isn't here, it's mine."

"Couldn't have said it better myself," Cooper mumbles and starts to pick his pace up again until he's back at the front of the pack. I let his words hang with me for a moment. I don't think he's mad at me for saving Zavy. I just think he wants to put up a strong front, be my tough older brother that wants to be in charge. I let myself scan over all of the groups' faces and can see their vacant expressions.

"I did this to these people," I think to myself. I let my mind go blank as I let the sounds of repeated feet thumping against the riverbank fill my head. I don't want to think about how I've ruined their lives. I didn't mean to mess everything up. I thought I was doing the right thing.

Mio finally calls for us to stop running when it's nearly noon and the sweat is dripping off of my face. "Everyone, drink some water. We won't be here for long. Sard is just another hour or so up ahead. Albert and Andy, prepare the last of the deer. We'll eat and make the last part of the journey," Mio instructs to a crowd of empty faces.

"Let's change and wash these clothes too," Cinder offers. "Essie, you and your sisters can set up over here." I watch Cinder lead the three sisters to a shaded part at the edge of the river. I hadn't noticed the large wooden baskets they'd been carrying before. They've cleverly fastened them to the back of their bags. I watch them unclip them and fill them with the river water. I look up and over their heads and see we are just at the base of the mountains. I was right about not having to climb them. There's a large dip straight ahead if we follow the river. We'll still have to climb, but not nearly as high.

Albert and Andy start building a fire to cook the meat and I go to the river to fill my water bottle with fresh cold water. I'm disappointed to find it already warm from the baking sun above us. Warm water is better than no water I remind myself. I turn around and sip on my water bottle looking at everyone's blank stares. The news that we are close to Sard should have made everyone happier, but they look even more upset.

"What's the deal with everyone?" Zavy asks as she joins me. We retreat to the privacy of the woods to change into the spare outfits they had packed in our bags. The quality of their clothes isn't nearly as nice as the ones from the bunker. I notice Zavy chooses to wear the extra pieces she had brought with her instead of the rags Cinder had given us. I pull on the large white tank top and soft black cloth shorts. I try and tie the tank top up on the side so it fits better, but it still hangs off my shoulders.

"Cooper doesn't think any of them will be allowed into Libertas now that we lost Alexander," I say bluntly back to her.

"That can't be true! They promised them," Zavy says shocked.

"They promised them in exchange for me and Alexander. No offense Zavy, but you in exchange for Alexander isn't exactly a fair trade," I say with a flat tone in my voice.

"We'll just have to make a new deal with the people at Libertas when we get there," she says simply.

Zavy and I don't say anything else. We come out of the woods and back to the bank of the river. I scan the clearing and see that everyone has gotten to work and changed into fresh clothes as well. Albert, Andy, Bren, and James are cooking. Essie, Cassandra, and Sarah are washing clothes. I don't want to feel useless to the group that has already given so much to me. I know they may be angry with me for losing Alexander, but I need to try and make things right. I cross the clearing toward the sisters.

"Would you like some help?" I ask as I stand over Essie while she works, scrubbing our dirty clothes.

"Oh no," she starts. "You don't have to help. We can take care of it. It's our job," she says, gesturing to her sisters.

"Please," I cut her off, taking a seat across from her. "I need something to do." Essie gives me a soft smile and says I can start with my shirt.

"Dunk and scrub," she instructs. I take a brown rough brush and soak the shirt in the water.

"I used to help my mother clean clothes," I say as I work away on my shirt. "Well, not really." I laugh, remembering how little I actually did. "She'd fill one bucket for clothes and one for me to play with," I start to explain. The three sisters have fallen silent eager to listen to a story of my past.

"I used to have these little toy boats. I had been walking the streets with Alexander, no Cooper," I correct myself quickly. "And we wandered into the toy shop on the edge of town. It was my favorite place to go." I pause, remembering all the times we had gone there. Basically any day we didn't have school Cooper would take me there. "Anyway," I say, continuing, "We'd just wander around and look because we could never afford the toys. I had found these beautiful white boats in the back of the store. They were tiny, just the size of my hand, and there were little blue waves painted on the sides."

"How'd you get them?" Essie asks me in a soft voice.

"Cooper haggled with the owner and got me the boats," I explain.

"What did he give in return?" Cassandra asks, listening in on my story.

I smile, remembering. "A gold necklace our father had given him for his birthday. Even then he was making stupid decisions to make me happy."

"Your father must have been upset," Sarah offers, but I shake my head.

"He didn't notice. Cooper just said he had lost it in our room," I say.

"Believable because our room was a disaster," Cooper chimes in as he walks over to our group. He's probably been listening the whole time.

"Just your side," I say back to him and he lets out a half laugh. Maybe he can forgive me for messing up their plan. Maybe I can still make this right.

"So anyway," I say, drawing my attention back to the clothes, "My mother would do laundry and I would play with those boats."

"That's a lovely story," Essie says smoothly.

"What about you guys?" I ask. "Three sisters, your mother must have had her hands full."

The three of them laugh. "We were a lot to handle," Essie admits, nodding her head.

"We didn't have an older brother to take us on cool adventures," Sarah offers, glancing up to Cooper. His cheeks have blushed red.

"We mostly played dress up in our mother's clothes," Cassandra continues.

"Our mother worked in the bakery so she was lucky enough to afford such luxuries like dresses and jewelry," Essie notes.

"We'd each take turns dressing up and being whatever we wanted," Sarah explains the game. "Most of the time I'd choose to be a princess." She stands and twirls in her rags pretending they are a big ball gown. The three girls giggle and Sarah sits back at her bucket.

"I actually preferred being a teacher," Essie admits softly.

Her sisters respond in unison, "Boring," and the three of them burst out laughing. This must be something the three of them joked about a lot because Essie doesn't seem to take offense at the insult.

"No one dressed as a baker?" Cooper jokes and the three burst out laughing again. I assume he's heard these stories before.

"I miss that," Sarah says and the moment settles as the three of them hold on to that feeling of playing dress up and being a kid.

"Remember when you taught me to braid hair?" Cassandra asks Essie and her smile widens.

"You can braid?" I ask and turn to Cassandra.

Essie and Sarah shout, "No!" at the same time and then start laughing again.

"Cassandra can't figure it out to save her life," Sarah jokes.

"I've had to brush out many of her attempts," Essie adds.

"But you can braid?" I turn my question to Essie and she nods yes. "Will you do mine? My mother used to."

Essie cuts me off, "Of course I can." She smiles and it feels genuine. All of them do, maybe I can still save this group of people. The mood in the air seems to shift a little and there's a sign that things could still be okay.

We spend the rest of the afternoon cleaning clothes while Essie braids all of our hair. She does mine straight back into one long tail. She even teaches me how to do it myself, but I don't pick it up very quickly. Essie reassures me that I'm better than Cassandra and with practice, I could be as good as her.

Albert calls us all to come and eat when the meat is ready. Everyone eats in silence and after we have all finished Mio has us up and running again.

"I can't believe we are actually running in this heat," Zavy mumbles.

"Do you realize how often you complain?" I ask her honestly. She doesn't respond but shoots a cold gaze in my direction.

Suddenly the ground starts to make a steep incline and we are all running uphill and turning in and out of trees. The river here is roaring louder than ever and my legs are starting to throb. We continue straight up this section of the mountain and the river breaks off to our right. I glance up and see the pouring waterfall spilling from the mountain's peak. I only have a second to take in its beauty before I'm back to weaving in and out of trees and it's hidden from my view.

When I'm not sure how much more my legs can take I feel the ground flatten out beneath my feet and nearly run into Zavy before I realize everyone has suddenly stopped running. I push through the crowd to see what everyone is looking at and feel the air get sucked right out of me.

"That's Sard," Cooper says as he takes a step next to me. We have run up a short nook in the line of mountains. To my right and left they tower above us, but we are high enough that we look down on Sard. The mountain range seems to encircle the city giving it a natural barrier of protection. I look out over the tops of the trees and can see the tall industrial buildings lining on the shore of the Island. I take in a sharp breath when my eyes land on the ocean. I made it to the blue. After all those years of dreaming and wondering if I'd ever get to see it, I am here. My eyes fill with tears remembering how I used to beg my mom and dad to bring me here.

"I made it mom," I say so softly it's inaudible. She would have been so happy, and I wish more than anything that she could be with me now.

"I've never seen buildings like that before," I breathe heavy.

"That's how all of the buildings used to be before the asteroid shower. When the Hawaiian Islands couldn't get the resources they needed to continue this style of buildings they had to refer back to the Roman style that we are more familiar with in Garth. Almost all of the industrial buildings have collapsed over the years because they didn't have the right materials to repair them. No one knows exactly why Sard still stands," my brother explains.

"It's amazing," is all I can manage to say.

"Come on everyone," Cooper turns and addresses the whole group. "Just down this slab of mountain is one step closer to your future."

Chapter 19

The beauty and magnificence of Sard seem to change the overall mood of the group. Many people point in awe of the city that seems to rise out of the island. Everyone is as mesmerized as I am by the blue ocean. It's something I know we grow up hearing about, and are always told we'll probably never see. Toby is so young he thinks the water is trying to swallow up the island, which he also thinks is really cool. Zavy and him walk off to the side and she reminds him of the asteroids and how these buildings are from a world before ours. It reminds me a lot of when I would teach Titus in the cell, and I'm so happy Zavy has her little brother. The thought that I could have been showing this to Titus sends an overwhelming wave of mixed emotions over me. I walk in step with Cooper as we make our way gradually down the side of the mountain and into Sard.

"So we'll leave for Libertas today?" I ask Cooper.

He laughs and says, "You're getting a bit ahead of yourself Adaline. We can't just walk through Sard. The entire city is filled with people working for King Renon. On the outskirts of Sard is an abandoned factory that is starting to collapse. Inside that building is a tunnel that runs under the city and goes to a building that is on the shore of the island. We have connections there that get us a boat and the materials we'll need for the trip to Libertas. The journey underground will take up the rest of today, and we can't sail out in the morning without driving attention to ourselves."

"So we'll leave tomorrow night?" I ask him.

"If all goes to plan, hopefully," he says.

The ground beneath our feet starts to level out, as we are approaching the edge of the forest. When we get to the edge Mio has us stop to take a break. I look out past the last of the trees and see the glint of the sun shining off of the buildings that are directly in front of us. I gaze up the buildings and have to shield my eyes from the sun to see its entire structure. My stomach tightens as I look out at the city. I've been in the cover of the woods for at least a week now. The idea of Sard, a city made up of people serving King Renon frightens me enough, but just the general idea of being back in civilization and out from the trees' protection makes me sick. The pale faces around me suggest they are all feeling the same thing. They haven't left these woods in seven years. I can only imagine what they are thinking.

"It's incredible," I hear Zavy say and look at the shock on her face. "I can hardly believe they're real."

"I know, me either," I unclip my water bottle and take a few sips of water. The nerves inside me are threatening to make me lose what food I've managed to eat today.

Mio starts to explain our next steps, "We're going to have to run out to that building." He lifts his finger and points out to the closest of all the buildings. This one is a bit shorter. There is colorful paint sprayed on it and yellow caution tape wrapped around the base of the building. This must be the abandoned factory Cooper was mentioning.

"We can't risk getting seen by the guards that patrol this side of Sard," Mio continues. I look out and catch the hint of a guard on top of a building a little to our right and another on a building to our left. They pace the roof of the buildings back and forth looking from the mountains to the ocean and then back again.

"We will run in pairs right when the guards turn the other way. When you get to the building stop outside and look back. I will let you know if the guards saw you or not. If they did, well then we have a problem on our hands. Just whatever you do, if the guards see you do not go into the building because you'll risk exposing the rest of the group," Mio says coldly.

"So what do we do?" I hear Toby ask.

"You'll have to fend for yourself. Remember the only person who has to get to Libertas is Adaline." The group falls awkwardly silent as everyone drops their gaze from mine. Mio continues, "Cinder and I will go last. Cooper and," Mio pauses, scanning his eyes around the group until they land on me. "Cooper and Adaline will go first. Why not get the only important one out of the way."

I try to bury the fear creeping inside of me. I shrug my shoulders and take another sip of my water. I close the bottle and clip it back to my bag. "Let's go," I say, and even I believe I'm not the least bit nervous.

Cooper's at my side and we turn to face the abandoned factory. We stand ready and watch the two guards pace along their buildings waiting for them to turn around.

"You know I can just use my gift and put us there," I say to him as we look out at the building. "I mean I could try to."

"That wouldn't be a good idea," Cooper says.

"Why?" I ask, turning to look at him.

"King Renon is on to the fact that people with gifts are fleeing to Libertas and traveling through Sard. He's put a force field sort of device around Sard. It won't stop you from using your gift, but it can detect when the gift is being used. Kind of like an alarm system."

"Seriously?" I ask, hardly believing what he's saying.

"Seriously," Cooper says. "One of these buildings is where King Renon is having scientists constantly researching gifts and how to get rid of them. The alarm is still new, but they're supposed to be putting one around Garth soon. Mio came down here a couple of times to see what advancements have been made."

"That's crazy," is all I can manage to say.

"Ready?" Cooper asks and we look back out and see that the guards have turned their backs to us.

"Let's go," I say and feel my legs push off the ground. My heart rate instantly doubles as we sprint across the clearing. One foot in front of the other. My tattered old shoes from the bunker fly through the yellow-green grass. I can see Cooper out of the corner of my eye. With his hair blown back, the intricate cut swirls stick out. The muscles in his neck bulge with each breath. My legs shake, but I keep pushing. My brother and I, together again.

When we reach the building we push our backs up on the side and hold our breaths waiting for Mio to give us the all clear that neither of the guards saw us. Mio's face comes into view and he gives us an approving nod. Cooper and I both let out a sigh of relief.

Cooper slides into the building first and I follow behind him. The sounds of the howling wind increase when we walk into the building, echoing through the deserted place. There is debris piled up throughout the room. Piles of dusty rock and metal grow from the floor, towering up to my shoulders. In the rubble of the building there are pieces of paper scattered over the floor, signaling whoever was here left in a hurry. I assume the collapse of the building wasn't planned, and I wonder if anyone was injured in its destruction. It seems as though it's been empty for years. I guess they have been using this as an entry point to Sard for many journeys dating back who knows how long. If there was anything of significance here I'm sure it was removed and cleaned out ages ago. Still, curiosity wins out and I start searching through what's left of this place.

Different metal desks are spread around the edges of the room. I walk around and look at each desk, not finding anything all that interesting. There are some papers scattered on the desks and the floor. I pick one up and notice how clean the print is. I don't understand too much of what is written on the document. I scan down the page and the words "research" and "gift" seem to stick out to me the most.

I put the page down and pick up another more crumpled one. I flatten it out and see it's a diagram. It's a chair with wires coming out of it. The words "The Test" are printed above the diagram. There's a list of words I assume are chemicals needed to perform the test. I feel the wind creep up my back. What was this place? I look up and I can see the blue sky above me; I hadn't realized there wasn't a roof on this building and no other floors remain after the collapse. Bare rafters expose themselves, crisscrossing over my head. Chunks of cement from what used to be the roof balance above our heads.

I spin around at the sounds of footsteps behind me, but it's just Zavy and Toby. I put down the papers and join Zavy, Toby, and Cooper. We all huddle in the center of the building and wait for the rest of the group to get to the building, not daring to say a word in case someone could possibly hear us. Soon, Mio and Cinder bring up the rear of the group and we are all standing together, the sounds of our breathing are the only noises in the building.

Mio starts handing out a plastic object that he explains to be a flashlight. He shows us how to turn them on and off and no one asks how he got them or why they work in fear of being overheard, but then Toby whispers to Zavy "Why's everyone so quiet?" Except it's not much of a whisper in this hollow concrete block. Zavy doesn't answer him but just puts her hand over his mouth out of instinct.

"Yes, why is everyone so quiet?" I hear the deep sound of his voice, driving a chill up my spine. I turn around and bring my eyes to meet his golden gaze.

"Paylon," I breathe. My first realization is that Alexander's not with him, and then I realize neither is Chadian. He's alone. Mio draws his sword and steps into Paylon's path. He begins to charge Paylon, but I watch as the commander doesn't even flinch at the attack.

"Oh, now that won't be necessary." I see Paylon lift his hand and slide past Mio's attack. As he sidesteps Mio he brushes his hand across his back and instantly Mio's sword crashes to the ground.

"He's controlling him," I think aloud. That one small touch was all Paylon needed to control Mio for that brief moment, and then I remember Codian's necklace in my backpack.

A rush of adrenalin courses through my body. I swing the bag off my shoulder and unzip it all in one movement. I whip out the green necklace and meet Cooper's gaze. He draws his sword and I toss the necklace to him. He clips it around his neck and stands to face Paylon.

"Now things are a little more interesting," Paylon says as he draws his sword and there's an instant sound of metal clashing as Cooper charges Paylon.

Paylon holds Cooper's impact and says, "Oh, come on. Even your sister's little boyfriend could do better than that." Paylon pushes back and Cooper falls to the ground.

"What did you say?" I ask, getting Paylon's attention.

"I said your little boyfriend put up quite the fight," Paylon says as he walks toward me. That's when I notice the dried red blood on his silver blade and I can't catch my breath. "Lost me my second best marksman, but you already knew about the first, right?" His golden eyes stare deep into me.

"You were controlling them. Codian and Chadian. You ruined their lives," I spit back at him.

"Well, a life for a life I guess," Paylon says smoothly as he twists his sword in his hand.

"What does that mean?" I ask. I move my hand and squeeze the butt of my sword as Paylon creeps closer.

"Chadian for Alexander. Codian for you," Paylon says and he swings his sword at my neck. I quickly pull mine from my belt and the metal clashes together.

"He's dead?" I ask, and my voice is very weak. My arms shake at the pressure of our swords together.

"Don't be surprised. You felt it didn't you? He's been dead for days, Adaline," Paylon says, sliding his sword along mine and coming in for another swing. Paylon becomes fuzzy in my vision. Alexander is really dead? I already knew that, but Paylon saying it makes me feel it all over again. I hear the crash of my sword on the ground. He's gone. I look back up at Paylon and watch as he swings his sword to my neck. I can't make my body move. I'm just stuck. Just as it's about to strike Cooper pushes me out of the way and takes the blow to his back.

I crash to the ground on my side and hear Cooper scream behind me. I turn over and watch as Cooper whips around and starts to charge Paylon again.

"Everyone into the tunnel!" Cooper yells. I turn and see that

Cinder is already clearing pieces of paper, revealing a round plate in the ground that resembles something of a sewer lid that we have lining the streets in Garth. Cinder pulls the lid off and throws it to the ground. I pull myself to my feet and balance on my shaky legs. I pick the sword up and it feels twice has heavy in my numb hands. We all start filing down a ladder into the dark tunnel below. I'm the last to go down besides Cinder and Mio. I look back at Cooper and Paylon, hesitant to leave him.

"Go, Adaline! He'll catch up," Cinder says. I bite my lip, remembering what happened the last time someone told me they'd catch up with me, but eventually, I start descending into the dark tunnel and slide my sword back into my belt. When my feet finally hit the ground they splash in a shallow puddle of who knows what. The smell almost makes me lose my breakfast. A couple of lights dance across the side of the tunnel and I remember the flashlights Mio had passed out. I reach for it in the side pocket of my backpack and click it on, illuminating a couple of inches right in front of my face, but not much more. I can see that a shallow amount of dark brown liquid covers the entire floor of the tunnel.

I look up and see that really, we are more in a large pipe. Different symbols are sprayed in paint along the walls. I immediately recognize them as the symbols for the gifts. It takes me by surprise to see them in person, this detailed in a hidden tunnel under Sard. Each gift has its own special symbol painted in a muted color.

Enhanced sight is painted in yellow. It's a single, wide eye with curling lines. Enhanced touch is a small orange hand with its finger pointed out. Hearing is a green ear, taste is a brown smile, and smell is a red nose. Each with such specific details, and I wonder who took the time to put them here. They are patterned together on the wall to make an abstract face.

For me this journey has always been for my safety, my freedom. But details like this make me understand this is more than that. The gifted are fleeing as groups. They are working together, starting a movement to free our kind. It feels weird to lump myself into that group of people, the idea is still too new to me.

Cinder and Mio splash to the ground and Cooper is immediately behind them. I can see blood smeared on his face and his clothes. His sword is still dripping red droplets into the liquid of the tunnel. He seems to be in a trance as if he isn't completely sure of where he is as he slides the sword back into his belt

"Let's keep going!" Cinder yells, her hard voice replacing her normal soft tone. "It's a straight shot from here." We start at a steady jog and begin splashing through the tunnel, our lights bouncing along the walls.

Chapter 20

After a little bit of rearranging, I'm able to fall instep with Cooper. In the round tunnel, it's hard to run side by side with anyone, but we manage to.

"Are you okay?" I ask him over the splashing of our feet.

It takes him a couple of seconds to respond. He blinks a few times and seems to come out of the trance, "Yeah, yeah I'm fine."

"What happened up there?" I ask, not sure if I should push him.

"All I can say is that you shouldn't have to worry about Paylon following us," he says and lets out out a heavy breath of air. He removes the necklace I had given him and hands it back to me.

"You killed him?" I ask, gasping and I shove the necklace back into my bag.

"No," Cooper says flatly. "He's injured though. There's no way he could last more than a day. I cut him pretty deep in the leg and I got his neck, I couldn't even imagine him living another hour, to be honest." Cooper's eyes glass over and I know he's remembering the fight. I imagine Cooper swinging his sword and driving it deep through Paylon's leg. Paylon falls and Cooper swings back slicing across his neck. The irony of it is Paylon may get his life for a life I guess.

"When we left he was crawling back into the forest, but we can't be too safe," Cooper's voice fills the tunnel. "All we can do is move as fast as we can and hope we can get out of here before word spreads. But Adaline, he used his gift. The people of Sard already know something's up." Suddenly Mio stops running, causing the rest of us to bump into each other.

"What is it?" Cooper asks and he makes his way through the group to the front and I follow behind him. I shine my light directly in front of me and when I get in front of the group I see them. There's just five of them sitting on the dirty floor of the tunnel, shivering. Children. They are all girls and can't be more than ten years old.

"What's going on here?" Cinder asks, her sweet tone returning. She steps forward, but the girls sink away from her. A confused look settles on the girls' faces.

I lift my hand and wave to them and my shadow dances in the light on the tunnel. At the sudden movement, they all look at me and surprisingly wave back. "I don't think they know how to talk," I offer as I study their faces.

"Adaline, that's silly. They're grown kids, they can speak," Mio says.

I step forward and kneel next to them. "Do you girls understand what I'm saying?" I say, shaking my head yes and no.

Four of them shake their heads no back to me, but the fifth girl who had her face in her hands looks up and says, "I can."

"You can?" I ask and she nods her head. "Can you tell me who you all are?"

"May and April are sisters," she says, pointing to two blonde-haired twins sitting by each other. Then, she points at the other two girls, one blonde and one brunette and says, "Lilly and Sam are sisters. All of our mothers worked together at the food storage units. One day their mothers brought them to my house and then my mother brought all of us down here. She told us that we had to stay here no matter what. We've been here for about, wait what's the date?"

"5019. It's mid-July. Now nearly August," I say hesitantly back to her.

"Three months," she responds, not believing it.

"You've survived down here for three months?" I question.

"When my mother brought us we had lots and lots of baskets with food and water, but we just ran out of the food yesterday," her voice draws distant as her mind surely reminds her how hungry she is.

I look at the hollow cheeks on her face, turn back to my group, and ask, "Do we have any food?"

"I have some berries," Cinder says, reaching into her bag. She pulls out a skin full of berries.

"Let's stop and rest for a minute," Mio says and everyone takes a seat, sipping on their water. This part of the tunnel is dry from the liquid we'd been previously running through. Mio and Cooper walk off from the group and I watch as they move a few paces deeper into the tunnel. Cooper takes off his dark shirt and turns around. I see the gash on his back from fighting with Paylon. I hear Mio ask him if he was hit anywhere else and Cooper says he wasn't. Mio pours water down Cooper's back and cleans the wound a bit before wrapping it in a white fabric. It immediately dyes red with his blood, but it seems to stop the bleeding from progressing.

"What happened to him?" The one who speaks asks in a soft voice as she works on the berries we've given them.

"We were being chased by a bad guy," I say and her eyes widen, "but he saved us. He's my brother." She looks from me to Cooper before turning back to her berries. She doesn't say anything else for the moment and just focuses on filling her empty stomach.

I turn back to the other girls and see that Cinder is handing out more of the berries. I walk over to Zavy and ask, "You could talk to these girls, right? With your gift? You said you were a Communicator, right?"

"Yeah, I could try," Zavy says, her eyes not meeting mine.

"What's wrong, Zavy?" I ask. She doesn't respond and I realize that she also doesn't know how to use her gift. "You don't know how to use it do you?" I ask her, not able to believe it. Zavy made me feel stupid for not being able to use mine and she can't use hers either.

"I said I could try," Zavy says, brushing me off. The five girls devour the berries. I move to sit next to the girl who I was talking to and Zavy moves to the pairs of sisters. "So what's your name?" I ask.

"Molly," She says between mouthfuls of the last of her berries. When she finishes eating she says, "Can you take me back to my mother?"

"Well, I'm not actually from here, so I'm afraid I don't know where your mother is, but I think we can take you to someone who might know," I say and glance up to Mio and Cooper who have rejoined the group. I look to him for his approval, not that I've needed it before to bring new people with us. He gives me a nod of approval and I look back to Molly.

"Okay, her name's Eleanor Fisher," Molly says in a small voice.

"I'll make sure to find out where she is," I promise her.

Then Mio's voice echoes through the tunnel saying, "It's time to start moving if we ever want to get out of here." I stand up and help Molly to her feet. Her thin little legs can hardly hold her own body weight. She moves and walks with her friends huddled together at the front of the group.

"We might want to take it slow Mio," I say, worry on my face. They seem frail, even for being children. We start walking at a steady pace further into the tunnel.

Cooper comes in step with me and asks, "How'd you know they couldn't understand us?"

"It was something in their faces," I explain. Titus had a similar look a lot when mother and I would talk in the cell. He really only knew how to ask for more food."

"I'm sorry," Cooper says and looks at me.

"It's okay," I say, breaking his gaze.

Zavy comes in step with us and I ask her if she was able to talk with the other girls. "A little bit. They can talk and understand some of what we say. Food and water. Family."

"Did you find anything else out about them?" I ask.

"All of the sisters are only five. Molly is the oldest. She's ten," Zavy says.

"How can they be five, but not be able to understand much?" Cooper asks.

"They never went to school," Zavy says. "Their parents all hid them in their homes. I couldn't tell, but I think I was getting that Molly's mom was a Future Holder. I could have been reading it wrong, but I think that's what I was sensing."

"What do you mean by sensing? How does your gift work, Zavy?" I ask her for the first time.

"Like this," she says and takes my hand in hers. "Hey, Adaline." I hear in my head, but Zavy didn't say it out loud.

"Whoa," I say out loud and Zavy laughs, dropping my hand.

"It's freaky, right?" Zavy laughs, "I was trying to talk to them and they were responding, I think. I just don't know how to use my gift so I don't know how much of the information I got right."

"It's like talking through your thoughts, right?" I ask, trying to understand it, and Zavy nods.

We walk in silence for what feels like hours. The sounds of our footsteps clicking on the cement floor fill the tunnel. Every few minutes there will be the marking of a gifted painted on the side of the tunnel, confirming we are moving in the right direction. Some of the group members have started humming a new camp song they must have learned one of the many nights they spent out in the woods. It's a simple but beautiful melody only made up of a couple of notes. The magnificent part is when they layer the melody and the notes overlap they create stunning harmonies. I realize how much I miss music. With my memories restored I'm reminded how much my father loved it.

Mio doesn't want to stop to eat again, so instead, we eat as we go. We pass Cinder's bag of berries around the group and take handfuls. Mio promises us there is a real meal waiting for us when we get out of this tunnel. The time seems to drag on and on and I know we must have walked miles. I feel guilty knowing it is only taking this long because the girls can't go any faster. I'm the one who said they could come with us. I look forward and see Molly stumble along with the group, her legs giving out. I run up to her and let her lean on my side.

"Mio, how much longer?" I ask and I'm beginning to worry these girls won't be able to make it much farther.

"It should be right," Mio starts and takes a few more steps forward until finally the flat end of the tunnel is illuminated, "here."

A smile falls on my face, "See, you made it," I say and look at Molly who seems to have found a second wave of energy and stands up on her own.

Mio climbs up the ladder and pounds three times on the ceiling of the tunnel. We stand in silence for a second until the tunnel becomes illuminated in a blinding white light. I blink a couple of times to clear my vision and watch Mio climb the rest of the way up. We wait until Mio yells back down to us that it's all clear to come up. I help Molly up onto the ladder and then follow behind her.

When we surface outside of the tunnel it's like we've climbed into a different world. The building Cooper mentioned is more like a home. We've climbed up into what seems to be the living room. The wood floor is a nice change from the cement tunnel we've been in all afternoon. Different white glowing lights hang from the ceiling and plush elegant couches are placed throughout the room. I turn around and see large glass doors that open to a deck that looks to the ocean with the stars reflecting into the water. It's breathtaking.

For a second I'm just taking in the amazing room that has manifested in front of me, but quickly my mind comes back to life and I'm back in survival mode. It's night. We've been in the tunnel all afternoon. I look down at myself and then scan the rest of the group. I am shocked by how awful we all look in this very clean and polished home. Our faces are caked in dirt, our shoes are soaked in dirty water, we have mud dried to our nails, and knotted hair. We hardly look human.

"I see we've had some additions to the group," a questioning voice asks and I turn to see a man about Mio and Cinder's age standing next to Mio. He has short brown hair and dark brown scruff down the sides of his face.

"We do. Sorry if it's an inconvenience. Some things change after seven years," Mio says and glances at me. "Everyone, this is my little brother Leo."

"Brother?" Cooper asks.

"Little?" Leo scoffs. "Just two years."

"Who'd you think I would have connections with here?" Mio asks.

"It's nice to meet you," I say and shake Leo's hand. "When we were traveling through the tunnel we came across these girls." I place my hand on Molly's shoulder and say, "Molly is hoping you know her mother, Eleanor Fisher?"

"I can't say I've heard that name in months," Leo says.

"Did you say, Eleanor Fisher?" a woman's voice rings into the room as she enters. "Oh, sorry. I'm Leo's wife. My name's Kimberly."

"Yes, do you know why that name sounds familiar?" Leo asks her.

"Well yeah, she was one of those three ladies that were executed a couple of months back for stealing from the food storage unit they worked at. Why?" Kimberly asks and turns to us.

"Executed?" Molly asks in a broken voice. "Adaline, that can't be right."

"Molly, I'm so sorry," is all I can say. I tighten my arm around her shoulders. Kimberly gives me an apologetic glance, not knowing it was Molly's mother we had been talking about.

"What are we going to do?" Molly asks with her face buried in my side. I look up to Mio and see him roll his eyes because he knows what I'm about to say.

"You can come with us and I'll see if I can find somewhere for you, okay? You don't have to worry, I'll take care of you," I say, feeling a sort of protection over her, much like the one I once felt for Titus.

There's an awkward silence that falls over the group. Leo pulls Mio over to a door in the other room and starts to talk in hushed voices. Then Kimberly says, "You guys are probably exhausted and well in need of a shower."

"A what?" Zavy asks confused.

"Right, I'm sorry. All of this technology is new to you. You would like to clean up I'm sure." We all nod our heads in agreement.

"You can all follow me," Kimberly says. Molly walks over to the other girls she was in the tunnel with to try to explain to them what we are doing. Zavy offers to help, but I tell her to let Molly do it. While Zavy may be able to get the message to them it will be received better if it comes from Molly.

I bring up the rear of the group, but when we pass Mio and Leo I overhear Leo say, "We've got a problem, Mio."

"A problem?" I ask and stop. Leo and Mio look from each other to me and know that I'm not going to budge.

"Someone came through the tunnel yesterday. I'm not sure how he found it or how he knew to come here. We tied him up immediately and threw him in here. We don't know what to do with him," Leo says. He turns the knob and pushes the door open. My first thought is that Paylon sent Chadian into the tunnel to ambush us here. I draw my sword, ready to finish off what's left of King Renon's search group.

The light from the living room seeps into the dark cellar room. I follow Mio and Leo and take a step inside. My shadow grows with the light across the floor. Metal shelves line the walls filled with cardboard boxes of different items. I see him hunched over in the back of the room. He's sitting on the floor with his head hanging. There's a dirty cloth tied in his mouth and his feet and hands are bound together. He lifts his dirty face and shakes his matted hair, his green eyes meeting mine.

"Alexander," I say, the air leaving my lungs. My sword clashes to the ground and I push through Mio and Leo and run to him. I throw my arms around his neck. I can't contain the tears that start to roll down my cheeks. "You're alive. I thought you were dead. Paylon said you were dead," I say into his shoulder. I pull away from him and pull the cloth from his mouth.

"Hope you didn't miss me too much," he says in his broken voice and I can't help but laugh, so relieved to hear his voice again. "Paylon found you guys?"

"Yes, but Cooper cut him. We're sure he's dead by now," I say wiping the tears off my cheeks and I notice my hands are shaking uncontrollably.

"Did I seriously just lock up," Leo starts.

Mio laughs and says, "You sure did."

"Boy, why didn't you tell me you were Alexander?" Leo asks, untying his feet and hands.

"Well, you didn't give me the choice, now did you?" Alexander says as he gets to his feet.

"You should go catch up with the others. Go clean up before

dinner." Mio says, placing a hand on Alexander's shoulder. We both turn to leave, but the adrenaline from seeing Alexander alive has faded and the heavy awkward air between us has settled again, but I don't mind. As long as he is alive and with us, I couldn't ask for anything more.

Part 3: The Journey

Chapter 21

Once Alexander and I catch up with the group Kimberly splits us up. She leads the girls further into the house and Cinder takes the boys down a short hall to our right. I'm reluctant to part with Alexander so soon, but I know I don't have to be worried about his safety here. I'm lead down a long hallway in the back of the house with the other girls. I manage to catch up with Kimberly at the front of the group and we file into a room on the right side of the hallway. Once we have all been ushered into the large tiled room that has twenty or so stalls Kimberly starts to go over what all of these new appliances are and how we use them. Then, we are each assigned one of the stalls and told that dinner will be ready when we are finished. Kimberly collects all of our backpacks and says she will store them for us. Reluctantly, I let her take my sword. I know I won't need it here, but I've grown attached to that weapon.

I walk into the stall I was assigned and see all the new technology that Kimberly had briefly explained. Something called a 'toilet' is sitting on one side, we would call it a waste bucket back in Garth, with a 'sink' across from it. It does slightly resemble the spigot I had at home. Above the sink is a mirror. I step in front of it and am shocked to see who is staring back at me.

The last time I saw my reflection was when I was just nine years old. Even that mirror doesn't compare to the tall shine slate of reflective glass hanging in front of me. The only mirror we had in our house was a small round mirror that was built into the desk in my mother's room. It had brown spots around its edges and a yellow reflective tint. In the mirror in front of me, I see a crystal clear reflection staring back. My skin is blotchy with red patches from being exposed to the excessive amount of sun. My skin isn't used to that from being in prison for so long. My long brown hair is matted and strands of it have fallen out of my braid, but my green eyes are magnificent.

I take off my poor excuse for a shirt and pants, remove the sewer water soaked white shoes and socks, and step into what Kimberly said was the shower. I push the button she directed me to do, and warm water starts to stream out of the ceiling of the shower. It's amazingly refreshing after everything I've been through. It's a warm summer rain shower right here in their house. I use the different buttons to dispense a liquid form of soap for my hair and massage it through all the tangles, gently untwisting the braid. When I use the soap designated to remove the dirt from my body I notice how pale and fair-skinned I really am under all the dirt. I watch as the last of the dirt circles down the drain, as if washing off the last seven years.

I press the same button I had used to turn on the water and the warm rain halts. There is a thick grey towel hanging on a metal bar and I use it to dry off. I step out of the shower and open a compartment in the stall. I expect to find a new clean ragged shirt and pair of pants but am surprised to find an odd pair of clothing. More similar to the clothes we had found in the bunker.

It appears to be a shirt and a long pair of pants, but both are made out of a stretchy fabric like the ones Leo and Kimberly were wearing. The pants are a jet black and the top is a light shade of pink. I put them on and am surprised at how well they fit. At the bottom of the compartment is a pair of long black socks with a pair of short black leather boots. I slip on the socks, lace up the boots, and pace around the stall, breaking them in.

I step back in front of the mirror and feel like an entirely different person is looking back at me. I pull on the mirror to open it as Kimberly had instructed. I scrub my teeth and brush out my long, wet, and tangled hair. The first time I have done either in a very long time.

Then, at the last minute, I see a small light reflect off the metal pair of scissors at the bottom of the cabinet. I pick them up and close the mirror, looking at my reflection once again. The only parts of me that look the same are my magnificent green eyes and my long dark hair.

Something about my hair holds too much from the past, probably because of how my mother used to braid it, and unbraid it, and then re-braid it to pass the time in the cell. I raise the scissors to my hair and snip away, watching chunk after chunk of my hair fall to the ground until my hair is cut into a sharp 'V' form, short by my shoulders and growing to a single point. I put the scissors down and step back to admire my work and I couldn't be happier with the change.

I throw my hair clippings in the bin by the toilet and hang up my used towel. Then, I step out of the stall and notice everyone else has already made their way back to the dining room. I walk out of the tiled room and back down the hallway toward the sounds of laughter and soft music.

I step into the dining room and look around at the magnificent and detailed pieces in the room. The table is a grand long rectangular slab of dark polished wood and stands in the center of the room. Dark wooden chairs line all sides of the table, and there's a royal purple carpet that runs under them. It makes my stomach turn because I know that is the color of our nation. They aren't supposed to be supporting the King, but they do live in Sard. I assume they've had to put up an appearance here in the city in hopes that no one would suspect they were the ones helping the gifted escape. Still, it reminds me of the floors of the castle and I hate that I have to be in the same room as it. The walls compliment the rest of the space and are a warm yellow with large chandeliers hanging over the table.

When I step into the room, all conversation stops. I look around the room and see that everyone else is wearing similar clothing to mine except they vary in color. I look to Alexander and he motions to my hair and I realize how much of a shock it must look like.

"Just thought I needed a change," I mumble under my breath and everyone falls back into their conversations. I make my way over to an empty chair next to Alexander and can feel his and Cooper's stares burning into the side of my head.

"You hate it don't you?" I ask and turn to them. They both shake their heads no and smile.

Alexander says, "I like it."

Cooper adds, "Yeah, it gives you an edgy, fierce look." I laugh and turn my attention back to a group of what looks like servants coming through two double doors at the back of the room. They remind me of the lower help from the castle that would work around the prison and I wonder whose house we've come up into. How highly ranked is Mio's brother to live in such a magnificent home with people serving him? Each server is carrying large platters of food and I simply can't believe my eyes. They lay the plates of food out in front of each of us. I've never seen this much food in one place, and I don't even recognize half of it.

Everyone seems to be as hesitant as I am as if we're waiting for the catch. Then, the help returns with silver metal tools, I assume we use to eat with, and clear glasses full of a dark bubbly drink. Mio, Cinder, Leo, and Kimberly enter the room and fill up the empty chairs at the table.

"Good we're just in time," Leo says as he lifts the silver tool with pointed ends and uses its side to cut some sort of meat with an odd red sauce on it. He uses the tool to pick up a piece of the meat and place it in his mouth. He looks to each of us and is confused when he sees we aren't eating. "It's not poisoned, I promise," Leo says with a mouth full of food.

I tentatively pick up the same silver tool that Leo did and try the foreign piece of meat. My eyes widen at the explosion of flavor when it hits my tongue. The food seems to simply melt in my mouth.

"What is this?" I can't help asking.

Leo looks at me confused and says, "Well, it's just meatloaf. Have you never had any?"

I shake my head no and ask, "What are these?" and I wave the silver tool in my hand.

"You don't have silverware in Garth?" Kimberly asks, looking to Mio and Cinder for an explanation.

"It's much too expensive for most people to afford," Mio says.

"That's absurd," Kimberly says shocked.

"Life in Garth is not what it use to be," Cinder offers as some sort of explanation.

Kimberly shakes her head in disbelief and turns back to me to answer my question. "That's a fork and the other one," I look down to the other round silver tool, "is a spoon. You use the fork for most solid foods like the meatloaf or the pasta salad and you use the spoon for most liquid foods like the vegetable soup." I look down at my plate and match the names of the food Kimberly said to their forms. I take bite after bite of the rich food until nothing remains on my plate or in my bowl.

"I feel like I'm going to be sick," Zavy says as she finishes off her food. We all laugh and slouch back in our chairs knowing we are all feeling the same as her. I feel as though I have just eaten a month's supply of food from the castle all at once. First, I just feel full, but then a pang of guilt washes over me as I remember all the people left behind in the castle. None of them will ever get to know the feeling of a full stomach. I wonder if King Renon thinks some of them helped me escape. Could he be punishing innocent people because of my actions? I dismiss the thought quickly because Paylon knows I'm a gifted, and that's enough explanation as to how I escaped. King Renon may be evil, but killing innocent people for no reason wouldn't sit well in Garth.

"This was always my favorite part of this job," Mio says, letting his fork clink down on his empty plate and everyone starts to laugh again. The depressed mood throughout our group has quickly vanished now that Alexander has returned and they will all get their fair shot at getting to live in Libertas.

The servers that brought out our food circle back around to collect our empty plates and bowls. They leave our glasses behind so I continue sipping on the dark fizzing drink. It bubbles and tickles my nose each time I take a sip and I wonder how it is made. I've only had water for most of my life with the occasional milk if we could afford it. Just as I'm about to ask if we could go rest for the night the group of servers return carrying armloads of more food.

"You can't possibly expect us to still be hungry," I exclaim, shocked that there's even more food being placed in front of us.

"You can't leave here without at least trying this dessert. It's our famous red velvet cake," Kimberly says, diving right into the dessert as if she hadn't just finished a plate full of food just seconds before.

I lift my fork and scrape a small bit of the white paste off the top of the cake. I lick it off the fork and am overwhelmed by the sweet and smooth dessert. Against what my stomach tells me I eat the entire dessert until I'm scraping my plate clean. I look around and see that the others couldn't resist the sweet temptation either.

"I don't imagine we'll be eating anything this extravagant on the boat," I say. Mio and Cinder both laugh and shake their heads no.

Mio says, "It's probably a good thing though. You think you're having a hard time holding your food down now, just wait until you get out on the sea."

"It's hard to keep anything down on the water," Cinder adds. Mio and Leo start discussing plans for our departure tomorrow. I overhear them explain that we will rest, and to my surprise eat more food. Alexander clumsily drops the cloth napkin he was using and bends over to pick it up.

When he bends over he whispers in my ear, "We need to talk. Tonight, after everyone goes to bed, I'll come find you." He sits back up and looks away quickly. What does he want to discuss? I don't argue though because I have some questions I'd like to ask Alexander, and I'd rather not do it with a crowd of people.

Once everyone finishes off the last of their food we are separated into groups and are taken into different rooms that we will be sleeping in. Zavy, myself, Essie, Molly, and two more girls from the tunnel walk into a room on our left, and the other girls we met in the tunnel are led into a room across the hall with Cassandra and Sarah. The younger girls seem skeptical to split from one another but Molly assures them they are safe with our older members. Our backpacks from the journey here are hanging on hooks along the wall. There are a total of 6 beds in our room, and they are set up with one stacked on top of the other.

"Yes, bunk beds!" I hear Molly's young voice squeal.

"Bunk beds?" I ask in a questioning tone, and I can see the confusion on Zavy and Essie's faces as well. How could we live on the same island as this city, and yet know a completely different lifestyle?

I claim the top bed of the set that's closest to the door, and then Kimberly comes around and gives us extra pillows and blankets since she has taken the dirty ones from our backpacks. I take my bag from the hook and double-check to make sure nothing else was taken. The clothes from the bunker that I had cleaned yesterday are still folded and tucked at the bottom of the bag. I find that my photograph, gold coin, and Codian's necklace are still hidden away in the secret inside pocket of the bag. The rations from the bunker are still tied together in the front pouch with the cental-straw packed neatly on top. I exhale with relief, knowing nothing else in my bag has been taken. I know Cinder's intentions were good, but these are the only belongings I have in this world.

We all climb up into our bunks and Kimberly flips off the light. She cracks the door just enough so a single sliver of light stretches across the floor. My eyelids start to get heavy and I can feel myself falling into a deep sleep, my exhaustion taking over. I remind myself to stay awake because Alexander will come for me soon I assume. All of the other girls in the room have already fallen asleep and just as I'm about to as well I hear hushed voices approach my door. My eyes shoot open and I think it's Alexander, but the harshness in the voice tells me it's not. It's Mio and Leo, and it sounds like they are making their way down our hall.

"We've got a serious problem, Leo," I hear Mio whisper and continue, "Not only did Paylon see us come through the tunnel, but he used his gift and I'm sure the alarm they have this city under notified the officers. Now, we saw him run back into the forest, but there's no telling what he's going to do."

"We could all be in danger," Leo whispers, fear creeping into his voice.

"I'm sorry I didn't mention it sooner, I didn't want to worry the kids or Kimberly," Mio apologizes and continues, "Cooper's pretty confident he got him deep enough, but Paylon might have still gotten the word out about our arrival."

"They know don't they?" Leo asks, and I'm confused by what he could mean. Who knows? What do they know?

"They have to know. If it were anyone else they'd just let them go," Mio says flatly.

"All right. I'll stay up and keep watch in case someone finds us," Leo responds. "You should get some sleep. You have a long journey tomorrow."

"Leo, I think you and Kimberly need to come with us. We might make it through the night without them finding us, but they'll track every inch of those tunnels until they find it leads to you," Mio says desperation creeping in his voice.

"You know I can't possibly ask Kimberly to do that. You know she already has a hard enough time letting them stay here. She never wanted any of this," Leo says in a small, weak voice.

They are quiet for a second until Mio finally says, "You better hope they don't connect this place to that tunnel."

"We'll be fine Mio." The brothers don't say anything else, and after a second I hear their footsteps lead into separate directions, and that's when my fatigue pulls me into a deep sleep.

Chapter 22

There's a soft tap on my shoulder and my eyelids flicker open. A pair of dark green eyes are looking back at me in the dark of the room. Alexander. Right, I was supposed to stay awake and meet with him. Without exchanging any words I quietly get up and leave my bed. I wait until we are out in the hall to make any sound. Alexander starts to head toward the front of the house and I grab his arm, stopping him.

"We can't go up there," I whisper, remembering what I had overheard between Mio and Leo before fatigue pulled me under. "Leo is staying up tonight to keep watch. Here," I say and guide him back, deeper into the house. After I had showered I remember passing a room that looked like a sitting area. It takes me a minute to find my way back to it, but when I do I'm surprised to find it full of books. I see a small switch next to the door and when I flip it on the room ignites in a blinding white light. It's a small and dark wooden room. Books line the shelves that circle the entire room. There are couches and tables spread throughout the room. On the far wall is a wooden door that leads to another room, but I'm not sure where.

Alexander and I click the door behind us and make sure no one else is in the room before speaking.

"How did you know to come here?" I ask him in a shocked whisper, finally getting out the words that I've been thinking since I saw him chained to the floor of Leo's storage room.

"That's actually what I wanted to talk about," Alexander says. He goes to a couch that is placed against the far wall and removes his backpack before taking a seat. I know Alexander may have been to Sard before when he worked for King Renon, but this is far too complicated for him to have just figured out. I cross the room and take a seat next to him. "I had some guidance," he says vaguely while scanning my face. I'm sure my expression asks for an explanation so he asks, "Can I see your mother's journal?"

I'm confused by his request. I sit up a little straighter and say, "I destroyed it."

"You what?" Alexander asks shocked.

"I didn't like the pressure hanging over every decision I made. The second-guessing of my every move was too much," I explain.

Alexander nods his head, understanding. "Well, that's how I got here," he says and explains how he had read my mother's journal while I slept the last night in the bunker. "I opened it and it started with 'Alexander,' like she knew I would read it," he explains.

"She did," I say and shrug my shoulders.

"Are you mad I read it?" he asks me gently.

I shake my head no and say, "The idea of knowing the future is tempting. So my mother told you to come here?" I question.

"It was more complicated than that," Alexander says and he pulls a few tanned pages from the bag at his feet. "She told me to take them," he adds defensively before handing them to me. I take the aged fabric and a feeling of dread washes over me. Her perfect handwriting scribbled across the page makes me nauseous, and I'm wishing I hadn't destroyed the journal. I miss her so much, but I know it was the right decision. I couldn't live with the pressure of knowing the future depends on my every move. While that may still be true, at least I don't know what those moves have to be. I start reading my mother's delicate handwriting and imagine Alexander reading this next to me while I slept in the bunker.

Alexander,

I have some important instructions for you, but you need to keep them a secret from Adaline. The fewer people who know the more likely this will work out. You and Adaline will be tested whether to save Zavy or travel safely to Libertas. For me, I beg that you just go to Libertas, but Adaline will never leave a friend behind. Go with her and protect her. You'll need to split up and draw Paylon away from his camp. Here is a map of how to get to Sard.

Below her handwriting a dashed out sketch is etched into the tan paper. It shows the river we followed with an X through it. Then, a rock path is marked out through the ink drawn trees.

Follow the stone boulders. They will lead you to Sard. Do not return to the river. Paylon will be following you closely, and we can't risk you bringing him to the path Adaline and Zavy will be taking.

I note how my mother specifically didn't mention anything about Cooper or the search group in her plans. Only telling Alexander enough information for him to not ask any questions. It's incredibly manipulative. I had no idea my mother had that side to her.

If you hurry the journey will take you 48 hours. Take enough water and rations for the trip, because you don't have time to hunt and you won't find another water source on your route. When you get to Sard locate the abandoned building on the edge of the city. Inside you'll find access to an underground tunnel system.

My mother then proceeds to give Alexander step-by-step instructions to Leo's home. "You went right past Molly and her friends," I say softly.

"I didn't even see them," Alexander admits. "I knew I had to get to you. I didn't know you were behind me."

"Paylon said you killed Chadian," I say, lowering the papers. I had forgotten until now. "He said you killed Chadian so Paylon killed you." Alexander squints at me confused. "What happened after you left me?" I ask, handing Alexander my mother's pages. "I don't want to know what my mother has to say. I want to know what actually happened."

Alexander nods, taking the pages back. "I did what I told you I would do," he begins to explain. "I traveled a mile or so south of Paylon's camp and started a fire. I added as much green as I could to make the smoke visible. I picked a couple of trees and lit them on fire," Alexander pauses as my eyes widen. "Isolated ones, so they would fall and catch Paylon's attention."

"It worked," I say. "We heard the tree crash and he left with Chadian."

"I waited until I heard his horse, and then I ran," Alexander adds.

"You let him get that close?" I ask, upset.

"I had to be sure before I left. Then, I took off running. I never saw him or Chadian. I assumed they saw the destruction and figured it was a trap. They must have went back to their camp, but you had already rescued Zavy and left."

"And I killed Codian," I admit. Alexander is silent and I make my eyes meet his.

"He fought you outnumbered?" Alexander asks and I shake my head no. I wish he had fought because then I wouldn't feel completely responsible for what had happened.

"He threatened to kill Cooper if I didn't kill him," I say and my voice shakes. "He wanted to die." I take a deep breath and say the words I've been fighting internally for the last two days. "And I know I could have tried harder to save them both, but at that moment I couldn't think straight."

Alexander puts a gentle hand on my arm. "It's okay Adaline." I take in a deep shaky breath, knowing I can't change it now.

"So then you ran?" I ask.

"Yes, and your mother was right. I didn't find any water or food. That's also why I was running so fast. I had run out of water after 30 or so hours. It was either run here and get water or die in the woods." Alexander says flatly.

"How bad was it?" I ask Alexander because he seems to be sparing me the details. I remember how hot the last couple of days have been. I know it couldn't have been an easy trip.

"Bad," he lets out an exhausted breath. "I've never had to go a day without food or water. I wasn't prepared for the effects." I nod remembering the first days after my mother lost her job and we had nothing to eat. I know it's only been a few days, but Alexander does look like he's losing weight. Maybe it's my imagination, but his face does seem thinner. "The dehydration was the worst part," he admits. "I stopped feeling the hunger after a while, but my sandpaper tongue wouldn't stop begging for water."

I imagine Alexander running through the scorching sun panting, but no water to refuel himself. "My mother sent you on a death mission," I say irritated. "She knew you may not make it, but was willing to risk your life to save mine." Disgust bubbles inside me, but Alexander's gentle hand on my wrist calms me.

"I would go back and do it all again." His green eyes stare into mine.

"All of it?" I ask softly, and he knows I mean more than just leaving me to help Zavy. I mean it all, helping me flee the castle, leaving his safe life, and becoming a traitor. Since the return of his memories, I've wondered if he does regret helping me.

His grip on my wrist tightens and he says, "All of it."

I smile and try to make myself believe it so I don't have to carry the guilt that my mother and I may have ruined his life. Now that Alexander has caught me up with what happened to him I share the major events of the last few days for my traveling group. There's not much to share though. Most of the time was spent thinking about Alexander and wondering what we were going to do when we got to Libertas without him.

I tell him about Paylon ambushing us, and I know he thinks it's his fault. Paylon was following him and was probably waiting for us to get there. I tell him about finding Molly and her friends in the tunnels and he's surprised that Mio was so quick to agree to them joining us. I tell him I was bringing them no matter what Mio had said and he had probably known that too. After Alexander is up to speed we walk back to our rooms. I leave Alexander at his and we stand in silence in the dark for a moment.

"See you in the morning," he finally says softly. Then, he sinks into his room and I make my way back to mine alone. When I get back in my bunk I'm reminded how little sleep I've gotten since this whole journey started. When I finally find sleep my last thought is of the red velvet cake and how I hope we get more tomorrow.

My eyelids shoot open at the thunderous sound of someone banging on the front door. It sounds so unbelievably similar to the night when the guards came to my house seven years ago. I hear

Leo's faded voice welcome whoever is there. A stern voice responds and asks if he can come in. There's a pause before I hear the door creak open and I sense Leo hesitate before allowing him in.

"We've been notified of escaping prisoners from Garth," the stern voice says to Leo. "We are supposed to investigate all homes."

"No," I whisper into the night air. Tears brim my eyes and my heart quickens. Images of the guard ripping me from my bed start flashing before me, and I can't help but feel like that helpless nine-year-old girl again. I can't believe I'm about to be taken in as a prisoner again. This can't be happening. I look around the room and see the other girls have woken up and are looking at each other frantically.

"They must be important prisoners for King Renon to make such a big deal about getting them back," I hear Leo say as their voices grow down the hall. Everyone's eyes seem to land on mine, all of them looking to me for what we should do. I lift a shaky finger to my lips and remind them to stay quiet. It's the only thought my terrified mind can process. My eyes lock with Molly's and tears roll down her cheeks.

"Yes, if they get away it is feared that they have the power to destroy Garth," the officer says in a flat voice

"Well that's kind of extreme," I hear Leo say, his voice right outside our door.

"We aren't taking any chances," I hear the officer respond and suddenly the room is washed in bright light from the hallway. I close my eyes and hold my breath, hoping somehow he can't see me.

"Why do you have so many empty beds?" I hear the guard question and I'm confused about what he means by empty.

"My wife wanted lots of kids, but she isn't able to have any. It's been hard on us. I've been meaning to get rid of them, but she doesn't want to let them go," I hear Leo's voice grow distant as he leads the officer out of the room and farther down the hall. The room falls eerily silent once Leo and the officer have made their way further into the house. Even though it sounds like the officer has moved away from our room we stay completely silent and frozen in our beds. After a couple of minutes, I hear their voices surface again when they make it back to the front of the house.

"We'll be making rounds hourly, so expect another officer here soon," he says in a more sensitive voice.

"That's fine, the house will look the same," Leo says in a light voice.

"I know it's annoying for people like you who would never bring in prisoners, but it's routine," he adds sympathetically.

"Like I said, I understand. Take it easy," Leo says and I hear the door creek open and click shut again. The house falls back into being silent, and then Mio bursts through our bedroom door.

"Up," he hisses to us. "Don't speak and don't turn on any lights. We're leaving. Now." He turns and pushes through the door into the other girls' room. I get out of bed skipping every other step on the ladder.

I throw my boots on and lace them up, and everyone else is doing the same. Zavy helps Molly and her friends get up, their small bodies shaking with fear. I sling my backpack over my shoulder, place my sword back at my hip, and file out into the hallway.

The guys are coming out of their rooms and making their way down the hallway. I fall in step with Alexander and feel him take my hand in his. We both look at each other and know, without speaking, that we aren't losing the other again. I notice his bag and sword have been returned to him since Leo freed him this afternoon.

Everyone walks and huddles in the center of the living room where we came up when we arrived. I look around the room and count to make sure everyone is here. Zavy is at my side with Toby tightly holding her hand, tears rolling down his cheeks. His eyes are wide with fear. I turn and see the other girls from the tunnel have made it out of their room and are huddled together. Molly locks her eyes with mine and I try to calm down and show her I'm not scared, but I'm not very good at it. Our heavy breathing fills the room, but we don't dare say a word.

Mio surfaces in the center of the group and says, "We're sailing out tonight. It's too dangerous for us to stay here now that they have the word out of our arrival."

"Kimberly and Cinder are packing up the boats now," Leo says, joining Mio in the center. "We're going to file through the back door and onto the docks. Leave the flashlights off and stay silent."

Mio and Leo push through the group and slide open the glass doors I'd looked through earlier. The cool night air rushes in and sends a chill creeping up my neck. We fall into line behind Mio and Leo and follow them down the deck and onto the soft sand, but when we hit the sand we are completely exposed in the moonlight. Mio and Leo break out into a sprint to the dock and we all quickly follow. When we hit the wooden dock we stop running, partially hidden under the canopy and posts around us. I take in deep breaths of the salty air from the sea and count to make sure all of my group made it here too. I won't lose anyone. I can't, not when we are this close.

"Everything's ready to go," Kimberly says as she comes out of the boat to my left, and then Cinder climbs out of the boat to my right.

"Everything's set over here too," Cinder adds. I look down at the boats and see that they aren't much. Each has an upper level on the backs of the boat where a tall black sail is flipping in the wind. The rest of the boat is a simple wooden frame, and I can make out something that resembles a propeller and motor at the rear of the boat. Wooden benches line the edge of the boat with the food being stored inside them.

Mio turns to us and says, "Cinder and I will each run a boat. I want Cooper, Adaline, Alexander, Zavy, Toby, Molly, Lilly, and Sam on my boat. Cassandra, Essie, Sarah, James, Bren, Albert, Andy, May, and April on Cinder's boat."

We all start to file into our assigned boats when Mio steps in front of Alexander and stops him. "Have you been on a boat before? With the castle's army?" Mio asks.

"Yeah, I've helped with boats like these before," he says.

"So you know what I mean when I say I need you to get us out of here by manipulating the motor to be as quiet as possible so we don't draw attention to ourselves. I can't do it because I need to get some papers straight now that we are leaving earlier than planned."

"Yes, I can manipulate this type of motor to get us far enough away from shore without it making much noise," Alexander responds, and hints of an officer shine through. He was trained to take orders. I watch him climb to the upper level on the rear of the boat and take a seat in front of a small control panel. There's not much on there. A button or two and a small switch.

"Are you sure you don't want to come?" Mio says, approaching Leo and Kimberly.

"We're sure," Leo says strongly to Mio.

The two stare at each other for a long while until Mio finally turns away, coming onto our boat, and saying, "Then let's get going." Mio and Cinder both undock the boats and we start to float deeper into the dark depths of the ocean. Mio sits toward the front of the boat. I try to see what papers he was talking about, but I can't make out what he could be reading.

Alexander starts flipping switches on the small control panel for the motor and slowly but surely the boat inches along silently in the water. I glance across the water and see that Cinder is doing something similar to Alexander.

I look out at the ocean and can hardly believe that I am on a boat. I think back to mine and Alexander's first night together in the forest and remember talking about going to Libertas together. After a week of fighting Paylon, finding Zavy, and meeting my brother again we are finally doing it. We actually made it to the ocean and are on our way to Libertas. To freedom.

I look back to Sard and watch the moonlight dance across the tall metal buildings, and in my head, I beg that no officers see us as we leave.

Chapter 23

After what seems like an hour or so, I turn and glance back in the direction of Sard. It's only a small glowing light off in the distance.

"All right, we'll turn on the motors now," Mio says, breaking the cool silence as he walks to the back of the boat. Alexander flips a switch and the motor comes to life with a low hum. He relaxes and moves to sit on the edge of the upper level, hanging his legs over the side.

The group falls silent again, except for the sounds coming from the motors of both boats. I look into the horizon, letting the wind flip pieces of my hair around my head and blow a light mist of seawater on my face. I can barely make out hints of sunlight breaking through the night sky, signaling a new day is arriving.

"We'll have two people stay on watch while the rest of us get some sleep," Mio says.

"What are we watching for?" Molly's little voice says almost humorously as she lets out a large yawn. She's taking this abrupt leave awfully well. I assume she doesn't really understand the caliber of King Renon's forces that are looking for us. Even all the way out here in the middle of the ocean I feel the need to glance over my shoulder every once in a while.

Mio drops his voice and says, "Creatures lurk in the depths of these waters. You can never be too safe, Molly." He gives a low chuckle, and Molly sinks deeper into her seat.

"That's not funny," I mumble, shooting him a glare. We're quiet for a moment until I say, "I'll keep watch."

"Great, we can keep each other company," Mio says.

"No, I'll keep watch with Adaline. You should get some rest, Mio," Cooper says.

"You both should get some rest, you've done too much for us as it is," Alexander speaks up.

"Well, I'm not going to say no to sleep," Mio says as we rearrange ourselves.

"You wake me up when you want to switch," Cooper says, meeting Alexander's gaze.

I join Alexander on the perch of the boat and we take our seats along its back edge. I watch as everyone else spreads out from lying on the side benches to the floor with the clean blankets and pillows from our backpacks.

Alexander and I sit with our backs pressing against each other so we can each watch a side of the ocean. On my side, there is an infinite stretch of calm seawater. On Alexander's side is Cinder's boat, and it looks like Cassandra and Essie are taking their first watch. We sit like this, soaking in the ocean breeze and silence until it seems like everyone has fallen back to sleep.

"What's your favorite color?" I ask Alexander.

I hear him huff a small laugh before responding, "Blue. What's yours?"

"Yellow," I say simply.

"What's your favorite animal?" Alexander asks.

"When I was growing up, I had a book of all these animals that lived in the world before the asteroid shower. The red panda was my favorite," I say, and the thought of the old book makes my chest feel heavy. I wonder if it's still buried deep in the drawers of my bedroom nightstand.

"So specific," he responds, and I feel his laugh shake against my back.

A smile falls across my face, and I can't help but laugh too, "You'll find that with me even the little things have a very specific and deeper meaning."

"So then why's your favorite color yellow?" he asks.

"Because my mother would always pick the yellow flowers around our house, and she would keep them in a vase inside. Yellow was her favorite color," I say, reliving the happy memories. "Why blue?" I ask him, wondering if he has a reason behind his favorite color as well.

"Because whenever life got hard, I'd always just look up into the sky and remind myself there was more out there than the awful cards I was dealt," he says.

We're quiet for a moment before I ask, trying to keep the conversation going, "So you like light blue?"

"Yes, light blue like the sky," he says.

"And what's your favorite animal?" I ask him.

"Birds," he says shortly.

"Any specific type of bird?" I ask, curious.

"Every once in a while I'd see a red cardinal fly by my bedroom window. Cardinals are my favorite because on this exotic island they seemed so out of place. The only explanation is that they've traveled here from another place on Earth. So, there is hope that there's more than just Garth on this planet," he explains. I shake my head. We're lucky these islands survived the asteroid shower, he shouldn't be hoping for the impossible. I've found though, with Alexander, he seems to always be hoping for the impossible.

"So then a lot of what you like has to tie into the fact that you just want to leave the life you had?" I ask for clarification.

"Basically," he says shortly.

"So then this whole journey is good for you?" I ask gently, noticing we are delving into much deeper waters.

"In a way," is all he offers to me.

"You don't have to explain," I say, letting the topic go.

Alexander turns from the side of the boat to face its front. I turn to face him, and he says, "I want to tell you."

"You can tell me if you want," I reassure him.

He pauses for a minute and places his arm around my back, and I let my head rest on his shoulder. The wind picks up a bit, and Alexander loosens his muscles against me. Whatever he wants to tell me he doesn't want the others on the boat to overhear, and the wind will cover his words. "My current mother and father, the one who traveled to Libertas with your father and worked with me in the prison, aren't my real parents," he says, his voice breaking as he speaks, and my heart hurts for him. I take my hand and grab his.

"Do you know who your real parents are?" I ask softly, my eyes dancing along the stars glistening in the water, not wanting to meet his eyes. I know this is hard for him, and he doesn't want me to see him upset. He's always tried to be strong and not let me see a weak side to him.

"Yeah, I do," he says and pauses, taking in a deep breath. "I'm King Renon's brother."

"What?" I whisper, shock running through me. I lift my head off his shoulder and look at him. "You're what?"

"I'm Renon's brother. When I was just a baby, Renon took me from the castle and left me in the woods to die. He didn't like the idea of sharing the royal title, so he got rid of me. My now mother and father found me wrapped in a blanket that was embroidered with my name and the royal family's markings. They brought me back with them and raised me as their own. When I was ten years old, and I went to work for Renon, my father told me the truth, and then my memories were blocked from me and your mother made me believe I was your childhood friend."

"So when we restored your memories, that was the last real thing you had from your life?" I whisper.

"Yeah, that's why I was in so much shock. I didn't know what to do. I've never had the time to process this because the moment I learned the truth, it was taken from me." He pauses and then continues, "So when you ask me if I think this journey is good for me, it really isn't me living a new life. Yes, meeting these new people is good for me, you are good for me, but I'm still Renon's brother on a journey where I am running for my life. Nothing about that is new for me."

"Does he know you're his brother?" I ask suddenly.

"I don't think so. There's no way he could know. I just think he wants me dead because I'm one of his guards and I betrayed him," he says. I know Alexander is right. They don't resemble each other in the slightest. Tears brim in his eyes and his hands shake.

"What is it?" I ask him.

"I'm sorry I didn't tell you this right away. I'm sorry I had such a hard time getting myself to tell you this. You think of me as this good guy who is just as innocent as you in all this mess, but I'm not. I come from such a dark and evil family," he says, tears running down his cheeks

I reach up and place a hand on his cheek, "Your family doesn't define you, Alexander. You are still a good person." I rest my forehead against his as he cries. "You are a good person."

When his tears have stopped coming, I move my head on his shoulder again. "I won't tell anyone. We can keep this between us."

"We need it to stay that way," he says, his voice broken.

Then after a long moment of silence, I finally say, "Alexander, can I ask you something?"

"I guess," Alexander replies, his voice a little hoarse.

"What's going on between us?" I ask, simply too tired to care anymore.

"What do you mean?" he asks.

"You know what I mean," I mutter, looking up into the sea of stars above us.

"Not really," Alexander pushes.

"All right, let me put it like this," I say. "I've never known who you were before this trip and now, suddenly you're with me every day, and while I still have the feeling we are strangers, there is something else here. Let's call it the endless feeling of butterflies I have when I'm with you."

I pause for a second before finishing, "I don't know Alexander. I feel like I like you more than just a friend or companion, but I don't know how you feel. I know you told me you feel protective over me, but I don't need another older brother," I say, glancing down at Cooper, still fast asleep. "And you told me that before you had your real memories back." I wait for Alexander to respond, but he doesn't so I push, "Can you please just tell me how you honestly feel about me?"

He's quiet for a moment longer. He rests his head onto mine and grabs my hand in his. "Let me put it this way," he starts, "Once upon a time, I was supposedly best friends with this girl when we were little. One day she gets thrown in prison, and me being the hero of the story, I go to her rescue to break her out of the prison. My plan to do this is by working in the castle. Unfortunately, it was going to be a lot harder to rescue her than I had thought.

So, I had to plan and wait for the right time. Well, me being the awful hero that I am, waited seven years to do anything. By this point, she had just rescued herself. When I met her again she wasn't a little girl anymore. Now she is this gorgeous woman who has had to go through so much pain, and the kicker is I don't even actually know her." He pauses again and I let his words crush against me before he clarifies, "but I want to know her. I want her to be a part of every day of my life. I just have this feeling we are supposed to be together." A smile falls across my face until he says, "But-"

I cut him off and say, "Oh can't you just let us enjoy this moment before the 'but'."

He laughs and pushes forward, "But I also know how much it would kill me if I let us get even closer, and then she's taken away from me. I'm afraid to let myself admit to loving her because once I do, there's no going back, and right now I'm not in a place where I'm secure enough to let myself truly love her."

We both fall silent after he says this because it's true. As much as I hate it, I know Alexander's right. I can't let myself care anymore for Alexander when I have to live a life not knowing if he'll even be here tomorrow. Instead, I'll just enjoy what we have while he is here. We stay silent, just enjoying being able to sit here together, but in the silence, my mind wanders. I start to analyze our relationship and how I feel about the cards life has dealt me.

If I had never left my cell that night, I never would have even known I had an older brother. I never would have gotten to see Zavy again. I never would get to have this connection with my father.

Before, he was just someone who had left me, but now, even though he is still gone, this journey was something he planned for me. So I feel this connection to him that I didn't have before. This doesn't mean I'm not still mad at him for leaving me. I still blame him for my mother and Titus dying, but at least now I know why. At least now I can connect to him and know what he was thinking when he made that decision, and I think knowing that will help me be able to let him go.

And Alexander. If I never left my cell that night I never would have met Alexander. His memories would never have returned. So many good and bad things have happened to me from meeting him. It's odd to think I can't even picture my life without him now. It's hard to believe that our relationship all originated from lies my mother had planted in our heads. We were given these false memories to allow us to trust one another, but what I'm sure no one expected was that we would still feel the same about each other after the false memories were gone and we got to create new, real ones together.

Some would say we're lucky. We get to fall in love with each other twice. I don't know if I'd say we were lucky. I think we got dealt with these cards and a lot of things could have gone wrong. Like incredibly and awfully wrong. I think each of us on our own walks through life with a tragic story. We are both broken and lost, but also hopeful and strong. And I think that's what it means to be in a twisted love. A love where you can be broken and strong at the same time. Where you can be lost in life, but hopeful that at the end of the day you will find your way. I don't think we are lucky. I think we are dangerous to each other because somehow we are both able to look at the other person, see their twisted life, see the warning signs, but still go hand in hand over the edge.

We aren't lucky. We're idiots. You go through this life destined for death. Smart people try to prolong that inevitable end. But idiots, see idiots can't understand the difference whether they die today or ten years from now. We are these idiots because we are so twisted in our broken, strong, lost, and hopeful mess that we can't see or comprehend the difference of dying today or years from now. So we look at each other and walk into the battlefield together with no protection and no weapons, but death will catch up to us. I would rather fall in love once and live out a long, happy, and simple life. Trust me. I think people who can accomplish that are truly the ones who are lucky.

People don't ask to be broken. We don't ask to be given the cards that will send us into a twisted life where we don't care if we die today or tomorrow. It's a tragic and dramatic life that is destined to have some highs but also to have some really low lows. So when you live this twisted life, you have to learn how to let the few highs balance out all the lows. It's tragic, sad, and dramatic, but it's mine. And it's Alexander's. With all the lows that come from loving someone as twisted as yourself, there are some beautiful highs that will keep you going.

So every time he breaks my heart when he tells me he has feelings for me, but the timing is wrong, I have the high of the comfort I feel when my hand is in his. From the lows I'll have when he can't talk to me about his past because it's hard, I will have the high of being able to look into those green eyes, knowing that I can trust them with my life. It's a crazy adventure, sure. It's up and down. It's tragic and sad, but it's also amazing and powerful. It's a bond I never would have been able to have if I wasn't here right now walking into this new life.

My past was a warm, sunny day all the time until the prison, and since then this new life has been a storm, and it changes day to day. Some days it sprinkles, and some days it pours. Some days it doesn't rain at all. It's just an eerie warm air that swallows me, and I live the entire day in fear of a storm that will eventually come. There's thunder and lighting, and it's dark. It's so dark all the time, but there are moments, specifically right after the worst storms, where the sun peeks through the clouds as it does in every storm. Just a glimpse of the light and those are the highs.

The highs. They don't last long, but the effect they have on you does. So you learn to enjoy the highs and to make them last as long as possible, but you also learn to love the rain. You learn to love the sound of it as it pours down on the rocks and the creek. You learn to love it like a song the clouds above are singing for you. And that's how you survive. In this hand of cards, you don't live. You survive. And I think that's been the hardest part of it all. To go from being a kid, living a safe and stable life, to being tragic, broken, and having to just simply survive. Just survive.

Chapter 24

After awhile Cooper wakes up and tells Alexander he should get some rest. Alexander doesn't argue, and as soon as his head hits the pillow he falls instantly asleep. I turn so that I can rest my back on the side of the boat and look out to the other side of the ocean. Cooper sits next to me, facing forward. I pull my knees up to my chest and wrap my arms around my knees as if I was just a little girl.

"Why's your hair cut like that?" I ask, looking closely at the intricate swirls cut into Cooper's hair.

"Why's your hair cut like that?" he shoots back to me.

I laugh and say, "Seriously, why'd you cut all the different swirls?"

"When you're put in a group of people who are all really the same as you, you have to find some way to show that you are more important then they are," he says.

"That's awful," I gawk at him.

He laughs and says, "I know," as he runs his hand through his hair. "I'm actually waiting for it to grow out."

"Why's it so important that Alexander and I get to Libertas?" I ask him flatly.

"What?" he says surprised.

"I know that father was the head person in charge of getting people out of Garth, and so if he says Adaline and Alexander better get brought to Libertas then it better get done, but this has turned into so much more than the regular trip to Libertas. Now these innocent kids have been dragged in, and Paylon and King Renon are coming for us, and it just seems that it's overly important we get to Libertas."

Cooper pauses before responding, "It's kind of complicated. I mean seven years have passed since they made a big deal out of getting you to Libertas, so things in Libertas might have changed. It may not be so important that you make it to Libertas. That's what still scares some of these people. They're banking on the fact that it's still incredibly important that you get there so that they can stay as a reward."

"But that doesn't tell me why it's important," I push.

"I can't say, Adaline," Cooper says sharply.

"Sorry I asked," I mumble.

"I just promised our father I wouldn't tell you in case we get there and things have changed," he mumbles.

"I understand," I agree. We stay quiet for a second longer until I ask, "What's going on with you?"

"What do you mean?" he asks.

"What happened with Paylon? You seem different since then," I say carefully.

"I'd thought I'd killed him," he says flatly.

"So you're upset you didn't kill him?" I ask.

"At first it was eating away at me that I had killed him," he says in an empty voice.

"It was self-defense," I cut in.

Cooper shakes his head no and says, "It doesn't matter Adaline. The feeling you get when you pull the life out of someone is something you can't shake by giving it an excuse."

"I know," I say as I remember the hallucinations I had when I'd killed Codian.

"The thing is, I was sure I had killed him, but now I come to learn that he's not dead. I don't feel relieved Adaline," he says, looking at me. "I wish I had killed him. Then, Sard would never have known we were there."

"We're out of Sard now," I say. "Paylon is the least of our worries."

He swallows, but the muscles in his neck stay tense. "Yeah, I guess you're right."

We let the sounds of the ocean surround us, and I look back out toward the horizon and can see hints of pink stretching into the sky. Mio wakes up and insists that I sleep for the few hours of the night that remains. I find an open spot on the floor of the boat and try to make myself comfortable. Even out here at sea, I keep my sword attached to my hip, just in case I need to draw it at a moment's notice.

I lay my head back on the pillow and look up into the night sky amazed that, if I could block out the sounds of the water, I could really be anywhere. I understand now what Alexander meant when he said that blue is his favorite color, so he can look to the sky and know that there is more to the world than this life. Looking up at this night sky I could be lying on the forest floor, looking out my old bedroom window, lying out in the field behind my house.

Somewhere someone is looking up at the same night sky as me, and while we may be a small dot in the center of the ocean, this night sky connects us with everyone else in the world. I drift to sleep consumed by thoughts of my mother, father, and Titus enjoying this night sky with me.

When I force myself to squint open my eyes I'm nearly blinded by the sunlight shining down on me. I sit up and look around the boat, which seems a lot smaller in the daylight. My face feels raw from the burning sun and my clothes are damp with sweat.

Most everyone is already awake and eating what must be our breakfast. I roll up my blanket and pack it with my pillow in my backpack.

I take a seat on the surrounding benches next to Molly and her friends. Cooper comes over and hands me a handful of berries that Kimberly had packed for us. He also hands me a handful of dry oats. When I pop some of the dry oats into my mouth I'm surprised by the sugary sensation that follows. I look down at the oats more closely and see that they have a glossy glaze on them.

"It's cereal," Molly says. "You eat it with milk." She holds up a little box that holds the white milk with her cereal floating inside.

Cooper returns to me with a similar box to Molly's and a spoon. "You open the carton like this," she instructs pealing back the tab on the carton. "Then you add your cereal and berries in." I do and watch the pieces float on top of the milk. "Then you use the spoon to eat it." She says as she fishes out a spoon full of her own cereal.

I lift my spoon and fish it through the milk to pick out the cereal and berries. "Thanks, Molly," I say and smile to her.

"I can't believe you've never had cereal before," she says in her light little kid voice. She finishes her cereal and looks up to me.

"I didn't grow up in Sard, so I don't know a lot of the things you probably do," I admit to her and she ponders this idea for a second.

"So you came from Garth?" she asks softly.

"I did," I tell her.

"Where are we going now, Adaline?" Molly asks me.

I realize that no one probably explained it to them. "There's an island out here called Libertas. My father organized this group of people to take me and my friend Alexander there before he," I stop myself still not fully able to talk about my father's death. Even though it has been seven years, I just found out days ago.

"Before he what?" Molly asks innocently.

"Before his ship crashed on his last trip," Cooper finishes, taking a seat next to me.

"And your mother?" Molly asks curiously.

"She passed too," I say.

"So we both don't have families," Molly mumbles, stirring her milk with her spoon.

I put my arm around her shoulder. Molly reminds me so much of Titus. They were about the same age and just as innocent in this world. She's surely much smarter than him, growing up in Sard. I know I couldn't save him and bring him to safety, but I can help Molly. "We're each other's family now," I tell Molly and I mean it. I'm going to protect her like I would have protected Titus, like I should have protected Titus. Molly smiles up to me and I say, "Here, I'll take your carton and throw it away." She hands it to me and I walk over to Mio who is sitting next to a large black bag.

"Adaline we need to talk," Mio says not looking up to me.

"What is it?" I ask, throwing my trash in the bag and taking a seat next to him.

He hesitates and says, "I can't promise those girls are going to get to stay with us in Libertas."

"What?" I ask shocked. Just seconds ago I promised her we were family and now Mio wants to tell me she won't get to stay in Libertas.

"I don't get to say who comes and goes to Libertas. When we get there I'm just another person without a gift that is trying to get in," Mio says tensely.

"Why is it so impossible for people without gifts to get into Libertas?" I ask.

"It's complicated. The main reason is Libertas is somewhere for people with gifts to go so they aren't taken in by King Renon. The rest of us don't really have that problem so we are expected to make it work back in Garth. Plus, if you let one person in you have to let them all in." Mio turns and scans Cinder's boat, taking in all the people who may be turned away.

"But it's important Alexander and I get there, right?" I ask, the gears starting to spin in my head.

"Yes," he says questioningly, wondering where I'm going with this.

"Then you all should get to stay as a form of gratitude for getting us there," I say simply.

"Those girls didn't help you get there," Mio says, meeting my eyes.

I look away and say strongly, "They wouldn't force children to go back without parents."

"You'd be surprised what some people are capable of," Mio says and stands. He walks to the center of the boat and draws all of our attention to him.

"We should be pulling into Libertas early tomorrow morning. If you're not Adaline or Alexander I need you all to line up so I can distribute some paperwork to you for applying to reside in Libertas."

"But Toby and I are gifted. Do we still need to fill out the paperwork? I thought this was a place for people with gifts," Zavy asks.

"You two weren't part of the original plan so yes you need to fill out the paperwork, but you will definitely be granted access. It's more of keeping track of who goes into Libertas." Zavy nods her head in response. Mio walks to the back of the boat and pulls out a grey binder from his bag with a black pouch, and everyone moves to line up to receive their paperwork. Mio begins to pull thick packets of paper from his binder and one by one each member of our group starts to fill out the papers that will determine their future.

Alexander and I move to the front of the boat to get out of the way. We sit side by side and look out into the horizon, the wind flipping pieces of my hair off my shoulder.

"I can't believe they aren't guaranteed access to Libertas," I mumble.

"Maybe they'll make an exception when we get there. This could just be a policy everyone has to follow," Alexander says.

"I don't know, I don't feel like this is going to end well," I say. I look over to the other boat and see that they are all filling out paperwork as well. I look back at our boat and see that Zavy is helping the younger girls fill out their paperwork since they can't read or write. I remember that Zavy has an enhanced sense of hearing, and more specifically is a Communicator. Her gift might not have been extremely helpful before, but now she's making good use of it. She still seems to struggle a bit with getting clear information from the girls, but she's getting better at it. I glance back at the other boat and notice Cinder is doing her best with May and April as well.

"None of these people have anywhere else to go," I say to no one in particular. Cooper comes up and sits next to Alexander and myself. "What kind of questions are they asking you on this paperwork?" I gaze over his papers.

"Just the basics. Our name, age, the date, if we have a gift or not, why we should be given access, how many others we arrived with, grades we got in school, previous jobs we've held. Kind of weird stuff to ask I guess," Cooper says and starts filling out the paperwork.

"Do you think Mio's right about not everyone getting to stay?" I ask Cooper.

"We'd be lucky if half of us get to stay," Cooper says sharply. I look away from him and let the chill of his words settle on me.

Half. We're at seventeen right now, not including Alexander and myself. Could I really cut that down to eight or nine? I take count of my traveling group again and feel nauseous at the idea of having to get rid of some of them.

"Who decides?" I ask Cooper and he looks off in the distance trying to process his next words.

"There's supposed to be a council that will review our answers," Cooper explains. He squints in the sunlight and looks to me. "I actually don't really know who will decide. I really don't have any idea what Libertas is even like." I nod, and as of right now I'm not getting the best first impression of the place we are hoping to find freedom at. They seem to isolate themselves and think that they are more deserving of a better life just because they have a gift. Life in Garth is awful whether or not you have a gift, because truthfully the King is watching us all in case we make one wrong move.

"Adaline and I will do everything we can to make sure you all get to stay," Alexander says over to Cooper. Cooper just nods his head as he continues working through his papers.

Again I put myself in the shoes of the council at Sard. Which eight would I be willing to let stay? The leaders of the group? Maybe the hunters that kept everyone fed? I understand what Mio meant when he said he was afraid the younger girls would be the first to get cut. What have they done to help get me to Libertas?

Abruptly I get up and walk over to Mio. "Do you have an extra application or paper?" I ask him and he tilts his head a bit confused.

"I do," he says and hands me a blank sheet of paper and pencil. I take them and return to Alexander and Cooper without giving Mio an explanation.

I list out all seventeen members of the traveling group, excluding Alexander and myself, and start to decide why they should get to stay. I go down the list to each person and write down what they did to help me get to Libertas. The council will have to hear my explanation as to how this trip went, and they will want to know who I think deserves to stay. So, I will be ready to fight for every single member here, because like I told Molly we are all family now. I'm not losing my new family. Not a single member will be shipped back to Dather. We will stick together because I can't bring myself to have to lose anyone else.

Chapter 25

"Would you and Alexander like to make yourselves useful and file these papers?" Mio asks, standing over us. Mio had been sailing our boat while the others worked on their paperwork. "Cooper, manage the sails this shift," he adds and turns to head back to the end of the ship. Alexander, Cooper, and I get up and follow him. Cooper heads to the upper level where the sails are controlled and we take a seat on either side of Mio. He pulls his black bag up onto his lap and hands us each a pile of yellow manila envelopes. "When someone finishes their papers place them in the envelope, seal it, and print their name on the front of it."

"All right," I say and look up to see that Mio has started to fill out his own paperwork. Not even Mio is guaranteed a place in Libertas.

"Mio," I start. He pauses from writing and looks at me. "I overheard you and Leo talking last night. What did he mean by Kimberly not wanting us there?"

"Well, when Leo and Kimberly were dating he didn't tell her he had the gift. He's able to make things appear invisible. He's a Vision Shifter, with an enhanced sense of sight." He clears his throat before continuing and I wonder how his brother got the gift but he didn't. "So when he finally told Kimberly about his gift it took her a long time to accept that. She knew that meant she'd have to live her entire life keeping this a secret and if it got out it would result in their deaths. When she finally came around to the idea I was just starting to work with your father. So she not only had to accept Leo's gift, but also housing runaways. As you can imagine this new life was far from anything she could have imagined."

"So Leo's gift was why the guard couldn't see us?" I ask.

"That would be correct," Mio says, writing in some more of the answers.

"So, your brother has the gift but you don't?" I ask Mio bluntly.

Mio lets out a dry laugh and says, "Please, don't remind me." I scan Mio's face and see his mouth set in a thin line. I imagine that was a constant topic the two argued about growing up.

"If Leo has the gift why doesn't he want to come to Libertas?" Alexander leans in and asks.

"It would mean he'd have to leave Kimberly behind," Mio says, still not looking up from his own paperwork.

"After all that she's done to help people get to Libertas, they won't let her in?" I ask.

"We've requested it many times before," Mio says, and disgust fills his voice. "I asked them to come again because I was hoping maybe this time things would be different, but Leo doesn't want to drag Kimberly out here again just to be turned away."

I'm silent for a moment as the realization that Libertas has turned away someone as significant as Kimberly in the past weighs on me. She's been helping people escape for years and she still hasn't earned her place.

"What did Leo mean when he said, 'They know'?" I ask, remembering that part of their conversation. Mio glances up at me and I know he's lightly scolding me for eavesdropping on him and his brother. A long silence follows and Mio doesn't answer. "Mio," I start to push.

"I'm not sure I should tell you this," he says, hesitating.

"What do you mean?" I ask in a broken voice because I can't believe no one will tell me when it seems to have everything to do with me.

"You and Alexander are very important to Libertas," he says, carefully thinking through each word.

"I've figured that much out," I say.

"Well, now we think King Renon figured it out as well," he says.

"Figured what out exactly?" Alexander asks. Mio starts to backtrack when Alexander pushes, "No, I want to know just what these people in Libertas are expecting from us."

Mio is quiet for a minute before letting out a long breath. "King Renon's family is known for not only having ruled in Dather but the very first ruler, his grandfather, was a future holder like his wife." Alexander tenses at the mention of his family's history. "His grandfather, King Lux, had many visions of disaster for his family in the distant future. To warn his later family he wrote his visions into a prophecy that has been attempted to be deciphered for years. The prophecy was simply titled *The Prophecy of Saviors*." He pauses and pulls out a worn piece of cloth from his bag. He hands it to me and I carefully unfold it. As my eyes gaze over the black ink Mio's voice reads aloud:

Related to me, you must read
A warning you see, pay attention to thee

Years will come, and years will go
Deep in the future, you must go
We rule with power and rule together
But one will ruin our family's honor

Again a warning I am sending
Pay attention, I am begging

They have value
Use them wisely
Keep them close, don't let them go
They hold the string that ties the nation closely

A warning has been noted
Your actions will not be forgotten

But if they go, and take the string
There may be hope for thee

A boy and a girl keep watch for them
They hold great power that can save our rem

Fate is set and can't be changed,
But think again my family's end

The boy and girl hold the key
Kill them off to guarantee
That life in Dather will always be
The way it was from sea to sea

Mio stays silent and lets Alexander and I digest the words. "That's supposed to be us?" I start. "Alexander and I are supposed to be this key?"

"Yes," Mio says shortly.

"With what proof?" Alexander huffs. "Just because our fates were tied? That could literally be anyone."

"Show me your arms," Mio says flatly.

"What?" I ask.

"Your right," he points to me. "And your left," and points to Alexander. "Put them out," Mio commands. Alexander and I both extend our arms to him. Mio reaches into his bag and pulls out a small brown bottle.

"Give me your other hand." We both put out our hands and he pours a white cream from the bottle into them. "Rub it into your forearm."

We begin to rub the warm cream into our forearms and are shocked by what's happening. A dark brown figure is starting to appear, spot by spot. I continue to apply the lotion until the entire image comes into view.

"A key," I say amazed. I examine the dark brown figure inked in my skin. It's not a perfect key. It's a bit abstract, but it's still obvious to me.

"You were both physically marked with the key when you were born. Your parents took it as a sign that you were the ones King Lux was writing about." I glance back up to Alexander and see his eyes are wide. Mio means his parents that he grew up with, but I know he's thinking of his real parents. They must have noticed the birthmark, what did they think of that? "They then took you both deep into the forest where wizardly magic is secretly practiced and had your birthmarks disguised until it was safe again to show them. I still probably shouldn't have told you this," Mio says, contemplating if he made the right choice.

"We should know what we're getting into," I begin to say and Mio shakes his head agreeing.

"I promised your father I'd let him tell you when we got to Libertas, but since he's gone I figure that promise doesn't stand," Mio takes in a deep breath and I see the weight this secret has had on him.

Alexander begins to speak, "How'd King Renon figure it out though?" His eyes scan my face. If King Renon knows that we are the keys in the prophecy, and he remembers his brother being marked, then King Renon knows Alexander is his brother now. Although, King Renon was only six when he abandoned Alexander in the forest, so I don't know how much he may remember about his little brother.

"Your guess is as good as mine, Alexander. I suppose he didn't want to take any chances. I mean, a female prisoner with her fate set to die and yours set to serve the castle is suddenly broken, it follows the prophecy loosely I suppose," Mio says, trying to make all the pieces fit.

"What is it talking about when it says 'they are valuable'? Who are they?" Alexander asks.

"People with gifts," Mio says and suddenly the prophecy begins to make sense to me.

"King Lux was trying to warn King Renon of letting people with gifts get out of Dather, but he took it the wrong way. He started to imprison them to keep them close, but that is what started the fire. Now people with gifts are fleeing from Dather, and this is going to lead to its destruction." I look up to Mio and see the answer on his face. "A rebellion."

"I think you're on to something," Mio says, staring back at me.

I keep working the prophecy aloud, "People with gifts are fleeing to Libertas to plan a rebellion against King Renon, and Alexander and I are the keys to the rebellion. If King Renon kills us the rebellion will die as well. That's why we are so important to both sides."

"It would seem so, wouldn't it?" Mio questions and I nod.

"We don't know the first thing about leading a rebellion," Alexander says shocked. I glance at him and agree. I don't know how to do anything except run. Alexander has had some training, but not enough to make him a leader of an army of gifted soldiers.

"Oh trust me, I know," Mio says sarcastically. "Not even with all the training in the world could you lead a rebellion. Your places in this rebellion are unknown. They know they need you, they just don't know what for."

Mio goes back to filling out his paperwork, and I continue to rub my fingers over my birthmark repeating the lines from the prophecy in my head, suddenly realizing we're in a much deeper hole than I could have ever imagined. The rest of the team on our boat has finished filling out their paperwork and one by one they bring us their packet of papers. Alexander and I take them, file the papers into their own yellow folders, and label them with their names.

"You're up again, Alexander," Cooper says, coming down from the sailing perch. "Keep us heading straight ahead, directly east."

Mio takes the folders from Alexander and I, and he files them back into his bag. I move with Alexander and we sit on the wooden level that stays clear for the one sailing or the lookouts at night. The small boat is starting to feel a little overwhelmingly full. Especially with nerves running high on who gets to stay in Libertas. "Want to teach me how to sail?" I ask as we sit on the rough wooden beams where we sat to take watch last night.

"It's easy now that we're going," Alexander starts and he points down to a bronze compass that is fitted into the control panel. "Just watch this needle to make sure we keep heading east." I note the needle wobbles around the curly printed *E* on the white background of the compass. It's much simpler than the one my father used to carry. "If it starts to shift too far from east you adjust your sail."

"Why would it shift?" I ask and realize it was probably a dumb question. If it was Alexander doesn't say so.

"Rough currents could pull us off course, or a strong wind," he begins to list off a few examples.

"So you have to be adaptable," I conclude, cutting him off. As Alexander nods a cool burst of wind sends the sail into frantic ripples. I tense and see the small arrow on the compass swing halfway to the *S*. Alexander remains calm and moves to the ropes at the edge of the platform. He unwraps them and repositions them so the needle sits steady on the *E* again.

"Want to try?" he asks over the wind and curiosity crawls across my skin. I don't know when I'd ever get the chance to again so I go and stand by his side. He hands the ropes to me and when I take them in my hands there's an instant force ripping me forward. "Pull back," Alexander instructs. He lets his right hand sit gently on the rope so he's there to take over, but still leaves me in control. My arms shake, but I manage to pull the rope back slowly. "Good, now anchor it there," he says and motions for me to tie the rope back down. Once I secure it I look down at my red palms.

"That wasn't so bad," I give a wide grin and breathe through my smile.

"You did good," Alexander says and we take our seats back on the rough wooden beams.

"Did you learn to sail when you worked for the castle?" I ask gently as I bring up something from his past.

Alexander gives a sharp nod. "When I was signed on officially we had to go through two weeks of intense training. The first week was spent in Garth. We became familiar with the different chambers in the castle and we searched through the small radius of the forest, looking for runaways."

"Like us," I joke and his lips crack into a smile.

"I never would have guessed I'd be on the other side of that," he says, processing the irony. "Then, week two we were in Sard. We got an overview tour of the city and the different jobs we may be assigned, and finally training in sailing. Not for combat, but to travel between islands."

"You've been to the other islands?" I ask and my eyes widen at the impossible thought, but Alexander shakes his head no.

"I've just sailed around Dather's coast. I could have been assigned to a troop that traveled between islands, but I was too new." I nod, remembering the guards from the night I escaped the castle. They had left Alexander alone on night duty outside the castle because he was the newbie. I realize how different this all would be if they hadn't done that.

"We're going to the best island now though," I offer and Alexander nods. Previously our only other islands were Sone, Hamni, and Garge, and all of them imprison the gifted just like Dather. Even worse, King Renon has them all sent to him so he can keep the other islands weak. So far they aren't used in Alignmass, the battles to obtain rule. This is where a nation's strength is decided. Men still believe one on one combat of skin and muscle should determine leadership.

Still, the regular soldiers of Dather beat any other islands' forces. For now, gifted are enslaved in Dather. Some are used for tracking, like the Hounds that worked with Paylon. Many are used for tasks around the castle and town. If we ever needed to protect ourselves from an invasion I'm sure they would be used then too, but that has never happened. No other island has ever challenged Dather in war. We win Alignmass fairly and continue to rule. We sit in silence, both examining the markings that weigh on our wrists. The thought of Libertas, a home for runaways, trying to start a rebellion against the largest force in the world seems idiotic, but when you have nothing to lose you're willing to risk it all.

Chapter 26

When Mio releases Alexander and takes the next turn at controlling the sails I move over and begin to help Cooper prepare lunch.

"What did Kimberly pack for lunch?" I ask, looking over Cooper's shoulder into the storage bins.

"Don't worry, it's nothing magnificent," Cooper mumbles pulling out a loaf of bread, thinly sliced meat, and yellow slices that I don't recognize.

"The bread looks funny," I say, taking it from him. "It's already sliced?"

"Yes, it makes preparing a sandwich much easier," Cooper says and he lays out our supplies.

"A what?" I ask.

Cooper begins to laugh at my confusion. He takes a piece of bread from the loaf and says, "Bread, meat, cheese," as he assembles the meal.

"You're telling me that's cheese? Everything in Sard is so different," I mumble.

Cooper finishes the sandwich by folding it in half. "Everyone line up to get lunch," Cooper announces. "Here," he says and hands me a slice of bread.

We both begin to assemble sandwiches and give everyone two of them. After everyone has received their lunch, we make ourselves some and eat in silence. The dry bread causes me to have to finish off what was left of my water. I begin to wipe the beading sweat off my forehead and realize I'm going to need more water soon.

"I'm sure Kimberly packed water, right?" I ask hesitantly.

"Of course," Cooper says. He reaches down into the bench and hands me a cool clear bottle.

"How's everything staying cold?" I ask, sipping on the icy cold water.

"We have coolers stored under the benches," he says and when he sees the confusion on my face he adds, "Just another one of Sard's weird inventions." I nod my head in response.

I look out at the sun glistening off the calm blue ripples of water. The boat bobs along slowly, just simply gliding into the infinity of blue. I imagine what the rest of today will be like. Maybe I'll help Alexander sail some more later. I'd like to talk with Molly, Lilly, and Sam to make sure they are doing all right. I can't imagine what they must be thinking, so much has changed for them in the last few days. I see that the other boat has finished filling out their papers as well. I assume Cinder helped Molly's other friends finish theirs.

Somewhere out here an island filled with gifted rises from these waters. I stare out into the thin horizon line and imagine it appearing before my eyes. My vision begins to blur in the bright sunlight and I almost miss a hint of a black figure coming up out of the water and then back into it. I blink hard and scan the distant waters again. "Cooper," I say. "I think I saw something," I hesitate, not sure if my eyes were playing tricks on me. Then, there it is again. It's a little closer this time, but I can't tell what it is. It just grazes the top of the water before diving deeper down. I turn and see Cooper saw it too.

I watch as Cooper's eyes widen, realizing what he just saw. "Mio," Cooper starts to say and suddenly the ocean begins to shift from its calm state into wild ripples.

"I figured they'd find us eventually," Mio says.

"Who?" I ask and I feel the adrenaline bleed into my veins.

"Remember how I told you the waters were cursed with enchanted creatures?" Cooper asks and I nod in response. "Well, they've found us." Just as the words leave his mouth there's a large thump on the side of the boat. I look over its edge and see a scaly body flopping through the water. It couldn't be any bigger than a snake.

"That can't be what you're afraid of," I say.

"Oh no, that's the baby. And where there's the baby." Cooper doesn't need to finish his sentence. The mother creature lurches out of the water, her body as round and wide as the tunnels we were in under Sard. She resembles something of an eel and lets out a low screech as she dives back into the water causing a large wave to crash against the boat, soaking us all.

"Everyone put these on!" Mio yells as he throws neon orange

vests to everyone. "It'll help you float if we go overboard." There's another thud against the bottom of the boat that launches me forward against Cooper, and we both crash to the bottom of the boat.

"Sorry," I mumble, rising to my knees. I wipe my soaked hair from my face and see that Cooper is bleeding from his forehead.

"It's okay," he starts to say until we are thrown down again by another thud. The eel continues to knock against the boat repeatedly sending it left and right, up and down.

"You're bleeding," I say. Cooper's hand wipes the red blood down the side of his face.

"I'm fine, I just hit it when we fell," Cooper mumbles and he tries to stand with wobbly legs. "Everyone, try to sit on the bottom of the boat. Get as close to the center as you can," Cooper commands over the screeching of the eels.

"The only thing we can do is wait them out," Mio huffs.

I crawl on my knees to the center of the boat next to Alexander. "Is there anything you can do with your gift?" Alexander asks me. I look out into the water and try to freeze the sea creatures, but as quickly as they come up they go back under and waves crash onto the boat.

"I can't," I say. "I can't see them so I can't control them!" I yell back to Alexander. Salty water launches at us, drenching us. The water is starting fill the boat. I try and use my gift to lift the water out of the boat, but it just rises and falls back on board. Slowly I'm able to splash some out, but not as quickly as the eels are sending it in.

Wave after wave, and after what seems like an eternity the water returns to its calm nature. We are all coughing up seawater and gasping for air; our hair and clothes soaked in saltwater.

"Are they gone?" Zavy bravely asks. I stand and look around. Somehow we have managed to stay close to Cinder's boat through the chaos.

"Mio," I say shocked by what I'm making out off in the distance. "What's that?" I ask and point out in front of me. It appears to be an island of some sort.

"Well, that's not Libertas," he says. "We must have been knocked off course, not really surprised though." When we finally get our breathing under control I see a large shadow begin to spread across the boat. I glance up and see the mother eel stretching into the sky.

"Watch out!" I hear Mio distantly yell. I watch, as if in a trance, her body crash down on Cinder's boat, completely demolishing the wooden frame. In the impact, another powerful wave is sent into our boat knocking as all to the ground. I pull myself to the edge of the boat and suck in deep breaths of salty air. I see three or four orange vests bobbing in the water, but there are many I can't find. The dark figure of the eel weaves under our boat and I look frantically around to see if there's anything we can use to stop this beast. My sword at my side is the only option I find so I draw it and watch the scaly body launch itself out of the water and over our boat in a clean arc. I swing my sword up and cut a giant gash in the creature. Dark red blood from the monster coats the boat and my sword, and it dives back into the safety of the water.

"What are you doing," Mio yells and grabs my wrist.

"Trying to stop this thing from attacking us. We can't sit here and do nothing," I scream back and rip my wrist from his grasp. I spin and scan the water, looking for the beast, and then the shadow crawls across the floor of the boat. I spin and see the eel tower up into the air. Before I can tell my arms to move and position for another attack the monster crashes into our boat causing it to crumble and suddenly I'm pulled underwater. Salty liquid engulfs me. My eyes burn and I fight the urge to scream or suck in a breath of water. My head is pushed back above water by the life vest and then pulled back under with the current.

I finally come up next to some debris from the boat and latch onto it, coughing up mouthfuls of saltwater. When I finally catch my breath I glance around at the disaster. Both boats have been completely destroyed, and now four or five eels are lashing in and out of the ocean. The water around us is dyed a dark crimson. Blood.

My eyes are scanning through the water, looking for Alexander. Suddenly someone surfaces next to me gasping for air, "Alexander!" I yell over the chaos, his green eyes lock with mine and he grabs onto the debris with me.

"We need to get out of here," he yells to me. I look back out to the island I'd spotted moments before.

"I could use my gift," I say and begin to work out a plan. "I can transport us to the island."

"But?" Alexander says, seeing the hesitation on my face.

"I'm not sure what'll happen when I do it. It knocked me out last time and paralyzed me. That was just the two of us, who knows what could happen now."

"I've got you," he says, grabbing my hand. I close my eyes tightly and start to picture everyone being put on the island. I run through the list of everyone in my head as I had seen them the night we were assigned our boats, careful not to forget any one: Cooper, Zavy, Toby, Mio, Cinder, Molly, April, May, Lilly, Sam, Essie, Cassandra, Sarah, James, Bren, Andy, Albert, Alexander, and finally myself.

Suddenly my world becomes deathly silent. A warm sensation is pressing against my cheek. I crack my eyes open and can see the stretch of white sand meeting the calm ocean water and then my world goes black.

Chapter 27

When I finally come to I flutter my eyelids open and a roof of green leaves hangs over me. My body is pushed into sandy dirt. I try to sit up, but find I can't. My breathing quickens when I realize I am unable to move any part of my body. I try to yell for help, but no words leave my mouth. Then Molly's young face comes into view above me.

"You're awake," she says and a soft smile falls across her face. Her cheeks look stained with tears and her eyes are red. "You guys, she's awake!" Molly yells. Suddenly Alexander and Cooper appear on either side of me. I feel Alexander take my hand in his and give me a tight squeeze. I urge my hand to squeeze back, but I'm unable to.

"It's okay," he says, noticing my panic when I still can't move. "Mio says you'll get back full mobility with a lot of rest," Alexander says.

"Just take it easy Adaline," Cooper says. I notice he has a damp white wrap around his forehead and I remember him hitting his head during the attack. "We've already had to resuscitate you twice. We were so close to losing you," he says with a tight voice.

Alexander finishes for him, "You were so weak you couldn't even keep your own heart going."

"But we saved you," Molly pipes in. "I'm your doctor for this shift, and I request much more rest so you'll have to visit later," she says looking between Cooper and Alexander.

Dark spots form in my sight and I can feel myself getting pulled back to sleep. I try as hard as I can to stay awake. I keep blinking, trying to clear the black dots that clutter my vision, but they continue to grow until my whole world is dark again.

"Adaline, wake up," I hear Alexander's voice say softly. My eyelids crack open and the rosy pink sky bleeds into view. "Guess who's your doctor now," he says with a light laugh to himself. "You need to get some water in you." He presses a water bottle against my cracked lips. Slowly I sip on the cool liquid, and then I hear Mio and Cooper yelling somewhere off in the distance.

"There's nothing on this island to eat!" Cooper yells at Mio.

"Well, I'm sorry she didn't think to bring some of our food when she zapped us here," Mio yells back.

"Not even Toby can find something here to get his hands on," Cooper mumbles.

"I can try to catch those birds again if you want," I hear Toby's childish voice say softly.

"No Toby, you tried your best. They need to stop pushing you so hard," Zavy's voice says sternly.

"It's a little chaotic here," Alexander's warm voice says, bringing me back to him. "Don't worry about it, you just need to rest," he finishes and pulls the bottle away from my lips.

I try to ask him how long I've been out, but find I am still inaudible. I try to move my arms or legs, but they are still frozen in place. I find that I'm able to twitch my fingers on my right hand and am relieved with this little sign of movement.

"That's a good start," Alexander says, looking at my progress.

I use my fingers to spell out *T.I.M.E* in the sand. He looks at it questioningly and then says, "You've been out since around noon, so it's been about 6 hours. Mio's hoping by tomorrow morning you'll be able to walk around." He pauses and shuffles around in his backpack, and I realize I must have pictured us all with them on when we were getting assigned boats. I remember using that memory to go through everyone who is here with us so I didn't forget anybody.

"This is all I really saved," he says, pulling out a small handful of berries. "You need them the most." Slowly, I'm able to chew the berries. "I'm not letting you go, okay?" his voice sounds small and weak.

I urge myself to tell him I'm going to be okay, but the more I push the more tired I get. I begin to get pulled back to sleep. The black specs start to fill my vision, and I yell at myself over and over again to stay awake.

"Stay," I hear my voice croak out.

Somewhere in the dark distance, I hear Alexander's voice say,

"Always." And that's the last thing I recall before I'm pulled back under.

When I wake again my vision is filled with darkness. I feel my fingers grip the sandy dirt as my heart quickens at the thought of being permanently blind. Carefully I push myself up onto my elbows and am relieved when I see glints of a fire in front of me. I look down to my left and see Alexander sleeping. It must be late at night because I can't make out anyone else moving around. Many people lay near the fire, but I assume Alexander refused to leave my side. I think Mio's dark figure sits against a tree down by the coast.

I stretch out my arms and am happy I'm able to move them again. I try to bend my legs, but find that they still can't move. I use my arms and pull my knees to my chest to stretch them out. I can't help but feel worry rise inside me at my limp legs. I have to keep reminding myself that it will get better. I will be all right.

I see Alexander's water bottle lying where he left it this afternoon. I sip on some of the water and debate about trying to force myself to try and stand or just go back to sleep. My mind tells me I really should try to sleep through the rest of the night, even though I'm not a bit tired. I lay back down next to Alexander and my mind plays out what little I know about the situation we are in now. Our boats were destroyed and I brought us to this deserted island that has no source of food. I'm not even sure they have found drinkable water yet. At the end of all these thoughts is one reoccurring regret. I never should have destroyed my mother's journal. She would have been able to warn us about the creatures. She may have known what I need to do now to help get my group to Libertas. She could have at least told me she loved me. Tears weld my eyes, and eventually I fall back to sleep with a hurting chest.

My mother comes into view. Brown and warm yellow hues start to paint themselves into a familiar picture. She's sitting in an old wooden chair. The rest of the room starts to fold into view, and I recognize it as my kitchen. My small little home on the edge of Garth. I spin around the room confused how I can be here seven years later. The door to my left creaks open and I watch nine-year-old me walk into the kitchen. I take a seat in the wooden chair across from my mother and see she is holding Titus in her arms. This is the night the guards came to get us.

"Is father home yet?" my little self asks her in a soft voice.

"Adaline, it's been three months. Your father isn't coming home," my mother says with no emotion in her voice.

I watch my younger self trace the circles on the wooden dining table. I miss that table. "Sometimes I think that's what you do in the middle of the night. You just sit up and wait for him." Little me pauses and a wall of silence settles between us, and young Adaline adds, "I wait up for him too."

"Well you shouldn't," I hear my mother say shortly. "And trust me, Adaline, I'm not waiting for him." She's about to get up from the table and take Titus to her room. I remember this night so clearly. I have to warn them, they need to run.

"Mother!" I say to her, but she doesn't hear me. She stands and turns to go into her room. I run in front of her and yell, "Stop! The guards are coming. Mother, they're coming! We have to leave, please. Please leave tonight, don't let them take us."

For a moment I think she sees me. Her blue eyes look at mine. She knows. I can see it on her face now. She knew they were coming. She wasn't waiting up for my father to come home, she was waiting up to see if tonight was the night the guards would come for us.

She walks right through me, and into her bedroom to lay Titus back down. Then she comes back to the kitchen to get younger me and leads her back to my room.

"You can't do this," I say to her and follow her into my room. The floorboards squeak under my feet. The same little floorboard at the edge of my bed. It always squeaked. I used to hide trinkets under it.

"We can make it mother. We can go on our own to Libertas. Please mother," I keep begging her, tears streaming down my cheeks, but she still doesn't hear me. She tucks the blanket around young me and kisses my forehead before turning and leaving. I follow her back out into the kitchen and in a broken voice I say, "Mother, please."

I watch my mother pause in front of me. She turns and looks at me. "I'm sorry, Adaline," she says, and then she starts to walk into her room. I hear the thud on the door of the guards, and then the dream slips away.

"Morning," I hear Cooper's voice say when I open my eyes again. The morning light shines through the branches. "Sleep well?" he asks, taking a seat next to me.

The dream of the night I was taken to the prison leaves me feeling a bit nauseous. I push myself up into a sitting position and lie, "You could say that." And am surprised to find myself able to talk again.

He hands me some cooked meat and berries and I take them graciously. "Have some breakfast," Cooper says.

"What's this?" I ask as I chew on the unfamiliar meat, remembering what Mio and Cooper had been arguing about yesterday.

"It's some kind of groundhog that burrows deep in the sand. That's why we couldn't find anything yesterday, we were looking in the wrong places." I nod my head in response and finish eating. Cooper hands me a water bottle and I carefully sip on it trying to saver the water.

"Have you found freshwater?" I ask, knowing we can only go so long without it, and I don't remember bringing it here with us. Based on Cooper's facial expression I know my worst fears are true.

"No, we haven't yet. Some of us are going to walk through the island later to look," Cooper says.

"Can I come?" I ask, excited to move around again.

"If you're up to it. Alexander, Zavy, and I were about to go," Cooper stands and pulls me to my feet. I stretch out my legs and walk around. "Good?" Cooper asks.

"Yep, good as new," I say. It's not entirely true, but I'll say anything to do more than lay in the sand.

"Come on," Cooper says and I follow him across the clearing we're in. I look around, taking in the area for the first time. They've set up camp on a clearing that meets the sand and stretches out to the ocean, I think that camp is empty until I notice Bren sitting against a tree in one of the few shaded spots. His leg is wrapped in a dark red fabric that I realize used to be white.

"Bren, are you okay?" I ask and kneel at his side. He tosses his head in my direction and I see how pale he is.

"Fine," he chokes out in a weak voice.

"I wanted to tell you later," Cooper starts and leads me away from Bren.

"Tell me what?" I ask, glancing over my shoulder back to Bren. "Why are you pulling me away?" I stop and free myself from Cooper's grasp.

"He lost his foot in the attack," Cooper whispers harshly in my ear. "Essie says he's losing a lot of blood and probably won't make it much longer."

"Well, we have to do something!" I scream and Cooper motions for me to quiet myself.

"Bren asked us to leave him alone. There's nothing we can do for him here except try and get him to Libertas as quickly as possible," Cooper explains to me. "We are working as quickly as we can to collect enough supplies to take with us to survive the last part of the journey. Until then, Bren asked to be alone."

"He's just going to sit there until we are ready to leave?" I ask bewildered.

"Adaline, you have no idea what we went through yesterday when we got to this island," Cooper says, and we start walking along the coastline again. "Between Bren's foot and your failing heart we've had our hands full trying to keep what's left of this group together."

"What do you mean 'what's left'?" I ask Cooper.

Cooper stops again and drops his head. "Not everyone made it," Cooper says almost inaudibly as he looks back up to me.

"What do you mean?" I ask again, my voice cracking.

"We lost a lot of people when we were attacked at sea," Cooper starts to say, but I cut him off.

"That's impossible. I made sure I got everyone here." My mind searches for the memory of the battle, confirming I had remembered everyone.

"You did Adaline. Everyone made it here, but some of them were already gone when you moved us," Cooper says, choosing his words carefully.

"What?" I ask, not wanting him to sidestep anything with me. "Stop trying to talk around what happened," I say harshly to him.

"They drowned, Adaline," Cooper says flatly and meets my eyes. "Some of them drowned, those who were the most unlucky were torn to shreds by those creatures." When Cooper says this I'm reminded of the dark crimson water before I had moved us. I feel the blood drain from my face and a cool sweat bleeds on my neck.

"Who?" I ask, my voice shaking.

"All of the younger girls Molly was with," Cooper starts to say. My heart seems to have stopped beating in my chest. My hands shake and I struggle to breathe. I remember when I first came to and Molly had looked so sad. Cooper continues to list people, "Essie's sisters Cassandra and Sarah, and Albert's brother Andy." Cooper pauses and then finishes, "We lost 7 Adaline."

"Why didn't you tell me?" I ask.

"Mio wanted you to rest, I'm sorry," Cooper says, and then moves in to hug me. I fall into my older brother's arms.

"I just feel like I'm missing a piece of me," I say to him when we pull a part. "I didn't know a lot of them, but they spent seven years of their life sitting in the woods waiting for me, to help me get to Libertas. It was all for nothing. They'll never get to live in Libertas," I say as more and more pain washes over me. "They died helping me," I say more to myself than Cooper, and then I realize how many people have died because of me, because of this journey. I remember sitting on the boat yesterday morning wondering which members I would cut when we got to Libertas, and am sickened by the thought that the universe decided it for me.

"They chose this path Adaline. We won't let them be forgotten, okay?" Cooper says and I nod. Cooper clears his throat before adding, "There's something else." I hear his voice tighten in his throat. I can't get myself to speak so he continues. "Molly is starting to get sick." My mind races and words fumble on the edge of my tongue. Inaudible words break in my throat and Cooper tries to calm me down. "She's fine, Adaline. Essie has been keeping an eye on her. She just says her throat is sore and she's more tired than usual." Cooper's explanation does little to calm me. I've seen enough people die in the prison from what started as a small cold. If it's untreated it can get out of hand fast. Cooper knows this and says, "We're keeping a close eye on her." I give a forceful nod and we continue to walk down the coast.

I see Albert is walking along the shore pulling up wooden pieces of our boats that have floated to shore. "He's hoping he can somehow put the boats back together, but he knows it's going to take more than just labor. He's going to need your help," Cooper says and meets my eyes. "But not until you feel that you are strong enough to use your gift," he quickly adds.

"I don't feel weak actually," I add. "I mean I've literally been resting for almost 24 hours, not doing anything. I'm definitely getting stronger with it." I look out at where Albert is sitting on the beach waiting for the rest of the boat to wash in. I can see the pieces of wood bobbing around in the waters. I watch as I wash them into shore. Albert runs out and scoops them up and looks over to me. "It's like it can recharge itself, if that makes any sense," I say back to Cooper.

"Well I would save it up for when we need you to magically build us some boats," Cooper says flatly. We continue down the coast between the sand and line of trees when I see Zavy and Alexander up ahead. At the sight of me, I see the muscles in Alexander relax. He's been worrying himself sick over me and I can tell he's gotten very minimal sleep.

"Glad to see you're on your feet again," Zavy says and embraces me in a tight hug. "Have I thanked you yet for saving my life once again?" she adds.

"You don't have to thank me. Anyone would have done it. We're all in this mess together," I say tightly.

"Where's Toby?" I ask her and before I can fear the worst she smiles softly.

"He's helping James hunt some more," Zavy says. "You were smart to picture us the night we left Leo's because we have what little weapons and hunting gear still with us." I nod agreeing that what we have is minimal but better than nothing.

"We did lose the spears in the crash though. We tried to repair them, but the bow and arrows work better anyway," Cooper adds.

I move and hug Alexander and he whispers into my ear, "Thank goodness you're okay, Adaline."

"You can't get rid of me that easy," I say back lightly. Since our talk on the boat the first night everything with him seems to finally be like it's supposed to be. The awkward heavy air is long gone and I feel as though we are working toward a true, genuine relationship. Though I know it's unlikely to become anything more soon, at least I have him as my friend. At least I have someone I can trust and depend on.

"Cooper, did you tell her?" Alexander asks and I nod. "I'm sorry, Adaline. I wish we could've saved everyone."

I just nod because nothing we say will bring them back. It's sad to say it, but I'm starting to get used to losing people. People are in my life and then they're gone, and it seems to get easier and easier to just let them go. I turn to Cooper and ask, "So do you know where we are going?"

"Not at all. Instinct tells me there's got to be some kind of river or freshwater source running on this island, we just have to find it," Cooper responds, and with that, we all turn and head deeper into the forest.

Chapter 28

"I think I can see a clearing up ahead. We can break there," Cooper says from the front of our line. We've been hiking through tangled vines all morning and it has to be nearly noon. We are all dripping in sweat and are parched, but we are far too scared to take a sip of what little water we have left. This island seems to be much more humid than Dather. The air is extremely thick and my clothes are soaked.

Cooper continues to swing his sword in and out of vines to clear a path for us to walk. Finally, he slashes the last few out of our way and we step into a clearing. We all freeze and scan the area at what lies ahead of us. None of us say a word to the others, and an eerie silence falls over the island.

Scattered in rows across the clearing are large and small boulders that almost appear to be headstones as if this were some kind of graveyard. Finally, Zavy speaks up and asks, "What is this place?"

"It looks like a graveyard," I say, admitting my first impression of the clearing. I walk to the nearest boulder and kneel next to it. Alexander, Zavy, and Cooper follow and kneel next to me. I take my hand and brush away the vines and moss that are suffocating the stone. *Martin Core* is jaggedly carved into the rock. There's some kind of symbol sketched under his name, and it takes me a second to recognize it as the symbol for a gifted with an enhanced sense of touch.

"I don't understand. All of these people died here?" Zavy asks to no one in particular.

"I think there's something more to who these people are," Cooper says in a low voice. He stands and moves to the next boulder and brushes away its overgrown vines and says, "Sarah Temp, she had an enhanced sense of hearing."

"Thomas Shepard, enhanced sense of sight," Alexander says as he kneels at another rock.

I stand and walk through all the rows of boulders and glance over them. "They all have symbols of gifts on them," I say and I try to work out the details in my head.

"I thought Libertas was where everyone with gifts went," Zavy says confused, and then asks, "Are we sure this isn't Libertas?"

"Are we too late?" I ask. I turn and see the shock set on Cooper and Alexander's faces.

"This doesn't make sense, our father planned for us to come in seven years. We aren't late. We are right on time. This doesn't add up," Copper says.

"Then what is this place?" Alexander asks the open-ended question that we can't find an answer for.

"These markings look older than seven years," I add and run my hand over one of them. "These look like they've been here for decades."

"I think you're right," Alexander adds. I watch as he places his hands on the stone. "I'll try to use my gift to pull some information," he starts to say, but suddenly there's the sound of a branch snapping off to our left where we entered the clearing.

"What was that?" Zavy asks in a low voice and takes my hand in hers.

"Who's there?" Cooper yells and him and Alexander both draw their swords. Suddenly, there's another snap to our right and then another and another all coming from different directions.

"We're surrounded," I say.

"Who's there?" Cooper yells again, but there's no response.

We all stand completely still, and the world falls back into silence. Just when I'm about to say that we should go back to the camp a large vine shoots out of the woods and twists itself around Alexander's wrist.

"Alexander!" I yell and run to him, but before I can get to him a large green vine has wrapped itself around my waist. "Cooper! Help!" I shriek and watch as he runs toward me with his sword, but it's no use. Another green vine comes in and twists itself around Cooper's ankles and pulls him to the ground.

"What's going on? It's like they have a mind of their own!" I yell out to the group. Zavy runs over to Cooper and takes his sword from his hands. "Zavy, look out!" I yell at her. She whips around and slices through the vine just as it lurches out to her. She makes awkward stiff swings with the sword, showing she's clearly more comfortable with her old bow and arrow. I try to wiggle free from the vine that has wrapped itself tightly around my waist, but the more I fight it the tighter it squeezes.

Zavy starts running to me with the sword to cut me free, but as she raises the sword I watch another vine lurch out and twist itself around her wrists. "Don't fight it, it just holds on tighter," I say to them, but instinct has taken over and everyone is twisting and trying to pull their way free. The vines start to drag all of us in separate directions into the woods.

"What are we supposed to do!" I hear Zavy yell, and before I can answer, a figure jumps into the circle. Her long golden hair peeks through the hood of her cloak. She pulls a long sword out from her cloak and starts slicing into any vine that launches out to her.

The vines around my waist begin to weaken their grip and eventually drop me to the ground. I gasp for air and try to fill my crushed lungs. Once I've gotten enough air into my lungs I race across the clearing, pull out my own sword, and back up the mysterious woman.

We slice our swords through every green image that falls into our path. I start to lose a grip on my mind and become completely engulfed in the battle. Vine after vine drops limply to the ground. My blood pulses through my body and my movements come in flashes. I never fully think of what to do, I just do it. At every flash of the green vines, my sword meets them instantly. Finally, the mystery woman says, "I think they've stopped." I drop my arm with the sword to my side and take in deep breaths to slow my heart rate.

"Alexander," I say and run to him as he is dropped from the vine's grasp. "Are you okay?"

"Yeah, I'm fine," he says and rubs his wrists. "Where'd you learn to fight like that?" he asks me.

"I don't know. I've never even used this thing before without also using my gift," I say, looking down to the sword and realizing for the first time that I actually didn't use my gift. "That's weird, my gift is always my first instinct," I say.

"You didn't use your gift because you can't use it against these vines," the woman's warm voice says to me. She turns to face Alexander and I, and for a moment we just look into her dark shaded face. Then, she takes her hand and brushes back her hood.

Her blonde hair blows back and her frail face comes into view. Her hazel eyes shine in the sunlight. "Mother?" Alexander asks, his voice cracking. Tears are in the woman's eyes and Alexander leaps off the ground and throws his arms around the woman's neck. "Is that really you?" he says between sobs.

"It's me. It's really me," the woman says into his shoulder.

Chapter 29

I can feel my own tears starting to fill my eyes because I can only imagine how happy he must feel to have her back in his life. Alexander's mother breaks away from him and says, "It's good to see some familiar faces." She glances between Cooper and Alexander.

When she gets to me she pauses and says, "Adaline, it is so good to see you." She embraces me in a tight hug, and even though I truly don't know who she is I feel as though I have known her my whole life. She just seems to be one of those people who are so welcoming to others. I can already tell she is so selfless and caring of not just her own family, but also everyone she comes in contact with.

"Marin, we need some answers," I say to her as I pull away.

"I know," she says and then continues, "I need some answers myself. I can start by telling you all that I know, but first I want to know what you guys are doing out here."

"The eels attacked our boat on the way to Libertas," Cooper explains and Marin nods, seeming to understand. "Adaline got us out of the destruction and brought us here. We've been here almost two days now."

"Did you all make it?" Marin asks her question innocently.

"We lost seven. Four you didn't know, we picked them up in Sard," Cooper says. "Cassandra, Sarah, and Andy didn't make it either."

"I'm sorry, we knew this trip would be dangerous," Marin begins to say, but Cooper cuts her off.

"Marin, it's all right. Everyone knew the stakes when we signed up," Cooper says.

"We've been looking for freshwater. We are running dangerously low," Zavy says after a moment of silence, and then adds, "You must know where some is, right?"

"I do," Marin says in her strong voice, pulling her mind away from the deaths of the kids she left behind, and then explains, "I built my camp near a creek that runs through the island. I'll take you there." She places her sword back in her cloak and starts taking large strides back toward the woods. We all run and fall into step with her and then she starts telling us her story.

"I'm sure that Cooper has told you all that he knows about the night that we brought everyone out into the woods, so I'll just pick up from when we left the camp," Marin says. "After we left you with Mio and Cinder, your father, Derith," she says, looking between Cooper and myself, pausing for a second, "and I headed deeper into the woods for Sard.

We got there without any trouble, and Leo had us on a boat in no time. Derith seemed oddly off the next day and I couldn't figure out why he was like that, but when we were just a couple of hours or so from the shore of Libertas the creatures in the sea attacked our boat. Part of me thinks that Derith knew they were coming, and that's why he was so on edge the entire time." I nod, not completely surprised. According to Cooper, he was a Future Holder and probably did know they were coming.

Marin continues explaining, "For awhile we managed to stay on the boat and keep everything in one piece, but that didn't last long. The moment the creatures snapped our boat in half I was knocked unconscious and I can't remember a thing. When I woke up I was on this island."

"We heard about the crash," Cooper says and I watch him pull out my father's compass that he had shown me. "We found this washed up with the debris from your boat."

Marin takes the old compass and her face sets in a soft smile before she hands it back to Cooper. "He wouldn't go anywhere without that thing," Marin says. "There was no one else here on the island with me, trust me I've walked every inch of this place. I had no way out of here so I've just been trapped here for seven years. Now it's starting to make sense why Derith was so on edge and wouldn't tell me why. He probably saw that you all would end up here on your journey to Libertas and he needed someone to be here when you arrived. I wish he just would've told me he needed me to stay here, but to be honest if he'd asked I would have said no. This island isn't exactly the number one place for a vacation," Marin says as she begins to make the pieces fit on her end.

"What is this place?" I ask Marin, curious about what exactly those vines really are.

"This used to be Libertas," Marin starts explaining. "Those people who are buried back there are the very first generation of people who had fled from the Kings of Dather to save themselves. The problem was, when they died and were buried, their body decomposed and the atomic matter that was in their bloodstreams, what gave them their gifts, was absorbed into the island. This caused the island to literally come to life.

That's why those vines seemed to have a mind of their own because they kind of do. At this point, the people who lived here started to understand what was happening to their island, and so they were forced to flee and find a new place to colonize which is where the current Libertas is located."

"I don't think I realized how long people have been fleeing from Garth," I say, processing the information.

"How have you managed to live out here?" Alexander asks, concerned.

"I did just that, I managed. I only took what I needed from the island and nothing more. They're very smart in that way. You try to use your gift to control them but then they use their gifts to control you. It starts to cancel itself out." Marin finishes and pushes hanging debris out of the way before walking into a large clearing. There's what must be Marin's shelter near some trees. She's managed to drape branches over each other to make a roof, and there's a quiet stream of water running along the side of the clearing.

"You can fill up your water here," Marin says to us, and we each reach for our backpacks and pull out a couple dozen empty water bottles that we had brought from camp. I can tell Marin is doing the math with the water bottles and how many people she'd left in the forest seven years ago.

"We've picked up a couple of people along the way," I say to her. My heart drops, remembering seven of them are no longer with us.

She nods her head sharply and says, "I figured as much when I saw Zavy with you." We walk over to the creek and dip in each bottle one at a time, letting the cool water run into the bottle and over our dirty fingers.

"Have you found a source of food?" Marin asks and I watch as she rolls up her belongings and packs them in her backpack.

"Yes, we found what appears to be a groundhog. It's a different kind of meat, but better than nothing," Cooper says.

"It's the only thing on this island I've found that's safe to eat also," Marin adds zipping her bag and coming over to help us fill the last of our water bottles.

"How'd you find us?" Zavy asks as she finishes up filling the last of her bottles.

"I was heading that way to do some hunting when I heard you all screaming," Marin explains. She adds, "I assume you all have some sort of plan or way to get off this island then?"

"Well, we have pieces of our boat that we can put back together, but I don't think we really know where we are going anymore. How far off course is this island? Do you even know?" I ask Marin.

"We are less than a day's trip from Libertas. It's directly east of the island. If we leave tonight we will be there by morning," Marin says, handing me the last of the now full water bottles.

"Well, then we should go back and tell Mio now! The sooner we get off this island the better. I don't know how much longer this island is going to allow us to stay here anyway," Zavy says, flinging her backpack over her shoulder.

"Slow down there, Zavy," Cooper says. He walks over and clips an additional water bottle to her bag. "Some of us are still recovering."

"You can recover on the boat," she shoots back at him and starts marching back into the woods.

"She's right Cooper. If we hurry we may get Bren to Libertas before it's too late," I say.

"What's wrong with Bren?" Marin asks, and I'm sure she's picturing the ten-year-old boy she left in the woods years ago.

"He was injured in the attack, and we aren't sure he'll make it without professional medical attention," Alexander explains and Marin nods.

"Then let's move a little quicker," Marin agrees, not wanting to lose any more of the kids she left behind. Without another word, we begin to file after Zavy and back through the woods toward our camp.

Marin falls in step with Alexander and myself and asks with a stone voice, "Alexander, did your father make it out of the castle?"

"He did," Alexander says in a shallow voice.

"And he found you guys?" Marin asks and nods up toward Cooper.

Alexander squints his eyes in confusion. "No, I haven't seen him since he left the castle."

Marin drops her head and says, "I was afraid of that."

"What are you talking about? Did he see something in the future?" Alexander starts to ramble off questions.

"He told me he wouldn't see me again the night I left," Marin says softly. "I just thought maybe it still would work out."

Alexander reaches into his bag quickly and hands Marin the tattered piece of cloth. I don't have to ask to know that it's the note his father had left for him. "Can you explain this then? He said he would see me."

"Alexander," Marin says and I watch as she transforms her emotions back into her stone front. She hands Alexander the note back and says, "The future changes in seconds. Every little thing changes the outcomes Future Holders see. George knew the plan, he knew where he needed to go." Alexander takes the note back from his mother and places it in his bag. He doesn't seem to get caught up on the fact that his mother is telling him his father must be dead. Alexander is in denial, and I understand the feeling.

"What gift do you have?" Alexander asks his mother, trying to change the subject. Cooper already told us she had an enhanced sense of touch, but I know Alexander wants to hear it from her.

"I'm a sensor," she says and nudges Alexander. "Just like you." Alexander gives a small smile, but the comment, I'm sure, just reminds Alexander that Marin is not his real mother. He didn't get this gift from her. Marin knows that, but I wonder if she knows that Alexander knows the truth. His father had told him the truth when they worked in the castle, but Marin was long gone before then. She must not know she doesn't have to keep this secret from him anymore. I'm debating about catching Marin up when she says, "I'm so sorry we had to leave you. You can't possibly think that it was something we did lightly." Marin's face tenses and I can see the regret in her eyes.

"I know. I just wish we could get that time back, you know?" he asks softly

"I know, Alexander. I'll make it up to you. I promise." We are silent for a second until Marin suddenly asks, "Your memories? Are they fixed?" Alexander and I both shake our heads yes and Marin adds, "That's good. How's your mother Adaline?" I look up to her as if what she was asking was a joke, but I can see the sincere concern on her face. She must have no idea what has happened to her, just like Cooper hadn't known.

"She's dead," I say weakly.

"What?" Marin asks, horror spreading across her face.

"We were thrown in prison after my father left us. Seven years passed and on Parting Day she was taken away to be executed. When they executed my mother Titus and I took the opportunity to try to escape, but when we tried Titus was killed. I broke out of the castle that night and ran into Alexander, and you know the story from there."

"I had no idea, Adaline. Derith never told me that your mother and little brother would die," Marin says in a weak voice.

"I don't think he knew," I say softly, trying to believe that my father wouldn't send us all to prison knowing we were going to die. "But I think my mother knew," I add. I pause and then ask, "What do you think happened to my father? You washed up here, but could he have survived?" The question makes my stomach turn in knots. I wish I would stop asking if he was alive, because I know deep down he's not.

She's quiet for a second before saying, "Adaline there's no way he would have survived that. When the creatures attacked us we were completely knocked off course. I was washed up here, but simply by luck because we were so close to the island when the boat finally gave in. Libertas would be much too far away to drift to. I've had to accept that for a long time, Adaline."

"I've had to accept he was dead a long time ago too, Marin. It just never seems real," I add. We are all quiet for a moment longer until we come through the edge of the woods and our feet sink into the sandy beach as we walk into our camp. There's so much more we need to discuss with Marin, but I see that what's left of our travel group has started packing up. Mio must want to move soon.

"Man is it good to be back," Marin yells out, and Mio turns to meet her eyes.

"Marin?" Mio exclaims, shocked to see her.

"I know, not exactly the place you thought you'd find me." Marin approaches her old friend and adds, "I'll explain everything, but first let's get this boat together so we can get out of here."

"About that," Mio says and the happiness he had to see Marin washes away.

"What is it?" Cooper asks him. Mio takes in a short breath and before he can say anything I notice Molly crying by Bren's side. We push past Mio and make our way to Bren, but Cinder steps in our path.

"Cinder, please tell me he's okay," Cooper says, and I watch as my brother starts breaking down.

"He's gone," Cinder says softly. Cooper lets out a muffled cry and pushes around her. He collapses in the sand by Bren's side, and I watch as he shakes with sobs. I feel frozen in the sand, tied down in this spot. If I walk up there and see him then it's real. If I stay here then it's not.

Slowly Zavy, Mio, and Marin make their way to Bren's side, but I stay put. Alexander puts a strong arm on my shoulder and helps me move forward. Through a pool of tears in my eyes, I make out the boy's ghost of a body sitting in the shade of the tree where we left him.

Cooper continues to sob and my heart breaks for my brother. They must have been so close. You spend seven years living with someone that closely you're bound to grow a strong relationship. Toby comes to Zavy's side and he leans against her. All of us circle Bren and silently say our goodbyes to him. Most of us are quiet, but Cooper's sobs have grown more powerful and he throws his fists into the sand and lets out a yell of rage.

"Cooper," Cinder's soft voice tries to calm him.

"This isn't fair!" he yells defensively. "We can't keep losing people. I don't want to lose anyone else!" He pushes out of the group and makes his way to the edge of the water. I watch as he kneels into the shallow waters and I see him shift his anger back to sadness. I look to Bren one last time and whisper a small goodbye in my head. I add his name to the list of those who have died either at my hand or because of me indirectly.

"We'll bury him before we leave?" Molly asks in her smallest voice.

"We'll bury him with the others," Cinder says, and that's when I notice the heaps of unpacked dirt a few paces back in the woods. The rest of our team lies buried there. Mio moves to grab a shovel, but I pull up the dirt with my gift. James and Albert carefully lay him in the earth and we all help in burying him. Mio goes to Cooper to see if he wants to say goodbye, but Cooper says he's said all he needs to.

Most people wander back to cleaning up their belongings to get ready for our departure, but I sit with the dead a little longer. Just like that, in a matter of 24 hours, we lost half of our team. Everyone else has had time to say goodbye to the other members, but I haven't yet. So I take a moment to go to each mound of dirt and say a soft goodbye to each of them. I thank them for their efforts in trying to help me. I apologize that my father brought them into this mess, and I cry for each one of them.

Chapter 30

I follow Albert out to the shore where he has started to lay out the pieces of our boats. There's a pile of cracked and soaked wood along with one torn black sail. I notice we are without a motor and realize, even though we are close to Libertas, it will be harder to get there without assistance from the motor.

It's odd to see Albert without his brother. My heart aches for him, and I wish there was something I could do. I know how it feels to lose family. Albert is putting up a strong front though, and I wouldn't expect anything less.

"This is all I found," Albert says, and I can tell he's hoping I can perform some sort of miracle. I see that there's only enough wood for probably one boat. With only 11 people left, 12 now that Marin has joined us, it'll have to do.

I take pieces of the boat and line them up with each other. When I start to get the pieces to fit I watch as the cracked pieces become one whole piece again, and eventually, a brand new boat sits in front of us. It's one of the best things I've been able to do with my gift. I'm starting to figure it out, slowly but surely. I start to feel lightheaded, and I feel Albert grab my side and lower me into the sand.

"Are you okay?" Albert asks.

"Yeah, I'm fine," I say and rub my eyes until my brain clears again. "How does it look?"

"It looks like a brand new boat," he says back to me. I tilt my head and reexamine it. It's not as good as he's making it out to be, but it's better than I could have hoped for.

"I'm sorry about your brother," I say and look over to him.

"Thank you, Adaline," Albert says and then adds, "I still see him everywhere, but I know he wouldn't change anything." Albert walks back into camp, cutting the conversation short. I know it's hard to talk about and we aren't exactly close. I wish he had someone he could talk to about this, but I guess that person would have been his brother.

"Are we all ready to go now?" I hear Molly's little voice ringing in the air as she runs up to the boat.

"I think so," I say and stand back up. I take Molly into a tight hug and she squeezes me back with her little arms. "Are you okay, Molly?" I ask her and look down at her.

"I miss my friends," she says and looks down at the sand and then back up to me, "I'm glad you're alive. You're like my big sister," she says in the smallest and frailest voice.

Tears brim my eyes and I pull her into another big hug. "And your cold?"

"Essie says I'm doing okay," she gives a small cough to clear her throat. "I don't feel much better though."

"When we get to Libertas we'll find someone with stronger medicine," I say and she gives me a weak smile. I walk over to Mio to see if he needs any help moving things to the boat, but then remember we don't have much more than our backpacks and a few weapons. "We're ready when you are," I say to him.

"Sounds good, Cooper and Toby are cooking the rest of the meat and bringing it with us. It should be enough. We really only have dinner left and then we'll be in Libertas," Mio says and we are quiet for a moment letting the sounds of waves crashing on shore surround us. "Thanks for getting us out of there, Adaline," Mio adds.

"Don't thank me. It was just an instinct," I say shortly.

"I know you heard me yelling at Cooper about how you didn't think to bring the food with us, and that was wrong. It was crazy out there, and I would have done the same thing," Mio says sternly.

"Like I said, my instincts just took over," I say with a small smile. It's probably the only nice thing I'll ever get out of Mio.

"The meat's cooked, and everyone should have packed up their things," Cooper says, walking over to us. His anger from earlier has faded, and I see that he's trying to be the strong leader the others need.

"All right, then let's get out of here," Mio says and we walk down to the boat. Mio and Cinder both walk the boat out into the shallow part of the water, and we all climb into the boat.

"Want to give us a little push Adaline?" Mio asks, and I respond by providing us with some steady waves until the ripped sail starts to catch the breeze. Marin takes her place on the balcony and navigates the boat in the right direction, carefully guiding the sail in the breeze.

As we head deeper into the ocean I look back and watch the island sink out of view. "It's crazy, all those people who are buried there, one day no one will even know they're out there," I say to Alexander.

He takes my hand in his and squeezes it. "It's an awful thing; to die and then be forgotten forever," he says and looks back toward the island.

When the island has faded completely out of view I turn and see the sun starting to set in the other direction. "I never get tired of looking at the sunset," I say to him. "I've spent seven years without them. Something so simple, and yet so beautiful."

Alexander leans his forehead against the side of my head and says, "Just like you." My heart flutters and I remember the night in the bunker after I had stopped him from turning himself into Paylon. He had used that same response when we were talking about the glittery ceiling. It's comforting to hear him say things like that now that his memories are corrected.

"I'm far from simple," I say and smile to him, and we both start laughing. The butterflies explode again as they always do when I'm with him. We might have told each other we couldn't form a further relationship with the other for fear that we may not survive this mess, but we can't stop the feelings from forming. It's a dangerous path we're trying to walk down, somewhere between friends and lovers.

"Alexander. Adaline," Marin calls down from the perch and

motions for us to join her.

I'm about to stand when Alexander tightens his grip around my wrist and whispers in my ear, "Don't tell her I know she's not my real mother."

"What?" I ask, confused why he'd want to keep that a secret.

"I just got her back Adaline. I just want to keep things simple," Alexander pleads with me. I know he just wants to keep denying that he's related to King Renon, and I can't blame him. I nod and we stand together.

"Mio tells me he showed you the markings," Marin says as we join her on the balcony of the boat.

"Yes, he said that we are important to some rebellion. Can you tell us anymore about our markings?" I ask as we take a seat with her.

Marin begins to explain as the memory comes back to her. "Your father had been moving the gifted to Libertas, and they were searching for the ones who were marked with the key." Marin motions down to our wrists before continuing, "When you were born your father had seen the marking and had taken you to get the mark disguised."

"And you had done the same for me?" Alexander asks.

"Yes, I had helped Adaline's father with a couple of journeys before that, and when he showed me the prophecy about the gifted planning a rebellion I realized how important you were." Marin clears her throat, "I mean how important you would be to Libertas. Derith showed me where I could take you to get the mark disguised, and that's when we promised each other that we would take care of one another to keep our kids safe. We had to make sure that the prophecy could be followed out." I nod my head, better understanding where the tie between Alexander's family and mine came from.

"Do you know what they expect from us once we get to Libertas?" Alexander asks his mother.

"Not entirely. As far as I know, the plan was for Derith and me to get there and help get things set up for when you would arrive." Marin looks out over the side of the boat and I know she's thinking about the wreck on her journey. "Now that we didn't make it there, I hope they continued to move forward with the plan. Otherwise, we will be very behind schedule."

"What's the schedule?" I ask, trying to think about what they could have planned for us.

"Mio tells me that King Renon may be on to the fact that you both are the keys to the rebellion mentioned in his grandfather's prophecy. If that's true then he will already have his forces preparing for war. That doesn't give us much time to make the first move before they come to us," Marin says and I realize I'm not going to some safe haven island for the gifted. I'm walking into a trained army looking for a leader. My life is going to go from fleeing to attacking very quickly.

Molly comes over to the edge of the perch and stands on her tiptoes. "Adaline, will you play a game with me?" she asks over the edge.

Marin nods, giving me the sign that our conversation is over. "Sure, what kind of game?" I ask and climb down from the perch. We take a seat on the edge of the boat and Molly kicks her feet against its side while she considers what game she wants to play.

"A guessing game!" she finally squeals.

I laugh and ask, "Okay, how do we play?"

"I'll find something we can see, and I'll tell you what color it is. Then, you have to guess what it is," Molly explains. I remember doing something similar with Titus and it was always his favorite game to play in the cell. It never lasted long with so few items to guess.

"You can go first," I say.

"I see something blue!" Molly says.

"The sky?" I guess.

"Nope," she says and shakes her head.

"The water?" I guess next.

"Nope, try again," she laughs.

I let my eyes gaze around the boat searching for something blue when I look down and see that her shirt is a faded shade of blue. "Your shirt!" I say.

"Yeah, you got it!" she says. "Now you find something," she instructs, and I begin to look around the boat for something.

"All right, I see something clear," I say and let a small smile fall across my face.

"Clear?" she questions me and I can see the wheels in her brain start turning. "Air!" she shouts seconds later.

I laugh and tell her she's right and we continue to play the game until Mio is either completely annoyed with us, or he really does think it's time we have dinner.

I help Cooper pass out the last of our meat and we all eat it slowly. Cinder, Mio, and Marin move up to the perch. They tell us the adults need to work out some details so I take a seat with Alexander and Cooper. Molly is quick to join me, always staying close to my side.

"If we really do need more food we can always try to fish something out of the ocean," Alexander says to me, noticing that I've barely eaten any of the meat.

"I guess you're right," I say and start to eat the rest of my meal. Once we're finished eating we sit in silence except for the crashing of waves. "What do you think Libertas will be like?" I ask, breaking the silence.

"Mio said it's a world built on a mountain," Cooper says. "He's only been there a handful of times. He wasn't even allowed to get off the boat. Couldn't even set foot on the island." My lips form a tense line as I'm reminded that my group may still not get to stay after all.

"I picture it as a castle floating in the water," Alexander says and a laugh escapes my throat.

"You just think there's going to be a castle floating in the middle of the ocean? I ask him. Alexander's grin widens and he nods his head. We're quiet for a moment as I picture the unique image.

"What are you hoping it will be?" Alexander softly asks. I've been looking for freedom my entire life. Now that I'm just hours from it I don't know what I hope I see.

"When I think of freedom I picture the fields of flowers behind my house. I see an endless blue ocean. There will be music and dancing, and everyone will be smiling," I say and imagine a life where all that could be true.

"And mounds of red velvet cake," Zavy adds as she takes a seat in front of me. We laugh and our stomachs growl as we remember the rich delicacy from Sard. Our scarce dinner doesn't come close to meeting the standards of Sard.

"I hope I make some friends," Molly's tired voice yawns out. My heart tightens at the thought of her old friends that drowned in the ocean. I tighten my arms around her, doing everything I can to keep her safe.

"You'll make lots of friends Molly," I say as I brush her hair from her warm face. Her cold has gotten worse. A damp sweat keeps her hair stuck to her cheeks and forehead, and her skin is pale. It hurts, even more, knowing Molly is getting more and more ill, but all she cares about is making new friends. She is so pure and naive, and this world is too twisted and dark for someone like her.

"Time to get some rest," Mio says as he lays a heavy hand on my shoulder. Tomorrow we will be in Libertas. After all this, we will finally get to our destination. We move to get ready for bed and Mio announces that he and Marin will take the first shift tonight. I lie out my blanket next to Alexander's on the hard wooden floor of the boat and place my pillow down too. As soon as my head hits the pillow I start to feel myself being pulled under.

Today was the first time I stayed awake for more than five minutes, and it's definitely catching up with me. I look up at the stars and get lost in their beauty as I get pulled into a deep sleep.

"Look!" I hear Molly's little voice scream as I start to wake up. I break open my eyelids and white light from the sun rushes in. I prop myself up on my elbows and see that almost everyone else has gotten up and is looking at something in front of the boat. I get up and join Alexander at the tip of the boat.

"There it is," he says.

I feel my heart stop as Libertas starts to come into view. "It's magnificent," I say. From what we can see out on the ocean it seems that Libertas is completely closed in by a large stone wall. The island seems to just be one giant mountain, and as we look up the mountain you can make out the bricked pathways and houses that line the town.

On top of the island is a large castle that makes Garth's seem like nothing. As we get closer to the island a small docking area comes into view at the base of the rocky shore.

"And if you look to our right you can see the magnificent wall that surrounds all of Libertas," Mio says narrating our arrival.

A smile starts to break across my face and I throw my arms around Alexander's neck, bringing him into a tight hug. "We made it Alexander!" I say.

Mio and Cinder pull the boat up to the dock and tie it up. We all file out of the boat and onto the dock. The wall that surrounds the island is so tall that I have to tilt my head back to see the top of it. Every ten feet or so there is a guard post, and all eyes are on us.

I look forward to where the dock meets the stone wall and wonder how we get into this place. Marin leads the group and starts to walk down the wooden dock. We all follow in step behind her since she is the only one that's been inside the wall. When she reaches the wall she stops and starts to study the bricks. She raises a hand to one and pushes slightly against it.

Nothing seems to happen at first, but then suddenly a large section of the wall in front of us starts to sink into the earth revealing the breath-taking city behind it.

"It can read my fingerprints," Marin says, explaining how the door works, and I remember this isn't her first time at Libertas since she had been helping my father bring people with gifts here for a long time. This all seems normal to her. I lift my hand, examining the skin, and I wonder what the wall would read to unlock itself.

We all file in past the wall and see a woman is walking toward us wearing a fitted red dress that ends just above her knees. She has bright red lipstick to match and tall red shoes.

"Welcome to Libertas," she says, her voice ringing in my ears. Her red lips part into a large smile. "Quite the crowd you've brought us," she says to Mio. She curls her nose at him and scans the group, letting her curious gaze hang a little longer on the non-gifted members.

"We lost the paper work," Mio says as he approaches the woman. "Our ship was wrecked." Mio stops when the lady rolls her eyes, clearly annoyed with him.

"Excellent," The lady responds, the aggravation is clear in her voice. "We will have you fill out new forms right away," she says. Her eyes land on mine and I can feel a small chill run up my spine. "You must be Adaline," she says and walks toward me, shaking my hand. "And you must be Alexander," she says when she looks to him. "We've been waiting a long time for you two."

"We hope to help in whatever way we can," Alexander says.

The lady turns and starts to walk deeper into Libertas and we all fall into step behind her. I look back at the wall and see the spot that once lowered to let us in rise again. The lady leading us starts speaking, "You can all stay in the castle until your paperwork is filled out and reviewed, oh and you can call me Linda. I keep track of everyone who enters or exits the island."

As we walk together along the stone roadways through the town everyone's eyes are on us. It's a much different site than Garth. Everyone seems to be healthy and everyone has clothes on their back and clean skin. The stone architecture is magnificent. We have a similar style in Garth, but it looks like rubble compared to what they have done here. I grab Molly and usher her to the front of the group to Linda.

"Do you have medicine here? She's getting worse. It was just a cold, but now she has a fever." Linda lifts her hand to cut me off.

Without giving Molly more than a side glance Linda says, "The child will be fine. We have excellent doctors and medicine." I swallow and my tight throat relaxes. I fall back in step with

Alexander and let Linda continue to lead the way.

Children are running around playing, and everyone is smiling. I don't think I've ever seen this many people happy at the same time. I watch as pairs walk from store to store, shopping for who knows what. Each of them looks like what we would call wealthy back in Garth.

"I wonder how they survived out here. How do you go from nothing to this?" I ask Alexander.

"I'm sure it'll make a great story," he says, but the tone of his voice tells me he isn't all that comfortable with being here. He's just like me. We see this place and immediately have questions about how and why.

Linda stops next to a large wagon that is being pulled by two slick white horses. We file on and she tells us our next stop will be the castle. The wagon twists in and out of the tight brick path up the steep mountain. I look down and see the blue ocean water get further and further from us as we climb to the castle.

Everyone we pass freezes to see who has arrived. I wonder if there were more people like my father and Alexander's mother that brought people to Libertas, or were they the only ones? If they were the only people bringing in the gifted then these people haven't seen new faces arrive here in over seven years.

When we reach the top of the island I see the blue ocean come out from all sides. Lush green forest spreads down the island, and beautiful fields of flowers are grouped throughout the levels of the mountain. Although my gut tells me not to relax just yet, I let a smile spread across my face. It is just as magical as I had hoped our safe haven would be. I scan the faces of the group and everyone is just as amazed as I am.

When we reach the castle we are led in the grand doors and into a large hallway. Glossy stone lines the floor of the castle and blue drapes hang from the ceiling. Our steps echo off the stone floors of the castle as we make our way inside. Brilliant statues line the halls as well as different paintings of people I can only guess once ruled Libertas. I count three different past rulers.

"You can all wait down here," Linda says.

We walk under an archway and into a large room where the ceiling hangs high above our heads. Plush couches line the sides of the room, and in front of us is a grand double staircase that reaches up to the second floor.

Two thin men dressed in clean black suits walk down the staircase. My eyes lock on the second, his face is hollow and his brown hair is slicked back from his forehead. His emerald eyes land directly on mine and I feel as though the wind has been knocked out of me.

"We've got a lot of catching up to do," his familiar voice echoes through the room, the same voice that has been echoing in my dreams since I was a child.

My voice echoes over Alexander's, and in unison we say, "Father?"

My eyes flicker from my own father to Alexander's. Both of them are standing in front of us, healthy and alive. I bring my gaze back to my father's face and I watch him smile. His joyful eyes linger on me until his face shifts to a worried glaze as he focuses on someone behind me. I turn over my shoulder and see he's staring at Molly. I glance back to my father and his face has gone pale.

"What is she doing here?" His words are panicked and he yells, "She can't be here!" Two guards who had been silently lining the back wall walk up and grab Molly's thin arms.

"Stop!" I say, making myself speak over the shock of my father being alive. "We rescued her from the tunnels under Sard."

"She's working for King Renon, I've seen it in my visions," my father says, walking through our group and straight to Molly.

"No, I don't know what you're talking about," Molly begins to say and nervous tears fill her eyes. The two guards begin to drag her from the group and my father follows them.

"Leave her alone!" I shriek and start to run after them but my body freezes mid-stride. By someone's gift, the guard I assume, my feet are stuck to the floor. I watch as my father places his hand on Molly's forehead. "What are you doing?" I yell at my father.

"Removing the memories that King Renon had planted in her head," he replies. Molly screams in protest, her cries echoing in the stone room.

My father lifts his hand and her head drops limp. Slowly she lifts her head and scans the room confused. Her eyes land on my father and her breath comes short.

"Where am I?" her small voice questions.

"You're in Libertas, Molly," I say and find my feet able to move again. I run to her and put a gentle hand on her shoulder. She looks at my hand and steps back from my grasp. She spins around the room as if searching for something.

"Where's King Renon?" Molly questions, slowly backing away from us. "Where's my brother?"

END OF BOOK ONE

Printed by Amazon Italia Logistica S.r.l.
Torrazza Piemonte (TO), Italy

12955447R00219